INTO THE

REALM

THE BATTLE WITHIN

Diana Perez

D1566548

The content in this book is a work of fiction. Character's names, places and incidents are a product of the author's imagination or are used fictitiously. Any relation to actual people living or dead are solely coincidental.

For more information, you may contact:
author.dianaperez@gmail.com

Edited by Elizabeth Ortiz and Pastor Jenny Pineiro
Cover art by Pro_digitals

FIRST EDITION 2020

All scriptures used are quoted from NIV (New International Version), NLT (New Living Translation), NKJV (New King James Version), ESV (English Standard Bible), and NASB (New American Standard Bible)

ISBN-13: 979-8-6499-3649-1

To my husband David, you are my rock. Thank you for being the man of God you are. From friendship to marriage you have always been there supporting me in my dreams and encouraging faith.
I love you.

To anyone who has lost their way in the Lord, this is for you.

Contents

Acknowledgments

I am grateful for the many people who have supported me throughout this journey. They have motivated me, encouraged me, and listened to my rambles. First of all, my Lord. Without my God this story would not have come alive. In many ways, God woke me from my slumber. He reminded me of the gift He had given me and I am grateful for His love for me.

My husband David, he has really been an inspiration to me during this process. He motivated me to keep going when I wanted to quit. He believed in me even when I didn't believe in myself. He held me up, and always saw the positive when I couldn't. Whenever I would get stuck, he would always ask, "did you pray?" That was the question that stuck with me throughout this process. My two beautiful children, who have not only been patient, but motivating; I love you more than all the numbers in the universe, as my son would say. A special thanks to my family; my parents who introduced me to God as a child and have taught me the ways of the Lord. My brothers, my nephews and niece.

To my spiritual parents who have helped me come out of my shell and molded me into who I am today. They have been my spiritual covering through thick and thin. They have always been there to listen and advise not only me, but my husband as well. Pastor Robert and Jenny Pinero. They have truly been a blessing in our lives.

Pastor Jenny also edited my book along with Elizabeth Ortiz. Elizabeth has also been a mother figure to me. I am truly blessed. God has placed more than one mother in my life. I would also like to thank my sister in Christ, Arleen Soto. Whenever I needed spiritual guidance, I can always count on her. She is not only my friend but my photographer since my first born.

Thank you to my friends and family who have supported me throughout this process. Gaby Butler, Natima Wright, Daniel Bowens, Ezekiel Rivera, Jazmine Garcia, and Sarah Escudero.
Thank you everyone for your support and encouragement. You have all been a blessing in my life.

"Therefore put on the full armor of God, so that when the day of evil comes, you may be able to stand your ground, and after you have done everything, to stand. Stand firm then, with the belt of truth buckled around your waist, with the breastplate of righteousness in place, and with your feet fitted with the readiness that comes from the gospel of peace. In addition to all this, take up the shield of faith, with which you can extinguish all the flaming arrows of the evil one. Take the helmet of salvation and the sword of the Spirit, which is the word of God."
Ephesians 6:13-17 NIV

1. The Creature

A sword appeared in my hand just as I thought I needed some kind of weapon to fight this creature of the night. I ran with a speed I didn't know I had. I jumped into the air so high I thought I could touch the midnight sky. This creature was large and as tall as a redwood tree. But by some miracle I was able to reach its height to gain advantage over it. As I descended, I held the sword's hilt in both my hands, pointing the sword downward. With all the strength I had left in me, I stabbed the creature straight in the heart. It looked at me surprised and said *"I under estimated you."* As I stared at it, I said, *"Big mistake!"*

I then twisted the sword, the creature took its' last breath and fell to the ground, but before I could check if it was really dead – it vanished.

My battle was over, I thought to myself as I stood standing where the creature had just laid. I looked up to the heavens, and said

"Thank you Lord for your strength."

1

My body was starting to give out, I began to feel every cut and bruise, all the pain I had to endure from this battle. The adrenaline was wearing off, my body was feeling depleted, and my eyelids were heavy. I couldn't hold myself up anymore.

I let myself go, and I began to fall. I felt as if all the oxygen left my body as I hit the ground. I closed my eyes as I tried to breathe. A sudden jolt caused my eyes to open.

I sat up, taking in my surroundings. The glow in the dark stars on the ceiling above me tells me, I'm in my room. I really should remove those, I'm nineteen years old, not ten. Sitting up in my bed I realized, it was only a dream; a very realistic dream. I stand up from my bed, taking a look around — I see nothing out of place. "It was only a dream!" I tell myself. But then why does my body ache? The dream was so vivid, I even remember the smell of burning ash surrounding me. I run my fingers through my hair, its then I noticed I'm sweating. If I didn't know any better, I would say I really was in another realm.

My heart is still pounding just like I remember in my dream when I was fighting the creature. I don't even know what it was. The creature looked like a large dragon, but it spoke. Only in dreams can the impossible happen. I walked to the mirror across from my bed to assess myself. In my reflection, I'm wearing an armor, just like in my dream. Confused, I pat myself, trying to feel the armor but all I feel is the soft fabric of my pajamas. This dream is causing me to hallucinate.

I decide a cold shower might help me cool down. I walk across the hall to the bathroom. Turning on the water I thought I felt someone behind me, I turn to see nothing but my reflection in the bathroom mirror. I step into the shower, letting the cool water wash over me. Although the water is refreshing, I still can't shake off the memories of the dream that lingered. The realistic feeling, the breath of the dragon like creature when he spoke. How did it underestimate me? Why was I dressed like a soldier of war?

Turning off the water and stepping out of the tub, I get a strange feeling that I'm being watched. I return to my room wrapped in a towel, searching my draws for a new set of pajamas. From the corner of my eye I thought I saw a shadow move. Maybe I'm lacking sleep, and it's affecting my vision, still feeling confused.

Feeling unsure of what's happening to me I decide to do something I haven't done in a long time. I kneel down on the floor by my bed, looking around once more. I'm not sure what I expected to find, but I feel there's something out of place.

"*Hey God, it's me. I know it's been a while. I feel so silly kneeling here. I don't know if you can hear me anymore…I feel lost Lord…alone and confused. I have no one to talk to. No one who can understand what I've been through.*" I stop praying because I feel like I'm just talking to myself and I really don't know how to pray. I climb into my bed and I lay down, it's Saturday or Sunday now since it's after 3:00am. I have to be up in a few hours to get ready for Sunday service. Maybe God can speak to me there. I look around my room again just to make sure there's nothing here. Not seeing anything out of the ordinary, I realize I must be tired. I turn on to my side and fall asleep.

***

Walking down on a path in a big open field, I see someone up ahead wearing a shiny armor. I think about getting closer, but I'm not sure if it's a good idea. Whoever this person is, looks like a knight from a king's army. This knight looks my way from over his shoulder and begins to run away. Curiosity gets the best of me and I chase after him. He notices me running and he runs faster. He stops behind a tree and I slow down afraid of what may happen if I get closer. I stop right before I reach the tree, I must be dreaming again. I look up and around, trying to figure out why am I dreaming of knights now. I go around the tree, he's just standing there. As I study him, I notice his armor looks like he's been in many wars, tarnished.

As I take a step, the knight takes a step. He mirrors my movements. We come face to helmet, his face is covered by the helmet he wears. Neither one of us makes a move, we just stand there facing each other. I have this feeling we know one another.

I noticed the ground opened up behind him, and a stream begins to flow. Water starts pouring through the split in the ground like a river. The knight takes a step back and turns to face the river. He begins to walk toward it. I don't make a move; I just stand there watching to see what he intends on doing.

The knight jumps into the river, and the water stops flowing. I no longer see the knight. The river must be deep, or maybe his armor was too heavy to resurface. To my surprise he does, but his armor is not the same as when he went in. It's brand new.

As he climbs out of the river, it begins to flow again. The water not as clean as it was before the knight jumped in, but as the river continues to flow the darkness dissipates. The knight is now on the other side of the river, another figure appears; a man…I think. I can't make out his face, but I see his wings. He's an angel. Now I'm sure I'm in a dream. I know angels are real, but for anyone to actually see one in real life is highly unlikely.

He doesn't make any moves; he just stands there in front of the newly washed knight. The trees begin to open up allowing the rays of sunlight to shine down. Somehow I feel something is about to happen. The angel nor the knight move, it's like they are frozen in place. I feel something tugging at my leg. When I look down, I see a baby all dressed in white. When I look back to where the angel and knight where just standing, they were gone.

I look down to the baby sitting by my feet, I can't tell if it's a boy or a girl. It smiles at me and then I wake up. I lay in my bed thinking what this dream could mean. A baby means start of a new life, right? Will I be starting a new life?   I wish.

2. Morning Rush

Sunday morning. What a night that was! I turn on to my back, let my eyes circle the room. I'm still looking for something, something that feels out of place. I have to start getting ready for church. I hope today's service is better than last weeks. Not that it was a bad service, I just felt...out of it. Lately for me, it's just church, a building full of people with stories. My mom has been dragging me to church ever since I can remember. First it was just me, then five years later my little sister Evie. My father's not a religious person, he respects it, but he doesn't always join us.

My church is pretty active. We have a worship dance group, a choir of course, and once a month we'll have talent night. They like to engage in outreach programs. We have a lot of people of each age group: a few leaders, ministers, and one Pastoral Couple.

I wanted to be a Pastor when I was younger, but then I thought of the preaching. I'm not one for speaking in front of large crowds. I had a friend once; Rebecca, I would go over to her house and watch her father prepare for a sermon. Her father would tell us, *"It's like writing an essay for school. Pick a topic, do some research, and boom, you have a preaching."* He would say a little popcorn prayer and that's it, no science to it. At least that's what I thought. A popcorn prayer is a prayer without emotion, like a quick grace before you eat your food.

The Pastors have prayed for me, they used to say, *"Angel, you have a very special gift."* I'm still waiting to find out what that *special gift* is. My name is Angelisa Cruz, Angel for short.

"Angelisa!" My mom yells from down the hall. "Angelisa, get up! I don't want to be late again!" Ok so we were five minutes late last week, it's just a few minutes, how much can you miss in that time?

"I'm up mom, I'm going to the bathroom now." I answer her. I walk to the door of my room and walk out into the hall and find my mother about to knock on my door.

"Did you wake me up before Evie again?" I asked not understanding why I'm always the first one she likes to drag out of bed. Yeah I may be the oldest, but why do I always have to be first?

"Your sister is already at church, Lady picked her up twenty minutes ago," she tells me.

Lady is our next door neighbor, she's friendly...most of the time, but also very nosey. She knows everything about everyone. I don't think she likes me too much. My sister, she adores, but me... when I was learning how to drive a few years ago, her dog ran out in front of me. I got nervous, I didn't want to hit the little pug, so I turn the wheel and drove right into her rose bush. It was not my fault her dog couldn't control himself when he saw a cat. Wasn't it better that I destroyed her rose bush than hurting her dog? I guess I can't blame her for not liking me, but it really was an accident. Guess she never saw it that way.

"Why did she go to church so early?" I asked.

"Your sister had practice for the upcoming play, did you forget?" she answers.

Yeah, I guess I did forget about that. The special service.

"No mom, I didn't forget," I lied.

"Good, now hurry up and get ready."

"What's for breakfast?" I ask my mom.

6

"Whatever you decide to make yourself, just do it quick, we're leaving at ten thirty," she replies.

"You didn't make breakfast?" I asked confused with her answer.

"No, I did something I haven't done in a long time." I was almost afraid of her answer.

"I slept in! What a good feeling. So, I decided, you're old enough to make your own breakfast." Great, now I have to rush to get ready and make something to eat. I walk back into my room to check the time on the cable box, 9:58 a.m. I head back to the bathroom; guess I'll just grab a toaster tart.

I wash up, and return to my room to get dressed. Searching for clothes in my closet, *what to wear?* I ask myself. At least my church doesn't require a dress code. They're more of come as you are type of church, which is great. I can wear jeans and dress it up, it's so much easier to grab a pair of pants than to pick out a skirt and shoes and everything else that goes with it. Don't get me wrong, I don't mind wearing skirts and dresses, but I prefer pants, mostly jeans.

Ok, I'm ready, blue skinny jeans, a long-sleeved tan colored shirt with matching ankle boots. I combed my long dark black hair into a ponytail, and put on my big hoop earrings, and my gold necklace my father gave me when I turned eighteen last year. I did my makeup to match my outfit, I love how my gold eye shadow brings out my brown eyes. I'm done.

I look into the mirror and just stared. Sometimes I just don't recognize myself. Not my looks, but me. I don't know the person staring back at me. I check my outfit one more time, and decide its fine.

"Renewal Church, here I come, WOW me." I continue attending to keep my mom happy, but I don't belong there anymore. I don't belong anywhere, and everyone there knows it. My mom has no idea how I feel or what I've been through. She just thinks I have a broken heart because my ex left me. At least that's what I let her think.

I had been part of a world she knew nothing about. She sees me as a good girl, whom I once was…until I met Logan. My life changed completely, and I couldn't be who I was before because that girl was gone. Who I am today, is someone I don't even recognize.

I've done what many teenage girls do, experience life. Little did I know, that would lead me to where I am today; numbed from Christianity, and from the world. I'm somewhere in the middle, if that's a place. Neither side calls my attention anymore. I'm just living until the day I'm not. I have no purpose in my life, I walk around aimlessly.

The choices I've made, really did a number on me. But for my family's sake, I put on a happy face. The reality is, they have no idea the burden I carry.

If my mom knew, I'm not sure she would look at me the same. Why I feel God has turned His back on me. I'm a sinner, I don't deserve the right to repent. I've failed too many times. How many times will God forgive me? And I'm sure I'll keep failing, because that's just what I do; disappoint and fail. But for the benefit of everyone around me, I'll pretend. I'm a really good actress. I have been doing it for the past two years, no one suspects a thing.

3. Two Types of Christians

"Let us all stand to our feet and worship together," one of the choir members tells the congregation. I try to get into the worship, but I can't. I'm still numbed to it all, people around me are so touched by the spirit that they're dancing or speaking in heavenly tongues, but I'm just watching. I see my mom is worshiping, so why can't I? This is not my life anymore.

I decide to try again, but of course I don't want to stand up, I don't want people looking at me. They're always judging me, I can't say everyone here is, but a few. It's enough to make me feel uncomfortable. Some people don't want me around, I'm a bad influence they say. Yes, I made mistakes! I'm sure I'm not the first to do so, otherwise we wouldn't need to be here asking God for forgiveness.

I close my eyes again, trying to block out all the thoughts in my head, I try to focus on where I want to be; alone. I find myself in the middle of a meadow.

The sun is setting, there's a heaviness in the atmosphere, and the air is filled with anxiety. I stand still unsure if I should move.

I see someone up ahead, a girl. She's on her knees. As I walk closer, I can see she's crying. She has her face in her hands, shadows appear, and they begin to surround her. They keep circling her as she cries even more. I feel for her, she looks like she's in so much emotional pain. I walk closer to them, she lowers her hands and lifts her head, tears pouring from her eyes. She stares blankly ahead. What I see shocks me, this girl…is me!

The dark figures continue to circle her, she just kneels there, staring ahead. Her hands fall to her sides and then she freezes. The figures must be doing something to her, to me. She's me, I think. I don't understand this, I look away from her and look at the sun as it begins to rise now. Time must move differently here. All that comes to mind is the start of something new, but what? And to who, me or her? But I think she's me. I open my eyes abruptly, someone sneezed next to me and I lost my concentration, I was pulled out of what I think was… *a vision.*

The service continues on to the preaching. We should be ending soon. I look around and see some people on their phones, others having conversations. I mean if you made the effort to come to church, at least have the decency to pay attention.

I've always viewed Christians as two types of people; the religious and the faithful. Not everyone that goes to church is holy. Let's take the religious people for example, they go to church, they worship, preach, teach, to the normal eye they are Christians. They are I guess, but they lack something very important. They only 'serve' because it's what they know or have been taught, but they have no conviction or relationship with God. Most of them like to watch others and judge. Others may see a need and do nothing…they may talk about it but don't put in an effort to change it.

Some religious people see themselves better than most, others are just Sunday Christians, or just church goers. They believe that if they attend church at least once a week they are saved. Sure, if it were that easy everyone would do it. Praying at home, and reading the word of God is also something Christians should do to gain a relationship with God. Religious people are the reason many non-believers don't want to go to church. A lot of them don't like people that are not like them.

But then you have the men and women of faith. Those who truly live a godly life. You can tell by their actions, by the way they speak and by the way they carry themselves that they truly have the love of God in their hearts. In Matthew 7:16 it says *"By their fruit you will recognize them."* They have a relationship with God, and a desire to truly help those in need. Unfortunately, there aren't many of those in my church. Except for Pastor Edward, he has always been kind to me. I wonder if he knows what I've done.

I have to be honest, I know that not everyone starts out as a religious person. Sometimes they can be filled with the Holy Spirit, but when you work ministry in church you become busy and overwhelmed. The first love, the passion, begins to die and you begin to work out of your own strength. They've learned to manipulate, but I don't think they even realize it. You would think I'm an expert on the subject. I'm not, never had a relationship with God before. It's not from lack of trying, but I just never felt anything. Maybe that's why I ended up where I did.

Although I'm not feeling anything, at least I'm listening. Today's preacher is Brian. He's a nice guy who doesn't really like me, his sermon doesn't really call my attention. He's talking about getting caught up in the godless functions, to only surround ourselves with godly people. If God thought like that, He wouldn't have sent His only son to die for a bunch of sinners.

It's almost the end of the school year, prom season. I feel as if he's trying to discourage the youth from going to their prom. He's talking about how girls wear revealing dresses and guys rent the limos and how one thing can lead to another. He even mentioned the drinks may be spiked and they can get drunk. Instead of discouraging them about prom, why not just tell them to be careful, and not to do things just because others are doing it. Just pray that you've trained them well in God's ways. The more you tell someone not to do things, the faster they want to.

"Let's all stand as we close in prayer," he says.

"I see some new faces here for the first time, would anyone like to receive Jesus Christ as their Lord and Savior?" he asks.

The majority of the visitors are young, maybe they don't want to have to give up prom because none of them raise their hands or step forward. I know I'm not one to talk, being that I don't have that relationship with God as I wish I had. But I think dealing with new people, you have to be wise. I may have not been able to relate to most of them, but I can certainly understand where they are.

"No one? Not one of you will give yourself to God?" Brian asked.

Oh my goodness, he's looking right at the visitors, singling them out, putting them on the spot. I look to the new faces, as they lower their heads. I am in shock, you can't force someone to confess Christ. They have to come to it on their own. I look back to Brian, and he's still looking at them.

He shakes his head and says, "very well, let us close." He begins to pray and I am relieved he lets it go.

Just pray for them, and try to get to know them, maybe next time they will want to open their heart to God.

"Amen!" everyone says in unison.

People start to greet each other and make their way to the exit. I look back up to Brian, he's just looking at everyone. Then he sees me, and he shakes his head.

Brian is Rebecca's father. I use to be at their home all the time since Rebecca and I were very close. But one day we weren't and we barely say hello now. Brian preaches every now and then, he's one of the leaders in the church. Our pastors are away on a missionary trip. I guess Brian was put in charge until their return.

I don't really talk to anyone here anymore. So I lower my head as I walk out toward the parking lot.

I'm waiting in the car for my mom and sister. My father did not make it today. He's been having a hard time lately, I fear I am to blame.

I look around and set my eyes on the church. I remember when I was part of it, now I just go here. I made a mistake that I couldn't take back, and I lost myself. That was around the time of my senior year in high school.

I tried not to focus on my past, there was nothing I could do to change it. I had started college and was introduced to new things and I wandered even further away. My popcorn prayers went to non-existent, I hung out with a new crowd. Then I had lots of homework, studying and work. I couldn't handle it all, I lost my focus. Next thing I knew I was out the door. My so called *"Christian"* friends abandoned me when I needed them the most.

I felt that if I couldn't serve like I used to in the church anymore, I was worthless to the other leaders and ministers. I guess I blamed them, and just cut people off. I felt important when I was able to help in church. I did minor jobs, such as ushering, or passing out tithes and offering envelopes. I was in training for this program called *"Closing back doors."* That program was very challenging.

It was for the new believers, the ones that confessed Jesus Christ as their Lord and Savior. My church believed that when a new soul opens their heart to Jesus Christ, the son of God, that the devil places a target on them. The devil, we also refer to as the enemy, wants the new believers to cross back over to his side. There's a spiritual door that opens when you confess Jesus Christ, once you cross the threshold, the door does not close right away. The enemy begins his attacks to lure the soul back through that door.

Everyone that worked in the program, their job was to befriend the new believer. Gather their information, pray with them, and slowly introduce them into Gods ways, to start a new life. Teaching them how to pray, and how to use the bible against the enemy. The program is to show them a new way of living. It was also about fellowship, so they wouldn't feel alone during their transition.

It was a beautiful experience, but it was also difficult. People go through so much in life, which makes it hard to get pass certain experiences. I lived a pretty simple life, I didn't have much life experience to relate to most of them. I felt I had to withdraw from the program, one because I didn't feel qualified to be of service. Two, because I was beginning to lose faith. And three because instead of me helping someone cross over, I wanted to learn more about his world.

During the time I was a part of this program, I was doubting myself. Some of the new believers' life stories made me feel I should've had some kind of experience to relate to them. I didn't at the time, but be careful what you wish for. After the back door is closed, if you open it just a little it's not as easy to close it again. In my case, my door was closed, until one day curiosity got the best of me. I cracked open the door spiritually, and I didn't even realize it.

Let's just say I don't have that perfect background anymore. I was too ashamed of who I became so I left. Every day I drifted further and further away, and I guess I just fell into a spiritual coma.

I felt broken, the lack of prayer can really alter life. I live every day the same, like I'm on auto pilot. I listen to this song over and over again. It describes exactly how I feel right now, paralyzed. I feel this way not only in church, but even when I'm with my new friends. Sure I have fun with them, but I'm not really there. I feel nothing at all.

My mother and sister finally found the car and we begin to drive home. Mom cooks Sunday dinner, then we watch a movie together and head to our rooms after. I get into bed and fall asleep.

4. Magnificent being…and Coffee

I find myself in a strange place, lying down on grass that looks like it hasn't had rain in months, maybe longer. It's dry and brittle, at my movements I can hear it crunch. I stand up and look around, tall dry trees, I seem to be the only living thing here. I see no one, not even a bird in the sky, or a fly. Another dream I suppose, I keep having these dreams that feel so real. It's dark, and cold in this place. It almost looks like the place I was in my last dream, except this place looks dead. On the ground I see something shiny, but I can't tell what it is.

When I go to reach for it, I hear something running through the trees. I freeze and try to look where the steps were coming from. I can't see anything, I guess I'm not alone. Now I hear flapping from above, I look up to the sky. An angel, last night was the first time I saw an angel, and now I see another. I can't be sure this is the same angel from my last dream, I wasn't able to see his face. This one has a face I can see.

Still amazed, I stare at the magnificent being, I can't believe what I'm seeing. I watch him as he looks at me, studying me. His eyes are a deep grey, medium length black hair, fair complexion. He's wearing black leather pants, and a breastplate made of metal and leather, and he is holding a sword. He looks like he's attending a larping event. But the most admirable part are his wings. I watch them as they slowly move up and down to keep him hovering in the air. His big beautiful wings are white, they look like they can wrap around his whole body.

He breaks eye contact and looks behind me as if he sees something. I try to follow his gaze, but the way he tucks his wings behind and charges down, I can't tear my eyes from him. As he swoops down to come to my aid I hear the sounds of footstep coming from behind me. Before the angel can reach me, something hits the back of my head and I fall face down to the ground. After a few minutes, I roll on to my back, placing my hand to the pain in the back of my head, "ouch, that hurts." I say out loud to myself.

When I open my eyes, I'm on the floor, in my room.

"These dreams are all too real, and painful." I tell myself as I rub the back of my head.

Why am I feeling the pains of my dreams, and why am I having dreams like this?

I stand from the floor, and look at my alarm clock, 6:30am. Time to get ready for work. I have a really bad headache now, but I have to push through and make it to work. I go through my morning routine and walk out the door. I work a few blocks away from home so I ride my bike. I think about the strange dream, and how real it felt.

I don't understand why I'm having these dreams. Its two nights in a row now. Although it's not the same dream, at least I don't think it is. That was a beautiful angel, his wings were…wow. The way he was looking at me, studying me, wanting to protect me. At least, I think that was the case. The way he charged down; I think he was trying to protect me.

***

"Coffee, small, light, not sweet." A customer says to me. I work at an independent coffee shop called *'Caffeine.'* The owner was really creative with the name, not. But I guess it's inviting. It's always busy, mostly in the morning. People are so moody before they have their coffee. If I didn't know any better, I would think it was a drug, the way people act before they take that first sip of their coffee.

I say *'they'* because I am not one of them. I don't like coffee, none of any kind. Maybe that's why I'm so bad at making it. I hate when they put me to do the coffee in the morning. People are very specific as to how they want their coffee. *'Not too sweet, more milk than coffee, don't make it too hot'* they tell me. Isn't coffee just coffee? And now there's ice coffee! *'Don't put too much ice in my iced coffee'* they say. Oh please, that's like saying I want a bacon cheeseburger with no bacon. I don't get people sometimes.

In the middle of the day it gets better. The people that come at that time are more calm and relaxed. They order their coffee and sit at one of our tables and read a book, or a magazine, or are on their laptops.

"Small coffee, black!" A customer orders while he reaches in his pocket. He doesn't look at me, he keeps his eyes on his phone, as if he's reading something. He is one of our regulars, out of all of our customers, he stands out. He's not like the rest of them, at least not to me, he's different. I've never taken his order, until today. My coworker Elizabeth always catches him. I hand him his coffee as he swipes his card. He sits down, pulls out his laptop, and few books, then he spreads them all over the table. Maybe he's a teacher, but he looks young enough to be a college student.

He looks like he's researching. I wonder what he's searching for. Assuming he's searching, I mean he has notebooks, and post it notes all over his books. He really is a mess. I never really understand why people come to coffee shops to do work. Wouldn't it be more private at home, or even a library?

I feel a buzz in my pocket, I reach for my phone and see a text from my friend Val...well its Valarie but I just call her Val. We met my first year of college. She's a year ahead of me, but we had a class together and we just started hanging out.

Val: *are you coming over tonight?*
Me: *hey Val, what's going on?*
Val: *study party, want to come?*
Me: *depends, whose house?*
Val: *Alex, I know you don't like him, but he's really smart.*

Alex is also a year ahead of me. He's pretty well known, and rumors are he has the best parties. I've never been to any of his before, but he's been to other parties I have attended, and I didn't like how he treated people. He embarrasses people he thinks aren't good enough to be around him. I usually just stay away from him, but if he's hosting the study party I can't avoid him. Besides, I don't think he's that smart.

Me: *idk, I'll get back to you.*
Val: *come!*
Me: *we'll see.*
Val: *ok, text me. Bye.*
Me: *ok, bye.*

More customers coming in, better make more coffee. Why would Val want me to go to Alex's party when she knows I don't like him? I think he's just full of himself. I decide to go around to see if anyone wants more coffee.

"Can I get you more coffee?" I ask the guy with the mess of books.

Of course he doesn't look up, he just shakes his head no and keeps typing on his laptop. I start to walk away, but I found that so rude. I may just work here, but I am a person too. The least he can do is acknowledge my presence. I hate how people treat me sometimes when they come in here. I turn back to him, I know I shouldn't say what I'm about to say, but before I could stop myself...

"You could at least look at me and say no thank you!" It's too late, I said it.

He instantly stops what he's doing, slowly lifts his head to look at me. It seems he's noticing me for the first time. He doesn't say anything, when we finally make eye contact I can't shake the feeling like I know him. He's been a customer here, but it's something more, he's important. Deep grey eyes, black hair tied back into a ponytail, fair complexion. I feel my mouth begin to open, but I quickly close it. It's been a while since a guy can leave me speechless with his gaze. The way he looks at me, makes me feel uncertain.

"I'm sorry," he says finally. "I was not trying to be rude, I'm just working on something important, and I didn't want to lose my train of thought."

Now I feel bad, why didn't I just walk away? I don't even know what came over me. I just felt drawn to him.

"No thank you, I would not like any more coffee. Is that better?" He continues, still holding eye contact.

Why is he still staring at me? I want to walk away, but then I would be the rude one.

"Yes, thank you, I didn't mean to bother you." I turn to walk away, but "hey," he calls out. I turn back around and face him.

"What's your name?" he asks.

"Angelisa" I say.

"Angelisa, that's not a name I hear often," he replies.

"My friends call me Angel," I tell him.

Why did I just tell him that? I noticed his eyes widen as he hears *'Angel.'* I like my name, but really only my parents and acquaintances call me Angelisa. My parents didn't want a common name, they wanted something different.

"Angel is much simpler to say," I tell him.

He looks at me and smiles, nods his head and says, "Angelisa is a nice name, so if I call you Angel, does that mean we're friends?" he asks.

"Angelisa is fine too!" I answer.

He laughs at my response, "maybe when we get to know each other better I can call you Angel. But I like Angelisa!" he winks.

First he wouldn't acknowledge my presence and now he wants to get to know me? I really don't want to be distracted by a guy right now. My head is such a mess, my emotions are everywhere. A guy would just bring complications. But somehow I feel the corners of my lips curl up into a smile. Great, he's still staring, and smiling.

"What's your name?" I ask him to break this awkward silence. Teeth, now he's showing teeth, great.

He sits up straight in his chair, and says, "Ryan, not short for anything, just Ryan." Still with a grin on his face. Ok, time to get out of here.

"Nice to meet you Ryan, I should get back to work now. Let me know if you need anything else," I tell him and quickly turn around and walk off before he had the chance to say anything else.

I chance a glance over my shoulder to him as I walk away, and he's still looking my way with that same smile. For someone who didn't want to lose his train of thought he sure allowed himself to be distracted.

Finally, almost time to go, another half hour and I can walk out of here. I look over to Ryan's table, yup he's still here. Still on his laptop typing away. What is he doing? I guess he felt me looking because he lifted his head from his screen and looks right at me. I've been caught— great. I turn my face to the coffee machine and start to walk to it.

"Angelisa," I hear him calling me, shoot. I turn to look at him.

"Can I have another cup of coffee?" he asks.

"Black?" I ask to confirm. That's all he ever orders.

"Yes," he answers with a wide grin.

Perfect, just great, he might be thinking I'm interested in him. Don't get me wrong. He is good looking, and there's something about him that attracts me other than his looks. I just can't pin point it. But I'm just not interested in dating anyone right now.

I get his coffee ready and I start walking towards him. He watches me as I walk. When I reach him, he reaches out his hand to take the cup of coffee. Our fingers touch as he grabs the coffee from my hand, and I felt a shock. "Thank you Angelisa," he tells me.

"You're welcome." I wipe my hands on my jeans, and turn to walk away.

"Angelisa," he calls out to me again. Great! Now he says my name all the time. I turn around to face him, again he's smiling.

"Yes, can I get you something else?" He shakes his head no.

"This might sound crazy, but I need to tell you something," he tells me.

I'm confused, what can he possibly have to tell me? He doesn't know me.

"Angelisa, I feel you have been struggling with something, don't worry…it's going to get better. You have a gift, don't get lost in your surroundings." He says to me with a sincere look on his face.

What does he know about me? For some reason I feel my eyes begin to fill up with tears, and I feel goose bumps all over. I decide to break this odd feeling with a joke.

"A gift in coffee?" I ask him.

He laughs before he answers.

"No, not the coffee." He takes a sip of his coffee, and smiles.

"It's great by the way. But there's something special about you. Keep your eyes open, follow your instincts." I'm not understanding, but ok.

"Well, thanks for the advice. I have to go. Enjoy your coffee." I say to him as I walk away.

"Anytime Angelisa, have a nice evening." He replies.

What was he trying to say? I head to the back and gather my things, and clock out. I say bye to my coworkers, and head back to the front. I look to Ryan's table and he's gone. That was fast. It looked like he was going to be there for a while, especially since he had just ordered a fresh cup of coffee.

I grab my bike and begin to ride back home. I've been thinking about Val's invitation to the study party. I really need to study for the finals coming up, but I don't want to go to Alex's house to do it.

I reached my house, put my bike in the garage and head to my room. I feel my phone buzz in my pocket, it's Val.

Val: *"hey, I'm going to pick you up in an hour?"*

Have I decided I was going?

Me: *"I didn't say I was going, Val"*

Val: *"I know, so I decided for you. You know you need this study group, what's the worst that can happen?"*

I think for a moment, I do need to study.

Me: *"FINE! I'll be ready."*

I lay down on my bed to rest a little. I could use a nap, maybe I should start drinking coffee. Hmm scratch that thought, I don't even like the smell.

5. Alex's House

Val parks the car and turns to face me, "Angel," the way she says my name makes me wonder.

"Why do I feel like you about to tell me something I'm sure I don't want to hear?" I ask her.

"Don't hate me ok?" I'm sure I'm not going to like her next words. I should have followed my instincts, I just know tonight is not what Val said it would be, I'm sure of it. I turn in my seat to give her my full attention.

"What is it Val?" I say as calmly as I can, but with a tone that she would know I am not happy.

"I know you don't like Alex," she pauses.

"And maybe I should've told you before, but I really need you tonight. Please be nice to him, he has a friend named Mario and I really wanted to get to know him. Alex said he would set us up if I promised to bring you tonight. Please don't hate me!" she pleas.

"Valarie!" she knows when I say her name like that, I'm upset.

"I'm sorry Angel! I should've just told you before. I really like this guy, I just want a chance to get to know him. You still don't have to like Alex, but if you can just hang with him for a little while, I would have held up my end of the deal. Please don't be mad at me, you wouldn't have come if you knew I was kind of setting you up with Alex," Val says really fast. She takes my hands in hers and gives me the sad puppy dog look.

She's right, I wouldn't have come tonight had I known beforehand. I take in a deep breath,

"I am not kissing him! This is not a date for me," I tell her as I give in to her scheme.

I am upset with her right now, but she really is the only friend I have. I don't understand why she needed Alex to meet this guy. Val is beautiful inside and out, she's attractive all on her own. She doesn't need anyone to hook her up. If this Mario guy couldn't see that, then he's an idiot!

"Thank you! Thank you! Thank you!" she says excitedly as she throws her arms around me and pulls me into a hug.

"You're my best friend and I love you, but don't ever trick me again!" I tell her as I pull away from her hug.

"I won't, I'm sorry for using you," she responds.

We get out of the car and I stare at the house I assume to be Alex's. It's a simple house, for some reason I thought his house would have been...I don't know...fancier? Alex carries himself like he's better than everyone, I guess I thought he lived in a bigger house. The house is of average size for a New York Bronx house. Red bricks, small windows, two story house. He has a driveway, and from what I can see, a garage behind the house.

We walk into Alex's house, and of course no one is studying. They're either drinking or dancing. Why did I agree to this? I don't have time to party, I take my school work very seriously.

"Hey, I'm sorry I kind of lied to you about tonight." Val says to me.

I look at her, "Kind of? Val, let's just get this over with, I have to actually study tonight."

"I know, and you work so hard. Maybe you should try to loosen up a little. You have been so caught up in school and work lately, you could use a little break. Try to have fun tonight!" she pauses before she continues to speak.

"Alex has been asking about you for a while now, I kept telling him you were too focused on school and you didn't want to date. But sweetie, you haven't dated anyone in a while, I don't think that's normal for someone our age."

"If I wanted to date, I would've. I'm not interested and much less with Alex." I say to her, I'm still upset about how she got me here.

I'm going to do this for her. I think back to earlier today, when Ryan said to keep my eyes open, and follow my instincts. I'm not ready to date again. My last relationship…well my only relationship didn't end so well.

"Angel, come on, it's just for a little while. If you still want to go after an hour, I'll take you home." I look at Val, as she begs for me to stay.

"Fine, one hour and we are out of here." I agreed.

We walk into the living room, and spot Alex right away. He stands from the seat he was sitting on to make his way to us. When he reaches us, he smiles at me.

"Well hello ladies," he says. I can't stand the look on his face, he's so cocky.

He's a good looking guy, and maybe if I didn't feel so guilty I would give him a chance. Maybe not even, I don't know what it is, but he just doesn't sit well with me. I can't put my finger on it, I just don't want to get too close. I get a bad vibe from him.

I look up to him as he towers over me…he's tall, I guess that's why he's on the basketball team. I don't really follow sports so I'm not sure what role he plays.

He has a caramel complexion and dark brown eyes. His hair is cut low and he has a goatee. But he's not someone I would date, or mess around with just because of his character.

"Hi Alex," Val tells him.

"I bought Angelisa with me as you requested." She smiles at him, as she wraps my arm around hers.

She knows I don't mind my friends calling me Angel, but everyone else I do. I'm glad she remembered.

"Yes I can see that, thank you. Come on in ladies, the party is just starting," he says as he steps back for us to pass.

When we walk in I notice there aren't a lot of people here. Only a few guests, with us we'll make ten. Everyone looks paired off except for a guy standing alone at the fireplace. He sees us as we walk in and he smiles, more at Val than to me. I guess that must be Mario. He looks nice, cute. Tall, dark, handsome guy. *Good choice Val,* I say to myself. I hope he's nothing like Alex.

"Hey Angel, I'm going to go talk to Mario over there, I don't want to keep him waiting." Val says as she walks away, leaving me standing alone with Alex.

As Val meets Mario, I watch as he takes her in. It seems he likes what he sees. He should, Val has long brown curly hair that reach her waist. Her hair bounces as she walks, I always loved her curly hair. Her eyes are dark and her skin always looks like she has a summer tan. She's beautiful, he better treat her right.

Alex takes a step closer to me and puts his arm around my shoulders, I begin to regret agreeing to this.

"Want something to drink?" he asks.

I push his arm off me as nicely as I can, "sure, just water thank you."

I've been to enough parties to know how this works. Also seen a lot of movies, drinks at these kind of parties are always spiked. Most of the beverages are alcohol and I refuse to drink.

He looks at me and laughs, "water? We have beers!" I shake my head, "no thank you, I just want water."

He leads me to the kitchen, I sit on one of the bar seats around the island. The kitchen is pretty big, it has a modern look. His appliances are stainless steel, and the counter tops are black marble. He walks back to me with a bottle of water.

"Thanks" I tell him.

"No problem," he says with a wide grin.

"This is a nice place you have here, excuse me…your parents have." I tell him trying to make small talk.

He laughs, "Thanks, would you like a tour?" Heck no, I rather stay where everyone else is.

"Ah no, maybe later, when everyone else goes for the tour." He laughs, "I guess you don't trust me." His smile fades.

"I don't know you."

"That's fair I guess. We are alone here though, are you ok with that?"

26

"Yes, because everyone is right behind us. Why did you *'request'* for me to come?" I ask him. He places his hand on mines before he answers.

"Because you're beautiful! I see you with Valarie all the time, and I wanted to get to know you."
I remove my hand from under his,

"Thanks, where are your parents tonight? Do they mind you having parties when they're not home?" He looks confused by my questions.

"My parents are on vacation, work had them so busy they barely get to see each other. So they decided they needed some time alone. They'll be back tomorrow night. They trust me, but what they don't know, won't hurt!" he replies with a smirk.

"So what kind of party is this, and why on a Monday?"

"I don't really need a reason to have a party, let's just call this a get together. My parties are never this small." He answers.

"So I've heard."

"Your friend wanted to meet my friend so I set up a very small get together with a few of my friends!" he tells me.

"I don't think you've ever come to one of my parties before." He reaches for my hand again, I quickly pull back.

"I'm having one this weekend, you should come."

"I don't know, maybe." I tell him.

I didn't even want to come tonight, if it wasn't for Val I would be in my room studying. I reach for my phone in my pocket to check the time, it's only been fifteen minutes.

His eyes never leave me, "Well think about it." He reaches for my phone and starts typing something, then his phone vibrates.

"When you've thought about it, you have my number," he says as he hands back my phone.

I look at the screen and see that he texted himself so that we have exchanged numbers. He's very bold to just assume I wanted him to have my number.

"Okay," I say.

We continue to talk for a while, about school and favorite TV shows. I start to think...maybe he's not as bad as I thought.

"How about that tour now?" He asks.

I glance at my phone and notice more than an hour passed. Even though I'm not having a bad time, I know I have to go. I really do have to study.

I glance back up at Alex, "this has been fun, but I really have to go."

He smiles, "come see the rest of the house and then you can leave," he extends his arm toward the hallway.

I look back to Val, she's laughing as Mario whispers something in her ear.

I look back at Alex, "just a few minutes, then I really have to get home!" I tell him. He smiles and nods.

He puts his arm around my shoulders. I think about pushing it off, but I can't help feeling that I like it. I still don't trust him, and maybe I shouldn't be taking this tour around his house alone. I'm a big girl, I can handle this.

In the hall he points out the bathroom and his father's office space. He takes my hand and leads me up the stairs. Another hall way, this one has four doors. He opens the first door we pass as soon as we reach the top of the steps.

"This is my parent's room!" he says. The room is very large room with its own bathroom. We walk to the next door, "closet."

The next door is the bathroom, he turns on the light. "Need to go?" he asks.

"No, I'm good." He skips the next door and walks us to the window at the end of the hall.

"When it's a full moon, I like to watch it from this window." He tells me.

"It's not a full moon tonight, there's barely even stars in the sky," I tell him.

"No, but you can see the half-moon now," he answers.
I'm looking up to the moon, but I can feel his eyes on me.

"What?"

"You look even more beautiful under the moon light!" I smile, but he doesn't.

What a cheesy line. I think to myself. He leans in close to my face, I put my hand up to stop him.

"Sorry, I can't do this right now!" I tell him.

He pulls back, places his hand on my cheek.

"It's ok, I'll wait," he replies. I don't want him to wait. I pull away and start to walk back down the hall.

"Hey, I didn't show you my room!"

I knew he left that room last for some reason. "I really should be going," I tell him.

"Please, you don't have to go in if you don't want to," he stretches out his hand. I don't know why, but I walk back and put my hand in his. He opens the door and switches on the light.

"This is the real me, the one no one sees."

He walks in and I follow just a little to look around. He has shelves on the walls, trophies on each of them. Without realizing I walked in further. I get a better look at the trophies and awards.

"I knew you were athletic, but I didn't know you're really smart too!"

He laughs, "What? You thought I was just a dumb jock?" he asks.

I laugh, "Yeah, I did actually!" I answer him.

He walks closer to me, and without notice he presses his lips to mine. I wanted to push away, but I didn't. He pulls back to look at my expression. I don't react, he leans in again but a picture of Ryan pops in my head and I pull back.

"Alex, I can't!" I turn and walk out the room and head down the stairs.

Before I reached the last step, Alex is right behind me.

"Angelisa, I'm sorry. I just thought we had a moment, I didn't mean to cross the line. I was wrong!" He looks sincere enough.

"Its fine, I really have to go home. I stood longer than I should have!" I tell him.

"Ok, hopefully when you see me around you'll say hi now, and you'll come on Saturday. I'm not such a bad guy now that you got to know me right?" He says with a grin on his face.

"No you are not such a bad guy as far as I can see, but I still don't know you very well. But I can say hi when I see you." I tell him, not being able to stop from smiling.

"Good," he says as he puts his arm around my waist to lead me to where Val is sitting with Mario.

"Hey Val, Angelisa's ready to go. She might be coming to my party on Saturday."

He tells her. She smiles "perfect, let's go do some real studying." I shake my head at her. We head towards the front door.

"So?" Val asks.

"So he kissed me, he caught me off guard. He's not so bad, but I don't want to date him," I tell her.

"Wow, I thought you said you weren't going to kiss him?" I give her a mean stare, and she laughs.

I probably would've let him kiss me again if Ryan's face didn't pop into my head. What was that anyway?

"Ladies!" I hear Mario call out to us. Are we ever going to leave this house?

"Hey, what's up?" Val turns to him.

"One more stop before you go? I was having a good time with you, if this is to be our first date, I don't want it to end in Alex's house," he tells her.

Great, I'm going to get sucked into something else tonight.

"What did you have in mind?" Val asks him.

"Follow us in your car," he replies.

"Us?" I ask.

"Alex is coming too!" Perfect, I think to myself. So much for my getaway.

***

We walk into a lounge Alex wraps his arm around my waist. I try to pull away but he would tug me closer. Val really owes me for tonight. This was not part of the plan. According to Val, I've been so uptight lately. That's only because she doesn't understand what I've been through. I don't think anyone does, well anyone that wasn't a Christian first.

Losing sight of who God is in your life is like seeing your life spiraling out of control. My life lately has been like a roller coaster, with lots of loops and twists. Ever since I quit *'Closing Back Doors'* or I guess even before that, I have been through so much. I wish I could blame my self-destruction on my ex, Logan, but I can't put the full blame on him.

Something wasn't right with me before him. And now I feel as if I'm even further away from God than I was then. I was looking for adventure, and I found it. Although it wasn't the adventure I was expecting. I can't say I didn't enjoy most of it, because I did. But after the fact, I just knew something wasn't right.

30

"Have you smoked hookah before?" Alex asks me as he leans in.

"Nope, can't say that I have," I answer him. Hookah never really called my attention.

"Well, I'm glad I'm here for your first time!" he tells me.

I have no interest in smoking hookah, another thing Val is springing on me last minute. I don't answer him, I give Val an evil stare. She looks at me and winks, then cozies back up into Mario's arms. The things I do for my friends, correction... friend. I'm here that should be enough, I don't have to do what I don't want...*right?*

Alex finds us a table. I have to say, aside from the vibe I'm getting, this place is really nice. I like how the pink, purple, and blue lights mix together. The lounge is kind of dark, but bright enough to see.

On one side of the lounge there are booths, the seats are white leather sofas, and the tables are small, round, and black. I guess it's only made for hookah, since it's not big enough for plates of food.

On the other side, are normal restaurant booths, with regular sized tables, there's a big open space in between the two sides, enough for dancing I suppose. Of course Alex sits us on the hookah side, Val and I enter on either side first so we're in the middle of Mario and Alex. I don't like the idea of being trapped in the middle.

"Alex," I turn to him.

"I really can't stay long, and I have a class tomorrow!" He looks at me with a smile.

"We won't be too long, Angel!" he responds back.

I don't like how my name sounds coming from his lips. Calling me Angel feels like we're close, and well...we're not.

"Angelisa!" I correct him.

"Sorry, Angelisa!" he replies.

I hear Mario order a peppermint hookah. I didn't know they came in flavors.

"Do you like peppermint?" Alex asks. "I think for your first time, you should try a flavor you like," he continues.

"Yes I like peppermint, but I'm not--"

"...shh" he places a finger on my lips. He doesn't get it— does he?

I pushed him away the first time he tried to kiss me, and when he actually did get to kiss me I tried to leave. Why does he keep aiming for my lips?

"Alex, please don't do that again!" Val finally says something.

"She doesn't like to be touched like that," she looks at him as he lowers his hand.

"Sorry again, I just want you to try to enjoy tonight that was all!"

I turn away from him, still not getting the hint he puts his arm around my shoulders. This is going to be a long night.

The waiter comes with drinks and the hookah. He gives each of us a colored pipe, I assume so we don't have to share. Mario, Val and Alex each take a turn. Then Alex passes the hose to me. I haven't even opened my pipe yet.

I shake my head no, and Val takes it instead. They all get up to dance, Val in the middle of both Alex and Mario. Good thing I'm not interested because I would've been jealous otherwise.

As I sit by myself, I think about my life as of now. I realized, I haven't had fun in a really long time. I need to find myself, because I lost sight of who I was.

I feel like I don't belong here, but at the same time I don't feel like I belong in church either. I look down to my phone, I decide to send a text to my little sister. I tell her to call me in exactly one hour from now and if I don't answer to keep calling until I do. That way I have an excuse to get out of here. She responds with an *'ok.'*

I put my phone down and grab my pipe as I take the hookah hose. At first I choke on the smoke, the second time a little less choking. I finally figure it out, and it's actually fun. I keep at it for a while, until I notice there wasn't as much vapor as before.

"I didn't think you were going to try it, I guess we should order another one!" Alex says as he flags down the waiter signaling him to bring another one.

"I wasn't, guess I got bored!" I tell him. Alex sits down next to me again and checks the hookah that's on the table. He tries to show me some tricks, but it's not working. When the waiter comes back with a new one, he's able to show me the tricks. He tells me to try breathing it out my nose. When I do, I surprised myself. He laughs.

He takes my hand and leads me on to the dance floor. As we dance, he tries to pull me closer to him. I pull back a little. I don't want him to be too close. I'm still not interested in him, I'm just letting go a little. Trying to find what feels right for me, he definitely doesn't. Val and Mario come close to us, Val offers me her drink, and I shake my head no.

"It's just soda, I'm driving remember? No drinking!"

"How about we make a toast, so you must take a drink!" Alex tells us, to me mostly.

"And what would we be toasting?" I ask him trying to figure his angle.

"To you! For you finally loosening up!"

"I'm good, I don't need a toast," I tell him trying to get him off the topic.

"One sip, and you would have indulged me!" I look at him as I consider his offer.

"Fine, one sip!" I cave. He smiles as he grabs Mario's cup.

"To Angelisa, to a new circle of friends!"

"To Angelisa," they all say as one. Val and Alex hit their cups together, then they pass their cups to Mario and me. I honor my word and take a sip of Alex's cup.

We continue to dance for a bit, I drink a little more. I don't know why I never follow my instincts. It's like I never stopped drinking. I need a break. I excuse myself and head to the bathroom. I wash my hands and splash some water on my face.

I look in the mirror and just stare at my reflection.

"What are you doing?" I ask my reflection. I know this is not my life anymore, I don't want to be doing this. My mind must be playing tricks on me, because I swear I saw my reflection shake her head at me. Ok, that's it. Time to go home.

I walk out of the bathroom, and of course Alex is by the door.

"You ok?" he asks.

"Yeah I'm fine. I should be going," I tell him.

He leans in closer. This guy just doesn't get it. He hugs me, then he tries to kiss my neck. I push him back,

"Alex —"

He signs. "Yes I know, you're not ready! Ok, I won't push, let's head out!" he scoffs.

I know he's upset, but seriously, how many times do I have to tell him? Just on cue, my phone rings. I reach for it, and face it to Alex.

"My sister, I really should be home by now," I tell him. I answer the phone, I tell her I'm on my way, and hang up. We meet the others and say our goodbyes outside. I jump into Val's car, I'm hoping she wasn't lying about not drinking.

When we drive up to my house, I see my dad sitting on the front steps.

I turn to face Val, "you'd better go home, looks like he had a bad day." She nods as she understands. I get out of her car and she drives off. I walk up to the steps and sit next to him.

"Papi, what happened?" He doesn't answer at first, "I lost my job."

6. Reflection

It's Friday, my parents have been fighting all week. My father was fired from his job. He got caught with alcohol in his coffee. Someone reported him, and so he got fired. Apparently he's been drinking for a while now. I guess I should've noticed. He's been locked in his room when he was home, didn't want to go to church, not even on Sundays. He never had a problem with drinking before. It was my fault he started.

When I started college, I wanted to feel part of the crowd. Everyone around me was drinking beers and other kinds of alcoholic beverages. I didn't want to feel left out, so when they offered the drink, I absorbed it. At first I didn't like it but day after day I was drinking it, and I kind of got used to it. I wasn't a drunk, but as long as my friends were having it, I wanted some too. I wanted to belong. But I never really felt anything other than hangovers.

One day Val's cousin gave me a small bottle of vodka, and I brought it home. It must have fallen out of my jacket pocket and my dad found it. He said he wouldn't tell my mom about it, but I had to stop drinking. He made me promise, so I stopped. But I never knew that before I was born, my father was an alcoholic.

I guess having the bottle in his hands made him give in to the temptation. He must have had a taste and couldn't stop himself after. It's my fault he is in this situation now. He never told my mom where he got his first drink, but I'm sure it was from that bottle I brought home.

Now I have another burden to shoulder, I'm not sure how much more I can bear. Guilt grows within me, and I fear my mom when she finds out it was my fault. Maybe I should just tell her now. I can't. I can't bear the thought of her being angry with me, I don't think I could take it.

I make it to work, hopefully I can be distracted from what's going on at home. My sister Evie has been keeping herself busy, she's distracted with rehearsal for that special service tonight.

I hope my sister gets some rest. I need some too before tonight's service. I don't want to fall asleep while they're preaching. On Sunday they said this Friday's special service was going to be one not to miss. I wonder if it's something I should miss. What new thing is going to happen? All I know is that there's going to be a play. My little sister has one of the main roles. She always loved acting.

She's fourteen now, when she was younger she used to act out her favorite movies. She would stand right in front of the TV and recite every line of the main character. I thought it was pretty impressive. Over the years she would play theater with her friends in the back yard, she was always the star. The church opened up a drama club and she's been involved ever since. She's one of the Christians that can live in the church. Has she been *chosen?* I don't know, but she's enjoying it!

The pastor is always saying many are called but few are chosen. Am I even called? I feel as if I'm living in between two worlds. One that is all holy and godly, and the other is everything that is the opposite. I guess I'm in the grey area. Maybe one day I can figure that out. I just hope time doesn't run out on me.

Caffeine is pretty busy today, a lot of people are ordering coffee boxes to go. I haven't thought of my father's situation much, keeping busy is distracting. The front door swings open as Ryan walks in. He looks around until he sees me, and then he smiles. He walks to his favorite spot and sits down with just his laptop today. He lifts his chin to me, I guess that's my cue to bring him his coffee. He's come in a little later than usual today, I'll be leaving soon. I bring him his coffee, I place it down on his table.

"Thank you," he says.

"You're not working as hard today?" I ask.

He smiles, "no, I did my research, I'm just going over it."
I don't want to interrupt him.

"I'll leave you to it then." He nods and I walk away.
I feel a buzz in my pocket. I reach for my phone, a text from Alex.

Alex: *"hey Angelisa, have you thought about tomorrow?"*
Me: *"still thinking…"*
Alex: *"well, what if you came as my date?"*
Me: *"I still don't know if I'm going, and no offence but I don't want to be anyone's date."*
Alex: *"I understand, but come anyway, I want to see you again"*
Me: *"I'll let you know"*

I put my phone back in my pocket as I turn around to glance over at Ryan, I catch him looking at me. He's sitting on a slant, his right arm on the back of his chair and the other on the table. I feel like he's studying me.

"Can I get you something else?" I ask him since he didn't turn away.

"I was just thinking," he says shaking his head.

"About?" I ask.

"Do you want to have a cup of coffee with me?" he asks as he adjusts himself in his seat.

As much as I would like to, "No, I'm sorry, I really can't. My shift is almost over and I have to finish up, besides I don't drink coffee." He raises his eyebrows at my response.

"You don't drink coffee? But you work at a coffee shop?" he asks.

"It's a job, drinking coffee wasn't a requirement," I answer.

He laughs, then asks "what do you drink then?"

"Water! Why do you want to have coffee with me anyway?" I ask him, trying to cut to the chase.

"Sit, and maybe you'll find out," he answers with a smile on his face.

"I really can't, maybe another time. I really have to clean my station before I leave," I tell him regretfully.
He looks at me thinking of what to say next.

"Yeah I guess I better be going too. Rain Check? We can have coffee…and water!"

I try to keep a straight face, but coffee and water, I busted out laughing.

He smiles again and says "what did I say?"

"Coffee and water!" I say still laughing.

He begins to laugh, "Ok maybe that was a little corny, but I just want to talk to you."

"What are we doing now?"

"Talking, but I mean…really talk. I would like to get to know you."

"Well, you already know where I work, and that I don't like coffee. And I know you like your coffee black, and you study a lot."

"Have you been watching me?"

"I see you walk in here every day, ask for coffee and you start your…" I point to his laptop. "…whatever it is you are doing?" I see a smile tug at the corner of his lips.

"I can show you, but...you have to go."

"Yeah I do, I'll take you up on your 'rain check' another day."

"Ok, if I don't see you tomorrow, have a nice weekend, and I'll see you Monday?" I smile and nod as I begin to walk away.

"Or" I hear him say, causing me to turn back around. "Maybe, we can meet before the weekend is over?" He asked. I can't explain why, but I know I can trust him.

"Maybe. Give me your number, if I have some free time I'll text you." He agrees and gives me his number. I store it on my phone under Ryan Caffeine, not that I need to add that last part because he's the only Ryan I know. I would definitely remember Ryan, how could I not? He stands out, he's unlike anyone I ever met. We say bye to each other, I get my things and clock out.

***

Tonight's service, what should I expect? I'm only going tonight because of my sister. Otherwise I probably would have hung out with Val, but I don't think that would've been a good idea either. I've made such a mess of my life. I started drinking, drove my father back to his addiction and he lost his job because of it. There is other stuff I did that I'm not so proud of and I wish I can undo them. I can't turn back time, I wish I could.

I want to go back to my old life sometimes. But this new person I've become, won't fit in that old life. I go to all these parties and lounges with my friends, but I never feel comfortable. I feel so empty inside. I wish I knew how to fill this void.

I'm all already for church, I walk to my full length mirror for a final look. I'm wearing jeans…of course, with a simple black top and heals. I stare at my reflection wondering, who is the girl staring back at me? I truly am lost, and I'm alone. I can't help the tears that begin to fall from my eyes. It hurts so much to be alone and talked about. No one knows what I've been through, and other than my mom, no one seems to care.

In my mirror reflection, I see a hand wipe the tears from her face. I'm confused, I look behind me as if there was someone there in the room with me, since there seems to be someone in my reflection's room. The mirror version of me looks to the direction of the hand on her face, and smiles.

Then she looks back at me and tells me, "you have been chosen, believe that." She steps back and her outfit changes, she's wearing a suit of armor and is holding a sword.

"This is who you are!" she said. And just like that, it was back to my normal reflection. Just me again.

What was that? A vision? Was I hallucinating? I really should've taken that nap.

7. Talent Night

Everybody is in position to begin. The play is more of a musical where of course my sister has the main role. Not only can she act, but sings and dances too. She played a girl who was lost to herself. She danced a solo in the dark with only a spotlight on her. She was showing that alone she's left in the darkness.

When Jesus appeared to her, the lights came on to show He is the light. She then danced with Jesus following in His footsteps. They danced in tune for a while until she started to miss a few steps when she took her eyes off of Jesus. She began to dance further away from Him. When she realized where she was, she searched for Jesus, but He was too far from her. Her life distracted her from Him, but Jesus didn't let her go too far. He regained her attention, and they would be in sync again. The message was that no matter how far you've fallen, Jesus is always there to welcome you back.

No one knows what happened to me, oddly this play seems like my life. I know I'm not where God wants me to be, but I don't know if I'm ready to be. I know He will take me back, broken and all. I miss who people thought I was when I served here in the church. But I didn't really know God as others did, so this life I'm currently living may not quite suit me. But it's my escape.

I've adapted to a new lifestyle and I'm not sure I'm ready to give it up just yet. I guess you can say I'm in a weird place in my life, because although I come to church...I still participate in things that are not approved by the church. But in the world outside of God, I don't feel I belong there either. I'm in between worlds, unsure of which one is really the path I should take.

The curtains drop, everyone stands up and claps. I look around, there are some people crying. It was truly a powerful message, if only it were that easy. People are always talking about how it's easy to let God lead you, but it really isn't. I admire those that can follow God with all they have, but I just don't have it in me.

When I used to pray, I felt nothing. It felt as if I was talking to myself. I watched other people and they would speak in heavenly tongues, others would be very emotional. I've heard of people say God spoke back to them. Me? Just my own voice. Another reason why I left 'Closing back doors,' I didn't think I had the spiritual requirement for such a program.

Brian goes up on to the altar, he thanks the cast for their performance and gives glory to God for blessing them with the talents they have. He then gives a short prayer before he announces the guest of the night.

"I hope everyone has enjoyed themselves and has received God's message. It is not over yet, I would like to call up the guest of the night. Minister Gabriel, he is from Revival Church. He will be bringing the word." Brian said as Minister Gabriel makes his way up to the pulpit.

"Thank you Brother Brian," Brian returns to his seat in the first row.

"How many are ready to be spiritually awakened tonight?" Minister Gabriel asks, almost shouting. A lot of ministers are very loud and energetic, I like those. They keep your attention.

"Before we begin, I would like to introduce to you: my nephew. He had a dream, when he told me about it, I told him he should share it tonight. I believe his dream is a message for some of you here. He will be only a few minutes, then I will continue with the preaching. Ryan, will you come up here?"

"Ryan? What?" I see Ryan Caffeine walk up to Minister Gabriel. I can't believe he's here. His uncle pats him on the back and hands him the microphone. Ryan looks at the congregation almost as he's searching for someone. When his eyes land on mine, he nods as if he was looking for me. He begins to talk.

"Blessings everyone, my name is Ryan Rivera, my uncle invited me last week to join him tonight. I wasn't sure I was going to make it, but then I had this dream. When I shared it with my uncle he thought it was a message I should share here."

His eyes never left mine as he spoke. Did his dream have something to do with me? It would explain his reaction at Caffeine when he saw me, then just now.

He continues, "I decided I should just come, but it wasn't until right now that I see I was supposed to be here," he pauses. His eyes fixed on mine, he glances over the congregation before he begins again.

"Sometimes we may not understand God's ways, but it's not our job to understand, we just have to obey. God is always working. I won't take too much of your time.

In my dream I saw groups of people, some were praising and worshiping, others were just standing around watching. Those who were watching suddenly fell to the ground. Out of the group praising, a few fell down as well.

The Lord showed me people that have been falling asleep. He says it's time to wake up. You have been asleep too long, and you have let your daily lives take over His time. There is a spiritual war and you need to fight in it. If you want things in the physical to change, it needs to be won in the spiritual.

Whatever you are going through, everything you have been through was only to make you stronger. God has never really left you alone, you have let your problems and your situations keep you from God. Don't let the enemy win, God has already been talking to you, open your eyes, and be vigilant. Amen?"

"Amen!" I hear everyone say all at once.

"Thank you uncle for this invitation" he looks to his uncle as he walks back up to the pulpit. Minister Gabriel pats him on the back again as Ryan walks off to take his seat.

"I'm so proud of this young man. God has changed his life and molded him into the man he is today. My nephew's dreams confirms the message the Lord has given me for tonight. Time to wake up," he says.

He begins to preach, and my mind goes back to the dreams I've been having, the ones that felt so real. I think God is trying to talk to me. And Ryan, I knew there was something about him. I'm starting to think he has something to do with my dreams as well. He reminds me so much of the angel I saw there.

The service is almost over. I always liked preachers from other churches. Sometimes when in-house ministers preach, they talk about what they see and know of. Some ministers let their emotions speak louder than the voice of God. But when someone from the outside comes in, someone that doesn't know you preaches on what you are feeling, I believe it's more from God. That's just my opinion, may or may not be true.

Minister Gabriel is preaching about those that fell asleep. Not sleeping physically, but spiritually. Sounds like me, half of me asleep. It's like something died in me. I had a desire to work for the church at one point in my life, taking part in whatever I could. But one day my desire just turned off, and I never figured out how to turn it back on again. The saddest thing was no one cared to help me light that flame. They all turned their backs on me and I was left without a friend here. So I had to make new ones like Valarie. She's not perfect, but neither am I.

"You have to wake up! Your time is now! Tomorrow is not promised, Wake up!" Minister Gabriel shouts, he pulls me out of my thoughts. I know I have been sleeping, but I don't know how to wake up. Physically, I'm here, I'm awake but, spiritually, I feel dead.

"The Lord is already starting to wake your spirit," he says. Is he talking to me? I literally just thought that.

"You came here tonight hopeful for some message from God. He gave you a vision of who you are," said Minister Gabriel. Ok, he is speaking to me, that's God speaking to me. So He hasn't forgotten about me?

Minister Gabriel ends his preaching, and prays. Not a popcorn prayer, but a heartfelt sincere prayer. He prayed that God will give us strength for what we will be facing. He also said to allow our spirit to lead, and not our flesh.

"There's a war coming, and it's not against your flesh, but against your spirit. Do not lose faith and trust in your God. Amen." He ends his prayer.

"Amen." I say because somehow, I believe it's me he's praying for.

I see the *'closing back doors'* leaders ready to lead the new believers in their meeting area. My mom looks at me watching them, she leans in to whisper, "you should think about returning to the program."

I shake my head, "no mom I can't. I'm not that person anymore."

"You never really told me why you stopped going."

"It's just...it's not for me. It was too much work and I wasn't ready for it."

"I don't think that's why you quit, when you want to talk about it, I'm here."

I don't want to talk about it. There are new people there now. I don't even know their names. Some of them carry around the *'I'm holier than thou'* attitude. And others the *'do as I say, not as I do.'* Church is not meant to be for perfect people, because we feel lost or broken is when most of us go to church. But I don't believe that certain people in the church should be in charge of certain jobs.

Rebecca is one that shouldn't be working in that program. I know her secret, she's been putting the blame on me for her mistakes so her father wouldn't think less of her. I get why she would do that, but don't pretend you are perfect.

Guess I shouldn't judge, I made my own mistakes, no one knows of them, but it's a burden to keep them hidden. When I quit, no one asked why, all they said was *"God be with you."* I didn't know that when I quit, I would lose my friends. It was like I got pushed out and away from everything and everyone. I was spiritually broken, and they just left me. I know I'm a big girl, but even Christians can break.

As we're exiting the church, I search for Ryan. Minister Gabriel approached us.

"Hello, I was wondering if I may speak to you," he tells me. Before I can answer, my mom says, "oh sure, Angelisa meet me back at the car when you're done. And if you see your sister, tell her the same," she walks off.

I look at Minister Gabriel, "hi, I really liked the preaching." He smiles and says

"Thank you, but that was all God. He was talking to you."

"Yeah, I kind of got that. I've been feeling kind of numb for a long time. I guess I just got used to it."

He stares at me for a moment before he speaks again, considering his words I assume.

"He wants you to wake up, you were hurt, and you are ashamed. Instead of holding on to Him, you closed yourself off. You're hiding. You need to unburden yourself. Let go of the guilt. Your friends hurt you, but you're still here. You have let your light dim out. It's not too late."

I have no words, I feel tears rolling down my face. Where would I even begin?

"Keep your eyes open, both spiritually and physically. I promise, things are going to change," he says.

I can't talk, so I just nod. He reaches in his pocket for something, he pulls out his wallet and opens it. He takes out a card.

"Here," he says.

"This is my number and email. You can call me if you need to talk, or email me if you prefer. I get you feel alone here, but you can always talk to me if you need advice or prayer or whatever."

"Thank you, Minister Gabriel."

"You can call me Gabe, and you are welcome." He gives me a hug. I say bye and start to walk over to the car, when I see Ryan I pause.

He's not alone, he's with Rebecca and a few others by the small garden on the side of the church. I wanted to talk to him but I don't want to be around Rebecca right now, so I keep walking to the car.

"Hey! Angelisa!" Ryan shouts. I turn to face him.

"Hey," I whispered. I feel embarrassed of him seeing me this way.

"I saw you talking with my uncle, I was hoping we can talk now."

"I guess we should," I say not looking at him. I've been crying, I'm sure my mascara has run.

"I don't think us meeting here tonight was a coincidence, I knew there was something about you."

"Yeah I thought the same," I tell him.

"Are you ok?"

"Yeah, just… it was…I'm good."

"Want to get that coffee and *water* now?" He joked. I smile back at him.

"I think that would be nice, but I don't want water. Maybe a smoothie? Want to go to a diner?"

"Smoothies sound good."

"Let me just tell my mom, she's waiting for me in the car."

"Sure thing."

"Maybe you should walk with me, she should know who I'm going with."

"Yes, that might be a good idea, I should introduce myself. How old are you again?" He asked.

If I didn't know any better, I would think he's nervous about meeting my mom. But he doesn't strike me as the type of guy that's unsure of himself. The way he carries himself tells me, he fears nothing. He looks like he has an interesting past.

"I'm nineteen, why?"

"I'm twenty, so we're good. I just wanted to make sure there wasn't a big age difference that would cause your mom to worry!" he smiles.

Yes, that would make sense. He looks around my age, did he think I was younger than nineteen?

"I didn't think you were that much older than me, besides I don't think my mom would mind. She pretty much ditched me when your uncle wanted to talk to me," I responded.

"Yeah, but this would be different. A guy you just met wanting to take her daughter out at this time!"

"I hang out with people she's never met, later than this even. She trusts me…although maybe she shouldn't so much!"

"Why is that?"

"Nothing, never mind. There's my mom!" I answer him as we both reach my mom's car. Unfortunately, my mom is not alone, she's standing outside the car talking to Lady.

"Hey mom, this is…"

"Ryan!" my mom cuts in.

"Yeah, we actually met at work" I tell her.

"We wanted to go to the diner, is it ok, or did you need me to come home right away?"

I look over at Lady, she has a disapproving look on her face. She probably thinks I'll be a *bad* influence on Ryan. There has to be another reason other than her rose bush for her not liking me.

"Yes honey, go ahead don't be home too late." My mom says, she looks happy. I look over to Lady and smile.

"I won't mom."

I glance over at Ryan as we walk away.

"So what was all that about?" he asks.

"You caught that huh?" He nods.

"She doesn't like me. I drove into her rose bush and she's been mad at me ever since. Although I think there is more to it, but I have no idea what it is." I answer him.

He stops in front of a motorcycle.

"A bike huh?" He looks at me and grins as he hands me a helmet. Good thing I wore jeans.

"Yeah, do you like bikes?" I look over the bike as I nod.

"Yes, but I never road one before." He smiles.

"First time for everything," he says.

He gets on his bike and I climb on behind him. I can feel a lot of eyes on me. This will be the new gossip. Sometimes church people are the first ones to start the gossip, and they can be so mean. Ryan starts his bike and we take off.

8. What's Your Story?

I've always admired motorcycles, but I never dreamed I would ride one. I've heard so many stories about accidents that I feared them. Tonight, although I fear motorcycles, I thought why not try something new. When we first took off, I wasn't sure where I was supposed to hold on. Ryan told me I should hold on to him.

As the wind pushed against us I tightened my hold around his waist. The way the motorcycle cuts through the wind, speeding by the trees distracts me from my life. I can see myself riding a bike like this just to clear my head. It just feels right.

When he pulled over and turned off his bike I was a little disappointed, it didn't last long when I remembered he had to take me home after. I would have another chance to enjoy the ride. I hopped off his bike, then he does the same. He grabs my helmet and puts it on the bike. We walk inside and grab a table. We sit in silence for a few minutes as we look over the menus.

"Did your uncle have a ride back home?" I asked.

"Yeah, he drove himself there, but I should text him and let him know I left."

"So Ryan Rivera, what's your story?"

He straightens up in his seat, and says "before I get into my story, do you want to talk about what's bothering you?"

I look at him in surprise, I guess I really shouldn't be. I can't explain it, but it feels like he knows me...the real me. Either that or he really pays attention.

"Why do you think that?" I ask.

"I saw you speaking with my uncle, then you were wiping your tears."

"You saw me crying?" I'm modified. I hoped he didn't notice. I cover my face with my hand, as if that would change the fact that he saw me.

"Yes, I'm sorry. I didn't mean to embarrass you." He apologized. "Can I be honest with you?" He asks. "I hope I don't freak you out, but...I knew there was something about you when we first met. I just wasn't sure what it was. Then I come to your church tonight with a message and you were there. This message, my dream...it was for you. I strongly believe that."

I'm speechless, I contemplate on sharing what's been weighing on me for the past two years. I stare at him for a moment before I speak.

"I have been going through some stuff for almost two years now. And lately, I've been experiencing some strange dreams, and visions." I stop again, considering if I should share my dreams with Ryan. I decide against it.

"I'm really not sure what they mean, I don't want to get into them." He leans forward, puts his hands on the table.

"Maybe I can help you understand it." He smiles, "I'm good with interpreting dreams."

I shake my head.

"It's ok, when you're ready to talk about it, I'm here. I know you don't know me, but sometimes it's easier to speak to a stranger."

I consider his advice, it is easier to speak with a stranger sometimes. But I don't want Ryan to remain a stranger. And if I tell him all my dirty secrets, he might abandon me like everyone else. Will he think I would be a bad influence for him?

"But what if I do speak to you, and you decide we shouldn't be friends?" I break eye contact. "I know how people look at me, how members from my own church don't want to be around me."

"I want to be your friend regardless. I know there's a reason for our paths crossing. Whatever you want to talk about I promise, I won't turn my back. I know I can help you get through this." He says.

I look up again. "I'm not ready, I have a lot of baggage."

The intensity of his stare makes me uneasy, nervous. "How about I tell you a little about myself then."

I nod, that might be a start. "Yeah let's start with you. It never crossed my mind that you were a Christian?" I sit up and fold my hands on the table. "Again I ask, what's your story?" I guess I really shouldn't judge a book by its cover.

I'm use to viewing Christian guys with a clean cut, well dressed but nothing too flashy. In my church, they're as simple as can be. But Ryan, he's not as simple. For one, he has a motorcycle! He has long hair, which I kind of like. He has earrings, one on each ear. Nothing to flashy, but he has them. Ryan begins to laugh.

"Do Christians have a certain look?"

I shrug my shoulders. "I don't know! I just never really met a Christian guy that wore earrings or had long hair. I have nothing against it, I actually like it."

He smiles, causing me to smile. I lower my eyes to the table.

"But you been to my church, have you seen any of the guys there look anything like you? Try to understand where I'm coming from!" I answer.

"Our appearance is always a debate among the Christians. But reality is, what we look like doesn't save us. I could look like you think Christians are supposed to, and not have a relationship with God. My clothes, hair, or jewelry is not what's important. My relationship with God is what's relevant. We don't have to dress a certain way. But now, if God decides I should change my look, He will let me know." He pauses before he begins again. "Men in the bible had long hair, such as Samson and Absalom. What really matters is how I serve God!"

I nod. "I hope you don't take offense to my remark." I tell him.

"Not at all! I don't let words faze me." He grins.

"So why did you want to speak to me earlier today?"

"You didn't seem yourself. You looked sad, maybe stressed?" He answers.

"Stressed? How did I looked stressed?"

"You looked upset, and I knew something had changed from the first time we met."

He's very observant. "Hmm, you've been paying attention."

He leans back and smiles again. "Some might say its discernment."

"Right!" I grinned. "I learned something about my father. Something I did, made him what he is now." I'm not ready to confess my sin so I leave it there.

"So, back to you. Have you always been a Christian?" I deflect.

"No, I have not." He answered.

"Well, do you want to talk about it?" I asked him.

Before he answers he stares again. As if he's trying to read my mind. He doesn't pressure me to elaborate. "I was a messed up kid, always getting into trouble." He begins. "My parents had split up when I was thirteen, and I didn't take it very well. I lived with my mother, until I became too much for her to deal with and my uncle took me in.

He was a Christian, and he started taking me to church. Of course I wasn't too happy about it at first, but then it grew on me. The church had a lot of kids my age. A lot of them had situations similar to mines, and we became friends.

We had a youth pastor meet with us once a week, so we could talk about our frustrations. It was helping me with what I was going through, but I was still a kid, and was easily tempted. There was a girl, at the time I thought she was the most beautiful girl I've ever met." He smiles as he leans forward. "Recently I realized that wasn't true." He winks.

I smile and nervously begin to pick at my fingernails.

"I couldn't get her off my mind so one day I asked her out. The crew she hung out with in school were trouble, but I wanted what I wanted. She had accepted my invitation, we went to the movies. When we came out, her friends were in the parking lot waiting by my car."

"Wait, you had a car? How old were you?" I asked him.

"I was seventeen when this happened. It was my uncle's car, he let me borrow it for the night." He leans back in his seat. "I was still working with my issues, but I was getting better. My uncle trusted me and gave me the keys. So we walked up to the car.

The guys had a couple of six packs, and they offered me one. I knew I shouldn't drink and drive, but I took one anyway. I didn't want to look like a punk in front of my date. One beer led to another, and another. Next thing I knew the guys jumped me, and I was too wasted to fight back. They stole the car and my date went with them."

He pauses as he takes in the memory of his past, he takes a sip of his coffee. When he looks at me again he continues.

"I lost my uncle's trust, and that made me really mad. When I went back to school the next day, I walked right up to the two guys who jumped me and I beat them with my bare hands. I released all my frustrations on the two guys. I never touched the girls, I was angry, but I would never raise my hand to a female.

School safety agents had to peel me off of one of the guys. I stopped fighting, and looked down at them on the floor. I had broken one guy's nose and the other was curled into a ball on the floor. I had gotten expelled from school.

To make a long story short. Taking my anger out on those guys, didn't help me at all. I felt I was worse than I was before. I realized, I was fighting the wrong fight. When I got home, I didn't want to hear anything my uncle had to say so I went into my room. Funny thing is, I fell on my knees and cried out to God. I was asking for His forgiveness. I cried so much that night that I must have fallen asleep, because I couldn't remember anything after that."

I didn't speak when he stop talking, I didn't know what to say.

"I spent the next day locked in my room." He continued.

"It was Saturday morning, I woke up on the floor. I got up and showered, went back into bed. I felt the sudden urge to pray, so I got down on my knees and prayed. I didn't know how to start or what to say, so I stood in silence.

I had my eyes closed, all I remember saying was God, help me. All of a sudden, I felt as if I was in another place. I was standing, except, I wasn't. I was in a vision. I saw myself, and someone hugging me.

He whispered, *'I've got you my son, trust in me. Lay all your burdens at my feet.'* Again I cried, I felt His arms around me.

When He let go of me I pulled back a little, I saw my uncle standing behind Him. God told me, that he sent my uncle to help me. Suddenly I was back in my room, and I felt someone holding my hand, when I looked to my right, my uncle Gabe was there, praying with me. He looked at me, and hugged me. I cried again on his shoulders. And well, here I am."

"Wow, that's all it took? Prayer? You let everything go?" I asked him.

He grins. "Well it wasn't an easy process, it took some time. But I let God help me. I stopped thinking that I had to do it on my own. Sometimes we feel that if we get ourselves into messes; we should get ourselves out of them. Based on my experience, we don't have to do it on our own. We have to let go, and let God."

"I find that hard to do sometimes." I admit.

My phone buzzes in my pocket, maybe it's my mom. Nope it's Alex again, reminding me about the party tomorrow.

"Your mom?" Ryan asks me.

"No, a friend invited me to a party tomorrow, I never gave him an answer."

"Him? Like a date?"

"Oh no!" I cringed. "Defiantly not. Alex asked me to go as his date, but there's something about him that makes me feel uncomfortable."

"In what way?"
I wanted to tell him about the other night, but didn't.

"I can't explain it. He puts on this façade of being *the man*, a show off. But he seems kind when no one's watching. I don't like being alone with him."

"So maybe you should listen to your instincts."

"I'm only considering going because of my friend Val. She's the only friend I have right now that hasn't abandoned me. She's going to hang out with a potential boyfriend, I'm supposed to be moral support."

Ryan nods in understanding. "So you're going then."

"I don't know yet. Do you think I shouldn't?"

"That's up to you. There's nothing wrong with hanging out with friends, as long as you know your limits."

"I don't have many friends, my church friends disowned me when some stuff went down. I met Valarie in college, and we started hanging out. I met Alex this week, it's his party and the guy Val is interested in happens to be Alex's friend. I have to expand my circle of friends." I told him.

He leans back, looks down at his coffee then looks at me again. "Just be careful, and if you feel uncomfortable, then leave." He drinks his coffee. "Where is it? If you don't mind me asking?"

"Upstate New York, about an hour out."

"So you driving yourself out there?"

"No Val will pick me up, but if she doesn't want to leave early, I'll just call a cab." I answer.

"You can call me, if you don't want to stay. I'll pick you up."

"You would ride your motorcycle one hour away just to pick me up from a party?" I questioned.

"Think about how much a cab would cost you?"

"I can also take the train." I countered.

"You can just call me, or I can go with you. I can be *your* moral support." He offers.

"Thanks for the offer, but you don't have to do that" I say.

After hearing, Ryan's story, and feeling like God is talking to me, I'm not sure I really want to go to Alex's party. But I can't let Val go on her own. I wish I could invite Ryan, but I can't take him there. Besides, I think Alex might get the wrong idea, and it may seem rude.

"To be honest, I don't really want to go."

"So don't!" he replies. If it were that simple I wouldn't. I text Val telling her yes before I change my mind. I ignore Alex.

"I have to go, I can't let my friend go alone. I don't know her date well enough to leave her alone with him yet." I tell Ryan.

He nods, "I get it, just keep your eyes open."

"I guess we should go, don't want people to think wrong of you for hanging out with me."

He stares at me for a moment, then leans forward. "What is it you did that you think everyone is judging you all the time?" He whispers.

"Not something I want to talk about with you, at least not yet."
I joked. "We just met, I don't want to scare you away. I would like you
to know me now before you learn who I was then. And then you can
decide if I'm worth your friendship."

He meets my gaze, he doesn't say anything. I feel he's trying to
figure out my secret.

"That woman talking with your mom, is she the one you worry
about?"

"She's one, there's a few others."

He's quiet again, almost like he's studying me. "Would you
mind if I prayed for you right now?" He asks.

I look around the diner, there are a handful of people around
us. I hear him laugh, and I look back at him.

"What's funny?" I asked.

"You looked nervous just now. Are you afraid people will see?"
I take in a deep breath.

"Well, yeah!" I answered him. Won't people think we're weird?

"I just never seen someone pray in a diner before." I whisper.

"You can pray anywhere, I'm spontaneous. Don't worry, I
won't be loud!"

I smile, because he seems to understand my concern.

"Ok." He places his right hand on mines, lowers his head and
closes his eyes.

"Lord God, I thank you for this blessed day you have allowed
us to see. I give you praise and honor Lord. I present before you, your
daughter Angelisa. I pray you give her strength for the road ahead. I
ask that you may open her spiritual eyes Lord, that she may see what's
beneath the surface. Give her discernment Lord, that she may not be
fooled by the enemy. You have called her for a purpose. I pray that she
will begin to see herself the way you see her. I pray for healing of her
soul, that she may begin to unburden herself to you. Guide her steps
Lord. In Jesus name I pray, Amen!"

When he finished praying, I look around again. I didn't want
anyone looking at us weird, but it was as if no one heard. Ryan
squeezes my hand to regain my attention.

"Stop looking around, it doesn't matter what they think.
Besides I practically whispered it," he jokes.

"If you want to talk about it, I'll listen. I promise I won't
judge."

"Another time." I answer.

"You can talk to God about it. Yes He sees all and knows all, but sometimes speaking about it to Him is healing for you."

I nod as I consider his advice.

"Ryan, I really should be going. Don't want people getting the wrong idea about us if I get home too late." I tell him as I tuck my phone in my pocket.

"I can understand that. For everything else, you shouldn't worry so much about what people think. People are always going to find fault even if you doing the right thing."

He calls over the waiter to ask for the check. When the waiter returns with it I offer to pay, but he won't take my money. He said it was his treat.

"I could've paid. I don't want you to think—"

"Let me bless you tonight. It's my treat, don't take that from me." He tells me as if I offended him somehow.

I nod as he lays out the money. I kind of feel bad now. We head outside to his bike and head to my house.

His bike makes a lot of noise as we drive up to my house. I can see Lady peeking through the window. "We have an audience," I tilt my head in her direction. He looks over and waves at her. I laugh.

He looks back at me, "I'll pray for her too!" He jokes.

"Well, this was nice, thanks for the talk and for treating...the prayer, and the ride home!" I tell him handing him his helmet.

"Any time, maybe you should give me your number since you might not use mine!" He tells me. I laugh.

"I haven't had the chance yet." I exclaimed. I pull out my phone from my purse, and call him,

"There's my number!" He pulls out his phone, and starts typing. My phone buzzed in my hand.

It was him *"thanks"* the text read. I thank him again before I walk up to my house.

9. Feeling Judged

As I walk inside my house, I find my father passed out on the sofa in the living room. My mom is sitting on the other sofa watching TV, it looks like she's been crying. I walk into the living room and sit next to her.

"Mom?" I call as I reach for her hand.

"Are you ok?"

She looks at me and says, "I'm ok honey, your father and I were talking, and he passed out.

"I'm sorry you're going through this, I didn't know dad had a problem with drinking."

She puts her arms around me and brings me into a hug. "Of course you didn't, this was before you girls were born."

Guilt grows inside me as she speaks. She doesn't know why he started again. It's my fault, but I can't tell her that, I'm afraid she'll hate me. Pulling away from her hug I decide to change the subject, the thought of my mom being that upset with me saddens me.

"Where is Evie, asleep?" I ask.

"Yes, she was so tired after tonight."

I smile when I think of how well my sister played her role in tonight's play. She really touched my heart. I hope she'll never experience what I have. I'm supposed to be her example, she can never know what I've done.

"Yeah, I can imagine, she's been practicing so much I feel like I haven't seen her in weeks."

"So, tell me about Ryan, you never mentioned him before!" My mom's enthusiasm brings a smile to my face.

"It's not like that mom, he's just a new friend. He's been coming into Caffeine for a while now, we never spoke before. Monday was our first conversation. And it turns out he's a Christian, and he showed up to church tonight with his uncle. He wanted to talk to me earlier today, and since I was in a rush we didn't have a chance to. Funny how he ended up in church tonight."

My mom smiles and nods as if she approves of him.

"It's nothing romantic mom, we're just new friends, that's all!"

She smiles at me, "well I'm glad you have a new friend. I never understood why you and Rebecca stop being friends, did it have anything to do with Logan?" She asked.

"Yes and no. She's not who you think she is mom. I'm not ready to talk about what went down with us. I'm dealing with it in my own way." I tell her. My own way is shutting everybody out.

"You know you can tell me anything, I understand you need your space. But it's been almost two years now. Please just let me in, I liked Logan too. Did he do something to you?"

I know my mom is only concerned. I wish I could let her in, but she can't know. It would break her heart to know what I have done, and what I almost did.

"Logan and I broke up because he was going away to college!" I lied. He did go off to college, but that's not the real reason we broke up.

"Mom...I can't right now, in time when I'm ready, I will tell you everything." I promised.

I place my hand on hers as I stand. I feel tears begin to well, I can't let her see me cry. She's dealing with a lot right now. I smile at her before I walk away. As I walk up the stairs to my room, tears begin to fall. The memory of what I lost weights heavy on my heart. I go straight to my bed and fall asleep.

I'm dreaming again. I'm right where I was in my last dream. I don't see the angel anywhere. I hear this clinging sound up ahead, I walk towards it slowly. I see four figures and a knight fighting against each other. They're in the middle of a circle of people that are just holding hands as if they were praying. I don't want to be seen so I hide behind a tree. I feel a tap on my shoulder and I slowly turn around. *I've been caught,* I thought. Before I can see who was behind me, I wake up. It's morning. I can still feel my heart pounding in my chest.

Why am I getting these dreams? I go and wash up. I decided since finals are next week I should study before I go to the party. I go down to the kitchen and make myself some pancakes and return back to my room. When I'm done eating, I pull out my books and begin studying.

It's already noon, I need a break. I reach for my phone, I had it on mute so I wouldn't be disturb. I knew Val would be trying to reach me. I have four text messages:

Val: *hey, I just wanted to confirm, you are going tonight right?*
Val: *Hello!!!*
Val: *don't ignore me Angel, I'm picking you up at 6*
Alex: *can't wait to see you tonight…*

I did tell Val I was going last night, but I didn't tell Alex. I assume Val told him, unless Alex is just being cocky. I hope he understands I want nothing more than a friendship. I decide to call Val.

"Hey Angel! I've been texting you, why you didn't answer me?"

"Sorry I put my phone on mute, I was studying. Did you already tell Alex I said I was going?"

"Yes, he's been asking for you. I think he really likes you!"

"I don't see him like that Val. You know I don't want a relationship."

"Angel, you need to move on, maybe Alex is not the right guy for you, but he can help you move on. He's a nice looking guy and he's funny. You should really think about giving him a chance. I know your ex hurt you, but you can't keep putting your life on hold. Just give him a chance, I don't think it can hurt." Val tries to convince me.

Am I really putting my life on hold because of Logan? "Val" I say, "I understand and appreciate your concern, but Alex is not the guy for me, not even as a past time. To be honest, I'm only going to the party because of you. I don't plan on staying all night either!" I know Val means well, but she really doesn't know everything.

"Thanks for your support, I will not pressure you into dating Alex, but you are going to dress up right?" She asks. Dressing up is Val's thing, not mine.

"I'm not wearing a dress!" I declared.

"Yes you are, I was thinking that red one you have," she insist.

"NO! I don't want to wear a dress!" I snap.

"I'll be at your house around four, I think I need to help you get ready." She is so persistent.

"No dress Val!"

I can hear her laugh. "Ok, bye" she says.

"Bye!"

I walk to my closet to take a look at that red dress Val was talking about. Logan bought me this dress for a party at his uncle's house. It's a sexy cocktail dress. The dress is fitted and has a low cut in the front.

When I wore it, it hugged my curves. There's a soft knock on my bedroom door.

"Come in."

My sister walks in as I hang the dress back in my closet.

"Hey Evie, that was an awesome play last night!" She walks over to my bed.

"Thanks, it felt amazing to be part of it. But I'm glad it's over. It took a lot out of me!" She exclaims.

"Where did you go last night?" She ask me. I see my phone light up on my bed, I forgot to take it off mute. I walk toward it.

"I went…" I smile when I see who text me.

"Hold that thought Evie, let me check this." It's Ryan.

Ryan: *hey, how you feeling today?*

Me: *I'm good, how was your ride home last night?*
Ryan: *nothing like the wind blowing on my face.*
Me: *lol, nice.*
Ryan: *you going to that party tonight, right?*
Me: *yes*
Ryan: *be careful, let me know if you need a ride.*
Me: *thanks for the offer, but I think I'll be ok.*
Ryan: *if you feel you need a ride don't hesitate.*

I hear my sister clear her throat. "I'm sorry Evie, just one second!"

Me: *I'll be ok, but if I need a ride, I'll call you, ttyl*
Ryan: *ok, later*

I put my phone down, and face my sister "sorry."

"Was that the guy from yesterday, Ryan?" She asked me.

"Yes."

She looks a little displeased with my answer. "What's wrong Evie?" I ask her.

She stands from my bed and walks over to my window. Looking outside she said, "People were talking about you when you left with him," she turns to face me.

"They thought you would corrupt him like you did Logan," she cautioned.

"WHAT?" I shouted. "I'm sorry Evie, I'm not upset with you." I walk over to her, I took her hands in mine.

"You have no idea what happened between me and Logan." She pulls her hands out of mine.

"But Rebecca said—"

I cut her off, "Rebecca? You listening to what Rebecca is saying? Don't you know me?" She looks away from me again.

"I'm sorry Angel, it's just you are kind of an outsider, and she said just maybe you shouldn't hang out with someone like Ryan because you're going to drag him down." she whispered.

I can't help the tears coming down my face. I can't handle my sister thinking this way of me. I feel both hurt and angry right now. I need her to leave. I'm not upset with her, I'm afraid I may take out my anger on her.

"Evie," I call her name as I walk over to my door.

"I think you should leave my room, I have to get ready."

She looks at me, "just tell me Angelisa, did you drag Logan down with you?" I wish I can tell her what happened, she's too young to understand.

"Evie, things happened, and I can't talk to you about it because you wouldn't understand. But no, that's not what happened."

I turn to my door and open it for her to leave. When she looks at me, her face is a mix of emotions. Then she walks out. I shut the door behind her and lean against it as I slide down to the floor. I begin to cry. I'm so tired of being judged. I didn't provoke what happened. If this is what people think of me, maybe I shouldn't try so hard not to be.

I get up, and decide I'm going to wear the red dress. I look for shoes to match, I found my black heels with an ankle strap. I search through my accessories, and pick out a pair of big gold hoop earrings and a black leather choker. I walk back to my closet and pull out the dress again, a black leather jacket and a black purse. I lay everything I chose on my bed. I walk out of my room and into the bathroom, I take a shower and wash my hair. I'm so hurt by the conversation with my sister.

When I return to my room I throw something on, towel dry my hair and walk down to the kitchen to get something to eat. My mom and sister are both sitting at the table. I don't want to say anything to them. But I guess my sister filled my mom in on our conversation.

"Angelisa, please tell me what happened with Logan," my mom urges.

"Mom, please just leave it alone." I begin to make myself a sandwich.

"Angelisa, I have left you alone about this for a long time, now people are saying things about you, and I don't know what to believe."

I finish building my sandwich, I look over to where both my mom and sister are. I look between them. I can't believe this is happening right now.

"If you don't know what to believe, then I guess you really don't know me." I snapped. I'm fuming right now. I can't wait to get out of here. Where is Val?

"I have to get ready," I storm off.

"I want the address to that party," she yells behind me.

"I'll text it to you!"

I get my phone to text Val to hurry up, and to send me the address to the party so I can give it to my mom. Val texts me back right away with the address and says she's on her way. Thank goodness, I have to get out of this house.

10. Letting Loose

We arrived at the party. Val was happy I decided to wear my red dress, I find it a little shorter than I remember. Val is wearing a black fitted short dress, with red pumps. She did my makeup and my hair before we left. With Val nothing is ever simple. My hair, we both agreed to leave it down, she curled my ends. But my makeup, she decided on the smoky eye look, mascara, eyeliner; the works. I can't complain, I like the way I look tonight. I just hope Alex doesn't think I dressed up for him.

As we walk in, I feel as if everyone's eyes are on us. I'm not use to all this attention. Alex walks up to us and holds out his arm so I can slide mine in his, reluctantly I do. He leads me to the kitchen. I look back and see that Mario has escorted Val to the dance floor. Alex offers me a drink but I don't take it.

"Just water," I told him.

"Come on…it's a party," he teased. I shake my head no, I'm upset, but I'm not stupid.

"Maybe later then," he said. He extends his hand out for me to take, "want to dance?" he asked.

"Sure." Anything so I don't have to talk.

A merengue song is playing as we reach the dance floor. We join everyone else by getting into the rhythm. We dance a few songs to this genre. Then they play some reggae, I think about walking off the dance floor, but Alex moves in closer, encouraging me to continue dancing. He pulls me in closer, I can feel him on me. I pull away some so he wouldn't be so close. He gets the idea and remains his distance. My feet are starting to hurt with these heels, so I take them off and hold them in my hands.

A slow song comes on, Alex pulls me closer and we sway side to side.

"You look so beautiful tonight." He whispers in my ear. I smile.

"Thank you." I feel his hands slide lower, so I take a step back so his hand will go up. His gesture makes me uncomfortable, did he really think just because he gave me a compliment that he can touch where he wants?

As if he senses my unease he asks, "You want to take a break?" I nod.

"Yes please, my feet are killing me."

He grabs a water bottle and a red plastic cup from the kitchen's island. Then he reaches over to the snacks on the other side of the island and grabs what looks like chocolate cake, well more like brownies. He offers me one and I take it, I could use a little sweet. As I take a bite he asks if I like it, I nod. Either it's really good, or I was hungry. He asked if I would like another one, I feel a little guilty as I nod. I shouldn't have another but I'm feeling a bit peckish. He must see my guilty expression because he starts to laugh as he hands me another.

"You into junk food tonight?" He asks as he brings his laughter to an end.

"I didn't realize I was hungry."

"Well there's more snacks if you want something else. There's what you Puerto Ricans call pastelillos, do you want one?"

"You should have offered that first, I'm not sure I can eat more of anything after those two brownies I just ate."

"Did you eat before you came here?" He questions. The look he gives concerns me.

"No, why do you ask?"

"You should eat something else and drink a lot of water."

"Why do you say that?" I asked confused.

"Because you just ate two brownies…"

I grow more confused, am I missing something?

"The brownies are actually edibles. You know…weed brownies. I didn't realize you didn't know what was in them. Melissa baked them, and she always adds more of that *"special"* oil than she should."

"WHAT?" How could I have been so stupid? "What does it do? What affect would it have on me?"

Alex laughs, "don't worry, nothing crazy. You're just going to feel giddy. You might actually enjoy yourself." He bites his bottom lip,

"Maybe you would let yourself have fun with me tonight." His eyes drift from mine to my lips then back up again.

He takes my hand and leads us toward the back of the house. There's a few people by the back porch smoking hookah. Alex asks if I was ok, I nod. He introduces me to a few of his friends. I smile as I greet them, I didn't want to be rude but I wasn't interested in meeting his friends. They kept trying to pass me the hookah hose, but I refused every time.

After a while, I couldn't stop laughing. I have no idea what's so funny, but I couldn't control myself. I start to dance on my own, but soon after Alex joins me. As we move together I feel his hands all over. I know I don't want this, I try to move away but I begin to feel lightheaded.

"Are you ok?" Alex asked as he places his hand on my back.
"I'm not feeling so good, I could use some air." I answer. He nods in understanding and takes my hand to lead me out of the crowd.

We head outside, and sit by the pool. Sitting by the water is refreshing. I take in a deep breath and release. *Where is Val?* I wondered. I haven't seen her since I got here. I glance over my watch, I've been here for three hours. I didn't even noticed. Alex offers me a bottle of water, I quickly take it and drink the whole thing nonstop. I feel so sleepy all of a sudden.

I lower my head and close my eyes. I wish I could take a nap. Alex sits closer to me, he strokes my hair and tucks it behind my ear. With his fingers he strokes my neck then he leans in to kiss me. I didn't want to kiss him, but I let him anyway. When he tries to deepen the kiss I pull away.

"Sorry, I'm not really ready for this," I apologize. He pulls back, "I thought we were having a good time?"

I sit back, "we are, I just don't want to be doing this."

He sighed as he looks toward the pool. "Don't you like me?"

I breathe in deep. "I do, but not in the way you're thinking." He faces me.

"Alex, my last relationship changed my life, and I'm just not ready to put myself out there yet, I'm sorry if I gave you the wrong idea."

"I thought maybe you were going to let me try to erase the bad memories. You look tired, there's a room upstairs if you want to rest."

He stands and smiles, "I can take you up there if you want."

I know that's a bad idea. I shake my head.

"I can't remember a time when a girl turned me down. You're kind of killing me here!" I look away from him.

"Angelisa, I understand. I'm not looking for anything serious. But I get it, you're just killing my ego!"

I laugh "I'm sorry, that's not my intention, but all I can offer right now is friendship. And I doubt even that would be very good!" I tell him truthfully.

"As a friend, will you have a drink with me?" He laughed.

"One drink, then you can take a nap upstairs until the effects of weed wear off."

I smile at his request, "I'll have one drink." I told him.

"But I will not be going upstairs with you or alone. I'm not feeling good, I might just head out soon." One drink can't be that bad.

Everyone already thinks the worse of me, I just don't want to care. The way I feel, a drink may really erase the disappointment from my family, even if it's just for a little while.

"I don't think Val is leaving anytime soon, so you might as well relax. I'll be right back!" He walks back into the house.

Suddenly, I get this weird feeling as I stare into the pool. Something in the water calls my attention. An image of sorts; me. As I try to make out what I'm seeing, I realize it's a vision. What I see causes me worry, but I wonder if I'm hallucinating because of the brownie cakes.

I see myself passed out on a bed, but I'm not alone. Alex is standing over me. I close my eyes and shake my head. It must be a side effect I try to convince myself. But then why would I be seeing what I'm seeing? I thought I might see pink elephants or even mermaids in the pool, instead I see myself about to be taken advantage of by Alex. I open my eyes hoping the image is gone, but it's not. Alex moves closer to the bed and places a knee on one side as he's about to climb over me.

I begin to feel lightheaded again, placing my fingers on my temples I hear a voice say, *'time to go.'* I turn around, but I'm alone.

I quickly get up, but the quick movement almost makes me stumble since I am not feeling a hundred percent. I grab on to the back of one of the patio chairs to steady myself, I then grab on to the next one then lean my hand on the wall leading back to the house.

As I step inside I find Val, she's about to go into one of the bedrooms with Mario. Mario stops to talk to another guy before he enters the room, giving me enough time to reach Val before she goes in. When Val notices me, she meets me half way.

"Are you ok, Angel?" She signals to Mario to give her a minute as she walks me to a seat nearby.

"I'm feeling a little lightheaded. I had some brownie cakes."

Val laughs. "I should have warned you about those. Where's Alex?" I look over my shoulder wondering the same thing, but I'm hoping I don't see him before I head out that door. I shrug my shoulders.

"Val, are you and Mario about to…?"
She nods biting her lip before I could finish asking her my question.

"Angel, you may not approve but I'm a big girl, I know what I'm doing!"

"I know," I look over my shoulders again. *"I just got a bad feeling,"* I whisper.

"About Mario?"

"No Alex, I just want to go home. Alex keeps encouraging me to go upstairs and sleep it off, but I'm worried what would happen if I do." I tell her looking over her shoulders.

I don't want Alex to find me.

"I'm going to find a ride home. I assume you don't want to leave yet?" I ask hoping she would offer to take me home. But I don't want to ruin her night.

"Would you consider me a bad friend if I stayed?"

"No, I totally understand. Don't worry I'll find a ride. I'll text you when I'm home."

"Ok, do you need me to walk you out?" She offers a hand.

I take it, "No, I'll be fine. Really, it's ok."

"Be careful." She tells me as she hugs me. "Maybe I should just take you home myself."

"No it's ok if you want to stay. I can find my way." I reply. I pull out my phone to text Ryan as I walk towards the front door.

When I walk outside, I sit on one of the chairs on the porch trying to figure out how I'm going to hide from Alex while I wait for Ryan to get to me, if he's still willing to pick me up. He did offer more than once, I'm sure he would. I'm starting to regret wearing this dress, jeans would've been nice and warm right about now.

A roar of a motorcycle calls my attention from my phone, when I look up I see Ryan right across the street. I smile as I put my shoes back on to walk over to him. He returns my smile with his.

His eyes travel quickly to the length of my short dress causing me to tug the hem down. His smile disappears and I fear I may have given him the wrong impression of myself with this outfit. It wasn't until I felt an arm wrap around my waist from behind me that I noticed Alex found me. *Shoot.*

"Hey, I was looking for you." He offers me a cup filled with a dark red substance, the smell of liquor is strong.

"What is it?" I cringed.

"Cranberry juice…and henny. You promised me a drink, you didn't tell me which."

"That smells really strong, I don't think it's a good idea to drink that. Especially after those brownies—"

"Come on, one drink, you promised!" His expression changes as he offers me the cup again.

"I know, and I'm sorry, but I can't drink it." He tightens his hold around my waist, as he slides in front of me and backs me up against one of the pillars on the porch.

"Alex please, let me go." I say as he presses himself up against me now.

"Alex," He spills some of the drink on me as I struggle to get him off me.

He tries to make me drink what is left, I push the cup away and it falls to the floor spilling the remainder of the drink. I can't say I'm disappointed.

"Is there a problem here?" I hear Ryan ask. I didn't realize Ryan had made his way up to the porch. Alex looks Ryan up and down before he makes eye contact.

"Alex, just let go."

"There's no problem here," he ignores me. "This is my party, she's my guest."

"I believe she said to let go." Ryan barked. I remember his story last night, about him losing his temper. I don't want to be the cause of him losing control. Alex steps back some, to face Ryan, but he doesn't let go of me.

I have to defuse this situation fast.

"Alex, look at me." When he does I continue.

"If you care just a little for me, listen to what I'm telling you." He faces me completely, "I'm not feeling well, and I have to go home. Please, let's not make this a big issue."

He continues to stare at me, his eyes travel down to my lips then back up again, and then he nods as he loosens his grip.

"Thank you, I'll see you in school okay?"

He backs up from me as I walk closer to Ryan. Alex doesn't take his eyes off Ryan, or Ryan to him.

"Let's go," I grab his hand to pull him away and walk towards his bike.

He hands me a helmet as he looks down to what I'm wearing. He takes off his button down shirt and ties it around me like an apron. I didn't realize when I sit on his bike my dress would go up. He was thoughtful, I smile at the gesture.

70

He gets on his bike and I hop on behind him. I look back to the house, Alex is still standing there. Ryan starts his bike, I lean my forehead to rest on his back between his shoulder blades since I'm still not feeling well.

We take off, the air feels good, but cold. After we're a few blocks away, I yell at him to pull over. He stops up ahead. I have to call Val, I have to make sure she's ok.

"What's wrong?" He asks me. I reach for my phone in my purse and dial Val.

"I have to make sure my friend is ok."

"Hello?" She answers.

"Hey Val, you ok?"

"Yes, did you find a ride home?"

"Yeah, I had a friend around the area…" I face Ryan, I wonder how he knew where I was.

"He's taking me home."

"Ok, we'll talk tomorrow, get home safe." Val tells me.

"Bye, Val." I hang up, "how did you know where I was?" I ask Ryan

"What do you mean? You texted me the address, I assumed you wanted me to be around, I headed out here waiting for you to call me." He answered.

"I did not text you, I texted my mom the address." I looked at my phone and notice I did text him the address, and I never texted my mom.

"I was supposed to text my mom. I don't know what happened."

I lean up against a nearby tree. Rubbing my forehead brings me comfort. I feel so sleepy, but also hype. I don't want to lose control in front of Ryan, I have no idea what he's thinking of me right now.

"You ok?"

I feel Ryan in front of me. I nod, then I shake my head instead. I'm not ok.

"No, I'm not." I answered. He stands next to me, leaning on the tree.

"Want to talk about it?"

"No, not really. It's not so much about what just happened, it's more of me being so stupid." I open my eyes to face the ground in front of me. I can't bring myself to look at him.

"Why? For coming here? You had no idea what was going to happen." He tries to comfort me. I turn my head slightly to face him.

"I know that," I take in a deep breath.

"I knew better not to drink, but I didn't realize their snacks contained *"special ingredients"* I tell him. He gives me a questionable look.

"Let me guess, you had some special brownies or too much rum cake." I smile.

"Brownies." I look away again. "I thought I was being careful, it never occurred to me about the brownies. I was hungry."

He laughs, causing me to face him. When he meets my eyes, his laugh calms me down.

"I'm sorry, I just found it funny. I use to get caught up all the time. How you feeling now?"

"I can't lie, I'm starving right now."

"Then let's go grab something, I think there's a burger and shake joint around here. But a joint is probably the last thing you want to hear right now." He starts cracking up.

I want to be upset at him, but right now he's hilarious. His laughter is contagious. Didn't know Christians joke this way.

After we eat, or rather I eat, because Ryan just stares. I wonder what he thinks of me right now. I'm such a mess. He doesn't rush me, we've been here for some time. I just want to sleep. That's not an option since my ride home is a motorcycle.

"I think it's wearing off, but I'm just a little lightheaded." I tell him. He nods once and takes my hand to lead me to his bike.

"Come on, let's go. You just need some water and some pain killers, we can stop at a gas station on the way. I wish I would've borrowed my uncle's car." He said as he handed me the helmet again, "the ride home might be a little cold."

"Oh, here, let me give you back your shirt. Your arms are bare."

"I have sleeves, I meant for you. Besides you need my shirt to cover up as I'm sure you already noticed." I nod.

We get on and we take off. After a few minutes we found a gas station and stopped for what we needed, then we continued on our way.

The drive didn't seem so long going back, maybe because we were on a motorcycle. I am freezing, more on my legs than anywhere else. I had to hike up my dress to be able to sit on the bike. Luckily I have Ryan's shirt to cover up some of my legs.

My thoughts of the night are racing in my mind. I wonder what Ryan thinks of me now. I rest my head on his back as I fear we would no longer be able to be friends. He caught a peek of my life tonight, I won't blame him for not wanting to hang around. Maybe what my sister said earlier today was true, and maybe that's why it bothered me so much. I don't want to drag Ryan down.

We're on the highway and I see my exit coming up, but he doesn't get off. He continues to the next exit and drives to a house. As he turns off his bike.

He peeks over his shoulder, "this is my uncle's house, and he's having a vigil with a group our age. I thought you should come. But if you want me to take you home, I'll turn around."

I hesitate at first. Just the thought of being surrounded by more church people our age. What if they're like Rebecca and the others? But if I want Ryan to stick around me a little longer I should accept his invitation. He did bring us here in hopes I would stay.

"I guess I can stay a little while." I hop off the bike and he does the same. I untie his shirt from my waist and hand it back to him. He takes it, but doesn't put it on. The arms are wrinkle, I wouldn't put it on either.

He walks up to the house I follow behind him, he opens the door and walks in. Most of the lights are turned off, there's a dim light in the living room.

I can hear worship music in the background, but it's low. There are a few people praying on their knees. Gabe is standing facing the wall with his hands up. This was not what I was expecting when Ryan said vigil. Ryan places his hand on the small of my back to lead me in to the living room.

As I walk in I look down at what I'm wearing, I don't want everyone to look down on me because of how I am dressed. I have enough rumors going on about me, I don't want my outfit to confirm the rumors. I wouldn't mind using his shirt to cover up again.

I turn around to face Ryan, "I can't be here dressed like this." He takes a quick glances down the length of me, when he meets my eyes again he smiles.

He places his hands on my shoulders as he says "trust me, they are not looking at what you're wearing. You're fine, no one here will judge you. We're here to worship and receive from God. Just try to relax, give it a chance."

I want to believe him, "*ok*" I whispered as I pull down my dress so it seemed longer. Ryan leads us deeper into the living room.

"What should I do Ryan?"

He looks back at me, takes my hand, "let's just pray." In that moment Gabe turns around and smiles when he sees me.

"Welcome, come let us pray together," Gabe says. He extends his hand for me to take, I do. Ryan still holding my other hand, the others stand from their spots on the floor and join hands as well. We stand in a circle.

Gabe begins to pray out loud, and the others do the same. I still have my eyes open, observing everyone. Ryan leans in and whispers.

"Just close your eyes." I take another look around before I do as he suggest, I just listen.

It's beautiful the way they all sound. I've been to vigils before, but this one feels different. I continue to listen to them and the music in the background.

"Open our spiritual eyes Lord." I hear one of them say. I begin to feel this surge of emotions. I can't help to think, does God love me enough to forgive me?

I know He's a forgiving God, but why would He choose me? I don't feel as special as people have told me before. There's so many people that are better than me. I've been so guarded since Logan that I don't feel anything anymore. I'm afraid if I allow myself to feel, I would be overwhelmed. All those emotions I kept bottled in will definitely be too much.

I see myself again in this place, the place of my dreams. This time I'm not alone. Everyone I'm with right now is there, in a circle still praying. I look around and I see nothing but tall trees. It looks like I'm in the woods. I can hear the worship music in the background, and Gabe praying about guilt. He was saying guilt was keeping us down.

Suddenly, a creature was standing before me. It had a large head, its body looked like it was made of rocks. It had arms and legs but it did not have eyes. It had a large hammer in its hand, he raised it and was about to hit me with it, I screamed.

I feel as if I'm in two places at once. Here in the living room with everyone, and in another reality. Gabe was praying louder and both Gabe and Ryan's hands were holding mine tighter. I was crying, memories I didn't want to see were becoming visible in my mind.

My dad past out on our sofa, the look of disappointment in my sister's eyes. Even the events of what happened tonight with Alex. Another image flash through my mind, one I never want to remember.

The creature is still here, I scream again as he raises his big hammer. I try to shield my head, but I can't because I'm frozen in fear. I can't move anything but my eyelids. There was another figure coming towards me. When it reached the rock creature it stopped. I couldn't get away. I felt trapped. The creature manages to hit me, the blow feels so real. I fall to the floor.

I open my eyes, everyone is hovering over me praying. Gabe lets go of my hand, places his hands now on my head. He's praying over me, everyone is surrounding me placing their hands on my back and arms. I feel someone place a blanket over my legs to cover me. Ryan is still holding my hand. I close my eyes again and both the figure and the creature are still there. But they're not as close to me this time.

Images of my father passed out, the parties of me drinking, and of Logan still flood my mind. I can't take it anymore. I scream,

"NO! NO!" The voices are lower as I cry louder. Gabe tries to comfort me, "it's alright child. You are not alone."

I don't know how long I lay there, but when I come to, everyone is sitting on the floor around me singing along with the music. I sit up as I glance at everyone. I feel so embarrassed. One of the girls hands me some tissues so I can wipe my face.

"I'm so sorry about that. I didn't mean to react that way." I hide my face in the tissues.

"You have nothing to apologize for, this is why we're here. I know you might not be able to see now. But God has a purpose for you. What you faced just now is going to help you reach that purpose. You have been called, and you have been chosen. But you need to believe that for yourself." The girl who gave me the tissues comforts me.

Called and chosen, again I hear that phase. *'You have been called, you have been chosen.'* If I had a dime for every time someone told me that I would be able to pay off my college tuition. What does that mean anyway? Chosen for what exactly?

Doesn't matter right now, I feel foolish for how I responded to what I just experienced in front of a bunch of people I don't even know. I started to cry again. The other girl comes to me and hugs me. I cry more as I hug her back.

"Angelisa, you are holding on to so much pain. You have to let it go." Gabe urges.

"Do you want to tell us what you saw?"

I look at everyone, before I begin. I just hope they don't think I'm crazy. I go on to tell them about what I experience, leaving out the details of my memories. I tell them how I saw them there as well.

"Sounds like guilt and fear. It has power over you, a strong hold. It weights you down, holds you back from moving forward. You have to overcome it. Lighten the load by speaking about it. The bible says *'A person standing alone can be attacked and defeated, but two can stand back-to-back and conquer. Three are even better, for a triple-braided cord is not easily broken. Ecclesiastes 4:12',* share what you're feeling. Why do you feel so guilty?"

11. Surrounded By Strangers

I don't know if I'm ready to share my secrets with people I barely know.

"Do I have to share right now? No offence, but I don't know you, and not even my family knows anything about me anymore." I tell them.

"You don't have to share," Gabe assures me, "but I think you want to. You have been carrying around such a heavy burden for so long it's beginning to weight on you." He's right, everyday it feels worse than the day before.

"I just don't want people to think less of me than they already do," I whisper. Gabe places his hand on my arm.

"Dear child, just because we are Christians doesn't mean we are perfect. We all have a past. We all have something we battle with. Trust me, no one will judge you. Let us help you."

I glance around the room, all eyes on me. I want to speak, but instead I cry.

"If I tell you why I feel guilty, I would have to tell you the shame that led me to guilt. And that part, I'm truly not ready for." I stuttered. One of the girls moves closer to me and takes my hand in hers.

"Everyone has a story. We are not perfect." Ryan cuts in, "Maybe I should introduce everyone to you. This is Jason." Ryan points to the guy sitting in front of the loveseat on the floor.

He seems to be of average height, I can't really tell from how he's sitting. He has a light complexion, and dark eyes. His hair is cut into a low fade, dark brown, matching his extended goatee. He has earrings on both ears. He looks a little older than Ryan.

"Jason has been there for me since I started going to church. He's helped me deal with a lot of my issues." Ryan pauses as he looks at Jason. Jason tips his chin to Ryan, and then smiles at me.

"This is Marissa," Ryan says as he points to the girl sitting on the sofa across from me. Her face is serious. She has short hair shaved on one side, a dirty blond color. Her skin is fair, and she has light brown eyes. She offers me a tight smile.

"She's the drummer in our church, she's really good." She chuckles, "well thank you Ryan. I need you to keep up with the guitar."

"You play the guitar?" I asked Ryan in surprise.

"I've been practicing a few years now. I'll show you one day." Ryan winks. "This guy right here is Mike," he says as he pats him hard on the back.

He seems to be around Ryan's age. He has a short haircut, very light facial hair, black. Fair complexion and dark eyes.

"Mike is the coordinator to our 'New Beginnings' program." I look between the two of them, "what's that?"

"It's a group of people who guides the new believers to understand the road they are beginning with Christ Jesus." Mike answers.

"Oh, we have that in my church except, it's was called, Closing back Doors. I was in training, but I quit!" I tell them.

"Why did you quit?" The girl sitting next to me asked.

I looked over at her, then look down at my hands before I answered, "I wasn't ready for such a task."

Marissa leans forward, "Why?" I look at her, then at Ryan.

"It's where I fell." I answered lowering my eyes.

"How did you fall?" She asked again. My tears began to trail down my face. I couldn't bring myself to look at any of them. I closed my eyes when I answered.

"I wasn't ready to be part of it, I was weak. There was this guy and…" I took in a deep breath as the memory began to surface in my mind. His life seemed so intriguing, and I was led astray.

"But…" I shake my head at Marissa, she's about to ask another question, I cut her off.

"Please, I don't want to share all that right now."

"Give her some time guys. She's new, surrounded by strangers. When she's ready, she'll talk. My name is Ivy." The girl next to me said as she rubs my back. I shift my gaze to her, she's very pretty.

Her hair was long like mine, but a reddish brown color. Her eyes were hazel, her skin a mocha color.

"I have been a Christian for three years now. I'm twenty two years old, my mom died when I was ten. My father was never around and my emptiness was filled with anger. I use to fight anyone just because I felt like it. One day, I picked on the wrong person, and she sent me to the hospital. She had broken my arm and nose. Not to mention, a black eye.

At the hospital I met a girl. She was there because she was with her mother. While her mom had been taken for x-rays, she came to my bed and spoke to me about Jesus Christ. I accepted him into my life and I replaced that anger with His peace. He helped me change my life. It wasn't easy, the change didn't happen overnight, but I'm standing strong now. Instead of looking for people to fight, I look for people to guide them to Jesus Christ."

"Angelisa, God's been showing me your face," Gabe tells me as he comes closer to me.

"I don't believe it's a coincidence you meeting Ryan, and us ending up in your church last night."

Ryan clears his throat, "I've been praying for someone I've never met. When we first spoke in Caffeine, there was something about you, but I wasn't sure what it was yet. But then when I saw you last night, it was then I noticed it was you I've been praying for. God wants to help you, you have to let go, Angelisa. You don't have to tell us anything, but you should at least tell God. Yes, He already knows what happened, but you need to confess it to Him anyway. Trust Him to free you of it all. Your shame, your guilt, your sin."

"It's always hard in the beginning." Jason reassures. "I use to keep everything to myself, but God helped me find peace in Him. I trust Him."

"We will keep you in prayer." Ivy says. "We will give you your space." As she speaks, she gives everyone a stern look as if warding them to back off a bit.

"We have to close, it's getting late. But before we do, Angelisa, would you like to reopen your heart to God? To let Him in? He's been standing at the door of your heart for some time just waiting. He's already been talking to you, in dreams?" Gabe asks as if he already knows the answer.

I look right at him. Does he know about the dreams? My tears start to fall again, I nod my head.

"Stand child, let me pray for you." He reaches his hand out and I place my hand in his. I stand, and he begins to pray, everyone joins.

Every one gives me a hug, we all gather our things and head for the door. They all get into one car and drive off.

"Angelisa!" Gabe calls out to me. I turn to face him.

"The road for you is going to be a little bumpy, don't give up. God is with you." I smile.

"Thank you for everything!" I respond as Ryan and I walk to his bike.

"Ready?" He says as he hands me the helmet.

"Nope, but let's go." He shakes his head and smiles.

We arrive in front of my house, I can't help but notice Lady is already at her window, Ryan notices too.

"Is she always there?" Ryan ask me as I check my watch. Looking back up at him I nod. It's after midnight, I'm sure she was waiting to see who I came back home with.

"Yep," I answered.

"Thanks for everything tonight. I don't know what would've happened if you wouldn't have been there. I can't understand, how I'd text you the address and not my mom?"

"God works in mysterious ways." He answers.

"I was going to drink tonight, I was so upset when I left here. I had gotten into an argument with my mom and sister. They're starting to believe the rumors people in my church have spread about me. My sister also thought you and I shouldn't hang out anymore, because I might corrupt you. That's why I dressed like this and was ready to drink.

I figured if people were going to talk, I might as well give them a reason to. I'm tired of fighting to prove myself to them. But I realized that wasn't such a good idea, I shouldn't act out of spite. Yes, I messed up! But am I the only one that has sinned?"

"People always talk, and no you are not the only one. Sometimes it's easier for people to point at other people rather than look in a mirror and see themselves. They try to justify their actions by making others feel bad about theirs." He sympathize.

"I think I had a vision tonight at the party. When Alex went to get me a drink, I saw myself passed out on a bed and Alex standing over me. That was all I needed to see to realize I needed to get out of there. I don't know what his intentions were, but I felt I really needed to go."

"I'm glad you were able to get out, and that I had gotten your text. I was so angry when I saw him pressing himself against you that way, knowing you didn't want to."

"He probably just had too much to drink. I never really liked Alex, but I thought I was judging him without giving him a chance. Anyways, it's over now, thank you for being there."

"Anytime. You should go inside and get some rest. Maybe I'll pass by your church tomorrow, if you don't mind."

"That wouldn't be so bad. But I should warn you, people in my church are a little judgmental."

"I'll take my chances, what time it starts?"

"11:00am"

"I maybe a little late, I have to go to mines first." He says with a grin.

"You don't have to, people are going to talk. If you hang out with me too much, they'll talk about you too. I won't drag you down with me."

"Hey," he says putting his hand on my arm, "I don't care what people say about me, or you. I only care about what He thinks." He points up.

"I know God has a purpose in your life, and He wants me to help you. I am an obedient servant. I do as He ask." When he takes me into his arms to hug me, I feel a sense of peace.

Maybe God did send him to me to help me get back on track. He kisses the top of my head before I pull away, I smile and walk up to my front door. I turn to face him again, "see you tomorrow," he says as he gets back on his bike.

I walk inside and find my mom sitting by the window that faces the front yard. "Mom?"

"Why is he dropping you off? Did you take that boy to your party?" She snaps.

"No, I didn't take him to the party." I mumbled. I don't want her to get angrier than she seemed.

"Don't lie to me, I know what I saw." What exactly did she see?

"Mom, I didn't take him to the party. He took me to a vigil." She looks at me puzzled.

"Come again?" She asks.

"I felt uncomfortable in the party, I was trying to find a way back home, and he was around. But he took me to a vigil instead of bringing me home."

"Is that so? Explain how he happened to be there!" She still seems angry; she doesn't believe me.

"Mom, it's true. I meant to text you the address to the party, but I texted it to him instead. He thought I was letting him know I wasn't going to stay long so he rode up there and waited outside until he saw me." My mom looks so upset, she raised her hand and slapped me across my face.

"Mom!" I cried.

"You have a little sister to lead. I don't want her to be like you. Sleeping around with the boys from church, causing them to fall and leave."

I never slept around. I'm so tired of people talking about what they don't know. Sometimes I wish I wasn't a good person. I'm keeping someone else's secret and I get all the blame. I wish people would mind their own business. Why are they saying these things about me? To my mom? To my sister, she's so young, why pull her in to any of this?

"Mom, that's not true. But I guess you already made up your mind about me. Listen to everyone else, instead of recognizing your own daughter." I walk away from her and go into my room.

I throw myself on my bed and cry. I have cried so much today. My family turned against me now. Why is this happening to me? I stand from my bed, take off my jacket, get my earphones and put on some worship music. "I'm opening my heart to you God," I say as I lay down on my bed and fall asleep.

12. Encounter

I feel cold, darkness surrounds me. I try to see, but I can't. "HELLO!" I shout, hoping someone can hear me. Echoes of my own voice, there's nothing. Then suddenly I see a dim light ahead of me. Having no other options, I walk towards the light. There's a door illuminated by the light, I slowly reach out my hand towards the doorknob and turn it. I pull the door open and I quickly have to shield my eyes with my hand from the brightness of the sun.

After my eyes adjust to the light I lower my hand and continue to walk over the threshold. Everything is so bright, beautiful. I can hear birds singing, and there is a very pleasant smell, like flowers. I walk in a little deeper and turn slowly so I can see where I am. It looks like a garden, beautiful flowers everywhere, colorful butterflies, it feels peaceful. It's almost as it doesn't belong here on earth. I walk a little more into the garden, feeling the grass beneath my feet makes me stop walking. I glance down to my feet and notice I don't have shoes on.

It's then that I notice what I am wearing. A white nightgown, long sleeves, and the length goes down to my ankles. I'm feeling confused because I would never wear something like this, let alone go out in it.

There's a waterfall up ahead, I walk towards it to catch a reflection of myself. When I reach the water I look down and see a little girl. She has long dark hair, it's me, but when I was seven. I'm nineteen years old. What is happening? Where am I? How did I get here?

"Hello?" I call out hoping someone can explain this to me. "Hello, is there anyone here?" No one seems to be around. I start running hoping I bump into someone, I can't be alone here.

"Hello!" I call out again.

"Hello," I hear someone say besides me. I turn to face the voice, I see a man.

He's just standing there watching me. There's something about him, he's wearing all white like me, except it's not a gown. He is wearing a long sleeve button down white shirt, and white pants, no shoes. He has a glow around him. I can't really see his face, but by his voice, his posture and attire I can tell he's a man.

"I am not a man," he says to me. I stare. I'm confused, how did he know what I was thinking? I haven't said anything to him yet.

"You know who I am," He reassures me. Now I'm really confused. I can't even see His face, how would I know who He is.

"I'm sorry, I don't think I do." I answered. I can't really see Him, but I can tell He's smiling.

"Can you tell me where we are? I'm not sure how I got here. There was a door and I just walked through. But I don't even know how I ended up by the door. And why do I look like I'm seven again?" I tell Him really fast.

I can hear Him chuckle as He extends His hand out for me to take, "let's take a walk." I place my hand in His and we begin to walk.

"Do you know what happened to me? Why am I seven again?" I ask Him.

"Yes!" One word for all my questions. "You have been reborn, think back to last night."

How can I forget last night? So many things happened. But I think He means my last stop before going home.

"I was in Gabe's house, in a vigil." I tell Him. "But I still don't understand any of this." He chuckles.

"You opened the door to me." Confusion must show on my face. "Just before you fell asleep, you decided you were going to open your heart to me. You needed a reset." I did say that.

"I remember that," I responded "but I'm still confused, why and how am I here?"

We stop walking and sat down on a bench by the white roses. He begins to talk.

"I have been reaching out to you for some time now. You have lost your way. You wanted a chance to start over, you wanted to be reborn, and you opened your heart to me. You are seven years old again because you are beginning again. This is not your physical self." He reassures me.

"I'm sorry, I'm still confused. My physical self? What do you mean by that?" I ask trying to make sense of all this.
He takes both my hands in His and begins to speak.

"You were in a group called Closing Back Doors, correct?" I nod as I remember.

"Well you were in training to help those new believers cross the threshold and close their back doors. You witness the others work, and you thought you could handle it even though you were doubting yourself. By following the lead of others in that group, you took on a soul to consolidate.

You didn't do too badly on your own at first, but you weren't strong enough to stand on your own too long. Yes you had a seed planted, but it wasn't deep enough. Your seed was planted on hype.

You are very good with your words, you can convince a lot of people to do what's right. But when you encountered that situation, it was a little more than what you were prepared for. You were working on your own strength, and you burned out. You were trying to be an example for your sister. You even tried to preach to your father. You were giving others to drink from a cup that was almost empty. You dried out and drifted from me." He continued.

"At first you tried to fill yourself up with the lifestyle of your new friends. Parties, drinking, sex, but none of those things were satisfying you. You felt yourself slip further away. You needed me, I started to call out to you, but you couldn't hear me because your shame was louder than my voice."

"God?" I ask. He must be, this all makes sense now. I did feel lost, and empty inside. I feel my tears streaming down my face.

"Yes," he answers. "I was watching you, but I had to let you go just a little. When you were ready, you would return, like you just did. You can't just pray and walk away."

"I prayed every day, the others and me, we prayed together," I responded.

"You prayed, yes, but you didn't wait to hear me. You didn't let me guide you, you went ahead on your own." He pauses for a moment, considering His next words before He continues.

"You are not the only one that makes that mistake, others pray but don't wait for me to talk back. It's like a one sided conversation, you speak and I only listen. Having a relationship is not one sided, how can you know what I want you to do if you do not stop to listen? How can you get to know me?"

Now I see where I messed up. I'm not a patient person, I'm always in a rush and can't seem to slow down. I turn to face Him, "I'm here now, what's next?"

"You are in the beginning of your spiritual life. Think back to the conversations you heard while you were in Closing Back Doors, the leaders who ministered to those new believers, now you will be able to say you know what it's like. Right now you are like a child, as you mature spiritually, you will begin to grow." He answers.

"So what should I expect to happen here?" I ask.

"You are in the spirit here. This is the spiritual realm, you will be fighting for your blessing, for your soul, for your family. You will be facing different kinds of trials here and then in the physical realm, and each time you overcome them, you will grow.

You will need to arm yourself with my armor. As you face situations you will gain a piece. And when you are fully armed, you will face your biggest trial. I will also be with you, always just a prayer away. Just remember, what you do in the physical, will affect the spiritual, meaning you here."

He places His hand on my cheek, "I believe in you, you are more to me than you give yourself credit for."

"I guess I don't really think much of myself. I felt better of myself when I was in the *'hype'* as you called it. I guess I am really good at pretending. But since you knew I was in the hype, it wasn't truly spiritual, why didn't the other leaders figure me out? Maybe they could've seen the real me, and helped me before I completely died spiritually."

"As I said before, you weren't the only one. Don't worry about that, you are about to wake up. And when you do, it begins. Ready yourself for what's to come. Keep both, your spiritual and physical eyes open. Another thing, intimacy is the way to the heart that is very important."

"What do you mean by that?" I ask.

"It's not just prayer, think of it as this, when you are in love, most people want to express it. They listen to romantic songs, write poems, and give gifts. Well my way is, worship. Prayer and worship creates an atmosphere that will bring you here. A place for you and me, worship prepares the heart, and with an open heart you can receive what I have to offer you. Make time for me in your life the same way you make time for everything else." He answers me.

"So the only way for me to come back here is when I sleep?" I ask Him.

"No, I needed to get your attention so I allowed you a visit or two. The way to get here is through worship and prayer. You will soon figure that out. At first it may seem strange, but don't give up, you will get here." He answers.

"How do I start getting this armor?" I ask. He chuckles, and says, "You will not get all the answers in this one visit. But I will tell you only one more, you must face your sin. Only then will you gain the belt of truth. You will have nothing hidden."

I look at Him, and smile. I guess I did ask a lot of questions. Hey, I am seven years old here, isn't that what children do at that age, ask questions? I turn away for a moment, and when I look back He's gone. Everything starts to fade away, and I am now sitting on my bed in my room. I stand and walk to my mirror and see myself as a nineteen year old.

"It's time to grow," I say to my reflection.

13. Suppressed Emotions

Sunday service is the same again. There are a lot of eyes on me, I can only imagine what they're thinking. Most likely the same as my mom. I don't want to focus on any of that. It's time to wake my spirit up. I don't want to be a spiritual child anymore. I need to grow. I can't allow myself to keep living my life like this.

The choir is worshipping, I decide to stand and start to sing along. It's been a while since I did that. I would just sit in my seat and watch everyone else. But today I want to make a difference for myself. I have let what everybody thought of me keep me down, not today. Normally, I didn't care what people thought of me, but lately it's been weighting on me. I'm starting to feel emotions I didn't even know I was suppressing. What's worse than feeling numbed? Feeling everything all at once.

I've been numbed for so long, and in a few minutes of worship all those suppressed emotions are coming back. As I get into the worship, I can feel the spirit take over me. Tears run down my face as I remember when I had nothing to worry about.

There were no secrets separating me from my family, and when I wasn't alone. I had friends and I felt like I belonged. I realized I've been crying a lot lately. Last night I locked myself in my room and cried. I had learned to cover up my feelings, that I became very good at pretending I was ok. No one really knows what I was truly feeling. I'm not ok, God knows that, I needed that encounter with Him last night.

I keep worshiping, I tell God to show me what I need to do to be free. I tell Him to open my spiritual eyes, He does, and I find myself in the garden again. I still look like a seven year old. I take a look around, a few feet ahead of me I see a figure of something. I can't make it out. I walk towards it, as I get closer I start to feel cold.

The sky darkens, and the roses wither. The figure moves closer to me, the same one from the vigil. Suddenly I can't move. I'm frozen in place. The figure is like a shadow, it doesn't have a physical form. It doesn't even walk on the ground, it looks like its floating.

I'm afraid. It stops in front of me, just watching. I struggle to move, but I can't. I want to leave this place now. I thought I was ready, I'm not strong enough.

"Trying to be brave?" The shadow like creature mocked. "You think you are ready to fight us? You are no match for us. You are a sad, weak little girl." He laughs.

"*No,*" I think to myself.

"You have nothing, you are nothing, and you will stay as nothing." He indicated. I feel a tug on my hand and the garden fades away.

I open my eyes to find I'm the only one standing. I sit down and my mother whispers to me.

"Are you alright?"

I nod as I wipe the tears from my eyes. I don't think she would understand, much less believe me. I look over my left shoulder and see Ryan walking down the aisle with Ivy and Jason. My mom moves down so they can sit with us. Ivy sits to my right, Ryan and Jason to my left.

"Sorry we're late," Ryan whispers. I smile and look over to where my sister is sitting. She looks at me with disappointment written all over her face.

I can't help how she feels about me right now. One day she will know the truth. She's sitting next to Rebecca, I don't trust her with my sister. I honestly hope I'm wrong and that she does care for my sister and she's not just using her. My sister sees her as an example, I was supposed to be that for her. But she's witnessed my drunken nights more than once.

Brian is preaching again. Our pastor is still away on missionary work. I wish he would've left someone else in charge. Brian thinks I tried to corrupt his daughter. If he only knew the truth.

"Don't let your friends lead you down the wrong path." Brian says in his preaching. I'm not sure but, I feel as if he's referring to me.

"No one is perfect, but we need to try to be perfect. I've heard some of our youth are participating in activities of the world, and instead of falling on their own, they drag down their fellow brothers and sisters."

He is talking about me. How do rumors make it to the pulpit? I averted my eyes from Brian to Lady, she's staring at me. She must've told Brian about the last couple of nights she's been looking out her window.

I feel my face turn red from the anger I'm feeling in this moment. I look back up front to Brian, he's looking at me, then at Ryan.

"I see we have new faces here today." Brian says as he looks at everyone in my row. "Nice to see you again Ryan." Ryan smiles at him.

I just can't wait for this to be over. I don't know what else to do so people can stop talking about me. I don't want them poisoning Ryan against me, or Ivy and Jason. I could really use them in my life. The verse Gabe told me last night about a triple braided cord is not easily broken. I need them, they're all I have right now. I glance at my watch, it's almost one. It should be over soon. Our services usually are about two hours.

Brian makes an altar call for any new people who may want to accept Jesus in their hearts. But no one does today. Brian looks at us again, but he doesn't say anything. He closes in prayer. As everyone begins to exit they greet each other.

We start to walk out of our row when I see Rebecca walking towards us. I know she's not coming to me, because we haven't spoken a word to each other in almost a year, not even a simple hello. She must be interested in Ryan, I wonder if he might be interested in her. I glance at him then back at Rebecca. She glances my way but quickly looks away. I may feel weak and ashamed, but I don't let it show, to her she must think nothing fazes me, let her keep thinking that way. She will never know how much she's hurt me.

"Hi Ryan, nice to see you again!" She said, ignoring everyone else.

Ryan's eyebrows furrowed, "Nice to see you again…?"

"…Rebecca!"

"Yes, Rebecca. I'm sorry I couldn't remember your name."

"Oh, uh that's ok. Listen, some of us here were going to a BBQ after church. Would you like to come along?"

"Angelisa," he turns to face me, "you didn't mention a BBQ?"

"I didn't know. I guess I'm not considered part of the *'us'* here." I joked.

"Uh, well…" she hesitates. "It was just a few of us, not the whole church."

Ryan faces Rebecca again. "Oh, I see. Thank you for the invite, but we already have plans."

"Oh? Well another time then?" She questions.

"Yeah, maybe." He looks to me, "You ready to go?" I look over my shoulder where my mom was. She must have walked away while we were talking.

"Waiting on you."

Ryan places his hand on the small of my back to usher me out. Ivy and Jason follow us.

"I have to talk with my mom before we go."

"Of course, want us to come along? I would like to introduce Jason and Ivy."

"Yeah, that might be a good idea."

I walk to where my mom parked the car. She wasn't there. I look around and find her by the garden talking with Lady and Brian. I can only imagine what they're discussing.

"Hey, mom?"

My mom looks over to me than over my shoulder, "Angelisa, who are your new friends?" Both Brian and Lady are waiting for my answer.

"Well, you already met Ryan, this is Ivy and Jason."

"It's nice to meet you," Ivy extends her hand to shake my mom's.

"We're from Revival church like Ryan."

"We met Angelisa in a vigil last night, and when Ryan said he was coming to her church, we wanted to tag along." Jason said shaking everyone's hand as he greeted them."

"Oh?"

"Mom, they invited me to hang out with them for a little while, do you mind if I go?"

"Well, I suppose its ok. Don't be home to late. We need to talk."

"Ok mom, I won't." I said as I gave her a hug. I guess she believes I wasn't lying last night. We walk off, I was glad Jason mentioned the vigil.

"Where are we going?" I asked as we walk over to a black car.

"A few of our friends from church were meeting up at the skating rink. We like to fellowship every other Sunday. This is our fun." Ryan answers me.

"I haven't skated in a while, this should be fun."

"Well I hope you haven't forgotten how to skate," Ivy wraps her arms around mine.

"Because we like to compete with the boys. So you will be on our team."

"Great, no pressure."

They all laugh as we get into the car. I guess its Jason's car, since he's in the driver seat. Ryan sits in front with him. Leaving Ivy and I in the back seat.

14. Set Yourself Free

"Way to go Angelisa! You're way ahead of Ryan!" Ivy yells from behind the dividing wall by the roller skating rink.

"Yeah right, I think she's getting tired because she's slowing down." I hear Jason joke.

I'm about to reach the end of the rink, when suddenly Ryan is right by my side. I can't let him win, this is the last round. If I lose, the boys win. Why did Ivy insist that I be the tie breaker? I have to beat Ryan.

"OH MY GOD!" I yell. "Ryan look out!" I say as I point to his right. He looks over and loses focus. I skate faster and beat Ryan.

"YEAH!" I hear the girls yell and cheer. They all skate over to me and hug me. Ryan looks back at me and smiles as he shakes his head.

"You tricked me!" He said.

"Ryan, you should've stayed focus on the target." I joke.

"Oh don't worry, next time I will." He laughs. That was fun but I built up an appetite.

"Can we get something to eat now?" I ask.

"Yeah, I'm hungry too." Marissa agrees.

"Let's go to the food court." Jason says as he skates to the exit of the rink. He orders a couple of pizza pies, and pitchers of soda. We all sit down eating and laughing. I'm reminded how clean fun use to be for me. Just having a good time with people who like the same things as you. People who don't care what your past looks like, they just accept you for who you are.

"Hey Angelisa, on Wednesdays this whole group right here does a video conference. One of us brings in a scripture, and we study it together. Would you like to join us?" Ivy asks looking excited.

"Sure, sounds like fun." I say. I really believe this new circle of friends is good for me. They will help me get to where I need to with God.

Mike walks up to Ryan and hands him a set of keys.

"Here's your keys man, that ride was sweet. Thanks for letting me ride it out here." He tells Ryan.

"No problem. I hope it isn't scuffed anywhere." Ryan replies taking back his keys.

"Well…there was this turn…nah, I'm kidding." Mike jokes.

"Man you should've seen your face."

"Yeah, yeah whatever." Ryan turns to face me.

"You ready to go?" He asks.

"Yeah, whenever you are."

We say our good byes and head out the door. We walk up to his bike in the parking lot. I watch as Ryan checks it out. Looking for scratches I suppose. I can't help but laugh out loud, he looks at me puzzled.

"What's so funny?" He asks.

"You looking for scuffs?"

He looks back towards his bike. "Just making sure he was actually joking."

I decide to take a look at the bike myself. Towards the back of the bike, on both sides, I notice a design. Wings! He has a wing on each side of his bike.

"What's with the wings?"

He follows my gaze to the side of his bike. "They're angel wings. I always admired them, so I had them painted on my bike. I draw them all the time. I find them fascinating."

"I love angels too. I...never mind."

"You...what?" He asks.

"It's nothing, don't worry about it." I say. He doesn't say anything, he just stares at me trying to figure me out I guess.

"I had a dream last week, I saw an angel. He was beautiful. His wings were amazing."

"You dream with angels? What was he doing in your dreams?"

"Just looking at me. He was in the sky, his wings were keeping him up. He had a sword in his hand, it was just amazing to see."

"I see." He nods.

"What?" I asked.

"Nothing, we should go. Want to come to my house again?"

"When was I in your house?" I questioned. Then it clicked, he still lives with his uncle.

"Last night? The vigil?"

"I didn't realize. You live with Gabe?"

"Yeah, I told you I moved in with him when I was a kid."

"Right, you did. Sorry."

"No problem."

"What's going on in your house?"

"Nothing, I just want to get to know you a little better. My uncle should be home by now."

Considering his uncle will be home, I should be ok. Ryan is still new to me. I must be out of my mind going to a guy's house after only knowing him a couple of days. Normally, I would say no. But Ryan is different. I don't know what it is about him, but I know I can trust him.

"Ok, let's go."

***

We arrive at his house, he leads us inside. We walked into the living room. It looks brighter than last night. The sunlight shines through the windows illuminating the living room and dining room. I don't know what it is, but in this room I feel something strong in the atmosphere.

I take a look around, I don't see Gabe anywhere.

"Where's your uncle?" I ask.

"He should be in the study, I'll let him know we're here. Make yourself comfortable." He begins to walk away.

"Ryan?"

"Yeah?"

"Bathroom?"

He smiles. "Oh sure, it's down the hall to the right."

"Thanks."

I walk down the hall like he said and I find the bathroom. When I come back out, I see a door cracked open further down the hall. I hesitate. I don't know why I want to walk to the door. I can't help myself, I go towards it.

I push open the door a little. First thing I see is a desk. On the desk was a laptop, books, and papers. I guess this is Ryan's room. I want to walk in, but I hear footsteps. What was I doing? I'm not a snooper. I turn around and head back to the living room. Ryan just got there himself, he walks in with his uncle Gabe.

"Hello Angelisa, it's nice to see you again." Gabe tells me as he leans in for a hug.

"Nice to see you too, Gabe."

"I'll be in my study, let me know if you need anything Angelisa, Ryan." He nods as he addresses us.

I nod. Ryan and I sit down on the sofa as Gabe walks away.

"So, what you want to know?" I asked Ryan.

"You!" He laughs. "I want to know more about your dreams."

"Ryan! I think it's personal. I'm not ready."

"Any of it?"

"Last night, I got into a fight with my mom. She slapped me." I deflected.

"You ok?" He glances over my face.

"Yeah, I'm fine. Someone's been feeding her rumors about me. She was at the window last night. She saw when you dropped me off. She thought I took you to the party with me. She said I was going to bring you down like I did with my ex." I paused, I didn't mean to say that part.

"I was so upset, and hurt. How could she believe everyone else, then know that's not something I could do. I just walked away and went to my room. I put on some worship music and laid down. I had a dream, only it wasn't a dream." I watched as Ryan leaned forward as he seemed interested in what I was about to say.

"I saw God, except I couldn't see His face." I go on and tell him what had happened in the dream.

"It was my first encounter with God. I was raised in church, but I never really had an encounter."

"You're not the only one. Many people call themselves Christians, but they never really know God. It's a sad thing. They can live their whole lives following the ways of others, they don't let God be the one to lead them." He said.

"I'm starting to see that. Makes me wonder how can people speak on behalf of God, if they never really knew Him?"

"The main thing now is, you. You know now the spiritual realm exist. You know you have to grow, and that you will be fighting a spiritual war. The armor of God is found in Ephesians 6:10. I think, maybe you should start by studying that book. I will tell you now, the first thing you need to put on is the belt of truth. You need to start speaking of the things that happened to you. What are you trying to keep hidden? Set yourself free, and you will gain the belt of truth."

"The spirit of fear, it paralyzes me. I don't know how I can overcome it."

"*For God has not given us a spirit of fear, but of power and of love and of a sound mind.'* That's 2 Timothy 1:7. You have to believe in the power of God. He doesn't give you what you can't handle. You can overcome the spirit of fear."

I look at Ryan, I know he's right. But I'm scared. What if he doesn't like what he hears? No, I can't think like that, he's not like the rest of them. I haven't known him long, but I know he's different.

"Ryan, promise me you won't turn your back on me."

"I won't." He says. I take a deep breath and close my eyes. I can't believe I'm about to finally speak about it. I open my eyes and begin.

"I was part of *'Closing Back Doors.'*

"Closing back doors, please escort these beautiful new believers to the greeting room." Pastor Edward instructed from the pulpit. Rebecca and I follow behind the leaders of the program. We're still in training, so our only job was to watch and learn. Brian instructed Rebecca and me to consolidate a girl and a boy our age. We both looked at each other wondering why we were being assigned to the two new believers. We weren't ready for it.

"Angelisa, Rebecca, you're 17 and they look your age, I'm sure you can relate. You trained for weeks now, I think you're ready to handle this. This miracle catch was one of the biggest we had in a while. We need all the help we can get. All the other leaders have their hands full with other new believers. Please, we need your help." Brian urges us to move toward them. Rebecca and I look at each other.

"I'll take the girl, you take the guy. I don't think I can talk to him." Rebecca nudges me from the side. I look over at the guy, he's sitting on one of the chairs backwards. His arms rest on the back of the chair as he leans forward looking around as he waits for someone to greet him.

"Why can't you talk to him?" I asked her not understanding.

"Don't you recognize him?"

I shake my head.

"That's Logan Lopez, from school. He's on the football team."

I thought if I've seen him before I would remember. I shake my head, still not placing him. I never been to any of the games so I didn't know who he was, otherwise I would've remembered.

"Angel, please just talk to him. I'll talk to the girl." She pleaded.

"Alright, I'll talk to him." I caved.

I grab a chair to sit in front of Logan. "Hi, my name is Angelisa Cruz."

He smiles at me and I struggle to remember what to do next. His brown eyes fixed on mines made me nervous. How is it I never seen him before if we went to the same school?

"I'm Logan Lopez. I've seen you around at school."

I reach for one of the clip boards on the table near me. "Really? I'm sorry I don't remember seeing you around."

He laughs. "Seriously? I'm Logan, captain of the football team. You really don't know me?"

I nervously tuck my hair behind my ear as I shake my head. "I don't really go to the games, sorry."

He nods. "So why are we back here?" He asked as his eyes circle the room.

"Oh, well…you're here because you confessed Jesus Christ as your Lord and Savior. You opened your heart to Him and let him in. So I'm here to explain to you the process."

"I see. So that prayer was opening my heart to God?" He leans forward, lowering his head a little.

I sit up straighter in my seat. "Yes. Do you understand what that means?"

"I'm not sure, just that I want a fresh start in life."

"Yes, you have a new beginning. A chance to start a new life. You are acknowledging that Jesus is Lord, and you welcomed Him in to your life."

"Ok so what happens now?"

"Well, I'm supposed to ask you if there's anything you would like me to pray for?" He smiles at me causing me to fidget.

"Suppose to ask? Haven't you done this before? Or is it that I make you nervous?"

I look down at my clip board, I knew I wasn't ready for this. Reading the form clipped to the board, I remember something.

"I'm new at this, this is actually my first time. I usually watch others, I'm in training, sorry. Please bear with me. I'm supposed to get your information. Your phone number, email."

"I see. Yes I will bear with you!" He smiled again. He takes the clip board from my hand and fills out the form and hands it back to me. I look over it to make sure everything was filled. Name, age, email, but not his number. I look up at him again.

"You don't have a phone number?"

"Yes I do."

"Do you mind sharing it? We're supposed to call you tomorrow to check in. The church likes to keep contact with new believers and pray with you over the phone."

"Will you be the one calling me?" He asked grinning. He sits up straight in his chair.

"Usually it's one of the guys—"

"Nope, I want you to call me!"

"The guys usually call the guys and the girls call the girls."

"Well, I would prefer you call me instead. Then I would give you my number!"

I want to do my job right on the first day, so I agreed. He then takes the clip board back and adds his number.

"You're in church so you can't lie, I'll be expecting your call tomorrow!" He *winks.*

"Let's finish up for today, do you want prayer for anything?"

"My family."

"And I'm going to ask you to say the New Believers prayer with me again, now that you have a better understanding of what you did earlier."

He confessed Christ again, and I prayed a popcorn prayer for his family. I handed him a little bag that contained a small New Testament Bible and a worship CD. As we both stood up, he asked me for my number. He said he might not pick up a call from a number he did not recognize and he didn't want to miss my call. He pulled out his cell phone and handed it to me. I don't know why, but I added my number in his contacts. He then text my phone to make sure I gave him the right number. I reached for my phone and showed him his text. 'It's Logan.'

"Got it" I said.

"Call me" he said as he walked away.

Rebecca and I put our forms together to hand it to her father along with everyone else's.

"So how was it?" She asked me grinning.

"Good, I think he was flirting with me. He asked for my number, and he wants me to be the one to call him tomorrow."

Rebecca pulls me to the side. "Seriously? Maybe he was flirting with you. What are you going to do?"

I shrug, "I guess I'm going to call him." The memory of Logan when we first met makes me smile.

"Ryan, you still with me?" He nods.

"Yes, I'm listening. Continue." I took in a deep breath, this was only the beginning.

"The next day when I was scheduled to call him, he called me before I had the chance to."

"Hello?" I answered my phone.

"Hey, it's Logan. I was waiting for your call!"

"Hi, I was going to call you a little later. It's early. I still had time."

"Well, I wanted you to call me early. I thought maybe we could hang out today."

"Uh, well, the call was just to pray with you. We don't actually have to hang out."

"Is that not allowed?"

"We can hang out, but I'm supposed to ask you to come to church tomorrow. I should introduce you to the rest of the youth."

"Well, I'll make you a deal…you hang out with me today, and I will go with you to church tomorrow."

I think about his ultimatum. If I go out with him today, he'll go to church tomorrow and I can pass him to one of the guys to befriend him.

"Fine, church is at 11am tomorrow."

We made arrangements to meet by our school's football field. When I arrived, he was already there, waiting by his car.

"Hey Angelisa! Can I call you Lisa, or Angel? I think I like Angel."

"Angel is fine. So what do you have in mind?"

"Have you played football before?"

"No, I don't know anything about sports."

"Makes sense why you never came to any of my games. I'm still in shock that you never seen me before either."

We spent the rest of the afternoon on the football field, he taught me how to throw a football. We talked about who we hung out with to see if we had any friends in common. There were a few, but I spent most of my time with Rebecca.

"So basically you guys became friends?" I nodded to answer Ryan's question.

"Until, we became more than friends. The next day he went to church with me and then he started questioning the church life. He continued to go to church with me, but the more he saw the less he liked. He felt I was missing out on fun. He had told me I should enjoy my youth. To me, I had a pretty good life, I didn't think I was lacking anything. The church life was all I knew, I didn't think it was boring…but Logan did. He asked me, what the youth did for fun. My answer didn't impress him."

"What did you tell him?"

"What I knew…prayer, worship, bible class, you know."
Ryan shifts in his seat on the sofa before he asks, "Is that all you did at your church?"

"Then, yes. Now they have talent nights, dance, and plays."

"I see, please continue."

In school he would find me, walk me to class. The more we hung out in school, after school, the more our friendship grew. People started saying we were a couple, we weren't but I liked the idea of it. One day, while he was walking me to class he pulled me into his arms, stared right into my eyes before he kissed me. My first kiss, and I felt I was in love.

After that we started to hang out with his teammates and other friends, we were a couple. I started to feel a lot of pressure after that. His friends liked to drink and smoke, they love to party. They kept offering me drinks, I kept declining until one day...I felt I had to or I would lose him. I knew I was falling for him, I wasn't sure how he felt about me. Girls would always be around him, and I felt threaten by them. They were from the same world, in my mind if I didn't try I wouldn't be with him.

One of his friends Rob offered me a drink, he said it was juice so I took it. I had no idea it was spiked. I noticed his friends were laughing. Logan tasted my drink and told me what I was drinking. I looked at everyone around us before I looked backed at Logan. I took the cup from his hand and finished the drink.

"You didn't have to drink that if you didn't want to. You know I would never force you to do anything you weren't ready for." Logan took the empty cup back from my hands.

"I know, I didn't even taste it."

"Yeah it kind of sneaks up on you, so I suggest you stick to water."

I sensed his concern for me, but I didn't want him to feel as if he couldn't be himself around me, even though I wasn't myself around him. I would've done anything to be with him.

Rob offered me another cup, I took it without a thought and drank it. I can't remember how many drinks I had after that. Everything was a little fuzzy. Of course the next day I had a bad headache. Logan knew he couldn't have taken me home that night the way I was. He called Rebecca and asked her to cover for me. I guess he explained what happened and how to treat me in the morning. Because she was ready with orange juice and pain killers.

Apparently she told my parents I fell asleep on her sofa after Logan drove us to her house. Rebecca wasn't with us but she covered for me anyway. Her father was in a vigil that night so he was unaware of everything.

It seemed a lot of things happened that night, I couldn't remember much. But Logan set up a double date for Rebecca and Rob with us that night. He said she was feeling left out.

As we were getting ready for our double date Rebecca looked like she wanted to ask me something.

"Angel, tell me about Rob? I've seen him around, and I do like what I see. He's so cute. His light brown eyes and his caramel skin complexion, who wouldn't be excited to be set up with him? But I don't know much about him." *Rebecca asked as we walked to the front door to meet Logan and Rob.*

"He's a nice guy, I can't really say much about him because I'm usually with Logan most of the time."

"You know I've never been on a date before. My father doesn't even know the guys are coming along. I'm not sure what to do."

"Well, just be yourself. Most likely he'll just want to get to know you. He's really funny so I know he'll make you laugh." That seemed to calm her nerves.

We ended up going to the movies. Rebecca and I sat between the guys. Rob seemed to like her. During the movie I reached for Logan's hand, I noticed Rebecca did the same with Rob. Logan leaned in for a kiss, and when I looked back at Rebecca she was kissing Rob. It seemed as if she was mimicking everything I was doing. I didn't mind then, we were both new at dating.

"Ryan? Are you still with me?"
He nods as he answers, "yes, I'm listening." He rest his arm on the arm rest of the sofa.

"This next part is a little more intense, I think this is when things really changed for me, and Rebecca." I take a deep breath. "The night my relationship with Logan escalated."

"I see." He runs his fingers through his hair. I don't know why I feel like telling Ryan the rest. It may affect the way he sees me. But I believe this is the part that changed me forever. I stand from where I was sitting. I walk over to the window. I can feel Ryan's eyes follow me. I take in another deep breath.

"I'll meet you there Rebecca, Logan is on his way to pick me up and I'm unsure if I should wear the dress he bought me." I tell her on the phone.

"I'm sure it looks great! Just wear it, you'll make him happy."

"I got to go, see you soon." I hang up.

I take a long look in the mirror, this dress makes me feel like another person. I like the color, red always looks nice on me. But the length and the low cut in the front, I feel like I'm going to look like every other girl at this party. But Rebecca is right, it will make Logan very happy.

104

"That sounds like that red dress you had on yesterday." Ryan said as I turn around to face him. I nod. Before I continue, I look over to the kitchen. I can't look directly at Ryan as I say the rest of this story.

When I walked out my door that night, Logan was standing by his car. When he saw me, I knew he liked how the dress fit.

I hear Ryan clear his throat. I shift my eyes to my feet feeling my cheeks heat up.

I walked up to him, he was smiling. He took me in his arms and kissed me. He opened the door for me then he got in and drove. I felt his eyes on me most of the drive. He reached for my hand, he told me he loved me, and when I told him I loved him back he speed up pulling into a parking lot. I knew what was going to happen, I wasn't sure what I wanted but I didn't stop him. He turned off the car and started to kiss me, one thing led to another and we slept together.

I feared I said too much. Ryan shifts in his seat again. "Ryan?" When he doesn't answer, I feared I lost him. I don't say anything else, I'm unsure why this is the part he feels uncomfortable, I haven't even reached the worse yet. If I didn't know any better I would think he was jealous.

"I'm fine, sorry. Please continue." He finally answers. I shake my head no. "I just wasn't expecting that part, a parking lot? Your first time?" A parking lot wouldn't have been where I had expected my first time to be, but it happened.

I nod to answer him. "Wow, please continue." I shake my head again.

"Angelisa, I'm sorry for my reaction. I wasn't expecting to hear that." He stands to walk over to me by the window. "I know there's more you need to say, please finish." He takes my hand and leads me back to the sofa. I stare at the floor as I begin to speak again.

We make it to the party, and I'm happy, but I'm also ashamed. I felt as if I lost myself. It was so out of my character. I would've never done that in a car, not my first time anyway. When we go inside, he offers me a drink. I drank one, then two, I can't remember if I had more after that. I remember I was dancing with Logan, and Rebecca was there too. But I was too wasted to remember anything else that night.

The next morning, I woke up with another hang over. I was in Rebecca's room. I guess I was too messed up to go home. When I went to the bathroom, I threw up so much. My head was pounding. Rebecca said I was a party animal. Apparently I had danced with everyone and I was all over Logan. When she was filling me in about what happened the night before, her father Brian was listening at the door. He busted in the room and kicked me out. He said he wouldn't have a sinner like me around his daughter. He also blamed me for Logan's partying and drinking. I walked home in shame. I was so hurt and afraid of my mother reacting the same way.

Rebecca and I were still friends, we still went out on our double dates, but her father couldn't know. I was already a bad influence in his eyes. Logan and I were still sleeping together. I knew I shouldn't, but I couldn't control myself around him. I loved him, it felt right, and bad at the same time.

A while after the last party, we had a school dance. I of course went with Logan, and Rebecca with Rob. We were on the dance floor when I saw Rob lead Rebecca out into the hall. Logan told me of their plans. I didn't know if I should stop her or let her enjoy it. I decided she was a big girl, so I just kept dancing with Logan.

Some time had passed and they still weren't back. I told Logan to take me to where they were going. He leads us to the janitor's closet. He opens the door, and I found Rebecca not only with Rob, but another guy. When she sees me, she stops. She quickly pulls herself together and runs out into the hall. Running right into her father. He sees her all messed up and sees me walking out of where she just came from. And the three boys that followed. Of course Brian thought it was me, and Rebecca put all the blame on me.

I look at Ryan as he slouches back on the sofa.

"So that's why Brian doesn't think much of you, he thinks it was you with all those guys, at the same time."

"Yes, I never corrected him, but he wouldn't listen anyway."

"So why is Rebecca mad at you? You kept her secret it seems!"

"I don't know, maybe she started believing her own lies. To her, I'm to blame."

"And what happened between you and Logan?"

"Can we finish this conversation another time? I see it was too much for you to take in. Ryan, I know we all fall short, but I'm really ashamed of all this. I don't want you to be ashamed of me too. After Logan and I broke up, I haven't been with anyone else. I wasn't ready the first time, and I didn't want to lose myself again."

Ryan stands, and pulls me into a hug. "I'm not ashamed of you. We all make mistakes, we learn from them. Which I think that's what you've been doing. It's going to be ok. I'm glad you felt ready to speak. You can't hold it in, keeping it inside isn't going to make it as if it never happened. The truth shall set you free." He laughs.

"I hope so, I really want to be able to put all this behind me and move on. I love how easy and free you and your friends are. I want that freedom too."

"You will get there, and we will help you." He starts to walk to the kitchen. "I should start taking you home, do you want some water before we head out?"

"Yeah, sure. I do need to get home, don't want my mom getting another wrong idea about us."

He smiles "No, we wouldn't want that!" He gets me a bottle of water, and I drink it.

"I'm going to change my shirt, I'll be right back."

"Ok, I need to visit your bathroom again."

"You don't have to tell me, you know where it is now."

We walk the same direction, I stop at the bathroom and he keeps walking to the room I was looking into earlier.

When I'm finished, I see the door to his room wide open and the light is on. I walk towards it, when I reached the door I freeze. Ryan was topless, he had his back toward the door while he search through his clothes. I wanted to turn away but I couldn't take my eyes off of his tattoo; angel wings, a wing on each shoulder blade. It's not filled in, it looks like it's just the outline. Maybe that's what he was going for. His ponytail ends right between the beginnings of the middle of the wings. He looks over his shoulder and notices me looking. He quickly grabs a shirt off his bed and puts it on. I'm so modified.

"I'm sorry, I didn't know you were there!" he said.

"No, I'm sorry. I…" I cover my eyes with one of my hands. "Shouldn't have…so sorry, oh my God!"

He begins to laugh, "It's ok really. It's my fault, I should've closed the door."

"I saw the light on I just walked over here."

"I guess you saw my tattoo?"

"Yeah, it's… beautiful. I'm not big on tattoos, but those are amazing. You really love angels!"

"Something like that. Come in." He says, "Just leave the door open." I walk in and go straight to his desk. I look at all the loose pages, they're drawings; angels, wings, and crosses.

"I see you like to draw."

He walks over to the desk. "I do, but mostly the wings."

"Ryan?" I say facing him. "Last night, when we were all holding hands, did you see into…*the realm?*" I whisper that last part as if it were some kind of secret.

"No," he smiles down on me. "Why do you ask?"

"I didn't mention this last night, but you all were in there with me. But you had your eyes closed. I could see you praying, and I was able to hear you."

"That's interesting. I was just praying, I didn't see anything. I did here you scream."

"In one of my dreams, I saw people fighting in a war, I wasn't there long. Do you think people can go in together? Have you been there before?"

"I think if we pray for the same thing, being in one mind, in one spirit we can. And yes, I have been."

"Do you want to try?"

"You want to pray together?"

"Yes, I want to grow more."

Ryan laughs. "How can I say no to someone who wants to pray? Do you want some worship music?" I think about it for a moment.

"Yeah, if you don't mind." I answer him.

"Pass me my phone on the desk."

I do as he ask, I bump into his desk when I turn, knocking down some thing. I bend down to pick it up, a key chain with one wing on it. I stare at it for a moment, he *really* loves angels. They are beautiful.

"I guess I should warn you." He tells me while I put the key chain back on the desk.

"What?"

"Just be ready, you might face what you did last night. Just remember to keep praying."

He turns on his speaker, connects his phone to it, and plays worship music. He walks towards me and grabs my hands. He begins to pray, but I stay silent.

"If you want this to work, I need you to pray in one accord with me." He tells me. I'm a little shy to pray out loud, especially in front of him, but he's right. I begin to pray with him in a very low voice.

When I open my eyes, I see we're in his room still, but I also see a garden. Our physical selves are here in his room, but our spirits are not. We're in the spiritual realm, just outside the garden where I spoke with God. I'm still holding Ryan's hands, he's still praying. I actually have to look up to him because I'm still young here. He stops praying, and opens his eyes.

"Angelisa?" He asks me.

"Yeah, I'm here can't you see me?"

"Yeah, I can see you, you just look…like a little girl."

"Didn't I tell you, my encounter with God? I am a little girl because I haven't grown spiritually yet. Although, I think I am a little taller than the last time." I smile.

Ryan steps back, and I notice what he's wearing. A leather and metal breastplate, black leather pants, he has a sword hooked onto his side, and "OH, MY, GOD."

15. Anything's Possible

I see these big white magnificent wings unfold from behind him. He stretches his wings out and I can see just how large they are. He's an angel.

Ryan?"

I have to look up to meet Ryan's eyes, as he looks down to me. I'm still a young child in this realm. I strain to look behind Ryan, he has white feathers sticking out from behind him. Now I know he's the angel from my dream the other night.

"Why are you an angel here?" I asked Ryan. He glances over his shoulder confused.

"I'm not sure. It's the first time I see them." He stretches his wings open as far as he can. Amazing. I feel my jaw drop, Ryan must have noticed because he grins. I close my mouth at once.

"All I know is I have faced my fears and have gained God's armor. Maybe the wings are a gift from God."

He raises his eyebrow when he looks at me, "or maybe it's not about me, it's about you."

"About me? How so?"

"A bible verse comes to mind, Isaiah 40:31. *But those who wait on the LORD shall renew their strength; they shall mount up with wings like eagles, they shall run and not be weary, they shall walk and not faint.*' The way I see it, you're renewing yourself."

"Ok, that may make sense...but I'm not the one with wings." I cross my arms over my chest.

"I don't know, all I know is I didn't have wings until now. And to be honest...I don't mind them." He raises his wings high.

I reach out my hand to touch them, wondering what they feel like. It's soft, feels like rose petals, silky, delicate, yet firm.

"Can you use those to fly?" I asked him confirming he was the angel I saw in my dreams the other day. He doesn't say anything.
With a big grin on his face, "let's see."

He leaps up into the air, flapping his wings up and down. He looks so amazing. I still can't believe what I'm seeing. He flies around testing his new wings before he comes back down.

"I guess you can!" I say excitedly. "How is this possible?"

"In God, anything is possible. He must have a reason for the wings. We'll find out soon." He folds them behind himself, as he looks over at me.

"I've seen you before I met you... in a dream. I know you were put in my path for a reason. I believe, I'm here to help you. But I want you to know...I am human, not an angel. I don't know why I've been given this gift, I'm sure I will soon find out." He takes a look around the garden we're in.

"I've had to fight my own battles here."

"So is your war over?"

"No, as long as we still have breath, we will always be fighting a spiritual war. Our Physical form will always be tempted, and tested. I have to put on the armor daily. Just because you gain it once, does not mean you cannot lose it."

"This is so surreal to me. Do you think I will grow wings here too?"

"Maybe." He shrugs.

I look around, I wondered if I would see God again. I have more questions than I did the last time I was here. I find it crazy how I have been in church my whole life, and I have never experienced this before. I guess I was one of those religious people I spoke of. I only went to church, did as I was told. But no one really sat down with me to teach me about all this. I wonder if anyone in my church has been here before. I see now that you can easily get caught up in what you think is right, rather than waiting on God to lead.

"Ryan, where exactly is this place?"

"It's not really a place. It's like an atmosphere. Somewhere your spirit can go when you get lost in prayer and worship. It's also a spiritual warzone."

"I'm so new to all this, I feel like I shouldn't be. I grew up in church, I should've known about this place."

"Don't think like that. For some people, they have to go through an experience in order to have an encounter with God."

"Yeah, but shouldn't someone have taught this to me? Anybody?"

"May be they did, but you didn't understand. Or you really didn't pay attention before. It's nothing to be ashamed of, you're here now. That's all that matters."

"I suppose you're right."

We begin to walk, I'm drawn to a rose bush. It looks like the one from the garden where God and I talked. These roses are not white, they're grey. Somehow I feel the more we walk away from the garden, the closer we're getting to a battle field. To my left, I see that figure again. The shadow looking one. The spirit of fear.

"Ryan!" I say, trying to reach him. He must have kept walking while I stop to look at the grey roses. He turns to face me.

"You have to face your fear Angelisa." He says to me as he walks back to me.

I can see my mom, last night when she slapped me. The disappointed look in her eyes when someone misinformed her about my past. I can't move nor speak. The pain I carry with me every day is intensified here. My soul is bare, I feel it all. The pain, the guilt, fear, sorrow. I can feel every emotion surround me, through me.

Suddenly everything around me darkens, the day has become night. The wind blows creating a sound as it moves through the trees. The shadow slowly approaches me. A cold wind hits my face, my body. The wind surrounds me, whirling around me as if I'm in the middle of a tornado. The wind is so strong I strain my eyes to see, Ryan's not too far from me. He doesn't seem to be affected by this wind. Ryan's lips are moving but I can't hear what he's saying. I see the shadow, Fear, he's coming for me.

I try to move, but I'm frozen. Fear has paralyzed me.

"Afraid of me?" He grins. I can feel the tears sting my eyes. What is he going to do to me?

"I know your fears little one." He walks around me.

"Your mom turning her back on you when she finds out you were the one responsible for your father's current state. Your sister…taking you down from the pedestal she put you on. Even him over there," he points in Ryan's direction.

"When he finds out what else you did. He will leave you. You shouldn't bring him down with you. You will make him fall—"

"Like you did Logan, and you tried to do the same with your friend Rebecca. She got out in time." The creature from before cuts in. Guilt.

They're both in this tornado with me. I can still see Ryan, but he can't get to me. Both Fear and Guilt circle me.

A long chain appeared into Guilt's hands. He strapped it on my left wrist, then another on my right. Guilt begins to pull the chains from behind me. I lose my balance and fall to the ground. I still can't move. Guilt yanks the chains up in front of me to get me up on my knees.

"Ryan can't help you!" Fear whispers in my ear.

I want to get out of here. Why did I think this was a good idea? How can I fight this?

"We're glad you are here. We wanted to play with you." Fear said as Guilt continues to yank on the chains.

"He sees how weak you are, he will leave you here alone with us." Fear continues to taunt me. *'Ryan can't leave, he wouldn't.'* I think to myself.

"You're wrong, he will leave."

Did Fear read my mind? Is that possible? Fear and Guilt answer my question with their laughs.

Whatever I think, Fear responds back. What strength do I have here? My eyes sting from my tears. I try to loosen the hold I feel wrapped around my wrists. I feel as if I can't breathe. I look up to see Ryan flying with his sword in hand, he's trying to get to me. I need to find a way. If Fear can read my thoughts, then I can use my mind to call on Him.

"God, help me!"

"NO!" Fear yells! Fear begins to back away, but Guilt pulls on the chains harder.

"Lord, I need you!" I think in my mind. I know God can hear my thoughts, but here, so can Fear and Guilt. I begin to scream, I shut my eyes. When I open them again, I'm back in Ryan's room.

Gabe is here with us now. I'm on the floor curled into a ball. Gabe helps me sit up.

"Are you alright?" Gabe asked.

I still can't speak. I shake my head no. I may not be there anymore, but I'm still not ok. I can still feel chains on me. The words Fear spoke of my family and Rebecca, and...

"Will they forgive me?" I manage to ask.

"Who?" Ryan asks.

"Didn't you see Ryan?" He looks at me like he doesn't know what I was talking about."

"I saw you being attacked by the spirit of fear. But I couldn't see what he showed you."

"My mom, my sister, Rebecca...you. You all won't forgive me," I sobbed.

Gabe sits down on the floor with me.

"Angelisa, that's what the enemy wants. For you remain in your shame. He doesn't want you to move on, he likes you right where you are. You must face your fear. If you saw your loved ones, I believe it's time you spoke with them. It may not be easy, and you may be afraid of what would happen next, but only then, can you move on. The only one stopping your growth is you." Gabe is right! How can I move on if I'm still stuck in the past? I need to do this. May be it won't be as bad as I'm thinking.

"You're right Gabe. It's time I speak to them. I don't want to feel this guilt anymore, it hurts too much." I admitted as I stood from the floor. Gabe puts his arm around my shoulder,

"I will keep you in my prayers. I believe in you."

I nod. "Thank you." I turn to Ryan, "can you take me home?"

He reaches for his keys on his desk, "of course." He smiles.

***

We arrive to my house. I hop off Ryan's bike and hand him the helmet. I don't meet his eyes. I remember his face when I was telling him about my ex and everything that happened. I haven't even told him the worst part. I don't know if I should. What if Fear is right, I don't want to pull Ryan down spiritually.

"Hey," he says reaching for my wrist. He lowers his head to meet my gaze. I look at him.

"You ok?" He cautioned.

"Yeah, it's just a lot I've been holding in. Are we ok?" His brows furrowed.

"We're good, why you ask?"

"I'm a real mess, are you sure you want to be around me?"

"Of course I'm sure. I'm here for you, whatever you need. What ever happened in there, whatever Fear said, it's not true. The enemy wants you to stay right where you are. Don't let him win." Ryan cups my cheek in his hand, "ok?" I nod.

"I will be here for you." He pulls me into his embrace.

"I'm going to talk to my parents and sister about everything."

"Let me know how it goes."

"I want you to hear the rest of my story, but I think I need to talk to them first."

"That's ok, whenever you are ready, just let me know, and I will be here."

I pull away from him and walk up to my front door. I walk in and turn as I close the door to wave bye to Ryan. I see Lady at her door. I close my door and quickly walk over to the window to peek through the curtains.

Lady approaches Ryan, she's telling him something. I wonder what it is. I see him smile and shake his head no. She's still talking to him as he turns on his bike and puts on his helmet. He shakes his head no again and waves her good bye.

"Angelisa? What are you doing?" My mom asks.

"I was just checking if Ryan left yet. Lady was talking to him." I answered.

"She probably just wanted to know if he was seeing anyone." My mom tells me.

"Why?" I asked her.

"She thinks Rebecca would be a good fit for him." *Of course she would.*

"Do you?"

She shrugs, "I don't know, he seems fond of you." I look away from her, back to the window.

"It's not like that mom." I breathe in deeply, "mom…I'm ready to talk to you, about what happened. I'm not sure if you want Evie to hear it as well."

"How bad can it be? I'm happy that you finally decided to talk to us, but why now?"

"I was with Ryan and his friends today. They are so much fun, you would've never guessed they had a past. I just want to be free like them. They don't let their history define them. Then Ryan and I went back to his house, and we prayed together. It felt nice to have a friend who really understands you. Someone who knows exactly what you going through?" I pause for a moment.

"I had an encounter with God last night, and today at Ryan's I had a spiritual experience. One that made me realize the only way to be free is to finally face my past."

"Wow, an encounter with God! That's something."

"Mom, when we talk…there's a lot of things that happened you might not like. I had gotten so caught up in things, I felt I had no one to talk to."

"I know you probably felt you didn't have anyone, but I was always here. And I'm here for you now. I'm sorry I hit you yesterday. I was really upset about everything with your father, and what everyone was saying. When can we have this talk?"

"Tomorrow? Dinner?"

"Ok, tomorrow it is."

16. The Truth Comes to Light

I told Ryan about talking with my family at dinner tonight. I'm really glad we became friends fast, because of him I realized I can no longer hold this secret inside. I want to be free, I'm ready to begin the next chapter in my life. I can feel the call of God for me. I'm still not sure what that call is, but I can feel a tug at my heart. There's a desire in me to be more, to do more. I feel like I'm waking up from a spiritual coma. I don't want to let fear or guilt control my life anymore.

My mom has cooked up a nice dinner. Pernil (roast pork), arroz con gandules (rice and peas), potato salad, with sides of avocado and garden salad. My mom doesn't cook this meal on a week day. She usually keeps it simple.

Pernil and potato salad is one of my favorite Puerto Rican meals. I guess she's happy I finally decided to tell her about my past. I wanted Ryan to be here for support, in case my mom reacts badly. But I think this is something I have to do on my own. I want to tell him the rest of my past. I don't want to have to repeat it, but I think it's important that I do this just with my family for now.

I had a conversation with my dad about this dinner. I wanted to warn him that I will be telling my mom about the night he found the bottle of liquor in my pocket. I didn't want him to be surprise by it, and I know my mom will be upset that he hid it from her. I just want to come clean about everything. He wasn't too happy about it, but he understands.

My mom serves all of us and finally sits down. "So Angelisa, do you want to begin?" My mom asks me. I take a look at everyone before I start to speak.

"Before I get into any of it, I want to explain something. For the past two years, I've felt as if I was in a spiritual coma. I'm tired of feeling this way, and I know God has something special for me. I don't know what it is yet, but I do believe that everything I went through the past couple of years has been a learning experience. I need you to understand, that we all make mistakes. And before you hear what happened, I need you to understand that, I didn't mean to hurt you or make you think less of me."

"Honey, I would never think any less of you." My mom tells me.

"You heard what people have said about me, and you believed them. That hurt me mom. I know I kept the truth from you, and you may be really mad with me. But I understand that I have to live with the mistakes I've made. So although it was almost two years ago, I'll accept whatever punishment you have for me." I look at my mom, then my dad.

"I had an encounter with God and He told me I had to face my past to move forward."

I begin to tell them about Closing Back Doors and Logan. Everything I had told Ryan the night before. I watched all their expressions as I spoke. My mom was sad at first, then upset. I watch as they all exchanged looks.

"Well, I can understand why Brian would think you were a bad influence around Rebecca." My mom says.

"Yeah, but why would Rebecca say all those things about you, if she was the one messing around?" Evie asked.

"It's easier putting the blame on someone else I guess. But she could've just been afraid of how upset her father would have been with her. When you tell a lie enough, you start to believe it was true." I answered her.

Now I have to continue the rest of the story. *"After a while Rebecca wouldn't speak to me anymore. I don't know what she's told people about me. So I began to drift further away. I felt judged by Closing Back Doors, Rebecca started telling people it was me in the closet with the three guys. I tried to ignore the rumors that spread, I tried to keep working in the program, but I knew I couldn't anymore. I was in no position to help anybody, I still had a lot to learn and I knew I was living a life of sin. I didn't do what Rebecca said I did, but I was fornicating. They knew I wasn't right for the job anymore. I knew I couldn't help anyone if I couldn't help myself. When I told them I was leaving they didn't stop me. After that they didn't even look for me. So I got closer to Logan. He became everything to me."* I look at my dad.

"Dad, I'm sorry, this part is very hard for me. Mom…I closed myself off to you because I was afraid. I got pregnant." I paused, so that I can pull myself together and every one could process what I just said.

I chanced a glance at my parents, and my sister. I thought about Ryan, what he would think about this next part. For some reason, I really cared about how this part of my past would affect him.

I really don't understand why I feel like his reaction matters so much. I need a moment to recuperate. I never shared this with anyone. The way I felt when I found out I had a life growing inside me. I knew I was too young, but I couldn't help the joy I felt. It was a bitter sweet moment for me. My mom began to clear up the table.

"Can we go into the living room?" I asked my mom.

"I think that's a good idea." My mom answered me.

"Mom, are you ok?" I asked.

"I'm just processing this information. Is this it?" As much as I wanted to tell her yes. It wasn't.

"No mom, there's more. But I promise, I've only been with Logan." My mom nods.

"I need a minute, I'll meet you in the living room in a few." I say to my mom as I walk up to my room.

"Ok," seems to be the only word my mom can tell me. I know she's upset I got pregnant and that I didn't wait till marriage to lose my virginity.

My mom is old school. I made a mistake. I should've waited. But I thought I was in love.

I walk into my room and sat on my bed.

"God, I need your help. This next part is going to be hard to relive. I'm afraid of how my parents are going to react. Please just give me strength to endure my parent's wrath if they should have any."

I know I can't blame them for how they would react, but I'm still afraid of that part. I pull out my phone and text Ryan.

Ryan: *"Hey."*
Me: *"Hey."*
Ryan: *"How did it go? Talk over already?"*
Me: *"I wish, I only told them what I told you, and one extra part I didn't tell you yet."*
Ryan: *"So you almost done?"*
Me: *"No, I needed a break."*
Ryan: *"How did your parents take it?"*
Me: *"They're quiet, they haven't really reacted yet. But there's more to tell, it's going to be a long night."*
Ryan: *"Well, I hope everything works out. Hit me up when you can."*
Me: *"Thanks, I will."*
Ryan: *"Anytime, be blessed."*

I put my phone in my back pocket and head down to the living room. I hear my mother speaking.

"I can't believe she was pregnant! Where's the baby? You don't think she aborted do you?"

"I don't know Ramona, maybe she had the baby, or maybe she hid her belly well." My dad answers my mom.

"Then where is the baby now? I think maybe when Logan found out, they broke up and maybe she had an abortion." My mom responds back.

I didn't want them to keep guessing, so I walked in clearing my throat.

"How long were you standing there?" My sister asks.

"Long enough." I say trying to remain calm. "The pregnancy didn't last long. I was ten weeks pregnant, I still hadn't spoken to Logan about it."

I make my way to the sofa across from my parents.

"Logan was happy about college. He had just received an acceptance letter from the University he wanted to go. He had plans, and none included babies. I didn't know how to tell him. I was going to a University nearby. Although our universities weren't too far from each other, I knew we weren't going to be seeing each other as often. How was I going to tell him about the baby?

Days after graduation, some of his friends were having a party in celebration of graduating high school and Logan's acceptance to the University of his choice. He was talking to his friends about the next chapter in his life. Four years of college, getting a job in engineering, buy a house, get married and starting a family. I didn't know how to tell him he would be starting a family now. That was only if he wanted to stay with me. We went outside to talk.

"I know people say long distance relationships don't last, but I believe they can. I believe in us. Besides, we won't be that far from each other."

"Logan, I love you. But maybe we should break up. You have a lot of plans, you should focus on your future."

"You are my future, all that stuff I said inside, I plan to have with you."

"You have that plan all mapped out don't you? In that order?"

"Yeah, I would like to finish school before getting married. But I would also like to buy you a house before we get married. I plan to have kids as soon as we do marry. Is that wrong to you?"

"No Logan, of course it's not wrong. It's a great plan. But life doesn't always go the way we plan. Are you leaving room for mistakes?"

"Mistakes?! Like what?"

"What if I wanted to get married first? What if we have a baby first? What if college doesn't work out?"

"We'll just take one day at a time, let it play out. I'm willing to work out this long distance, aren't you?"

"No"

I told him it would be best is we just broke up. I wasn't sure what I was going to do with the baby. But I couldn't hold Logan back from his future. He thought I was joking and laughed it off. My face expression was serious, he noticed I wasn't joking.

"Why can't we just try it out before we decide it's over?"

"I don't know if I can handle it. Being away from you, wondering what girls are trying to get with you. I would be going crazy. I think this is for the best. It would just be better if we stood as friends."

That just made him upset. He got up and grabbed my hand pulling me inside the house where the party was. He looked at me and asked if I was sure I just wanted to be friends? I told him yes.

His expression was cold, he asked "well then friend, see that girl over there? I'm going to make out with her because I think she's hot!" He walked away from me, and he went straight to the girl, and did exactly what he said he was going to do.

I just stood there watching, frozen in place. Of course I didn't want to be friends. I thought I loved him. I wanted to be with him. But if he could replace me that easily, he never really cared for me as I thought. All his friends looked my way and they were all laughing. I finally moved from where I was, and walked out."

I couldn't stop my tears from running down my face. My mom sat beside me, and put her arms around me.

"Did you have an abortion?" She asked me in a low voice.

"I wasn't sure what I was going to do, I was so emotional and afraid. I was alone, I had no one to talk to about this. While I was walking, I passed the hospital. I went inside through the emergency room, sat in a chair and waited. I wasn't sure what I wanted to do. I was too young to have a baby. I didn't know how you guys would react. And I wasn't ready to give up on my own dreams.

I got up from my chair and walked to the reception desk, still not sure what I was going to say. I looked at the exit door, I just wanted to go home. I walk toward the exit, I didn't want to kill my baby. Before I got there, a lady bumped into me. She looked at me and apologized, and said 'it's all going to be ok.' I looked at her strangely. She walked away and suddenly I started having cramps. It felt really strong. I turned back to the desk, only to hold on to it. I was falling and I needed support. I felt liquid come down between my legs.

When I looked down, it was blood. I cried for help, a nurse came out from behind the desk and helped me walk to a wheelchair, but I didn't want to sit. Instead I climbed on to the wheelchair putting my knees to the seat and holding on to the back of the seat. I didn't think I could sit down. I just wanted to go to the bathroom.

The nurse rolled me into one of the examining rooms. I couldn't stand up, I was afraid to let go. I asked the nurse what was happening to me. She asked me if I was pregnant. When I nodded, she answered me.

"You're having a miscarriage." After a few more minutes it was all over. A doctor came in to see me, I recognized him. He was a friend of Logan's uncle. We met at one of his family dinners. He checked me, and gave me something for the pain.

"Is there someone outside waiting for you?" I shook my head.

"No, I'm alone, and I don't want anyone to know what happened." He nodded his head in understanding and told me he'll be right back.

The nurse helped clean me up and calmed me down. I didn't want to talk so I just stood there. The doctor came back in with a pair of sweats and a black tee shirt. He told me to get dressed and he would drive me home.

"You went through all that alone?" My mom asked me as she was hugging me. My sister came to sit on the other side of me.

"Angelisa, I'm so sorry. I had no idea." She said to me, how could she, she was only twelve.

"It's ok Evie, I didn't want you involved." I told her.

"Angelisa!" My dad yells.

"Don't think you have to go through something like that alone. We're your parents! We may not like what happened, but we will always love you." My dad said as he walked over to us and hugged all three of us.

I wish I had the courage to tell them then. What I did after that was to try to make me feel better. Drown out the memory of the last few months.

"Thank you papi, but I have to continue." I said.

"There's more?" My sister asks.

"Yes, there's more. After that day I had so much guilt. I was so upset, thoughts of aborting the baby did cross my mind. I didn't want to believe the father of my baby could replace me so soon, right in front of me and every one.

I thought that every time I would look at the baby, I would see the father and be reminded that I lost my youth raising a baby on my own. When I walked into the hospital I was unsure of my intention. When I was going up to the reception desk, I was going to ask for options. But then that happened. I was so heart broken.

I thought I was being punished, I made so many mistakes. I wanted to forget that day. I stayed to myself, as you all have noticed. I'd go to church, but I wasn't really there. Church was the last place I wanted to be." I wiped my face with my hand and just look at my sister, this must be too much for her.

"Evie, you're young, you might want to try things. Please don't make my mistake. I'm always here for you. Whenever you want to talk about anything, or feel confused about something. Trust me, it's hard to come back when you strayed too far." She takes my hand,

"I know Angel, I love you." She answers me.

Now to tell them about how my problem affected my dad.

17. The Battle Has Begun

"When the first semester of college started, I met Valerie. We became fast friends. She introduced me to her friends, and it just seem like a fresh start. I told her about the break up, but never about the pregnancy. Just what Logan did, and how my friends turn their backs on me. She told me I just needed to let loose and forget the past. It sounded like a good idea at the time. She would invite me to parties and I would go. College parties are nothing like high school parties. It's all about the drinking and other stuff.

I had one drink then another, and another. The times I didn't come home, I slept over Val's house. But it was because I didn't want you to see how wasted I was. Drinking helped me forget. And I liked how that felt. I didn't like the hangovers, but I didn't mind them as long as I had a night to free my mind." I look over to my dad who is now sitting right in front of me on the floor.

"I understand how addicting it can be Pa." I can feel my mom look from me to him.

"What happened next Angelisa?" My mom asks me.

"One night, at one of those parties, I got pretty wasted. I remember glimpse of things. I was drinking and dancing with a guy. I remember Val's cousin showing me a small bottle of liquor, he put it into my pocket." I see my dad tense, he knows what's coming next.

"After that I can't remember anything. The next morning I woke up in Val's cousin's bed. He wasn't in there. And I still had my clothes on. There was a knock on the door, it was him; Jose. He asked if he could come in. I thought it strange since it was his room. But I respected the gesture. I nodded and he walked in.

He gave me a glass of orange juice and painkillers. He said he thought I might have a hangover. He was right, I did. I asked him if I did anything reckless the night before.

He didn't answer right away. He said I almost did, and he had grabbed me, carried me to his bed and laid me down. He walked out the room and closed the door. He said if he didn't pull me out of the party, I would've done something I would've regretted. He said I had come on to him, and when he denied me, I went to another guy. The other guy was going to take me up on my offer, but Jose didn't let it happened. That's when he locked me in his room."

I needed to pause for a moment. I didn't want to remember everything. I just wanted to put it behind me. But I have to face my past, it's the only way I can truly be free. I see a lot of mixed emotions on my family's faces. I guess this was to be expected. I didn't want to talk about it before because I knew how bad it would sound.

"I guess we should be grateful you had Jose looking out for you." My mom said.

"Even though he gave you a small bottle to bring home, I'm guessing." I looked at my dad. I knew this was the hard part for him.

"I knew I shouldn't have continued, I meant to stop drinking. But later on that day I had a little more to drink. Not as much as the night before but I was a bit tipsy. I wanted to sleep in my own bed, so I asked Val to take me home.

When I walked in the house, I nearly fell. Papi was by the door and he caught me. Of course he scolded me for being drunk. I had completely forgotten about the bottle. It fell on the floor, and he picked it up. He did call my attention about having it. He helped me to my room, I went straight to my bed and fell asleep. The next morning when I saw him, I asked him about the bottle, he said it was gone."

My mom looked so angry. I believe at me, and at my father. "Now I know how you started with the drinking again." Her voice was cold.

"It was my fault, mom. I didn't know about his drinking, and I brought the temptation into the house." I told her trying to get all the blame on me and not on my father.

"You father is responsible for his own actions. He knows better Angelisa, and he should have never kept this from me. Victor we will continue this conversation later." My sister puts the focus back on me, "Angelisa, when did you stop?" Evie asks me.

"That was my last night. I stayed away from parties for a while. I didn't drink. I just focused on my classes and got a job. When I thought I was ready, I would go to a party, but I would not drink anything but bottled water. I didn't trust anyone to get me a drink in a cup. And then recently I started having dreams, and I had an encounter with God. My new friends have been helping me spiritually. And now I'm here, with you finally talking about the past two years of my life."

Wow, I did it. I let out a breath I didn't realize I was holding. I finally told my family and I feel so relieved.

My mom still looks upset, my father and sister look calm, surprisingly. *Thank you God for your strength to come clean with my family.* I say in my head.

"Is that everything? No more secrets?" My mom asked.

"No more secrets mom, that's everything. Are you mad? I can understand if you are." She reaches for my hand.

"Yes, I'm upset. All this was happening and I had no idea. What was I doing?" She looked so confused.

"Mom, you were really busy doing activities in the church, and work. You couldn't have been aware of everything, and I hid it very well." I answered.

"I shouldn't have been so busy to notice you were going through so much." She hugs me and begins to cry.

I knew this was going to be hard. We stay in the living room talking about how things could've been different if we spoke about what we were feeling. Or even prayed together. We always have dinner together, but we didn't take time as a family to seek God's presence together. My mom wanted to make a change. She wanted us to start being closer and seek God together. I liked the idea. We were starting to feel tired so we said our good nights and went to our rooms.

I throw myself on my bed, I guess I was expecting my mom to act differently. I was always afraid of her reaction. But now that everything is out in the open, I feel everything is going to fall into place. I still think about the baby I lost. I don't think I can ever forget about it. It was a wakeup call, one I didn't notice at the time. But I'm starting to understand now.

I always heard that God works in mysterious ways, He allows things to happen for a reason. We may not understand at the moment, but when you look back you start to fit the pieces together like a puzzle. Maybe I needed this to happen to me so I can grow. I never really knew God until recently. Many of us know of God, but we never *really* know Him. I want to build a relationship with Him. I want to walk with Him all the time, and have Him lead me. I see on my own, I mess up. I need to let go and let God just be.

***

It's dark where I am. Tall trees on both sides of the path I'm walking on. A cold chill surrounds me. I look up to the sky, it's bland. No stars, no moon or clouds, nothing. The road leads to a cabin. It looks abandon, I walk up to the steps and stop.

"Afraid to go inside?" A familiar sinister voice says from behind me. Fear! I turn around to face him.

"Did you think it was over? I'm still here and I'm not going away." He tells me before he appears behind me making me turn around again.

"I told my family everything, I'm not afraid of the truth." I answer.

"You may have told them everything, but you're still afraid. People still don't think much of you. You still fear what they would think when they find out you were going to kill your unborn child just because you were upset with your boyfriend." Fear tells me as he circles me.

"I wasn't going to kill my baby, I was uncertain, then miscarried." I retort.

"That may be so, but others won't see it that way. You went into that hospital with other intentions."

"I don't care what people think of me, I know what happened."

128

"Oh but you do care, you *fear* it. You fear your new friend's reactions."

"No!" I yell.

"You can say no, but deep down inside you know I'm telling you the truth." He vanishes and I wake up.

I was dreaming again. These dreams are too real, so vivid. Is Fear right, am I afraid? I thought I was good, and that I had overcame my fear. But maybe I just thought I did. I can't let fear stop me from moving forward. What was in that cabin? Was fear trying to stop me from going in there? Should I have wanted to go in? I wonder if I'll have another chance to find out. I will not let my fears control me.

It's Wednesday morning and I over slept. I rush to get ready and get to work. It's only been one week since all these things were happening, the dreams, and my encounter with God. I feel different, I see things differently. But to everyone else, nothing has changed. I get to work, it's already busy. I get started right away. I serve coffee to as many people I can as fast as I could. Finally the morning rush slows down and I can relax.

I sit at one of the empty tables and think back to my dream last night. It hits me what Fear was talking about. There's still a part of me that is still afraid. But I'm not afraid of what he thinks I am. I understand everyone has a past, some are darker than others. But why should I feel as if I'm the worse one of them all? My fear is not of what they think of me, it's because I don't think I have forgiven myself for my uncertainty. I was angry and I was hurting when I walked into that hospital. I just wanted to erase that part of my life. But you can't erase decisions you've made in the past. You can only learn from them.

"You look lost in thought." Ryan tells me. I didn't even notice him come in.

"Hey Ryan, I was just reflecting." I respond. Ryan sits down.

"About the other night?" He asks.

"Yeah. The talk with my family went better than I expected it to. I feel relieved that I told them everything. Now I know I have to deal with the after math."

"Well the good thing is that you did let it out, what's your next step?" Ryan asks me.

"I guess I should focus now on my relationship with God. My family wants to be more spiritual at home, so that will help me. I guess I have to go through the healing process." I tell Ryan not really looking at him.

"I'm here for you in anything you may need." I look at him.

"Thank you, I suppose we should talk next."

"I'm here if you want to talk about it. But you don't have to tell me anything if you don't want to."

"I know, but I need you to help me with the spiritual part. I think you would understand better if you knew what I've been through. Like last night I had a dream." I go on to tell him about what happened in the dream, what Fear was saying to me. When I was done, he looks down at the table.

"Maybe there's something more you forgotten or he can just be lying. We can talk later if you want."

"Yeah, I have to get back to work. Are you going to hang around here?"

"Yup, I'll be at my usual table."

"Want some coffee?"

"Of course, I'm sure you know how I like it." He grins.

"Yes sir."

I walk away and prepare his coffee. The day goes pretty fast, Ryan works on his laptop then says good bye. I stay behind to finish my shift. My mind wonders back to my dream. What was in the cabin? Was Fear trying to stop me from going in, or did he want me to go in?

***

Alone in my room, I turn on my speaker and play some worship from my phone. I close my eyes and just let the music take me. I sing along and begin to talk to God. I feel lost in His presence. Suddenly I find myself in the spiritual realm. It's beautiful. It looks like the garden I was in with God not too long ago. I see the bench where we were sitting, I go to it and sit. God appears next to me.

"Hello my child, you made it back." He tells me.

"I did, I just felt the need to pray and it took me here."

"When you get lost in prayer and worship, it usually does."

"I can get use to this."

"Good." He says laughing.

"God, my dream last night…what was happening?"

"You going to be fighting a spiritual war, you need to be prepared. Fear is going to use whatever he can to keep you at your lowest. He wants to keep you weak and afraid. He won't be the only one attacking you, keep your eyes open and be strong. Keep praying, read my word, ask for help when you need it. I will always be here. You know how to reach me, my princess."

"My battle is beginning?"

"No, it has already begun." Just as He says it, He's gone.

I stand from the bench and walk deeper into the garden. The sky begins to darken and the wind picks up. As I walk through the tall trees I have a familiar feeling, I've been here before. As I continue to walk I notice something on the ground, something shiny from underneath the dried up leaves.

I stare at it for a bit when I hear footsteps, crunching from walking on dried up leaves. The steps are slow, and are coming from behind me. I'm about to turn around when I hear the sound of flapping coming from the sky. I look up instead and see Ryan, his lips are moving but I can't hear what he is saying. This all seems familiar now. The dream I had a week ago.

If this is like the dream that means something is going to attack me from behind. Seeing the expression on Ryan's face I know it's near. The crunchy sound gets faster as if they're running and Ryan swoops down, I turn to see a dark creature running toward me.

I remember in the dream I never got the shiny object from the ground. But I still don't go for it. Instead I remain still. I will not show fear. Whatever this creature wants, it will not have it today. I am not the same person from a few days go. Somehow I feel empowered. I raise my hand in a halt position facing the creature and yell "Stop!" with an authority I didn't realize I had.

Ryan stops as he sees the creature stop. The creature stands in front of me now. Ryan is still up in the air, but much closer than where he was. He has his sword in his hand ready to strike.

"Who are you?" I ask this new creature. It doesn't answer right away. It just stares at me, like he's studying me.

"Who do you think you are?" It tells me.

131

"I asked, Who. Are. You?" I demand.

Its appearance changes, and now it looks like me.

"What is this?" I ask.

"I'm you. The real you. The one who likes to have a good time. You, that drinks and leads men on, and I'm you, the one that would kill an innocent baby. You, standing before me, are *nothing!* You are weak, and alone. You will never be the person *he* thinks you are meant to be."

It says that last part pointing to Ryan. I look up at Ryan, I'm confused. Who does he think I'm meant to be? Why did it take on my image, to intimidate me? I feel the tears begin to sting my eyes. I can't stop them from falling. I begin to sob. I fall to my knees, thinking about the baby I had once growing inside me. A life I wasn't ready to care for. I hear the creature laugh,

"As I said before, you are *nothing.*" Her laughter makes me angry, and her words makes me furious. I stand to my feet and lift my head to face this creature that wears my face.

"No, I am not weak! Not anymore. I'm the daughter of a king, He is my savior. You have no more power over me!" As I say this I feel the wind begin to pick up behind me.

The leaves are blowing everywhere. I turn around and look to where the shiny thing was. It is no longer buried under leaves and dirt. I can see what it is now; *the belt of truth.*

When I reach for it, it floats up and makes its way to my waist, it buckles itself. Amazed by this I look up to Ryan. He has a smile on his face. When I look back at the creature that wears my face, it looks upset.

"You think that's all it'll take? There are more of us. We will not leave easily." It says to me.

"I am ready to fight. I know who I am. So there is no more room for you or any of your kind. I am not that lost girl anymore. My life belongs to Him." I say this pointing up.

Just as I say it something comes flying my way. It attaches itself around my chest; *the breastplate of righteousness.*

The creature was launching towards me and quickly vanished when it saw what I was wearing.

18. Like old times with a Twist

The belt of truth and breastplate of righteousness. I finally received part of my armor, two down and only four more to go. Ryan did say that just because you have the armor doesn't mean you can't lose it. I will always have to work to keep it on. That was amazing. I thought I only had to deal with Guilt and Fear.

I still don't know what the creature was and how many more I will be facing. But like God said, as long as I keep praying and reading the word I will be ready. And He is only a prayer away. I look up to Ryan, he has a big smile on his face. He begins to descend but a knock on my door pulls me back to my room. I quickly open my eyes. I lower the music and open the door.

"Val?"

"Hey Angel, you never checked in with me, just wanted to see if you were ok." She said as she walks into my room.

"Yeah, sorry about that. Things just got really busy after I left the party. I had a long weekend."

"Yes, I heard about your ride. You really left with a guy on a bike? That's what Alex told me and Mario, he was super mad. What happened? And who's the guy?"

"The guy is someone I met at work. I accidentally text him the address to the party instead of my mom." I go on to tell her what had happened when Ryan picked me up from the party that night.

"Funny, Alex said it a little differently. Made it sound more like a jealous ex-boyfriend when he saw you two together, I thought maybe Logan showed up."

"No, it wasn't like that, and it wasn't Logan. I haven't spoken to him since we broke up. His name is Ryan, and he just didn't like how Alex was pushing himself on me. He knew I was uncomfortable and Alex wouldn't take no for an answer."

"Ok. So may be Alex was the jealous one? I guess he was hoping the two of you would hook up. I told him you weren't that type of girl. So did Alex cross that line with you? I just thought he liked you and that he was going to take everything at your pace."

"I knew that was his intentions. I had a bad feeling. That's when I went to find you. He was drunk and maybe he got the wrong idea about me. I'll talk to him tomorrow. I'm not mad at him."

"Ok, so tell me about this Ryan guy. Is he cute?"

"He is, but it's not like that."

"So what's it like then?"

How would I explain it to her without sounding like I have a crush?

"Would you believe me if I told you I think he was sent by God?"

She looks puzzled. "Like, your soul mate?"

"No, I think God put him in my path to help me face my past. I've only known him a week and he's helping me see things differently."

"You told him your secrets? The big secret you don't even want to share with me?"

"No, I haven't. I want to. I only told him about Logan, nothing else." I reassured her. "He's a Christian. He goes to another church, and he's helping me find my way back to God."

She nods. "Ok, if it makes you happy, I'm happy for you."

"It's actually a bit scary." I admit. "I find myself facing things I never wanted to think about again. But all those things are part of me now. I can't just act like it never happened."

She nods in understanding.

"Maybe you should hang out with us one day. I met a few of his friends, and they are all pretty down to earth. You might actually like them."

Her eyes widened a bit at my invitation." I don't know about all that, but I'll think about it."

We pass the time in my room watching YouTube videos. My mom walks in asking if we have any requests for takeout tonight.

"Pizza?" I asked. I've been craving pizza all day.

"I was thinking the same thing." My mom answers.

"Will you be staying Val?" She asked my friend.

"Sure, I love pizza." Val chuckled.

"Will you be expecting anyone else Angelisa? Like Ryan?" My mom asks me with a raised eyebrow. Of course Val is looking at me the same way. Why did my mom bring him up?

"I don't think so mom. I don't think he was coming over today. We were just going to talk on the phone...I think." I look at my phone as I tell her.

I forgot I had my phone on mute. I had a text from Ryan.

"Can we meet today?"

That was over an hour ago.

"Did you want him to come over?" I ask my mom.

"Sure, it would be nice to get to know him since he's helping you refocus your life."

Val looks at me.

"Yes, I would like to meet him too." She teased.

"I'll invite him, but just to be clear, he is only a friend and nothing more. So please don't get any ideas." I text Ryan back asking him if he would like to join us for pizza with my family. He answers back; sure.

"Ok he's coming." I tell them both.

"Alright, I will go order the pizza and some appetizers." My mom said as she leaves my room.

Val and I head downstairs to the living room, my father and sister are already there.

"Hey girls!" My father tells us as we walk in.

"Hey pa, what are you guys doing?" I ask them.

"I thought we could play a board game. How does a mystery game sound? I haven't played in years." My father says pulling out the board games.

"Sure, sounds like fun." I feel my phone buzz in my back pocket. A text from Ryan, *"I'm here,"* it says.

"I'm coming to the door" I text him back.

"I'll be right back. Ryan is here. You should start setting up the game."

I go and open the door. Ryan is getting off his bike and walks towards the house.

"Hey." He says as he gets closer.

"Hey, my mom wanted to get to know you since we've been hanging out lately. My father is setting up a game so we can play. Do you like board games?"

He smiles, "yeah, I might be rusty, it's been a while since I played."

"Yeah us too, but it should be fun. Also, my friend Val from college is inside."

"Nice, I would like to meet your friends."

"I told Val she should come with us next time we hang out, if that's alright?"

"Sure, that would be good. Is she a believer?"

"No she is not, would that be a no now?"

"Of course not, I was just asking. We can't only surround ourselves with Christians, we need to reach out to everyone. Sometimes fellowship is the best way. A lot of people have stereotyped Christians as judging, stuck up, boring people. It's nice to show them it's not like that. Christians can have fun too. Not everyone in your circle will be a believer. But they would respect you and your lifestyle, you just keep praying for them. Through your testimony they will come when they are ready."

I led Ryan into my house, I show him to the living room. My mom is there now. I introduce him to my father and to my sister. He already met my mom. Before I had a chance to introduce him to Val…

"Hi, I'm Val." She extends her hand to him. Ryan does the same, "Ryan, nice to meet you."

Val leans in to whisper to me, *"He's cute."* I don't think she whispered too well because Ryan smiles and thanks her.

The rest of the evening went well. We ate pizza and played games for a while. I forgot how fun it was. It was nice to be with my family. It felt like old times, with the exception of new friends.

"This was fun." Val says.

"But I have to start going, finals tomorrow. Are you ready Angel?" Good thing I was always ahead in my classes.

"Yeah I'm pretty much ready." But I do have a thesis to write.

"I'll be up all night finishing it, I'll be fine as long as I stay focus on the subject." I guess no sleep.

"I should be going too." Ryan says.

Everyone says their good byes, I walk Val and Ryan out. As we walk to the door, I look at Val, I'm so glad she's my friend. We may be different in many ways, and in other ways we're the same. And I hope I can be good for her now. I want to live by example. She always knew I wasn't meant for her world, but maybe she's meant for mines.

"Well, this was a fun night." Val tells Ryan and me.

"Yes it was, it was nice to meet you Val." Ryan tells her. Val looks at Ryan, her smile softens.

"I hear you saved my friend here the other night. Thank you for being around, who knows what could've happened if you weren't." Ryan looks from her to me and says,

"I'm glad I was there for her. She doesn't realize it yet, but she's special." I was stuck. What did he mean by that? Special how?

"That she is, I'm glad she's in my life. She's such a sweetheart." Val reassured. I smile at her, she's been good to me.

"I'm glad you two met, I won't have to worry about her so much now." She says with a half-smile. She hugs me and says bye to Ryan before she walks off to her car.

Ryan stays behind.

"Val seems like a nice person. How long have you known her?"

"Almost two years now." I smile at the memory of our first conversation.

"We met my first year of college, we complimented each other's hair, and then we just clicked."

Ryan begins to laugh. "Girls!"

"Whatever. Anyway, she's been great. She was at the party the other night, she wasn't ready to leave when I was. I told her I would check in on her and I completely forgot, so she showed up today to see if I was ok."

I still wonder what would've happened if Ryan wouldn't have been there that night. Would that vision I had, have come to pass? I shutter just to think about it.

"Are you ok?" Ryan asked as he reached for my arm.

"Oh, yeah, sorry. I was just shaking off a thought."

"I see. So were you praying earlier?" I was, but what would make him ask? Confusion must be clearly written on my face because he laughs.

"I ask because I was praying too. And well we must've been in the same spirit because I saw you, and I know you saw me." Ryan tells me as he starts to walk to his bike. I look at him confused.

"So you were there? I'm still a little confused as to how all this supernatural stuff works. We weren't even praying together."

"We don't have to actually be in the same place to pray together. I was praying for you, I assume at the same time you were praying."

"Ryan, I had a dream of that same encounter. I knew it was coming for me. I didn't know the creature would be me."

"Dreams sometimes are warnings. Sometimes our biggest enemy is ourselves. Sometimes we're the ones who put limits on ourselves. So I noticed you received the belt of truth and the breastplate!"

"Yes, but I'm not sure what it means."

"The belt of truth. Because you recognized who you are, a daughter of God. You told your family. You spoke the truth. You earned your belt. It's part of the armor. You have to keep being honest, and always remember who you are in Christ.

You received the breastplate, because of your purity. You gave your life to Christ again and He has made you brand new. The old you is no longer, you have been reborn. And now you have finally accepted it."

"I'm getting my warrior gear?!" I say excitedly. I couldn't stop myself from doing my happy dance. I wish I did stop myself when I see the look on his face.

"Ok then, enjoy your victory!" He smirks.

He hops on his bike, his features show concern.

"I really should be going now. Thanks for the invite tonight, it was fun." He puts on his helmet and turns on his bike.

"Yeah, I'll be writing all night." I give him a kiss on the cheek and thank him.

19. Be Careful Angel

Finally done with my last class. I'm pretty confident on how I did with my thesis. I head to the parking lot to meet up with Val. As I'm walking Alex comes up behind me. "Hey!" He shouts.

"Hey Alex, how are you?" He walks with me.

"I'm good. I wish you didn't leave the party so early the other night." The way he says it makes me feel uncomfortable, almost like he was expecting something to happen.

"I told you, I didn't feel good. All those brownies didn't sit well with me. I had to leave."

"Did Val fill you in on what happened?"

"No, not really. What did I miss?"

"Oh, you missed a lot. We all went skinny dipping."

"Oh, well in that case, I'm glad I left early." I cringed. "Not really my cup of tea."

"I thought you would feel that way. Val didn't participate, she was most of the night with Mario," he winks. "If you know what I mean."

I do actually. I just hope Mario is a good guy.

"So that guy you left with, was he your boyfriend?" Alex questioned.

"No, he's just a friend." I replied.

"You called him to pick you up?" He stares at me as we walk. "I thought we had something going on."

"Alex, I don't see you like that. I'm not looking for a fling or a relationship." I pointed out hoping he would understand.

"Coming to a party looking the way you did, says something different." He looks me up and down, taking me in. "I really thought you were impressing me, not that you had to go all out." He implies. "Plus the way you were all over me while we danced. You led me on."

"I'm sorry, that wasn't my intentions. I couldn't control my actions." I inform him. "I wanted to feel free, but not in that way. I'm truly sorry."

Alex grabs my arm roughly to stop me from walking.

"I really like you, why can't you give me a chance?" He snapped.

The look in his eyes scare me. "I'm dealing with some stuff right now Alex." I cautioned. "I don't want to be romantically involved with anyone. I'm flattered, but I'm not dating right now!" I yank my arm from him. "I have to go." I retort.

I walk away finally. Alex is really persistent. He really isn't someone I will go out with. I make it to the parking lot, thank God Val was already there. I get into her car and we drive off.

I tell Val what just happened with Alex.

"Angel, be careful with Alex. He usually gets his way. He's not use to hearing the word no." What was she saying? Will he try to hurt me? I can't be the first person who has turned him down. He can't be so naïve to think that.

Thinking back to the night of the party. I realized I made a mistake in dressing the way I did. I was just so angry and I acted out. What I didn't realize was that I put myself in that situation. Things we do or say have consequences, I'm beginning to understand that now.

"So what did you tell Alex about you not wanting to go out with him?" Val tells me.

"I told him I'm not interested in dating." Is it so rare for a girl my age not wanting to date?

"At some point Angel, you have to get over Logan." It's not just Logan.

"Val, I don't trust myself in a relationship, I don't want to deal with it right now." I see she wants to say something, but she stays quiet.

"Val, just say it."

She doesn't say anything right away, "what about Ryan? He seems really nice, and he's hot!" she finally says. "Those eyes, are they real or contacts?"

I couldn't stop myself from smiling. "They're his."

"You two would look cute together."

My cheeks warm. I hope she hasn't noticed.

"See, I know you like him!" She teased.

"Val, I can't admit or deny that right now." I look out the window. "I need his help. He came into my life in the right moment. He's been there for me in a spiritual way." I breathe in deep. "I need to get my life in order. I can't afford distractions."

Val doesn't say anything, although I can tell she wants to. I wish I can explain it all to her.

"You may not understand me, but I have been in the middle of two worlds. The one I was raised in, the church life, and the one I've recently come to know. Parties, drinking, and sex. I realized I was trying to fill an emptiness. I've been filling up with these things, but what I needed was God.

Although I was raised in church, I didn't know God until recently. Until Ryan helped me see that God was calling me. So yes I like him. I like that he's showed me how to be brave, how to be strong, and how to stay focus on what's important." We both stay quiet for a while.

"So you do like him!" She joked breaking the silence. We both laugh, I shake my head.

"Maybe Ryan is your guide, maybe he was sent to help you, and maybe after you get to where you should be spiritually and emotionally, you're meant to be together."

"Who knows, maybe you're right. But right now, that's not what I want. You may not understand me, but Val, I want to be used by God. I feel something inside me that's ready to explode, I have a desire for God's touch upon my life. Things are changing for me, and I like where it's going." I wanted to tell her about my recent experiences in the spiritual realm, but I don't want to scare her. I want her to come to Christ, and when the time is right I'll tell her.

"That's good that you found where you belong. I'm truly happy for you. I may not completely understand all of this, but if it makes you happy, I'm happy for you. I'll make sure Alex backs off." We both laugh and start singing to a song that came on the radio.

"So what you doing tomorrow night?" she asks me.

"My church is having a vigil, want to come?" She cringed.

"I don't think I'm the church type." She tells me.

"Everybody is the church type, they just don't know it. You should try it one day before you decide it's not your thing." I tell her.

"Maybe one day I'll go with you, but tomorrow will not be that day." She smiles.

I decide to drop it, I don't want to pressure her, when she's ready she'll come. I'll just keep her in prayer for now. I give her a hug and thank her for giving me a ride home.

It's still early, my mom hasn't come home from work yet. I find my father in the kitchen, it looks like he's attempting to cook.

"Papi? What are you doing?" He turns around to face me,

"Estoy cocinando! (I am cooking)" He exclaimed. He looks really happy, I'm glad. It's been a while since he's been in a good mood.

"What's the occasion?" I wonder if I missed their anniversary.

"Well, I just want to do something nice for your mom. I really messed up, and I know dinner isn't going to make everything better, but it's a start. I also started going to A.A meetings. I want to be better for you girls, for your mom, and for myself. I need to get my life back on track. I also have a job interview tomorrow morning. Keep me in your prayers."

"Wow pops, that's great! I'm happy for you." I watch my father as he prepares to cook.

"Papi?" I say "I'm sorry I bought that bottle into the house. I forgot I had it, and I didn't know you—"

"It's not your fault!" He cuts in. "I was the one with the problem. I should've resisted."

"But pa, I shouldn't have been drinking. I knew it was bad." He walks over to me and embraces me.

"You shouldn't have, but we all make mistakes. What we do after the mistakes is what matters. You, Angelisa Cruz are a very strong young lady. What you went through, you did on your own. What you were willing to do for Logan to have the future he wanted was very brave and selfless. You are beautiful inside and out. You make me want to do better. So thank you for the truth, I know it must've been really hard for you. I love you." I couldn't help myself, I started to cry.

"I love you too, Papi!"

I don't know how long we stay there hugging, I feel another set of arms around us, when I look to see who has joined us. It's my little sister Evie.

"I saw you guys hugging, and I wanted in." She says. We all start laughing.

"Ok girls, go do whatever it is you do when you come home from school. I have a dinner to cook!" My father said as he lets his arms fall to his sides.

"Papi, we can help you. We know how to cook." I said.

"No, I want to do this, but thank you. I have YouTube, and if I get stuck, I'll call you." He replies.

"Ok, have fun, cooking is an art." I tell him.

"I guess I never saw it that way." He smiles.

My sister and I walk up the stairs, she follows me into my room.

"What's up sis?" I asked her as I throw myself on my bed.

"I have to tell you something, it's about Ryan!" she answers.

"What about Ryan?" I ask confused. What would she have to say about Ryan?

"Well, you know Rebecca and I have been pretty close lately."

"Please don't tell me you told her anything about what we spoke about." I'm not ready for everybody to know my past. I didn't tell my sister not to tell anyone, I assume she would know.

"No, I didn't tell her about any of that. I wish you will let me call her out on the lies she's spreading. It's not right!"

"Let her talk, one day she has to come to terms with God. One of these days, I will ask her why she's made me out to be the only one in the wrong. But you said you have to tell me something about Ryan?"

"Well, Rebecca is in to him."

"Yeah, I figured. What of it?"

"Aren't you two a thing?"

"Friends! Just friends." I've known Ryan a week, why are people questioning our friendship. Can't a guy and a girl just be friends?

"Well, I just thought you should know. I like Ryan, and I think he's good for you."

"Thanks, but we are just good friends."

Evie looks at me. I wonder what she's thinking. She smiles and walks out the door. Strange little girl, but I love her.

20. The Vigil

My father drops me and my sister off at the church. The vigil is for the youth, so my parents have the house to themselves tonight. Mom was really surprised last night. My father's dinner was pretty good, not bad for his first time. I'm glad they are working things out, I feel like things are falling back into place.

The vigil has not started yet. My sister walks up to the front, she's part of the choir tonight. I stay seated in the back. I haven't been to one of my church's vigils in a long time. Tonight I thought I should come. I may have lost friends here, but I'm still part of this church.

There are a few people here who still wave and smile at me. Maybe I just need to make an effort, I can't always expect everything to just fall into my lap. I'm ready to start from scratch. Besides I'm not here for them, I'm here for God.

My phone buzzed in my pocket, a text from Ryan. I haven't spoken to him in a couple of days. With everyone lately asking about Ryan and me, I thought it best to pause for a little while. I didn't think I was showing any interest. Maybe without knowing, I was. I just didn't want him to get the wrong idea.

Ryan: *"hey, what you up to?"*
Me: *"hey, vigil in my church, you?"*
Ryan: *"nice, nothing much. I just thought I'd check in on you."*
Me: *"I'm good, thanks."*
Ryan: *"well, I'll let you get back to the vigil."*
Me: *"ok."*

I wasn't sure what to say after that. I tucked the phone back in my pocket. They turned the lights down and someone starts to pray on the microphone. I'm seated in the last row, I'll work my way up the rows when I'm ready. Right now, here is just fine. I can't seem to get in to the spirit. My mind takes me elsewhere. I start to wonder what everyone may be thinking about me being here tonight. I wonder if Rebecca spoke more about me. I open my eyes to look around, feeling like people are staring at me, but no one is. My mind is playing tricks on me.

I remember a time when Rebecca and I were so close, way before Logan came along. We did everything together. When we were in vigils we prayed together, for each other.

I see now it is important to have a spiritual family. It's important to have support from someone when you're praying or worshipping. Being surrounded by spiritual people helps you be strong when you're feeling weak.

I'm starting to feel out of place. Maybe I shouldn't be here. It feels like no one here will be my spiritual partner. I may recognize that I'm the daughter of a living God, but I'm still human. I'm still fighting insecurities. Everyone needs someone to lift them up when they're falling.

The choir sings a few old songs I remember. I sing along with them in a low voice. I'm watching everyone in front of me. Some people are standing up in front of the choir, some kneeling in their chairs praying. I'm not sure where I should be, I want to walk up to the front, but I'm still afraid. I decide to stay where I am.

I close my eyes, still singing low. I'm standing now, my hands gripping the chair in front of me as if I'm holding on for my dear life. I'm trying to hold on strongly because I feel if I don't, I will fall. Why do I feel like this here? I can't seem to get into the flow. When I'm alone at home talking with God, it's a different atmosphere. Here I'm surrounded by all these people and suddenly I feel like I'm not on their level, and maybe I shouldn't be here.

Mostly everyone here has a powerful calling, and I'm still not sure what mine may be. Everything I've been experiencing in the spiritual realm seems light to me when I'm around people who speak with authority.

"God is in this place!" Someone on the microphone prays.

"It's time to take your place in the kingdom! It's time to rise up! You know God has been calling you, don't let the enemy lie to you. He wants to see you down, but God wants you up!" the voice continues.

I feel as though I'm not enough, what makes me think I'm able to be here taking part with these spiritually mature people. Who am I to them? That confidence I just had a few minutes ago has faded and now I think I made a mistake in coming here. I'm weak, still struggling…I feel as if most of these people will keep judging me. I'm alone here.

"I don't know who I'm talking to here, but God says to you right now that you are not alone. Don't doubt what you've seen, what you felt, or what you have experienced. You are His, says the Lord almighty!" That same voice says.

God is talking to me, but how can I push these feelings away? How can I not let my emotions get in the way? I feel paralyzed in my own fears, why does God want me? So many people more able, more equipped…why me?

Tears stream down my face as those thoughts flood my mind. I feel a hand over mine, I don't open my eyes. I begin to calm down, my mind is not racing and I allow myself to feel the worship touch my spirit. After a few minutes, the person holding my hand interlocks their fingers with mine and tugs me forward to follow. I let myself be led. I open my eyes to see who's holding my hand; Ryan!

He's leading us to the group of people that is worshiping up front. He looks my way and winks. I'm surprised he's here. Why do I feel ease when he's around? He faces forward and closes his eyes. He sings along with the choir, then he raises his other hand in worship.

He's still holding my hand. I wonder if I should let go, I don't. Instead I close my eyes and start to worship myself. A few of the youth are taking turns praying on the microphone as the choir continues to worship in the background.

"Grab the hand of the person next to you. Let's make one big chain. We will pray together in unity, and that's what we are going to pray for...unity. We are one church, a house divided against itself cannot stand. Pray for your brothers and sisters. We are a family." The person on the microphone prays.

We all join hands, and everyone begins to pray out loud. After a few minutes of praying this way, I feel Ryan pulling my hand and puts another hand in replacement of his. When I look to see whose hand I'm holding, it's Rebecca's.

"I'll be right back," Ryan whispers in my ear as he walks away. I stare at Rebecca for a moment, she seems sad. When I offer her smile, she rolls her eyes. The look she gave me makes me feel uncomfortable, but I'm also sad for her. I decide not to worry about it. I close my eyes and continue to pray.

Rebecca lets go of my hand and walks toward the same direction Ryan did. After a few minutes, none of them had returned so I decide to take a walk that way too. When I get to the hall where the bathrooms are, I see Rebecca talking to Ryan. I don't go up to them right away. I wonder what they would be talking about.

I see Ryan is trying to walk away but she grabs his arm to keep him put. He's telling her something, but I still can't hear. I walk up to where they are.

"Hey, what's going on?" I asked them.

He looks at me, "nothing, let's go back inside."

I look at her, "I was just filling Ryan on some history!" she smirks.

I don't get it, we're in church, receiving from God, why is she acting this way?

"History on what?" I ask as I cross my arms over my chest. I decide to play her game.

"On you!" she retorts. She's trying to poison Ryan's head about me so she could have a chance with him. I was about to say something, but Ryan pulls me to his side and led us back to the vigil.

"Ryan—"

"Shh, it doesn't matter. The past is in the past, it's not who you are. I don't care what people say, I care about who you are now. As I told you before, I'm praying for you. I prayed for you even before I knew you. So please don't worry about her." *How could he have prayed for me before he met me?*

"Ryan, why did you come here tonight?"

"I may have sensed you were having a hard time connecting. I thought maybe I could help."

"I *was* having a hard time; I may have a harder time now." He takes both my hands in his as he steps in from of me. We're standing in the middle aisle a few feet from everyone else.

"Don't worry about her, forget what you think people are saying about you, zone everyone out and just talk to your heavenly father. He's all that matters."

He's right, why do I get caught up in what people think of me. I should only care what God thinks.

'Seek first the kingdom of God and His righteousness and these things will be added...' Matthew 6:33.

When we return back to the front, I see there are two circles now. One of girls, and the others are of boys. Ryan points with his head in the direction of the girls, as he walks over to where the guys are praying.

I took his advice about not worrying what people think of me and take part in that circle. I join in the prayer and as I let go of what I was feeling tonight, the Holy Spirit takes over. I feel a surge of power flow through me and my hands begin to shake. I start to feel a presence in the circle I'm in...someone's hurting. I can feel her pain.

I ask God to show me what to do. I look around the circle, a girl catches my eye. She must be new because I don't know her. She's about Evie's age...I'm drawn to her. I tell God to lead me in what I should do. I hear a voice say to me *'GO.'*

Without even realizing it, I let go of the two girls whose hands I was holding, and walk through circle to the girl. I take both her hands in mine, I open my spiritual eyes.

I find myself in the woods where I was fighting Fear. I can see everyone around us praying, just like the other night in Gabe's vigil.

The girl and I are in the middle of the big circle. Everyone is standing, but she's on her knees crying. Behind her I see the spirit of fear. He's terrifying her, she's shaking. I tell her not to be afraid. I open my eyes and we're still in the middle of the circle.

I look to them, "Pray against the spirit of fear." I tell them, some just stare at me and others start to pray. I see Rebecca in the corner of my eye, but I don't pay her any mind. I turn my attention back to the girl. I start to pray for her, pray for courage, and strength. I tell the girl that she needs to be brave. She shakes her head.

"I can't," she cried.

"Whatever you are going through is nothing God can't handle. You need to hold on to Him, He is your strength." I tell her, realizing I'm still fighting the same battle myself.

I may have overcome certain situations in my life, but they come back in other ways. I see now that you will always be fighting a war. God is my strength, as long as I have Him I will always overcome.

Spiritual eyes open again, Fear is right next to us. She looks at me, "I can't do this," she mumbles.

"Yes, you can!" I answer her. Fear laughs.

"You think, you're stronger now because you have those pieces of armor?" Fear sneers.

I look down, I didn't even realize I had on the belt of truth and the breastplate of righteousness.

"I am stronger! You don't scare me!" I tell him.

In that moment, a gust of wind blows, I see something flying in that wind. Something shining headed towards me, it lands in front of me. A pair of steel silver boots. I step into them.

I look at Fear, "looks like I earned another piece of my armor!" I shouted.

"I still have her, she's weak and I plan to keep her there.

I look at the girl, "you must face your fear, whatever it might be."

"I'm scared. I don't know what I'm going to do." She wailed.

"Don't let him hold you down, you are stronger than what you think." I tell her.

I see an image next to her. It's her, only she has a belly…she's pregnant. Her physical self begins to cry.

"I know what you're going through, I can help you. But right now, you have to face your fear." She looks at me wiping her tears. She stands up and faces Fear.

"Leave. Me. Alone!" she tells him. I admire her courage, the first time I faced Fear I was paralyzed. I already can tell this girl is stronger than me, she just needs someone to lead her.

I watched as Fear took a few steps back, he looked surprised at her boldness. I continued to pray for her until Fear disappeared. When I opened my eyes, everyone else was still praying. I look to the girl, she smiles sadly. I put my arms around her, and hugged her. I pray for God's peace over her.

Everyone stops praying and joins in the hug, one big group hug. After a few minutes, I pull away.

"What's your name?" I ask her.

"Jessenia," she answers.

"I'm Angelisa, we can talk later if you want."

She smiles, "yes that would be nice. I don't know who I can turn to." I understand her completely.

"Amen!" I hear a familiar voice say on the microphone. I look up to the altar. Its Pastor Edward...he's back. He looks at me and smiles.

"Let's all take a seat," he tells everyone. Jessenia holds my hand as I walk to an empty row, she sits next to me. Ryan finds me and sits behind me in the next row, my sister makes her way toward me and sits on the empty chair next to me.

"What an amazing vigil so far huh?" Pastor Edward says.

"I know I have been away for a while, but I do as the Lord asks. Everything has a purpose, I see we have a few new faces here tonight."

He looks at Ryan, "Ryan? Ryan Rivera is that you?" Pastor asks from the altar.

"Yes Pastor, it's me." Ryan answers.

"I haven't seen you since you were a young teen. Look at you now, I see an anointed young man. Tell your uncle Gabe we need to get together soon!" Pastor Edward tells Ryan.

I turn to Ryan with a raised eyebrow.

He leans in, "your Pastor and my uncle are good friends." Ryan whispers. So many surprises lately.

Pastor Edward looks around the church smiling, there are about thirty of us here tonight.

"I've missed you guys!" He begins to talk about his trip, and shouts out a few people thanking them for their help while he was away. He looks at me next.

"Angelisa, I told you before, you are special. God has great plans for you." He tells me in front of everyone. I can feel my cheeks turn red, but I'm glad I can finally understand what he means by me being special.

I'm glad I was here tonight. I was able to help someone, pray for her. I will help her deal with what's she going through. Pastor Edward keeps talking about his trip. I exchange numbers with Jessenia so we can keep in contact. She also exchanges numbers with my sister. If my sister doesn't know her, she must be really new.

As the vigil comes to an end, Pastor Edward asks the leaders to stay behind.

We all start to head out, "Angelisa! Ryan! I would like to speak to you before you go." The Pastor calls out. Ryan and I look at each other and head his way.

"Hi Pastor, it's nice to have you back." I tell him.

"Thank you Angelisa, I'm glad to see you back on your feet. Although I think you are in a much better place now than before. You look like a load was lifted off you!" He tells me.

"Yeah, I've been dealing with some stuff." It didn't occur to me I would have to share my past with Pastor Edward. I wonder if he was told about what I did or didn't do by anyone else. I respect this man, he's not like everyone else here in the church. Not just because he's a Pastor, because even Pastors can fail, but he's a man led by God. He's so genuine and kind. I am really glad he's back.

"Ryan! Always a pleasure to see you. How are you doing?" Pastor Edward asks Ryan.

"You know me, always well." I wonder why he called us both.

"I've heard you have visited our church a few times this week." He tells Ryan. *Great.* I think to myself…there has been talk, and it's reached the pastors ears.

"Yes I have. My uncle brought me along last week," he answers.

"And you kept coming back?" Pastor asked.

"Angelisa and I are friends, I came to keep her company," Ryan tells him.

"I see...well you are always welcomed." Pastor Edward looks at me then back at Ryan with a big smile on his face.

"I may ask you to bring a word one of these days!"

"Whenever you want, always willing." Ryan answers.

"Angelisa, I'm so proud of you. I'm glad you are finally stepping out of that shell of yours. I see Ryan is a good example for you. The Lord has been showing me...how you are growing. I'm glad, Ryan take care of her...she's special."

Ryan looks from the pastor to me. "I will, I have been and...I *know* she's special." My cheeks feel like it's on fire.

"Thank you Pastor." I cut in.

"It's been pretty interesting. I feel like a new person, but I still have more to unlock."

"Well you have a good guide," he said pointing to Ryan. This is getting awkward.

"You can always come to me or my wife if you need prayer or just to talk. I won't keep you, I have to go and talk to some of the leaders. Get home safe."

"Thank you, have a good night Pastor." I tell him. Ryan shakes his hand, right before we walk away. I look back to where the Pastor is meeting the leaders, Brian is one of them.

Once we're outside I look for Jessenia, I didn't really say bye to her. I find her by the curb, a car pulls up...I guess it's her ride.

"Jessenia!" I yell out to her. She meets me half way.

"Hey, I just wanted to say bye. Whenever you want to talk about your situation, just call me." I tell her.

She hugs me, "I will...thank you so much," she said. She walks back to the car and they drive away.

I find Ryan talking to some of the guys just outside the church.

"Hey!" I say more to Ryan than to the guys. They all stare at me before they all respond back with a, hey, or hi. I take a quick glance at them before I look back at Ryan.

"I'm going to call my father to pick us up, I just wanted to say bye."

I look back at the guys, "I didn't mean to interrupt." While I reach for my phone. Ryan gives the guys a palm as to say bye.

"You don't have to leave, I'm calling my father," I tell him.

"I can take you home" Ryan tells me.

"Thanks, but I don't think the three of us fit on your bike!" I laugh.

"I have my uncle's car tonight. Your sister can hop in the back seat, and anyone else you may want to give a ride to." I didn't expect him to have a car.

"Oh, well then ok. But just me and my sister, I believe everyone else has a ride."

I look around for my sister, when I spot her I wave her over. Before she reaches us, Rebecca shows up again.

"Ryan!" she calls. She really gets under my skin.

"Rebecca," Ryan answers.

"Thought about what I asked earlier?"

He shakes his head. "No, because my answer is still no."

"After what I told you, you still—" she pleas.

"... Rebecca!" my sister shouts.

"Give Ryan some space to breathe. You have been all over him since he started coming here."

Rebecca looks at my sister shocked. She looks between me and Ryan, she seems embarrassed. But then her demeanor changed.

"Evie, what are you talking about? Your sister is the one all over him. I'm just making sure he knows he has options." She tosses her hair over her shoulder.

"Let's just cut right to the chase," Evie turns to Ryan, "do you want to date Rebecca?" Ryan has a smile on his face as he answers my sister. I am surprise at her boldness.

"No, I don't date." His answer leaves me puzzled. He doesn't date? What does that mean?

"There, that should answer your question. So please just leave him alone."

Rebecca looks at Ryan, than at me.

"You choosing her? Over me?" She chided.

"Rebecca, I'm not choosing anyone. I'm not here looking for a date or a girlfriend. I came here as a friend for Angelisa." Ryan answers.

"So you two are only friends?" Ryan and I both nod.

"Ryan...can we talk alone?"

"I need to drive Angelisa and Evie home," he refuses to speak with her.

"Fine…well it's no secret I'm attracted to you." She admits. "I hope you would give me a chance. Can we hang out sometime?" She practically begs.

Why is she acting this way? She's not being very discreet about her feelings, and she's not understanding that Ryan just doesn't seem interested.

"Rebecca, I'm trying my best to make you understand, I'm not into dating. When it comes to my love life, it's in God's hands. You want to be friends? We can be friends, that's it. You want to hang out, sure we'll plan something as a group!" He fumed.

Rebecca's eyes widened. "No, I mean just me and you."

I watch them going back and forth, Ryan staying calm but I can see he's starting to get frustrated.

My sister and I had stepped back to give them some space. But now I'm thinking I should step in.

"Rebecca," I say, "don't you think you're over doing it? He's not interested, it's late…give it a rest." I interjected, I had enough.

I turn my attention to Ryan, "can you take us home?"

"Wait." She looks at me with sadness in her eyes. "Why you always get the good ones?" Rebecca asks me as I tried to turn away.

"Good ones? There was only one, Rebecca. Logan!" I noted. "And yes he was a good one, maybe he still is. But you can't force things to happen just because you want them to. Yes Ryan is a good one, but again he's only my friend."

"The way you two look at each other, and hold hands, I highly doubt you are just friends."

"Holding hands? We were praying!" I scoffed. "And if we weren't just friends, if you think we are something more, what does that say about you?" I retort. "You trying to come in between us? I'm going to tell you one more time. We are just friends, but no he doesn't seem interested in you. So maybe you should just lay off." I snapped. I forgot my sister and Ryan were close by, I look at them.

"Please give us a minute, I would like to speak to her alone." Ryan nods as he leads my sister in the direction of the car.

"Rebecca, I don't know what happened between us. We use to be very close. I've kept your secrets all this time, and you tell lies about me. Are you believing them yourself?" I ask.

"We were both there that night at the dance, you know what you did. I've only been with Logan, you were with way more." I accused. "I understand that you didn't want your father to know the truth, but the reality is, you're only hurting yourself.

Telling stories about me to hide what you did, is wrong. You can tell all the lies you want, but God knows the truth." I remind her. "I am working on my past issues, maybe you should start to do the same." I didn't give her a chance to speak, I walk toward the car.

I hop in the front seat and we drive away. It feels really good to be able to speak without feeling like I shouldn't. I am finally learning who I am, I have come to terms with my mistakes, and I am better for it. We all have to go through something in our lives in order to be molded into the person we're meant to be.

"So, what did you tell her Angel?" My sister breaks the silence.

"I basically told her she needs to move on," I see Ryan trying to hold back a smile. "And I also told her she needs to start facing the truth about her past. I confronted her about the lies she's spreading about me." My sister's jaw drops.

"What did she say?" Evie asks intrigued.

"I didn't give her a chance to respond, I just walked away. I think she should sleep on it."

"Maybe she'll stop, I don't know what's with her tonight. I mean, I knew she liked Ryan, but she was really pushy wasn't she?"

"She was, but I don't think it's really about Ryan." I answer her.

"Ryan, you're quiet." Evie tells him.

"I'm just listening. I agree with your sister," he glances over at me. "There's something deeper going on with her. Just keep her in your prayers. Don't push her away, she may need someone to talk to." Ryan answers Evie.

"She has other friends, she could always talk to them. I don't really want to be around her, especially after everything she put Angel through."

"Pushing her away is not going to help her, what she did to Angelisa was wrong. What she's *still* doing to her is wrong. But she needs help, until she's ready to admit that, she's always going to have those insecurities."

"I guess you're right!" Evie responds to Ryan.

It's a short drive from church to my house, Ryan pulls into the drive way. Evie thanks Ryan for the ride and heads inside leaving Ryan and I alone in the car.

"Angelisa, before you go…I just want to tell you something." He stares into my eyes. "Tonight, what you did for that girl…that's just the beginning of what God wants you to do. He wants to take you into the spiritual realm to reach the souls that are tormented by their past. He has so much in store for you. I know you are beginning to realize what you are capable of, but you haven't even gone beneath the surface yet. I know you feel this spiritual tug on your life lately. It feels like you want to do more, am I right?"

Considering his word, I know he's right. But am I truly ready for it all? Everything happens for a reason, what if what happened to me was so I can help Jessenia? Although I still don't know how I can help her. I still had no idea what I was going to do if I hadn't miscarried. But I do feel a pull on me, I want to do more, I need to do more.

21. What Are Your Fruits?

Everything that happened a couple of weeks ago at the vigil, keeps playing over in my mind. I was scared and excited all at the same time. What happened in the vigil was amazing, for the first time I felt like I could really see. I was able to discern that someone was in need of help. I was able to supernaturally see what she was going through. It was a tough start for me, but once I was able to push aside my own fears I realized, I'm capable of doing so much more with my life.

I think back to what Ryan started to tell me in the car after the vigil. This is only the beginning of what God wants me to do. I can't help but wonder what else He has in store for me. And I can't stop myself from thinking, somehow Ryan is part of this journey.

The timing of him entering my life in the exact moment God was speaking to me. And to think, I've seen him before we actually met. I don't know what came over me that day I spoke to him, I just felt I had to. God does work in mysterious ways.

I'm alone in my room and I feel the urge to pray, I decide to give into the desire and get down on my knees. I start by worshipping, giving God praise and glory. Since my encounter with God, and hanging out with Ryan and his friends, I have learned prayer is not just one sided. Prayer is like a conversation with people. You can't talk and not be willing to listen. Relationships aren't built that way. If you want a relationship with God, you have to learn to slow down and listen.

In Matthew chapter six, Jesus teaches how to pray. Verse seven taught me not to only talk, but listen as well. As I studied the Lord's Prayer I noticed an outline. Praising God's name, honoring Him. When God told me in my first encounter with Him, He said worship. We shouldn't just go straight to God and say what we want. We should praise His name.

As I'm on my knees I continue to pray, honoring my Lord, because He has blessed me and He has freed me. I can feel the presence of the Holy Spirit around me. I see myself in what I like to call my war zone. Every time I'm here, in this area of the woods, I'm about to fight something.

"It's been a while princess, we thought you were afraid to come back here to face us!" Fear says to me.

Behind him are two other creatures, Guilt and another I'm not sure who it is.

The third creature is as big as Guilt, but he's not made of rocks. He looks like a man, very buff, like a body builder. He's wearing black pants, his chest is bare. From his head to his waistband I can see his veins, they're black and his skin is red. His eyes are black as well, he's standing with his arms crossed over his chest.

As I continue to stare at him, he drops his arms and I notice his hands. He has long black finger nails. I think I'm starting to realize who he is, but I'm unsure as to why he's here.

"Have you met our brother Anger?" Guilt asks me as he noticed I haven't taken my eyes off him.

"I don't have anger issues!" I answer him.

"Oh, but you do!" He snares.

"You just hid it very well. But don't you know what happens when you suppress your emotions?" He begins to laugh.

"You...explode!" Fear responds making an explosion gesture with his hands.

"I haven't been suppressing anything, especially not anger!" I tell him.

"How do you really feel about your so called Christian friends that turned their back on you? Or how about your best friend who spread rumors about you? How about your ex, how he made you feel when he kissed that girl in front of everyone the day you broke up? Doesn't that make you angry?" Guilt taunts me.

I begin to question myself, have I been angry? I did pull away from everyone. And yes I was upset when Rebecca spread those lies about me. I stopped trusting people, I closed myself off and I went numb. I was suppressing my feelings, I didn't want to feel anymore. I closed myself off from…everyone and…myself. I felt lost and abandoned, thrown away like I no longer mattered.

The three of them walked closer to me, they circled around me. They were taunting me, laughing and whispering. I wasn't prepared for this. I had to think, I have come so far, I can't let this set me back. I have three more armor pieces to collect, I will not let this consume me.

I turn to face Anger, "you have no power over me!" I tell him.

"You're wrong!" he barked.

"Just wait and see, your anger will come out when you least expect it to." Anger continues as the rest laugh. The woods begins to fade away.

I stand from the floor, walk over to my mirror. It can't be true, I don't feel angry, I know I was before, but not now. I need to clear my mind. I don't usually go for runs, but I think today I'll start. I grab my earphones and head out. I've come so far for this to set me back. I have to deal with this anger I suppressed for so long. I don't want to blow up on the wrong person because I haven't dealt with it.

I start my run listening to songs about being a warrior and not being afraid, all the things I'm facing right now. I'm so lost in my music and in my thoughts I didn't realized how far I've gone, it's almost dark. I ended up in front of Rebecca's house, I don't know whether I should knock on her door or go back home. What would I say to her? I think I told her everything I needed to the night of the vigil. I haven't spoken to her since then. She wouldn't even look at me when we were in church.

I see Brian come out, knowing how he feels about me causes me to hesitate. He wouldn't appreciate me being here. When he notices me he walks toward me.

"What are you doing here Angelisa?" He sounds upset, he always sounds upset when it comes to me, thanks to Rebecca and her lies.

"Is Rebecca home?" I asked him.

"No, she is not home. I told you before, you are not welcomed here!" he replies.

"Brian, it's been two years, are you ever going to let it go?" I asked frustrated.

"I will not let it go, if I allowed you to keep your friendship with Rebecca you would have damaged her. I don't want you around her!"

"You think you know everything don't you? I've been quiet, I've let you think what you wanted to. But I'm tired, your daughter—"

"...what are you doing here Angelisa?" Rebecca asks me as she walks out her front door.

"I wanted to speak to you, but I'm still not welcomed here thanks to your lies!"

"What lies?" Brian asks.

"Dad, she's just upset. She wants to put the blame somewhere!" Rebecca laughs it off.

"I want to put the blame somewhere?!" I shout as I feel my cheeks burning up. The nerve of her trying to flip this on me.

"I think that's what you have been doing for the past two years. I'm tired of everyone thinking of me as they do. I didn't do all of those things, you di—"

"Angelisa! Don't, please don't do this," she pleas for me to stop.

I turn from her and face her father, "maybe you should check your daughter!" I tell him.

It's about time he knows the truth, but it's not my place to tell him.

"Anything my daughter has done is because you introduced it to her. My girl was a good girl until you started dragging her to parties. And the boy, Ryan, we both know you're not right for him. He needs someone like Rebecca, someone that won't pull him down. He's an anointed young man, the more time he spends with you, well...you know the rest."

As he said this, I feel anger rise. I know I'm not right for Ryan, or at least not ready to be with someone like him. But Brian thinking his daughter is better than me, who is he fooling? I'm about to answer him back when I hear a voice say *"Don't give in to your anger."*

I remembered why I needed a run. I am angry, and I won't let it get the best of me.

As I look between Rebecca and her father, I want to say everything I've been keeping secret. But as I think about it, a little voice inside me asks what would that gain me? I use to admire this family.

It's just Brian and Rebecca, her mom died a long time ago. Maybe that's why he's being so over protective.

"Brian," I say as calmly as I can after being so fired up.

"You have no idea what you're talking about. I have been through so much in the past two years. You as an elder of the church were supposed to be there for me, and instead you shunned me because you thought it best for your daughter.

As a man of God I expected you to be better than that. When I was in need of prayer and support, you turned your back on me. Your job is not to save the saved, but to reach the broken hearted, the lost and lonely, the damaged.

As Christians, we often make mistakes because we live in a world that draws our attention from God. We get caught up in situations around us, anybody, not just me, can fall into temptation.

Aren't we all sinners? Don't we all fall short? I'm not perfect, I wasn't then and I'm not now, but neither are you! Rebecca was able to make her own decisions. I did not force her to do anything. What she did was all on her, you can't blame me for her actions. She is her own person.

I died inside, do you understand what that is like? I felt nothing, I had nothing, and I was nothing. But God woke me up, I learned not to depend on anybody. I had learn to lean on God.

I didn't know how to do that then, I needed a guide, and that guide had to come from another church because you and others judged me. God sent me someone; Ryan, to show me I didn't have to stay dead.

Yes I made mistakes, none of which you think you know. I've been battling with a lot of stuff trying to get my life together. There's nothing I can do or say that would change your mind about me. But I hope and pray that one day you would push aside your stubbornness and see me as God does."

I face Rebecca, "I think it's time you come clean. You can't hide behind me forever." I look at Brian, he looks confused by what I said. Finally understanding is settling in. He's not a bad man, he's just led by his emotions.

My phone rings in my pocket, I reach for it; Ryan. Before I answer it, "I had no intentions of showing up here, I just ended up here. I hope you two can talk, and next time you want to pass judgment, look in the mirror." I tell them both as I turn and walk away.

Ryan wanted to meet up, I told him to pick me up from my house so we can grab a bite to eat.

***

"So where did you go today?" Ryan asks me as the waiter collects the menus.

"For a run," I answered. I go on to tell him about the events of the day. I leave out the part about Brian saying I'm wrong for him. I didn't see a reason why I should bring that up.

"I'm just tired Ryan, people always looking at me like a bad seed. I know God forgave me already, I know I'm passed that part. But it still hurts, I don't feel free to let go and move as God wants me to. I know the eyes that matters here is God's, but people could make you feel so insecure," I tell him.

"I can understand that, but you really can't let that hold you down. Not everybody is going to be on the same page as you. There's always going to be someone that wants to keep you down." I know he's right.

"Looks like our burgers are ready!" I say excitedly as I see the waiter coming to our table.

"I guess you were hungry!" he replies.

"Didn't I tell you I was running, I built up an appetite!" I laugh.

We sit there eating and joking about everything and nothing. I love how easy it feels around him. I don't have to hide how I feel or be embarrassed by it. I still haven't had that conversation with him about the rest of my past, but he doesn't pressure me about it. He says when I'm ready to tell him I will.

"Looks like you two are on a date!" A familiar voice says from behind me. Ryan stops laughing and looks up, I look over my shoulder; Rebecca. I didn't expect to see her again, at least not anymore today.

Why did we have to come to this diner? I wonder if this is all a test. Anger wanted me to explode, I'm not going to let him win, and I can control myself. What would Jesus do? That is what I would be asking myself when I feel anger begin to rise up in me.

"Rebecca, nice to see you again…today! It's not a date, as I said before he's my—"

"Guide! Isn't that what you said earlier to my father and me?" She cuts me mid-sentence.

"What do you want?" I ask her

"I came here to pick up some food, to get away from my dad and I find you. Can my night get any worse?"

"Did you speak to your dad?" I try to soften my tone.

"No, you think your little act today was going to make me talk? It's in the past, why bring it back up?!" She places her hands on her hips as she looks down on me.

Was I supposed to fear her? Her statement and her stances awakens something in me. I drop the fry I had in my hand on to my plate as I stare back at her.

"So it's ok for you to talk about a past I never had to make yourself look good?" I need to calm down, I'm starting to feel anger rise up.

"Ladies, I think you should really calm down, Rebecca why won't you sit down with us?" I turn my attention to Ryan. Why would he invite her to join us? I just want her to go.

"Thanks Ryan, but I don't want to ruin your *'date'* more than I already have." Rebecca replies.

Ryan looks from her to me, than back to her.

"It's not a date, please join us. It seems you two have a lot to discuss. You're both sisters in the eyes of God, you should try to work this out. You don't want to be friends, that's fine, but you can't allow bitterness to stop your spiritual growth." Ryan slides over offering her a seat.

Rebecca seems to consider his gesture, "Ryan, I really like you but, I can't deal with her right now." She tilts her head my way.

"I still can't understand why you would rather be with her?" Her remark causes me to look down, I consider my appearance.

My hair tied into a ponytail, I have no makeup on, and I'm wearing a red t-shirt and jeans. But I know she's not referring to my attire or my looks. She's jealous, or just angry at herself.

"Tell me Ryan, is this how you guided her?"

Ryan looks confused by her question.

He looks at me. "What are you talking about?"

"I see *he* doesn't even know," she tells me. She looks back at Ryan.

"My dad earlier said she wasn't good for you, and her responds was *'God sent me someone…a guide…Ryan'* something like that!"

I'm really getting upset now. Ryan looks from her to me, and I just can't help but feel embarrassed. But I shouldn't be, it's the truth, and I believe it without a shadow of a doubt. He's my guardian angel, I still didn't feel comfortable to confess that to him yet. My embarrassment lessens when Ryan smiles at me.

"Everyone knows she likes you, she's just making that up to feel better about it, but trust me she is not the right one for you!" Rebecca continues, content with herself. As if she caused a drift between Ryan and me.

"She's right Rebecca, what Angelisa said is true. God showed her to me before we met, I've been praying for her ever since. God put her in my path so we can meet, because she needed help finding her way to Him!" He tells her with his eyes locked on mine.

"But…fine maybe God did send you to her, but not like—"

"Rebecca," he faces her again. "You don't know me, and apparently, you really don't know Angelisa as well as you think you do. She's chosen by God, she's a powerful spiritual warrior. I think you need to come down from your own pedestal and talk to your friend as a woman of God." He tells her.

"I'm a woman of God too—"

"Are you acting like one right now? You do understand that just because you go to church doesn't mean you are a godly person, right? Anybody can go to church, but only if you have a relationship with God are you considered a woman of God. People need to see your fruits! Which are you showing right now? Because honestly, I can't tell. And I'm not saying this because I'm trying to make you feel bad, but because I don't think you know." Ryan tells her. She stomps her foot like a toddler before she storms off.

"Ryan, I—"
"Angelisa, it's ok. You don't need to explain anything. I know God sent me to you."
"Yeah but about what people—"
"Like I said, people will always talk. I can understand, how could you resist this face?" He jokes causing me to laugh.
"Seriously, it's ok. I'm not going to stop hanging out with you just because people are talking. I care about you Angelisa...you did well by the way. You didn't lose your cool, Anger didn't win today."
"I guess not, I think I can face him now." I tell him. I'm ready to fight.

22. Not Alone

Tall trees and fallen dried up leafs surround me, I'm standing in the center of my three foes. I'm right back where I was yesterday. But something is different. I can sense the atmosphere has changed. It no longer feels like my enemies are in control, in fact Guilt looks a little smaller than the last time I saw him. The guilt I've been carry around inside does not feel as heavy as it once did.

"What do you want from me?" I ask them, they're still circling me looking like they're ready to attack.

"Are you ready to fight?" Fear taunts.

"Well, it doesn't matter, you think you're so strong...but we know the truth!" He said once they all stopped moving.

"Don't you know?" I smile at them.

"You don't scare me anymore! There's nothing you can show me or tell me that would change that!" I quipped.

"You may have overcome some fears, but you will never be rid of all of them. New ones are born every day. Worry takes over and fear is back. Let's see how strong you are, shall we?" Fear exclaims.

He's trying to make me second guess myself. To them, our lives are like games, our situations are pawns for them. They manipulate our thoughts, try to set us up to fail. Not today! I stand strong and believe that my God will not leave me when I need Him the most.

My spirituality has grown in the past few weeks, I am no longer that seven year old girl when I first came here. I have been preparing myself to fight a war in the supernatural. I will not let fear take over me. God said I was chosen, and I believe that. Yes these creatures are fearful, but I serve the one they fear and I know He would not leave me to fight on my own.

Fear, Guilt, and Anger take a step back. They are preparing themselves, who would attack first, I wonder? Fear begins to wield the wind around us placing us in the center of a whirlwind just like before. The difference between then and now is I am not the same.

"Still not afraid I see," Fear teased.

"I told you, you don't scare me!"

Anger comes closer and shoves me to the ground.

"You should be afraid, did you think you really got over your anger? It's still there little one, and I'm still here!" Anger bellowed. He leans over me looking for a change in my confidence.

I can't let him get in my head, of course I still have anger in me, but it's how I handle it that matters. A long chain appears in one of Guilt's hands, I remember what he did with it the last time he had it. He swung the chain in the air aiming at me, I quickly roll out of the way. He yanks the chain back and throws it again, and again it misses me. Anger laughs.

"Can't dodge it forever." He said as he stands far back just watching.

I don't have much space to run since the wind is still trapping us, well more me than them. I have to find a way out of this tornado. Guilt comes at me again with his chain, Anger quickly grabs me and the chain wraps around my wrist. He got me, I have to find a way out. A dark sinister smile spreads across Anger's face as he sees I've been caught.

Fear steps closer, "did you really think you could take us on?" he mocked.

The wind gets stronger, Fear comes closer, and Guilt laughs. I see a version of myself, one of Fear's tricks. She's cradled like a baby on the ground, crying. Her arms wrapped so tight around her legs and her face to her knees. She looks terrified.

"What is this?" I ask Fear. "That's not me, I'm not afraid of you!"

"No, not of me dear girl, only of what I bring out of you! You are quite good at suppressing your emotions, your fears aren't gone as you thought, only hidden. But I can sense them in you." he taunts.

I look back over to the other me, still crying, I wonder what's bothering her. Guilt yanks the chain back pulling me to fall on my back. Anger approaches and kicks me in my stomach. I can hear all three of them laugh, what can I do?

"Now you look like her, you have no hope!" Anger taunts me.

"Still afraid, have no way out. You're in our playground now. We hold the cards here. You're out numbered!" Fear begins, I refuse to let him or the others get into my head.

I'm not afraid, I just don't know what to do. But then it hits me, why am I trying to fight on my own? As I try to stand Guilt pulls on the chain once again. *'Greater is He that is living in me'* He's in me, God is always with me.

Suddenly I feel strong enough to get up, I try once more to yank my arm out of the chain wrapped around my wrist without success. I refuse to give up, I keep pulling as Guilt continues to pull back causing me to stumble, but I do not fall. The others laugh as they watch this tug of war game play before their eyes.

Grabbing the chain with both hands, Guilt does the same, I position my feet to adjust my balance. A bright light distracts me from outside this tornado. As my enemies stand before me, I watch as the bright light begins to take the form of a man. Guilt takes advantage of my distraction and yanks the chain so hard I fall face down. I hear them laugh as I was defeated.

As I lift my head, light has consumed the darkness. I stare in the direction I last saw this light form into a man. My enemies turn to see what has caught my attention.

"No, it cannot be!" Anger yells. A sense of peace fills the air, at least for me. They may have knocked me down, pushed me around, but I will not stay that way. I stand, finally able to remove the chain with ease since Guilt is distracted with what's coming.

The light figure person somehow spreads itself like its wind itself, it surrounds my adversaries in another kind of tornado. The three of them are lifted up in the winds of this new bright whirlwind and are scattered through the air. The whirlwind Fear created disbursed and the bright figure was gone. At that moment I realized, this new creature was not an it, but a He. He was the Holy Spirit, He came to help me, because I came to the realization that I was not alone.

***

"I'm not fully armed Ryan, I need to grow more. I'm praying, I read a few verses a day. What else should I do? I don't want to be trapped by my emotions again!" I filled him in on what happen last night. As I sit down next to him on my front steps, my mind wonders back to the night before. I can feel his eyes on me.

"Why are you staring at me like that?" I drop my head into my hands.

"I can just see a warrior in you." He answers.

I feel physically, I'm not doing enough. God said what I do in the physical will affect the spiritual, so what am I missing? I'm not as strong as I thought I was, although I'm not as weak as I was before either. I have grown spiritually as well.

"Angelisa, you should study more the word, break it down. Faith comes from reading the word, the next piece of armor is the shield of faith," Ryan responds.

I haven't really been studying the bible. I use the bible app on my phone for the verse of the day. Sometimes I read a little more of the scripture, but I guess I'm not committed enough. I don't want to be corner like I was last night.

"If you want, we can study the bible together. I like to read the word of God a lot and take notes, I'm sure you've noticed. I can show you how to do that, if you're interested!" Ryan continues.

"I do need to learn more. I'm still struggling with a few things. Although it's not as much as before. The load feels a lot lighter than it once did," I tell Ryan.

"But I do know I have to be stronger."

"Just reading the word as a daily routine is not enough. You have to apply it to your life. In 2 Timothy 3:16-17 it says '...*the word of God is for teaching, rebuking, correcting, and training in righteousness.*' The bible is like an instruction manual for daily living, you need to know how to really read it and obey the word of God," Ryan instructs me.

We've been hanging out a lot more now, not just with him, but with Ivy and Marissa, Jason and Mike. Being with them shows me you can still have fun without participating in the sinfulness of this world, and you can still be separated for God.

I use to think, to be a true Christian, you had to basically live in the church and only surround yourselves with people that shared the same views. But it's not like that at all, having a relationship with God doesn't stop you from being who you are.

The only thing is, you don't feel the need to sin, or do things that you know God won't approve of. Smoking, drinking, sex before marriage, cursing, gossiping. All these things are not desired when you hold a relationship with God. I no longer feel as if I'm deprived of a youthful life. I have fun with my new friends. There's so much we can do that would not be displeasing in the eyes of God.

"May be we can start Monday, tomorrow is Sunday and I'm sure you'll have your daily dose. We can meet after your shift at Caffeine, what do you think?" I look at him for a moment before I answer. He really has been a blessing in my life.

"Yeah, that sounds like a plan!" I answer him.

"Good, come ready with a notebook and a pen, you'll be taking notes!" he says laughing.

"I got my phone!" I wave my phone for him to see.

"Trust me, it's not the same. Having a notebook full of the notes you take, the scriptures you study, is much better. In the future, when you look back into them, it's like a refreshment. A phone, you only have for a year or two, then you'll get an upgrade. Then the notes you have taken either get erased because you gave your phone away, or lost it. A notebook, you can have for a long time," he says as sincere as he can.

"So how many notebooks do you have?" I ask him laughing. He laughs, "a few," he answers.

"Ryan," I whispered as I look up to the dark sky. I can feel his eyes on me, I refuse to meet his gaze for what I'm about to say.

"I was pregnant once…I lost the baby." I don't know why I felt the need to tell him now, but part of me felt he should know. The other part feels like I made a mistake. He's my friend, I should be able to confide in him.

He looks up to the sky as I fill him in on the whole story of my miscarriage. I give him a minute before I speak again.

"Do you think because of what happened to me is why I was able to sense Jessenia's need?" I ask him. He doesn't answer right away, he just stared straight ahead dangling his keys. I assume he's digesting this new information.

"I really wasn't expecting that. The thought never crossed my mind that you could've…" he pauses again.

He turns his attention to me as he continues to speak.

"I believe everything happens for a reason, maybe you connected to her because you understood her fear. But also because you are growing spiritually, you may not feel like you are sometimes. Think of it like this…when a baby takes their first step, they try to balance themselves. They take one step, then another, then sometimes they fall. But they get back up and try again. You are going to have days when you're on a spiritual high, and other days not so much. It doesn't mean you're failing, you just have to keep going," he replies.

Talking about babies taking their first steps brings tears to my eyes. My baby didn't have a chance to have a first step, or cry or even sneeze. I'll never know who he or she would have looked like.

"It's just so hard sometimes. I don't know what I'm doing half the time, and I don't trust myself because I still have emotional baggage," as I tell him, I look away, avoiding eye contact.

"Everyone has baggage, don't think you are the only one. We don't have to be perfect, we strive to be, but if we were perfect, God would not have to send His son to die for us. If we were perfect, maybe we still would've been living in Eden. Don't be too hard on yourself, trust me. Just keep seeking God, and you'll see. I still go through things, I'm not a saint!" I didn't realize he still struggled.

I see him so calm and driven that I thought he was good. I can get so caught up in my own issues, I don't notice what other people are going through.

"Ryan..." I turn to face him.

"Sorry, I didn't realize. You're always helping me, and encouraging me I just thought you had it all together. I've been relying on you to guide me, to listen to me, I never asked if there was something going on with you!" I tell him. He looks like he's about to say something, but doesn't. He turns his face from me, and I suddenly feel as if I said something I shouldn't have.

"Ryan? What is—"

"I sometimes struggle with anger myself." He faces me again, something in his eyes keep me locked on his. The look in his eyes indicates he has a story to tell.

"I haven't seen my father since he left us, I felt abandoned...sometimes those feelings come back. I just don't let it take control of me. It's a constant battle, I'm always praying about it, the burden is not as heavy as before. God has filled that void, but I do miss my pops at times. I'm grateful for Gabe, he's been more than an uncle to me...he's a father." He looks away again.

"Is there something else?" I ask because it seems there's more he wants to say.

"There's...a new development I have to deal with!" he looks my way again.

"Which is?" Still holding my gaze in silence, it's me now that wants to look away.

"Don't take this the wrong way, but I can't tell you...yet," he finally says.

I lower my head to avoid looking at him. I shared with him more then I was comfortable with, but he can't confide in me? I feel a little hurt. As if he can sense what I'm thinking, he places his index finger under my chin and lifts my face so I can look at him.

"It's not you, I care about you, please understand that. This new…development, I haven't shared with anyone yet. I'm just leaving it in God's hands. When He deems it time, I'll tell you. For right now, all I want is for you to do what you need to, to be fully armed because you will be fighting a bigger battle soon. You're blessing is coming, that is why this is getting harder for you. So right now, let's focus on you. I'm ok, I promise!" he tells me.

The way he said that, and the gesture he made, under different circumstances, I probably would've kissed him. It would've been a perfect setting, but this was not his intention…I think. And it's not mine either, at least not for now. I don't even know if he would be interested in me anyway. I mean, most guys like their girls to be untouched, or maybe that's old school. I'm tainted. I turn my head to avert from his gaze. He lowers his hand and faces the direction I am.

"Sorry if I overstepped by touching you, I just—"

"It's fine, just…so," unsure of what to say next. I hear him laugh and I can't help but to look at him.

"What?!" I ask him, wondering what is so funny.

"Nothing, I just want you to focus on your mission. Great things are coming for you, ask God to give you strength because you're going to need it. So…Monday?" he asks. I just nod, I don't trust myself to speak. He smiles as he stands.

"I see I made you speechless!" He says as he extends his hand out for me to take. I place my hand in his.

"I should tell you, your pastor invited me to preach for some youth event you're having next month!"

"Wow Ryan, that's great! Do you get nervous when you have to preach?" I ask him. I get nervous when I have to do an oral presentation, I imagine preaching is the same.

"Nah, I like it!"

"So have you selected a topic to preach on yet?" He looks at me confused.

"What?"

"I guess everyone has a way to prepare for a preaching. I pray about it, and let God choose," he answers me.

"I was told it's like preparing for a thesis, studying the topic you choose!"

"Well, that's not how I prepare. I like to pray and fast, I let God tell me what His people need to hear. I don't know what they need, I can't just be led by my emotions."

"I guess it makes sense, but why fast? I'm a little embarrassed to ask, I've heard people speak of fasting but I never really understood the reason why." I asked because I'm confused what does not eating have to do with preaching.

"I see I have a lot more to teach you!" he laughs.

"Fasting is something that is between you and God. Not everyone around you needs to know you are fasting, unless you decided to do it as a group. In that case only your group should be the only ones to know. The reason for fasting is so you can weaken your flesh.

You feed your spirit with the word of God, and it sustains you. Matthew 4:4 says '...*Man shall not live by bread alone...*' you have to feed your spirit just as you feed your flesh. Reasons to fast can be many.

Some fast to get closer to God, to get stronger in the spirit. It's like taking a stand against the flesh and it's also to prepare you for battle. It helps you to overcome. There are also different types of fast. Not all of them have to do with giving up all food completely. Some, you can give up meat, or favorite drinks. You can also fast from social Medias, and TV. I can teach you all the different ways you can fast."

"So you don't only fast to preach I assume? Should I be fasting to help me fight spiritually too?" I ask him.

"You can if you want, it will help you be stronger. You can fast for any reason, I usually fast when I need to prepare for something like preaching, sometimes teaching. In my church sometimes we fast as a whole, meaning the whole church would do it together. We would take turns feeding each other. We would provide scriptures through text, and pray for each other.

I fast for me when God tells me or when I feel my flesh trying to overpower my spirit. The night I picked you up from that party you went to, my flesh wanted to take over. I couldn't stand the way that guy was pushing up on you. I can't say I know what would've happened if you didn't calm the situation down. I'm glad we went to the vigil after, but the next morning I felt I needed to fast. So I woke up earlier and did just that." he tells me.

"So what happened during your fast? Did God talk to you?" I asked him.

He searches my eyes then looks down to our joined hands. I don't know why we were still holding hands, but I didn't want to let go.

When I start to pull away, he tightens his hold, "I prayed, asked God for guidance. I asked Him to show me how I should help you. I also asked for forgiveness, He spoke to me. I went to my church still in fasting, then went to your church, and well you know the rest!" He lifts his gaze back up to meet my eyes.

"What did He tell you?" I ask him since he was very vague on that part.

"He told me what I needed to hear. I'm not ready to share that part yet. But as for helping you, He told me that you just needed a friend, that our friendship will help you grow. He wanted me to teach you what it's like to have a relationship with Him. And I hope I've helped you equip yourself with the tools you need to overcome these obstacles you're facing!"

"You have been helping me Ryan, if you weren't, I don't know if I would've come this far, thank you!"

He smiles "you're welcome, I know you starting to see, but I'm still going to tell you. You are going to be a great spiritual warrior, God is going to use you in ways you never even imagine. Get ready!" he tells me with a grin, like he can't wait for me to get there.

Honestly, I can't wait to get there either. I don't want to feel like I'm not enough.

"So Monday huh? And where should we meet?"

"I can come over here to your house, we can invite your sister."

"Yeah, that sounds good. I'm sure Evie would love that! So...six sounds good?"

"Six is fine."

"I'll take my dad's car to work, I'll bring home some coffee for the coffee lovers!" I mock.

"I can pick you up!"

"You do know I can drive, right?"

"I'm sure you can, but you see those rose bushes over there?" He points to Lady's garden. "I wouldn't want you to drive into them!" he teased.

"Hey! I saved the dog from getting hit by my car, isn't that what counts?"

"Well, just to be on the safe side, I should pick you up!" He states. He doesn't give me a chance to respond, he gives me a kiss on my forehead.

"I should be going, I'll see if I'll stop by your church tomorrow morning!" he says as he walks to his bike. I just nod as he rides off.

23. Standing in the Gap

Tossing and turning in my bed, I can't seem to fall asleep. My mind is flooded with my attackers in the spiritual realm, and the conversation with Ryan. I reach for my phone to check the time, 2:00am. I've been in bed since eleven, why can't I shut my mind off and go to sleep? I get up and head down to the kitchen. Maybe a glass of milk will help settle my unease.

I drink my glass of milk, start to head back to my room. Before I reach the first step I feel the sudden urge to walk to the living room. I walk toward it, no one's there, lights are off.

"Angelisa!" I hear my name being called. I look around, and see no one. I try to discern which direction the voice came from.

I walk further into the living room, I reach for the light switch, but before I have the chance to turn it on I see a glow illuminating the room. The living room is bright enough to see it's still empty.

Confused by what I see, I decide I should return to my room.

"Angelisa!" I hear my name again. I look around once more, and still nothing.

"Who's there?" I ask. No response. Strangely, I don't feel afraid. But at the same time I don't understand what's happening.

I turn to walk away again, *"Angelisa!"* I hear another time. I remember a story in the bible about a boy named Samuel being woken up three times in the middle of the night. The first three times he went to Eli's room thinking it was him that had called.

Eli, finally realizing what was happening, tells Samuel if he hears his name being called again, to say *'Speak, LORD, for your servant is listening'*. I doubt this may be the same situation, but it doesn't hurt to try. I walk into the center of my living room, look up as if God is directly above me.

"Speak Lord, I'm here listening!" As I say this, I feel silly, I lower my head and close my eyes.

"My daughter, why do you doubt?" God asks me.

"I'm nothing like Samuel, I was just unsure if this was the same case. I don't feel special enough Lord, I'm sorry!" I respond back.

"That is one of the things holding you back. You still can't see I have forgiven your past. I know you feel unworthy, but I see your heart Angelisa. I see you more clearly than anyone. People see what they want to see, they see with the eyes of the flesh, but you must look with the eyes of the spirit. I want you to live from the inside out. Forget what others want to see. Do you want to know what I see?"

I sit on the arm of the sofa closest to me as God continues to speak.

"I see how much you regret the things you've done, I also see how much you are changing. You know you are no longer that small child, you have grown!" I hear God tell me.

He isn't anywhere I can see, but I can feel his presence all around me.

"Angelisa, I need you to believe in yourself. You don't need anyone to tell you how you should be, you already know. Now, there is someone in need of your help. She's not ready to hear from me directly, she still needs someone in between, a vessel; you!" He tells me.

"Me? Why me?" I ask.

"Angelisa, you can't change your past. What you've done, doesn't define who you are now. I do not keep a record of your sins. But what you have gone through can now help someone in need of guidance. You need to step out of your own way!" God tells me in a still voice.

In that moment, I fall to my knees, and thank God. All this time He has been interfering in my life, and I didn't even notice. He didn't lead me into sin, I did. But He provided a way out. He showed me a door, and I walked through.

Once I crossed the threshold, my past life was left behind, and I no longer needed to carry it around. I didn't know any better, so I let the enemy continue to lie to me.

I begin to pray, and I don't let my thoughts lie to me about praying to what I can't see. I believe in my heart, God is listening. I just want to praise him.

"There's nothing I want more than you Lord, nothing more powerful in my heart. Be the fire that burns within me. The light on to a dark path. Show me the way Lord. There's nothing I want more than you right now.

Your presence surrounds me. It empowers me to move. Encourages me to speak in your name. Your spirit flows through me and I can't contain the warmth of your presence.

I need to believe in you, trust in you! Show me your way! Lead me, and I'll follow. Guide my steps Lord, I am here. I will trust in you, your words are true. I will not drown in my own self-pity. I let go, and trust in you."

"Yes my child, I am here. Your praise warms my heart!" I hear God. It's an amazing feeling, having this connection with the creator of the world. I continue to pray, and my prayers led me to a garden. Not to the garden I usually go to, it looks slightly different. The trees are full of brown leaves, they keep falling from the branches like rain. The bushes look like they are about to wither, it feels like autumn. Not one flower in sight. Where is this place?

I hear someone crying up ahead. As I try to find where the sound is coming from, a path unveils before me. I follow it.

"Jessenia?" She is cradling herself on the ground.

As I run up to her I ask, "What's wrong sweetie?" I bend down when I reach her.

She doesn't look up, "Jessenia?" still nothing. She can't hear me. Her cries are so loud I can feel her pain as my own. Her guilt, her burden is so heavy.

I realize what God was trying to tell me. I can help her, I know I'm not really here with her, but her spirit is in this realm and so is mine.

"Lord, I'm here with your daughter. I present her before you, I pray that she will feel your peace, that she will know her worth. I stand here with her, in her pain and worry. I pray that she will find deliverance in you my God!"

"Well, well, well!" A familiar sinister voice from behind me says.

"Look who it is, strong and almost fully armed!" Fear tries to taunt me.

I look back at him, "I am strong, and I will not let you hurt her!" I say completely facing him.

"Well, I am here for her but," he takes a step closer to me. "Now I have you as well!"

"You don't have me, and you won't have her either. To get to her, you would have to go through me!" I put my hands on my hips as I watch for his next move.

He lunges himself at me knocking me to the ground. As he stands over me he says, "Not as strong as you thought!" I kick my leg out knocking him off his feet.

"You're not so smart!" I tell him as I stand up. He comes at me again trying to wrap his arms around me, I duck down and he misses.

"You're not as fast either!" I retort. I can tell he's getting frustrated. He stands a few feet away from me, he stares at me as he raises both his hands. He manipulates the wind, causing the fallen leaves to sore around us.

"You want to play games?" He smirks.

"Let's see you outsmart this!" The wind circles around us causing Jessenia's fear to intensify. She tries to cradle herself tighter on the ground. Fear laughs at her reaction.

"I came here for her, she is mine to torment!" Fear says as he tries to get closer to her.

"You cannot have her," I tell him standing in front of her.

"Oh, but I will. She's already tormenting herself!" he comes closer.

182

"I'm here for her! I'll stand in the gap for her! I will fight for her!"

As I speak these words his appearance seems to change. When I faced Fear before, he was more transparent, like a shadowy fog. Now he looks more like a dark creature, not transparent at all. It's then that I realize, he is her Fear not mines. While he was fighting me, he was more translucent, because I was overcoming him, but since I'm standing in the gap for Jessenia, I see him as she would see him.

I give him my back so I can wrap my arms around Jessenia, I continue to pray. I know she can't see me, but I think she can feel me. I can feel her breathing deep under my embrace. I can feel all her worries, I pray for encouragement, peace and strength. I stay with her for a while, focusing only on her.

I know Fear is angry, because Jessenia is starting to calm down. Suddenly I feel a burning sting on my back, then another before I fall on my side.

"Don't turn your back on me girl!" Fear snapped.

I look over to Fear, he's standing with a flaming whip in his hand. My back was unprotected, I shouldn't have underestimated my enemy. I try to stand, but more lashes causes me to stumble and fall. My skin feels like it's been sliced open, the pain I feel makes me want to give up and cry, but if I do, he wins and that's not happening.

As Fear aims his whip toward me again, I roll out of the way and quickly jump on my feet. I reach Jessenia's side, this time I make sure not to give Fear my back. I kneel next to her and continue to pray. Once I hear Jessenia's cries subside, I know she's going to be ok. She's beginning to trust even though she still holds fear in her heart.

"Stop that!" Fear shouts!

"You are getting in my way, I'm not going to let you undo everything!" Fear said.

"You would have to go through me! She may not be ready to fight you, but as I said before, I'll stand in the gap for her!" I shout.

"Standing in the gap for others now?! My, my, how you have grown! Nevertheless, I have something that would bring you back down where you belong," He threatened.

"Shame!"

Confused by his outburst I stare at him. Seeing my expression, Fear laughs. Another figure appears from the darkness behind him. Fear must have conjured another one of his buddies, this must be what he meant when he said Shame. It was named, Shame.

Unlike the others, she wears my face. She looks like me, but then she doesn't. Her face is a little disheveled, her makeup is smeared. Her eyeliner and mascara have run down her cheeks as if she's been crying. She's wearing an oversized sweater, her hair hangs over her shoulders from underneath the hood on her head.

"Meet Shame! I'm sure you have some *shame* hidden in you!" Shame holds a rock in her hand, she throws it at me.

I raise my left arm to block it. I should have tried to dodge it instead but as I raise my arm, a large shield appears on my right arm before the rock Shame threw hits me.

I lower my arm with the shield, "looks like I just gained another piece of my armor!" I say it more to Fear than Shame.

"It appears so, nevertheless, you are in our playground! We can be very creative!" He replies.

Shame comes at me with a fist raised ready to punch me. I charge back raising my shield to block her. I use my shield to knock her to her feet. She stumbles back, but doesn't fall. I look over my shoulder to where Jessenia is.

She's still on the ground crying. I get down on one knee, I raise my shield and it grows to fully cover us.

"Jessenia, I know you have no idea what's going on, but I can help you. You need to overcome your shame, overcome your fear, your guilt. I'm here for you, God sent me to you tonight. You are not alone. God has forgiven you, you need to forgive yourself. You need to let God in!" I tell her hoping she understands why I'm here right now.

I look back at Fear, he's just standing there, watching. He's studying me.

"Indeed, you have changed. No matter, as I said, I'm here for her. I will get what I came for!" I stand, and to my surprise, so does Jessenia. I look back at her, I don't know if she can see me. I watch as she raises her hands in surrender and looks up to the sky.

"God! Please forgive me!" she sobbed.

"No!" Fear shouts! His wind dies out and he's gone. Shame is still there, but she doesn't move, she just stands, watching. Jessenia falls to her knees, the sun comes up and flowers begin to bloom. She's in a good place.

"Amen!" I say. My surroundings have changed, I'm back in my living room.

"God, are you still here?" I ask.

"Always." He answers.

"I have to call her, to see how she's doing." I tell Him.

"Yes," He responds. I run up to my room grab my phone.

"Jessenia, I'm sorry to call so late. Are you ok?" I ask as she answers the phone.

"Yes I am, for now. I had a strange dream, you were in it!" she goes on to tell me about her dream.

She's going through the same steps as me. But she is more open than I am. I feel as if we can help each other. I tell her my side of things about her dream, and explain the best I could. She seemed to understand.

As I hung up the phone I get back into bed. It's truly been a long night, I thank God for awakening me. I'm glad I was able to help her. I pray that God would continue to educate me to guide her. I still have some healing of my own, but I believe I'm almost there.

24. Losing Focus

Val invited me to another summer party. I've been hesitant about going, remembering what happen the last time I went to a party. I told Val I was unsure, the party scene really isn't me anymore, may be it never was. But at the same time, I feel I need to be there for my friend. I have to watch over her.

Ryan had texted me earlier to see if it was ok if Jason, Ivy, Marissa and Mike came over today to study the bible with us. I told him it was. I will be having full house tonight. This should be fun. I've never studied the word in a group at home before. I'm kind of excited.

It felt good the other night when I was praying for Jessenia, I really did feel like a vessel for God. I want to be able to do more. I decided I should add one more to the bible study group. I called Jessenia, she agreed to come over. I texted her my address and the time. Ryan came into my job today like every other time, to study on his laptop. Of course he stayed a little longer to wait for me to give me a ride.

"Since this is a group thing now, I invited Jessenia to come over!" I tell Ryan once we're in his car. I decided to bring home two coffee boxes for my coffee drinking friends. I originally intended to bring just one box for Ryan. But if his friends are anything like him with coffee, two would be best.

"That was a good idea," he tells me.

"I think so too, we can both grow together!" I tell him.

"Were you working on today's lesson?" I ask him as he drives to my house.

"Yeah, but we will all be taking turns. So, any questions you have, ask, it will be like a discussion," he answers me.

"Of course…so, what's the lesson?" he looks at me and smiles.

"Nice try, but you will have to wait just like the others!" he answers looking back at the road.

"Hey, you said if I had any questions, ask! So I'm asking!" I laugh, then he does too.

We arrive to my house, Jason's car is parked in front. When Ryan pulls into my driveway, Jason and the others meets us at the door. We greet each other, and I invite them in. Jessenia arrives shortly after. I introduce her to everyone and my sister as well, she was inside setting up the living room. Evie has worship music playing, and she set up the coffee table in the center of the living room with chips and dip. She also has sheets of paper and a few pens, I believe for taking notes.

"Wow Evie, thank you for setting up for us!" I tell her as I hug her.

"No sweat sis, I just can't wait to get started!" she tells me.

"Hi Ryan!" Evie greets him.

"Hey," he says to her. We all sit down and fellowship for a bit before Ryan starts.

"Alright, let's begin. Before we get into the bible, let's pray for a little," he starts. We all rise and join hands.

Ryan starts to pray, "Lord God we come before you as one. We thank you for this beautiful day you have given us, and this opportunity of us being able to come together to study your word," he keeps praying, and my mind starts to wonder somewhere else.

I start to think about how my friendship with Rebecca was before Logan, how I missed that version of her. Then I think about Val, my best friend, I wonder what she's doing now. Then Alex jumps in my head. He is the last person I want to think about right now. But I go back to that first night at his house, when he kissed me. Then the night of the party, what did he think was going to happen between us that night? Then Logan, he was good to me, until the end, but that was my fault. Why am I thinking about all this right now? I need to focus.

"Open our minds Lord, so that we may understand the word you bring to us tonight..." Ryan is still praying.

I wonder what Lady is thinking, knowing all these people are in my house right now. I know she must've been watching from her window. Oh my God, why can't I concentrate? I shouldn't worry about what Lady is thinking right now. "Amen!" I hear Ryan say.

"Amen." we all say. I can't believe I missed the whole prayer. I like to hear Ryan pray, his words, he sounds like a man after God's own heart, like David from the bible.

"I'm sure most of our bibles are on an app on our phones, so let's look up John 3:16-17. I know this is a very common verse, and pretty much everyone knows it. But do you? Do we, truly understand what it means?" Ryan begins.

"Evie, would you read it for us?" Evie stands and begins to read, *"For this is how God loved the world: He gave his one and only Son, so that everyone who believes in him will not perish but have eternal life. God sent his Son into the world not to judge the world, but to save the world through him."* Evie sits back down between me and Jessenia.

"Thank you Evie" Ryan tells her.

"Repentance! We have the opportunity to repent because God sent Jesus Christ to die for us. See, many people only read verse 16, but do not keep reading. God sent his son, not to judge us, but to save us. Many of us make the mistake of pushing God away when we sin because we're ashamed. Think back to Adam and Eve, they were afraid to come before God after they ate from the forbidden fruit. We tend to do the same. The enemy feeds us lies so we move away from God.

Another mistake people make when they sin is they think God would not accept them back. But if that were true, would He have send His son to die for us? *'For God so loved the world!'* He loved us, with all our sins, He loved us. He gave us Jesus Christ, not to judge us, but to save us. Many think that only those who don't sin deserves to have God's grace. But that's not true.

In Luke 5:31-32, Jesus said, *'it is not the healthy who need a doctor, but the sick.'* Jesus continues to say, *'I have not come to call the righteous, but sinners to repentance'.* First of all, we all sin, some sins seem bigger than others, but regardless, sin is sin. Second, He said He comes for the sick!" Wow, Ryan knows his stuff.

This is a great teaching. I did make that mistake. I knew I was going down the wrong path, but I just couldn't control myself. I was hiding from God. How silly was that, you can't hide from God. He sees all, He knows all.

Everyone starts in to a discussion, but I let my mind run again. How lost I was when I was with Logan, I do miss him sometimes. I wonder what his life turned out like. Does he ever think of me?

"Angelisa!" I look up, "yeah?" I say, because now I'm lost in whatever else was said.

"Do you want to share?" Ryan asks me, I'm completely clueless. I shake my head no.

"In Acts 3:19 it says *'Repent, then and turn to God, so that your sins may be wiped out, that times of refreshing may come from the Lord.'* True repentance is turning away from your sin, and making the decision not to sin," Jason takes over now.

"Some people ask God for forgiveness, but they still return to their sin. They ask for forgiveness again, and do it all over again. That is not true repentance. Trust in God that all your past is wiped clean!" Jason continued.

"I have been dealing with my past lately, it hasn't been an easy journey, I've been getting better." I tell them.

"I know the enemy is going to try harder, making me think that because of what I've done, I can't grow anymore. Every time I feel I'm one step closer to redemption, I'm faced with some memory of my past," I continued.

"Angelisa, we're always going to battle with our past, but we are not defined by it. God has refreshed you, you have a new start!" Ivy tells me.

My sister Evie hugs me, "I'm so proud of you Angel!" she tells me.

"Thanks," I reply.

Ryan wraps up, but we stay a little while longer just talking and laughing. This is fellowship time. My parents walk in and introduce themselves.

"Very nice to meet you all," my mom tells them.

"Ryan, a pleasure to see you again. Well carry on, we're heading out. Angelisa, not too late!" She tells me as she and my dad walk out the door. I turn to Jessenia.

"Hey, how you doing?" I ask her.

"I'm pretty good, I told my parents about the baby. They were upset at first, but then they told me to have the baby and we will deal with it together. I know things are going to change for me, but I'm ready to deal with it. God has been good to me!" she replies.

I'm glad for her, she is much braver than I was.

Everyone starts to say their good byes, my sister and I walk them to the door. Ryan stays behind.

"Hey, can we talk?" I nod, my sister tells Ryan good night as she heads inside.

"Are you ok?" he asks.

"Yeah, why?"

"Well, you looked distracted!"

"I was. My mind was just going everywhere!"

"Where?"

"Where what?" I ask.

"Where did your mind go?"

"I was remembering my friendship with Rebecca before boys, then I was thinking about Val, I haven't really hanged out with her in a while. I miss her. Then..." I stop, because I didn't think it would be appropriate.

I don't know why I feel that way, it's just Ryan, and we're friends aren't we?

"Then...what?" Ryan asks.

"Ryan, it doesn't matter. My thoughts were just scattered!"

"You can tell me." he wants to know. He's not going to let this go.

"Alex... my ex! I didn't want to tell you!" I snapped.

"Why?"

Now I'm getting frustrated. Why does he insist on knowing everything about me?

"Because, I don't like talking to you about my ex, or Alex!"

"Why is that?"

"Ryan! What's with all the questions? Sometimes, I miss my ex, ok? I miss being held and feeling loved. And Alex, I don't know why. May be I just liked the attention, because I know I don't like him. Are you happy now?" I don't know why I'm snapping at him.

I just can't help myself. I know he's only concerned. He doesn't say anything, I can just feel him looking at me. I refuse to look his way. I look up to the sky, then down to the ground.

"I'm sorry, I didn't mean to upset you. I just wanted to understand," he tells me. Now I feel bad.

"They enemy is plotting against you. The closer you get to your blessing the more he will come for you. Don't get distracted," he continued.

"I know...I'm sorry." I apologized. He reaches for my hand, and with his other hand he reached for my face, lifting my chin so he can look me in my eyes. "You're so close, don't lose focus." He tells me.

"Whenever you need to pray with someone, I'm here for you. If you feel embarrassed to come to me, Ivy or Marissa wouldn't mind praying with you." he continues.

"Why would I feel embarrassed?"

"Why didn't you want to tell me about you thinking of the guys? You didn't mind sharing your thoughts about the girls. I just assumed."

It really isn't what he's thinking, for some reason I really don't want to talk to him about guys. That's something more to talk to one of the girls, like maybe Ivy or Marissa. Besides, I really don't think he likes to hear about Logan, and mentioning Alex to him after what happened the last time he saw him, I didn't think it would be wise.

"I'm not embarrassed, I just…the last time I mentioned my ex, you tensed up. I didn't think you wanted to hear that he crossed my mind."

"I'm sorry for my reaction, but you can tell me anything. When you first spoke of your ex, I wasn't expecting what you said. It just caught me off guard, that's all." He lowers his hand from my face, but doesn't let go of my hand.

"He was your first love, it's ok to remember him."

"No, it's not that…to be honest, I don't know why he crossed my mind! Maybe you're right, the enemy was trying to keep me distracted!"

"It's going to get harder, if the enemy sees you getting closer to God he's going to use whatever he can to knock you off course. Distractions will come in any way, thoughts, desires, work, and family issues. Basically anything he can get you to focus on, anything that isn't about God. The enemy will stop at nothing, he doesn't want you to keep building your relationship with God."

That is what it felt like, my mind going crazy like that. It had to be the enemy, so that the next time I have to face my adversaries I would be off and they would have the upper hand. With only two more armor pieces to gain, I can't lose focus now.

"Thanks for tonight Ryan, I may have been a little distracted, but I was able to hear most of what you and Jason were talking about."

"Anytime, we should keep this going. May be invite your friend Val to join us, how she is doing?" he asks.

"As far as I know she's good. I will invite her, I doubt she would come, she has a boyfriend now, and she's preoccupied. Her boyfriend is having a party and she invited me, she's begging me to come. But with everything that's happened, that's changed with me…I'm just not sure. But then since we haven't hung out for a while, I kind of feel like I should go." I answer him.

"So, you're undecided!" he says. I finally pull my hand away, and adjust my ponytail.

"I don't know, Val has been there for me when I needed someone, I need to be there for her."

"I'm sure Alex will be going?" He sneered.

"Most likely, he is Val's boyfriend's friend. I think I can avoid him, or maybe invite him to church!" I laugh.

"Are you going to use your charm to lure him to church?" he smiles.

"You think I have charm?" I tease.

"There's something special about you. I'm sure that's why Alex is so drawn to you, well besides your beauty." He answers as he stares into my eyes.

I feel my cheeks begin to heat up. Is he flirting with me? The way he stares at me makes me feel as if the world around us fades away, leaving only the two of us. I have to avert my gaze from his. Even if he feels something for me, I won't be the one to make him loose his focus while he's waiting on God. I may be special, but I'm sure not for Ryan.

"Hey, for whatever reason he may go to church, may not be the reason he stays. What if I'm just a way for him to get to church, and there God will speak to him? Or is that being deceiving?"

"Anything is possible I guess. But don't tell him you'll date him just to get him to go," he answers me.

"I won't do that, I know better than to lead him on. He wouldn't let it go, and I'm not about to put myself in that situation again!" I tell him remembering what Alex told me at his party about me leading him on and the idea he thought I was leading to.

"Just be careful if you decide to go. There can be a lot of temptations there, and I wouldn't want you to lose your balance and fall." I can sense his concern for me.

I just nod, because he's right. I just want to hang out with my friend, I don't want to do any drinking or dancing. I just want to spend time with Val, and get to know her boyfriend.

Ryan and I call it a night, as I head up to my room I think back to what he said about being distracted. I don't want to lose my focus. I have to guard my heart, my mind. I can't let my thoughts get in my way, I can't let the enemy win this battle.

Diana Perez

25. Awaken by Whispers

I'm awaken by whispers, my room is so dark I can barely see a thing. It takes a few seconds for my eyes to adjust to my surroundings. I'm sitting on my bed, but I don't feel like I'm in my room even though I am, at least it looks like part of my room. I must be dreaming again.

Behind me is my purple wall with white framed water paintings. But in front of me, I'm out doors. I stand from my bed, trying to hear from which direction the whispers are coming from. I walk as quietly as I can, trying not to make a sound with every step. It seems I'm back in the woods, but this time it's different.

As I walk, a fog emerges…it's so thick it's hard to see through. I can hear the sounds of whispers get louder, I know I'm getting closer.

"We can use Rebecca against her, she was the one who started the rumors. May be we should be a little more...creative, let's not only use Rebecca...we can also use Lady. She despises Angelisa just as much as we do. We can make sure she sees Angelisa doing something. I'm sure Lady will let everyone know what she saw and more." I hear one voice say.

"Yes, we need to plan bigger, something that would make her break. We could also use someone else to cause her to lose her focus." I hear another voice join in.

The fog is still too thick to see through. They're planning something for me, they want me to fall back to where I was before. I walk closer to the voices, I stop behind a tree. I try to make out the voices, they seem to belong to my adversaries. I see three figures through the fog, they are standing in a half circle.

"Angelisa has become stronger than we anticipated. If she reaches her full potential, she will be a problem for us. Especially if she unites with that Ryan guy, we have to think bigger. She will be stronger once she receives the rest of her armor and she is almost there. We must dig deeper!" Fear tells the others as he paces back and forth.

"Maybe if we join our forces, create doubt, bring out her insecurities, her fears!" Shame tells Fear.

"We have to attack her physically," Anger joins in.

"Let's bring back some guilt!" Guilt says.

"I think I have an idea; she thinks she's overcome her past, but what if she faces her past? Giving her something to worry about will keep her more occupied on the problem than on her relationship with God!"

As I try to listen to more of their plans, Guilt fades away from the others. I wonder where he went. I feel a tap on my shoulder. When I turn around to see who touched me...Guilt.

"Well, well, well. What do we have here? Are you eaves dropping on our plans for you? We didn't even noticed you entered the realm," he tells me. I turn fully to face him. My back against the tree. He looks at me in surprise, I watch as he stands back and crosses his arms across his chest.

"You're cheating! You didn't get here by praying, you're dreaming! Which means, God led you here to spy on our plans? Well since you are here, let's make the best of it." Guilt takes a few steps back, a path appears through the fog leading up to where the others are.

When they see the fog has disappeared, they look my way. The three of them start to walk towards me. I step away from the tree, taking steps back away from my foes.

"You're here, let's play," Guilt orders.

As the four of them get closer I turn to run. The fog returns, thicker than before. I don't know where I'm going, as long as it is away from them, I don't care.

I miss a step and tumble to the ground, I'm on a hill and as I fell, I kept rolling down. A rock hits my head and causes me to stop rolling. I feel a warm thick substance run down my face. I touch my hand to where my head hit, when I look at my hand; blood.

After a few seconds I sit up to check my surroundings. Rocks upon rocks, where am I? Where are the others? I stand to my feet, I begin to walk exploring this new place.

I have no shoes on here, I can feel the pressure of the rocks as I walk on them under my feet. I'm in my pajamas, I don't have my armor on. I don't worry too much about that because I know if I need it, it will appear. God did bring me here in my dreams so I can be aware of the plans of the enemy for me.

I see the body of a girl laying on the grass. She seems to be asleep, I wonder who she is. As I get closer, I reach my hand out to touch her, to wake her. She feels ice cold, her skin is pale. I think…she's dead.

I roll her on to her back, her hair still covering her features. I dread to reveal her face. I gently remove the hair from her, it's me. I stand in shock watching as this corpse of mines transforms into a baby. Her eyes open and I jump back in surprise. She stares at me as if she sees through me. The look causing me to shiver. Who is this baby?

The baby begins to laugh and slowly sits up, she is about six months of age.

"Wondering who I am?" the baby speaks. Another shock courses through me. This visit is unlike the others I've had here.

"I'm told you came here to spy, did you find what you are looking for? You have no armor here, your God is not in this place. Here…you are alone," the baby snickers.

"My sweet baby, let's not scare her too much…yet. She thinks she's powerful. We will show her just how weak she is soon enough," Fear comes from behind me.

His voice sounding heavier than other times. I look at him from over my shoulder. He's standing proud, as if he's won some kind of battle.

I feel a jolt, and I'm right back where I started…on my bed. My room is complete, the door across from me, my dresser, my closet, it's all back in place.

I know the enemy likes to plot using anything to make you stumble and fall. All this time all I saw was how much Rebecca was trying to bring me down. Now I see, it wasn't all her own doing. I understand the enemy can't make us do anything, but he can trick us.

He plays on our weakness, and tempts us. Rebecca must have felt anger toward me and wanted to get back at me. The enemy must've seen an opening and played on her emotions.

We all make mistakes, I've made plenty already. I'll try to make amends with her, I have to push my feelings aside and give her a chance. We were good friends, I would like to be like that again, but for right now all I can do is pray for her.

The more I think about Rebecca the more I realize that it never occurred to me she was a pawn in their game. She gave the enemy a footstool when she fell into sin; as most of us do without realizing. She must have not been strong enough to overcome their schemes.

She hasn't been able to talk about what happened to her with anyone. Her father thinks it was me with those boys instead of Rebecca, she carries so much shame. She's been reflecting on me, and now she's being used by the enemy. I have to help her too. I have been judging her, I haven't been able to see that under all that hostility, she's just been hurting.

I told Val I would go to the party with her for a little, but I didn't plan on staying long. I tried to explain to her that parties aren't part of me anymore. At least not the kind that involve alcohol and drugs and all the other stuff I have yet to discover. I want to be able to put that part behind me.

She said she understood, but asked that I would join her tonight just for a bit. I hope I'm not making a mistake in going. I know I have control over drinking, I can turn that down and not think twice about it. I never did drugs so I'll be fine in that department. I know now to avoid brownies and rum cakes. I think I've been made aware of the things that would make me drunk or high. But avoiding Alex…that might be an issue. I just won't let him get too close to me, hopefully Val doesn't abandoned me like she did the last party.

I look through my closet to see what I would wear, I don't want to make the mistake I did last time and wear a dress that gives Alex the wrong impression. I'm undecided between a sundress and jean shorts, it is summer after all. Sundress should be ok, I pick out my teal and white sleeveless hi low umpire sundress, with my white espadrille wedge sandals. I'm happy with my choice.

I quickly get dressed and add on some accessories, I wear my hair down and I just curl my ends with my wand to get some soft bouncy curls. I walk down to the kitchen to say bye to my family.

"Angelisa," my mom says to me as she butters the bread roles for the dinner she made.

"Please be careful tonight. No drinking!" I look at my mom and take her hand, "mom, I promise I will not be drinking. I'm not that girl anymore, I've changed." I tell her.

She stays quiet for a second, then she takes me in her arms. "I know sweetie, but I'm still a mom and I'm allowed to worry."

"Yes, I know. Thank you" I tell her.

I walk out the door, finally I get to drive again. I appreciate Ryan picking me up when he does, but I do miss driving.

The party is in Mario's house, I've never been here before but by the looks of all the double parked cars I know I made it. I decide to look for parking around the block so I wouldn't double park.

I park behind a car that reminds me of Logan's. Of course it can't be his, I'm sure he would have traded it in by now. Although he really loved his car it's possible he just decided to stay with it.

My thoughts take me back to when we were happy together. I miss him sometimes, he was a good guy until I broke it off. I shake off the thoughts, I don't want to go back down memory lane right now. I'm in a better place, but I don't know what my reaction would be if I saw him again.

He doesn't know what I went through, why I really broke up with him. That is if his uncle's friend never mentioned it to him. I doubt he would've, he didn't even want me to tell him.

I walk up to the front door, it was already open so I just walk in. I quickly find Val and head over to her.

"Hey, I'm so glad you made it! I missed you!" she greets me with a hug. She has one of those famous red plastic cups in her hand.

"I miss you too, Val!" I look around, there are so many people here from college, and people I never seen before.

"Looking for someone?" Mario ask me with a smirk.

"No, avoiding someone, actually. Hi Mario, hope you taking good care of my friend!" I tell him as I lean in to kiss him on the cheek.

"Always, she's my queen!" he answers me.

"Hey babe, give me a few minutes with Angel, I want to catch up with her really quick," she tells her boyfriend.

He nods at her and she leads me to the front of the house, I guess it's the quietest.

"How you doing Angel? I feel like it's been forever."

"Yeah, I know. I've been good."

"Listen…Alex is here. He was asking for you, I just wanted to give you a heads up."

"He's still trying to get with me?"

"No one's really turned him down before, I guess you're like a challenge to him, he's determined." Great, why won't he take a hint? How many times do I have to say no?

"I guess I'll just have to be straight forward with him, I thought being settle was the best way, I thought wrong."

"He really isn't a bad guy, he's a little full of himself, but deep down he's a good person. Anyways don't worry about him, you have that Ryan guy don't you?" She winks.

"You should've brought him with you!" She teased.

"Val I told you, it's not like that with him! Besides I wouldn't want him around Alex after the last time."

"Ok, whatever. Anyways," she says looking inside the house as if she's looking for someone.

"I saw this really cute guy I've never seen before come in a few minutes before you arrived. Maybe you should meet him, I know you have this new life going on, but I think you can still date right?" I have to laugh at her remark.

"I guess, I don't know Val. I'm just not ready for any of that right now." I tell her. But I wonder, will I ever be? Sometimes I don't feel normal, girls my age have many dates. Me, I only had one boyfriend and I was so heartbroken, and so crushed with everything else, I just couldn't move on. Now I'm not so shattered, thanks to God for never leaving me. But I am still broken-hearted it seems.

"Come on, let's go back inside!" Val takes my hand and leads me in. We meet up with Mario who is talking to a few guys.

"Hey beautiful!" Alex whispers in my ear. I turn to face him. I smile at him to be nice, but I'm afraid anything I do or say will only make him think I'm interested.

"Hi Alex," I say to him. He grins as he eyes me from head to toe.

"Looking good!" He tells me. The alcohol is all I smell as he speaks. If he was a little aggressive the last time, I can only imagine how he would be now that he's drunk.

I told Ryan, I would invite him to church, it may scare him away from me, or he'll come because of me and actually accept Jesus Christ in his heart.

"Listen, I know you said you don't want to date anyone right now…but maybe we can just be friends," he says as sincerely as he can, while being intoxicated.

"Friends I can do!" I tell him, I'm happy we can find a common ground.

"Want to dance, friend?" he asks. I think twice about it, but he doesn't really wait for an answer as he takes my hand and leads me to where everyone else is on the dance floor. It's a bachata song, this should be fine.

We dance to one song then walk into the kitchen to get something to drink. The house has a lot of people, its summer and with people dancing it feels really hot. I need to hydrate. Alex offers me a bottle of water. I'm glad he remembered I don't like to drink. I feel like I can let my guard down a little with him. I take a look at the chips and figure the chips can't be spiked unless they baked them themselves. I take a handful and eat.

As Alex and I stand by the snacks we talk like we can be friends. He eats some chips as well. Someone pulled out some jello from the fridge, the red one. I love that flavor. I serve myself, as I take the first bite I notice something is off about it. I figure it's just the taste of the chips mixing with the jello. I serve myself another, it's pretty good.

"You really like that stuff don't you?" Alex asks. I nod since my mouth is full. He laughs.

"Want to dance more?" he asks me.

"No, maybe later." I answer him.

"Let's go out back and talk," he points his head to the back door, I nod.

He holds the door open for me, the backyard has a few lounge chairs. There's a few people out here dancing, at least we're not alone.

"What have you been up to?" he asks me.

"I've been on a spiritual journey finding myself," I answered.

"Is it working?

"Yeah it is. Still dealing with some issues, but I'm on the right path." We sit by a table that also had snacks. Gummy bears and worms. I start picking on a few.

"That's good, you look a little more at ease than before." He cracks up as I keep eating the gummies. I'm not sure why he's laughing so I just ignore him.

"I've been unburdening myself, I feel better!"

"Still not better enough to date?" he laughs.

"Nope, not there yet!"

"What is it you're looking for?" I must look confused so he continues.

"To be able to date someone. What are you waiting for?"

I don't know how to explain it. I'm sure it's not normal, but I can't help how I feel. I look away from Alex as I consider my next words.

"I guess I just don't want a temporary fling. I want something lasting, someone who will be there to help pull me up when I'm feeling down." I smile as Ryan's face flashes in my mind.

He would be a perfect match for me. But then I realize I may not be for him. If anyone has been called and chosen, it's definitely Ryan. He has shown me so much in the little time I've known him. He's been there for me. I'm sure God sent him to me, to guide me. I will always see him as my guiding angel.

"Basically, when I find it, I will know." I answer Alex.

"You will shortly. I believe you will be unburden soon enough." He tells me, I'm still not quite sure if we're talking about the same thing.

He's really enjoying himself, and I'm not sure why. Maybe he realized we're better as friends than having any romantic interest, or whatever he wanted from me.

After a while of talking and eating those gummies, I can't seem to stop myself from laughing. I have no idea what's come over me but I find everything funny. Who knew Alex could make me laugh so much. He stops laughing and just stares at me.

He stands from his seat, holds out his hand, "let's dance!" he pulls me to my feet and starts dancing.

I'm usually stiff when it comes to dancing, but for some reason I feel like I can really move. I'm not sure how many songs we danced to, I'm actually enjoying myself. It feels like my worries are a million miles away, and I'm just a young girl having the fun I'm supposed to.

It seems like innocent fun. We're laughing and dancing, having a good time. As we dance, I feel him leading us backwards. Next thing I know I'm backed up against a wall with Alex caging me in.

"Alex!" I say trying to get him to move back a little.

"Angelisa," he says as he strokes my skin just below my earlobe with his nose. It tickles causing me to giggle, why do I feel drunk? He raises his head to meet my eyes.

"Just give me a chance. One real kiss," he glances down to my lips, then back up again.

"If you don't like it or me, I'll leave you alone!" he tells me.

He's charming, in another time, I might've taken him up on his offer. I almost want to, I'm not feeling myself. I'm drunk! How am I drunk? Alex is also drunk, this won't end well. I don't like Alex the way he likes me, and I don't want to kiss him. I have to remove myself from this situation before we both do something we'll regret.

"No," I tell him low enough so only he hears. I don't want to embarrass him or cause a scene.

"Baby, just once!" he says trying to come closer. He kisses my neck as he wraps one arm around my waist tightly.

"I'm not your baby! Alex, I said no!" he pushes me against the wall roughly.

I try to push him off, but he's stronger than me. He presses his lips to mine, when he tries to deepen the kiss, I turn my face. He grabs my face roughly and kisses me again. I try to scream, but with this loud music I doubt anyone can hear me.

Tears run down my face as the pressure of his hand begin to hurt my cheeks. I try to push him off, but it's no use. An idea comes to mind, something I think might get him to back off. He's not going to like it, but what choice is he leaving me?

I try to relax, and let him deepen the kiss. When I feel his tongue slip into my mouth I bite it hard and make him bleed. He steps back releasing me, he spits blood on the ground. He curses.

Then he did what I wasn't expecting, he hits me with the back of his hand across my face so hard I fall down. I cover my throbbing cheek, it feels warm. I can't believe he hit me. I wasn't expecting a reaction like that.

When I look up, another shock…a face I never thought I would see again. Light facial hair leading up to his light brown hair, brown angry looking eyes; Logan. What is he doing here?

He walks right up to me, pulls me to my feet and takes me in his arms. He pulls my hand off my face gently to examine my cheek.

"Are you ok?" he asks. I'm still in shock from seeing him, and Alex's reaction toward me I can't voice my words. I nod.

But he knows me better than that, he leans me up against the wall to steady me, turns around to face Alex who is still spitting out blood. Logan punches him right in the mouth, busting his lip open. He pulls his arm back and punches Alex again so hard in the eye now. Alex falls to the floor.

Logan leans over him, "that's no way to treat a lady, don't you ever lay your hands on Angel again, or any female in front of me or I'll knock you out. And next time I won't stop until I'm sure you're out cold!" Alex's eyes widen when Logan calls me by my nick name, he knows there was something between Logan and I.

Alex must remember that I don't allow just anyone to call me *Angel.* Logan walks back over to me, wraps an arm around my waist holding me close to him. I'm reminded how safe I felt in his arms once upon a time.

"Come on Angel, let's find some ice," he tells me as he leads me back in the house.

I look back over to where Alex is still lying on the ground, he's holding his face. I didn't want this to happen, I thought he was sincere about being friends. I hoped we really could be, now I just feel naïve and stupid…and drunk.

Logan goes into the freezer and grabs an ice tray, he empties it on to one of the kitchen towels and places the towel on the right side of my face.

"Please don't tell me that guy is your boyfriend!" he tells me. Surprised by his statement I finally look at him, I've been avoiding eye contact. When I meet his eyes I lose myself in his dark brown eyes. I missed him so much. I try my best to look away but I can't. He still has that same affect on me as back then.

"No," I say.

"Oh my God Angel, are you ok?" I hear Val through the crowd as she makes her way to me.

It's then I notice I'm the center of attention. A lot of people are around me trying to find out what happened?

"I'm ok Val." I answer. Logan pulls the towel down off my face.

"You're going to bruise, but the ice should keep the swelling down." Logan tells me.

"Girl, when I said you should meet the cute guy, you could've just introduce yourself!" Val jokes. I try to laugh, but my face hurts too much.

"This is the guy I was telling you about," she continues. I look at Logan and see he's smiling at Val's comments.

"Val, this is Logan…*my ex.*" I tell her.

"Oh," she says.

"Hi," Logan tells her.

"Hello." She looks him up and down.

"You broke my friend's heart!" she snaps at him.

"Val!" I shout.

"What? He did!" I cover my face with my hands.

"I was a stupid kid, I'm sorry!" I hear him apologize. I lower my hands and look at him.

"We were both stupid kids." I tell him.

"Right, well rumors are spreading fast. Did Alex try to force himself on you? Because Mario is about to beat the crap out of him!"

"Tell Mario, Logan already did that. He wanted me to kiss him once, before I put him in the friend zone to see how I really feel about him I guess. He told me he would leave me alone after, but I didn't want to kiss him. I already made my mind up about him. I told him no, but he kept insisting."

"I should have never told you to come here. We could've hung out somewhere else!"

"It's fine Val, I was the one who accepted your invitation. I should've known better!"

"Who is this guy?" Logan asks.

"He's from college," I answer.

"Do you need a ride home, Angel?"

"I drove Logan, but thank you if you were offering!"

"Well, considering you killed a rose bush when you were able to see with two eyes, I don't think you should drive only seeing through one eye!" Val teased.

"Val, I can see! It just hurts."

"I can drive you, or Logan. Unless you want me to call Ryan?" Val just keeps putting her foot in her mouth.

"Ryan is your boyfriend?" Logan asks.

"No, he's a friend!" I answer Logan but I'm looking at Val trying to get her to stop giving out so much information. Logan left me, as much as I miss him, he doesn't need to know of my life right now.

"Ok, you can't drive yourself. I'll drive you home in your car. Let's not forget you're a little tipsy." I look between Logan and Val, still trying to figure out how I became intoxicated.

"Angel?"

"Were you drinking?" Val asked.

I shake my head. "How are you tipsy then?"

"I have no idea Val. I only drank bottled water. I didn't have any brownies this time so I have no idea."

Logan's laughs causes both Val and I to look his way.

"What?" Val asks. When Logan stops laughing he answers her question.

"Gummy bears and gummy worms. They were soaked in liquor. I saw Angel eating quite a few."

"I did notice they taste different. What about the jello? Was it made with liquor?" I asked.

Logan nods. Why do I keep putting myself in these situations? How could I not known?

"Come on, let me take you home. I'll have my cousin pick me up me up in my car. Logan insists.

Val hugs me, and walks me to the door. Logan hands me the towel with ice, "where you parked?" he asks.

"You drive the same car?"

He looks puzzled, "yeah why?"

"I think I parked behind you." I answer.

"I hope you didn't hit my car while parking!" He jokes.

We walk to my car and he drives us to my house. I look in the mirror, my eye is getting dark and so is my cheek. It stings, and it's still throbbing. I hope my parents are asleep. I really don't want to have to explain this tonight. Logan pulls in to my drive way and turns off the car.

"Why were you at the party Logan?"

"I was invited, my cousin is friends with Mario," he answered.

"Small world, I thought I would never see you again."

"I wanted to come see you, what I did back then was stupid. I'm sorry! I miss you," he admits.

I miss him too, but is that something I should tell him? I don't know what to do here. I don't answer him.

"I saw you, when you and that Alex guy came out back. I wanted to talk to you, but I thought he was your boyfriend by the way you were all over each other. I didn't want to interfere. But when I saw you were trying to push him away and then when he slapped you, I didn't care what he was to you. He wasn't going to treat you like that in front of me!"

"I bit him!" I face the window.

"It was the only way I knew I was going to be able to get him to back off. I wasn't expecting him to hit me."

"You did what you had to, how you feeling?"

"I feel stupid, to be honest. This wasn't the first time he pressed himself on me like that. My friend Ryan saved me last time. I just can't comprehend why he doesn't understand the word no?"

"Maybe he doesn't like that word."

"I guess not, I should go inside Logan." I open the door and step out of the car. Logan gets out too.

"I'll text my cousin to come and get me. Can we talk until he gets here?" I look back at him as I walk to the front steps.

"What's to talk about? We were two stupid kids, we moved too fast and we broke up. It's normal!"

"You hurt me too Angel! I just reacted. I was willing to work the long distance. I didn't understand why you wouldn't give it a chance!"

"I had things going on, I couldn't involve you. You had dreams, and my issues would have gotten in the way of it!" I still don't want to tell him about the baby. I don't know what reaction he would have. I just need some space to think.

"Angel," he says calming down. "Am I too late?"

"Late for what?"

"Us? I miss you, and I would like to try again. So tell me, am I too late? Is this Ryan guy important to you?"

"Ryan...Ryan is important!"

"Is he your boyfriend?"

"No, but—" Logan cuts me off with a kiss.

A kiss unlike Alex's I don't mind. I missed him, his touch. I pull back and I place my hand on his cheek. I look into his eyes before I kiss him again. It feels like we were back then, when nothing mattered. He deepens our kiss and after a few seconds, I have to pull back again.

"Logan, I'm sorry I can't do this. I do miss you, I miss this, but I don't think I can go back to the way things were. You don't know what I've been through, how alone I felt when we broke up. The road I took trying to forget you, I've lost a lot. I've been on a journey of spiritual healing recently, and I don't want to end up where I started." I tell him as honestly as I can without giving him too much information.

"Angel, I'm so sorry. I didn't want to hurt you like that, but you have to understand I was hurt too when you were trying to break up with me. I just wanted you to hurt the same way you made me hurt. I see now that was the wrong way to go. I never stopped loving you, I think about you all the time. I didn't reach out because I thought you were still mad at me. I was wrong!" He touched my face with his hand.

"I'm not the same person Logan, yes I broke up with you, but I was scared. I was dealing with something and I didn't know how to handle it. I felt so alone after, and things got worse for me. I just need some space," I tell him.

He wraps his arms around me embracing me in a warm hug. And for a moment, I just want to stay there. I would like to erase the past and just stay right here with him. But I changed when I was with him, I lost myself when I wasn't anymore.

He plants a soft kiss on my lips, "take some time, we can catch up when you're feeling up to it. I'm here all summer!" I stare into his eyes and just nod. I grab my keys from his hands and go inside.

I just left him standing there, I already feel like I messed up more than once tonight. I lean on the door and slide down to the floor. I can't contain myself anymore, I start to cry. I let out everything, I can't stop myself.

I feel as if I failed God again. I don't know if He'll forgive me after tonight. I can't blame myself for Alex's actions, but kissing Logan. And Ryan, should I tell him? What if Lady saw? She'll make sure to let him know. She'll let everyone know, and expand the truth to make me out to be the worst. Then I'll be right back to where I started. Alone.

26. The Wolves Are Coming

It's Sunday morning, I spent the day yesterday at home trying to avoid people seeing how my face looks now. I explained what happened with Alex at the party to my parents and Evie. I couldn't hide my black eye. My parents were furious. I told them about what I did to get him off of me, and about Logan being there to defend me. I even told them about him driving me home, but I didn't tell them about the kiss. I guess I'm back to hiding secrets again.

I am worried if Lady saw, not sure how she'll spin this. If she did see, she would use it against me; isolating me once again. I would now have two Rebecca's in my life.

Ryan wanted to pass by yesterday but I told him I wasn't feeling good. I wasn't lying, my face still hurts. I didn't want him to see my eye and have to explain to him the whole night. Of course Logan checked in a few times, but I didn't want to talk to him either. I have to figure out how to handle this on my own.

Last night I had a dream, I'm afraid of what it means. I was standing in the middle of the garden where I first encountered God. Everything was the same, warm breeze, scents, butterflies. Then a door appeared behind me. The door was a dark brown, almost black. I was curious about the mysterious door, so I walked toward it. Reaching for the doorknob I turned it, opening the door just a crack. The door flew open and darkness began to fill the beautiful colorful garden.

I woke up asking myself if I messed up that bad. What did it mean when the two worlds combined? I know I'm not to blame for Alex's actions last night, but was there another way I should have handled that situation? And what happened later with Logan, was God mad at me? All these questions make me feel fear and shame, even a sense of guilt. The more I thought about it, the angrier I felt. How can one mistake lead to all this confusion? Or was it more than one mistake? Suddenly I find myself questioning everything about that whole night.

I can't help but feel that maybe God has turned His back on me. But, it was just a kiss. I didn't let it go any further than that, I stopped.

As I get ready for Sunday service, I fear what people are going to think when they see my face. I tried to hide it under makeup, but I only seem to make it darker. I'll have to wear shades. I thought about just staying home, but I don't want to hide. I haven't been able to pray, I feel like I pushed myself backwards. I'm afraid I lost my armor. How would I face God?

We walk in to the church, I don't take my shades off. I wore my hair to the side to cover my eye, and I keep my head down. I feel shame, I know it was only a kiss, but it felt like I lost more. Everyone is praising, but I can't push my emotions aside. I feel worse than before. I'm not as strong as God said I was. My enemies were right, I am weak. Should I be so hard on myself? I am only nineteen, I'm allowed to make mistakes aren't I? But, why do I feel so bad?

I find lady in her usual seat, and Brian is sitting next to her. She whispers something to him, he looks back over to me. I knew it, she saw and is just jumping at the chance to tell people.

After they collect the offering, Rebecca sits by her father. I remember the dream I had about the enemy using her. I wanted so much to help her, but I felt too far gone in my own situation to even face her. Her father leans into her, then she looks back at me. And so the rumors begin. Why are Christians the first ones to judge? I try to ignore them and just focus on the preacher. I'm grateful Brian isn't preaching today, I'm sure he would have incorporated my weekend somehow.

My thoughts were so loud, I couldn't hear a word of the preaching. I'm worried, I feel as if something is very wrong with me; I'm dying again. Service is over, I couldn't wait to get out of here. I'm getting strange vibes, eyes are watching me. Making my way outside I don't make eye contact. To my surprise, Ryan is outside with his bike. I walk up to him.

"Hey," I say.

"Hey, I thought I'd pick you up, want to grab a bite?" Bite reminds me of Alex. The memory of what I had to do to get him off me. My vision becomes blurred as I remember the events of the night.

"Yeah, I need to tell you something!" I can feel someone standing behind me. "Hi!" I hear Rebecca say, I turn around to face her.

"Hi," Ryan and I both say at the same time.

"So Angelisa, I hear you and Logan are back together!" She was quick to blurt it out. Ryan's jaw tightens as he looks at her.

"Oh, you didn't hear Ryan? Angelisa hooked up with her ex this weekend. So I guess you two aren't a thing after all!" she gloats. Ryan looks at me.

"It's not what happened!" I want to explain, but Rebecca doesn't give me a chance to speak.

"Oh really, because Lady saw you from her window. She said the two of you were very close, she thought you were about to do it right there in the yard!"

"No we were not! You weren't there Rebecca, you don't even know what happened!" I shout.

"I will never be around a slut like you!" she retorts. People passing by stop to look in our direction. I can feel anger rising up in me. My skin feels like it's on fire. I don't hold back anymore. I had enough.

"A slut like me?!" I take a step closer to her.

"Was I the one locked in the broom closet with two boys doing what you were? I may have done things I am not proud of, but I was only with my boyfriend. The things I've done, I've only done with him. I highly doubt that falls into the slut category." Rebecca looks around, people are starting to gather around us.

"I kept your secret, but in doing so…it was my name, my reputation that was tarnished! I won't do it anymore. You need to come off your high horse and look in a mirror before you start pointing fingers!" I feel as if I'm about to burst like one of those cartoon characters on TV. All the pain I felt the past two years, all the rumors. The thought of my baby, and everything that happened since that day. All those suppressed emotions are beginning to surface.

Rebecca has no words, did she honestly think I would stay shut forever? Why would I protect her secret? She doesn't care about anyone but herself. Maybe people should know who she really is. Looking over her shoulder I see her father, and a few members of the church. I know they heard what I said about their *precious* Rebecca.

"How could you? I thought you would keep that between us?" Rebecca whispers. The nerve, is she serious? Why would I keep that between us while she spreads lies about me?

"Maybe I would have, if you wouldn't have tried to make me look like the slut. You talked about me, put me through the floor." I step closer to her, we're so close I can feel her breath on my face as she breathes heavy.

She's the one in the spotlight now. I should feel bad about this, but I don't. She's to blame for most of my pain.

"I tried to help you, instead you put all the blame on me!" I continued. She can't seem to look me in the eyes. Good! She'll finally understand what it felt like for me all this time.

"Well sorry, I'm not the one who did all those things you said, it was you!"

"Angelisa…calm down. You're up—"

"No Ryan! She can't keep treating people—me this way. It's about time everyone knows who she really is; a fake!"

213

In her anger she goes to pull my hair and in the process knocks my shades off. When she sees the bruise on my face she takes a step back, "your eye, what happened? Did Logan—"

"NO, it wasn't him!" I pick up my shades and attempt to put them back on, Ryan takes a hold of my wrist.

"What happened to your eye Angelisa?" His voice is a mixture of concern and rage.

I lower my shades, take a look around. I didn't realize how many people have gathered around us…waiting to hear what I say next. I don't want people to think Logan is capable of something like this, to me or to any female. He's a good guy. People are so nosey, they're so eager to know what's happening. I look back between Ryan and Rebecca, trying to ignore the crowd around us.

"It was another guy, at a party I went to." I make sure my response is loud enough so every nosey person can hear.

I don't mention Alex's name, because I don't want to shame him anymore than I already have. Who knows what the future holds for him, I don't know if one day he'll find God and end up coming to this church. I wouldn't want people to judge him for his past before giving him a chance.

"Logan was there," I continued.

"He punched the guy and drove me home!" I glance between Rebecca and Ryan.

Rebecca's face softens as she takes in my eye. And Ryan's jaw tighten even more. He seems to be holding back. I look over to the crowd surrounding us, they're just there. Watching, waiting to see what happens next. Not being able to contain myself any longer, I run. I don't like being the center of attention.

"Angelisa!" Ryan calls after me, but I ignore him. I keep running.

I'm sure they all are coming up with their own conclusions about me. They already thought the worse, what did I have to lose? What is wrong with me? I would have never acted out this way. I hear a motorcycle come up behind me.

"Angelisa! Stop!" I keep running. I don't know how to face him, he's going to ask about Alex, then about what Rebecca said about Logan and what Lady thought she saw. I can't bear the look of disappointment on his face. He rides up ahead of me and stops. I turn in the opposite direction and try to run off but Ryan grabs a hold of my arms.

As he stands behind me he tries to calm me down, "Angelisa, please don't run from me." I don't move, but I don't want to turn around.

"Ryan! Please I can't do this right now, I don't want you to see me like this." I tell him through my sobs.

"I just want to know that you're ok!"

"Ryan...I can't!"

He loosens his grip on me, but doesn't let go, I take in a deep breath trying to get myself to relax. I hear footsteps running from behind, then Ryan is pulled off of me.

"Keep your hands off her! What is it with you guys here? You don't understand when a girl isn't interested?" I turn around to find Logan staring at Ryan as if he's ready to fight. Then Ryan about to come back at Logan, I jump in between them.

"Logan, stop. This is Ryan, my friend!" I turn to face Ryan.

"It was Alex, he did this to me." I tell him taking off my shades. "I managed to get him off of me, and Logan beat him up!" I watch as Ryan looks from Logan, then back to me.

"I warned you about that guy, I should've been there with you. I shouldn't have let you go alone!" Ryan tells me.

"He didn't get too far, Angel took care of that when she bit him!" Logan tells Ryan.

"You bit him?" Ryan enunciated every word.

"That's when he hit me. I didn't expect that reaction. But I had to make him stop!" Ryan takes me in his arms and just holds me.

"I'm sorry," he whispers.

Ryan reaches out a hand to Logan, "I'm Ryan!" he tells Logan.

They shake hands, "I don't think he'll mess with her again." Logan tells Ryan. Pulling away from Ryan, I look between the two of them. I never thought I introduce these two.

"I should go, I need some time to process what I just did to Rebecca." I tell them.

"Rebecca? You're still friends with her after everything she's put you through?" Logan asks.

"No, we're not. But I just basically told the whole church her secret. She pushed my buttons today, and obviously I wasn't in the mood!"

"Come on, I'll give you a ride home." Ryan tells me. I nod.

"Thanks again for the other night, we'll catch up." I tell Logan. Ryan and Logan just nod at each other, I hop on Ryan's bike after he does and we ride off. I know Ryan has a lot of questions for me.

We reach my house, my parents are waiting for me outside. They're not alone, Brian and Rebecca are here too, and of course Lady. I'm sure Brian wants me to apologize for earlier.

"Mom?" I ask as we approach the group.

"Brian wants to talk to you about what you said outside church today," she answered.

"Maybe we should go inside." she tells Brian.

"No, I'm fine right here. Your daughter had no shame in embarrassing my daughter in front of everyone, we can clear her name in the open too!"

"What I said was true Brian, maybe I shouldn't have done it in that way, but I didn't lie." I tell him.

"My Rebecca would never do those things, I saw you walk through that door with three boys. That is the reason why I didn't want Rebecca around you, you're poison. All your wrong doings would have rubbed off on my daughter, and that, I could not allow. Do your parents know of your whoring? You're drinking?" Brian asks.

"I think you need to calm down Brian!" Ryan jumps in. I look over to my parents, I'm glad I told them the truth, but the expression on my father's face is disappointment. I hope he doesn't think I lied to him, because what I told them was true.

"Why are you with her? She's with you today but the other night she's with Logan? I told you she was not right for you. You don't want someone so tarnished!" Brian replies.

Those words, coming from his mouth shouldn't have surprise me, but they did, and it hurt. I feel ashamed for something that didn't even happen like how he was told. It was just a kiss.

"You have no idea what you talking about!" Ryan responds.

"I believe you to be a holy man Ryan, but if you keep on with her, that won't be you anymore!"

"With all due respect *Minister* Brian," Ryan says *minister*, as to remind Brian who he is. Who he supposed to represent. He takes a step closer to him.

"You have no idea who your daughter is. Since I first came to your church she's been throwing herself at me, and it seems you have been encouraging her."

He turns to face Lady, "and even you, Lady. Are these the way people of God act? What would He think of you right now? Have you ever sat down with Angelisa to find out what really happened that night you speak of? Or the other night you claim?"

"Well, Ryan, I was watching from my window. I saw them kissing!" Lady tells him. Ryan looks over my way. I lower my head. He knows it's true.

"Angelisa and I are only friends, she's free to date who ever she wants. But did you see this?" Ryan removes my shades.

"Maybe because of this, the person who did this to her, Logan came in her defense and old flames were ignited. Did you even ask if she was ok, or what happened? No, you assumed! You judged!" Ryan rebukes.

I feel my tears running down my face. This is too much for me right now! How did I let this one night screw up everything I've overcome?

I look up toward the drive way, as if this moment couldn't get any worse, Logan drives up. He's not alone. Val and Mario, and I guess his cousin, step out of the car. I suddenly find it hard to breathe.

"Oh look here, more of her lovers I assume!"

"Dad!" Rebecca finally speaks.

As Logan approaches us, he looks at everyone in attendance, when his eyes lands on Brian he asks, "What's going on here?"

"Angel, are you ok?" Val asks me as she takes me in her arms.

"They think Angelisa corrupted Rebecca back then, and is back at it because the two of you apparently made out the other night!" Ryan answers Logan.

"Logan, what are you doing here?" my mom asks.

"I just came to see if Angel was ok, I didn't know there was a party to dishonor her!" he deflected.

"Angel is now, and always was, a good girl. What happened the other night...no offence to you Mr. and Mrs. Cruz, is none of your business!"

He tells everyone else, "Angel is a big girl, and so is Rebecca. Whatever Rebecca did does not fall on Angel!"

Val continues to hold me, I'm not sure how much more of this day I can take. "Are you alright Angelisa?" Ryan asks. I nod.

"Angelisa...we're coming for you!" I hear that familiar sinister voice. I look around, as if they would be here in my physical world. I see nothing out of the ordinary.

"Ryan," I say looking right at him. He looks at me with concern.

"What is it Angelisa?" He asks.

"I hear them!" I whisper as I look around searching for the unseen.

"Hear who?" Val asks.

"Angelisa!" My enemies laugh as they call my name. I know I'm in no position to fight, not in the state I'm in right now.

I hear growling near me, but there aren't any animals around. The growls now sound like bark-howls; wolves. The enemy is coming for me in the form of wolves.

"Ryan!" I say taking a step back with Val still holding me.

"They are coming for me." I whisper. I can't keep my eyes open, I feel weak. My legs begin to lose their strength and I feel myself go into a sleep like state.

"Angel?! Help, I think she passed out!" I can hear footsteps come closer, another set of hands lifts my head from Val's and someone grabs my hand.

"Angelisa?" I hear Ryan call my name.

"What are you doing?" I hear Logan ask.

"Angelisa!" Ryan calls my name again shaking me a little to see if I wake up.

A sinister laugh draws my attention from my friends. I hear wind blowing, as darkness surrounds me.

"Angelisa!" a voice says laughing.

"You're not so strong now are you?" The same voice says again. It's Fear.

"Angelisa, if you can hear me...stay strong. You've been preparing for this, don't be afraid," I hear Ryan tell me.

Suddenly, strong arms lifts me up. "Open the door!" Ryan yells.

"We need to get her inside!" I hear keys jingling and footsteps running.

"Shouldn't we call 911 or something?" I hear Val.

"No, this is not physical, this is spiritual. Let's lay her down, someone get a moist towel to put on her head." I feel when he lays me on the sofa, I'm aware of everything going on but I can't open my eyes.

"He's right!" Fear tells me.

"This is spiritual, right now…you're in our world, and we're in control!" he laughs.

I hear them all laugh. I can't see any of them. I see the door from my dream last night. It's still wide open, still leaking darkness into the once beautiful garden. I can't help but feel responsible for what's happening to this place. It's because of me.

As the darkness fills the garden, everything begins to disappear. I'm standing in the middle of nothing, did God really turn His back on me? Is God disappointed for kissing Logan? Did He place me back in this hole of nothingness as punishment? Or was it because of what I did to Rebecca today?

I feel myself fall to my knees, my tears begin to spill from my eyes. I lost my way, if He would turn away from me, then how can I expect everyone in that room right now to believe that I've changed?

"Did you really think you can overcome us? You're drawn to that life without God, and hey we can't blame you…it is kind of fun compared to what you godly people enjoy doing. May be you should just accept the fact that this Christian walk is not for you. Save yourself the struggle, have fun, live your life like any other teenage girl. Your friend Val is enjoying herself, why don't you join her!" Fear tells me almost sounding sincere.

I consider his advice, may be he's right. Why should I fight the life that seems so easy to live?

"What's happening Ryan?" I hear my mom.

"She's been going through a spiritual journey, she's been battling with spirits that have been tormenting her. They finally got her where they want her; weak and afraid! They're toying with her," he answers.

"My poor girl, what should we do?" my mom asks.

"Afraid of what exactly? Being caught in her lies?" I hear Brian ask.

I can feel Ryan take my hand in both of his. He holds my hand up to his forehead, "Angelisa, I'm here for you. Don't give up this fight!" He whispers.

He stays quiet, an image of him flashes in my mind. He has faith in me, even with what he knows of me, he still believes I should fight.

"My daughter is not a liar," my father responds to Brian's questions.

"Brian, if you're going to stay, push aside your feelings and start to pray, this is spiritual warfare!" Ryan tells him.

"Evie, make a circle around us, those that know how to pray, please do so, if you don't just join hands and talk to God. We're praying for her. We need to help her get ready for war!" I hear Ryan again.

I don't know if I'm ready for this battle right now. Fear is going to sense it all, Guilt, Shame, they're going to have the upper hand.

"Father, I present your daughter before you…" Ryan begins to pray.

I hear muffle voices, but Ryan's voice is loud and clear. As he continues to pray, I feel my spirit going to where I usually go. There's something different here… it's snowing. It smells like something was burning.

Still on my knees I put my hand out, to catch some snowflakes. It's not snow, its ash. I hear laughter in the distance. They're waiting for me, they tempted me, played on my weakness and I fell right into their scheme. I'm afraid, I'm unarmed. I see them now, the four of them rising out of the shadows…they're coming for me. Fear appears before me first.

"Aww, poor little child. Where is that spunk you had before?" Fear gibed.

"She's weak!" Shame brags.

Guilt comes closer, *"not so tough now huh? You were suppose be a good person, you embarrassed Rebecca, and Alex. Now you're torn between Logan and Ryan. Oh wait, I don't think Ryan will want you now that he knows you and Logan had a moment the other night."* Guilt taunts.

He's going to make me feel guilty for what I've done.

"You're afraid! You feel everything slipping away. You should fear it, all that you worked for is now taken away," as Fear speaks, he begins to circle around me.

"Poor Rebecca, what must people be thinking of her right now?" Guilt joins Fear in torturing me. The pain I feel in my heart is too much for me to take. I begin to cry again. I'm trap, I want to wake up, but that seems impossible.

"Evie," I hear Ryan say.

"Take my phone, call Jason. Tell him to call everyone and have them come over now!"

"Ryan," I say in my spiritual form, but I can feel my lips move as I call his name in my physical body.

"Help," I cry.

"I'm here, hold on. Don't let them taunt you, you are not weak!" he replies to my cry.

"What's going on?" I hear Logan.

"She's being tormented by her fears, and guilt. She's fallen weak, she's doubting herself and the enemy knows it. They're trying to keep her down," Ryan answers.

"Don't forget, God has not left you!" Ryan speaks to me again.

I feel so alone here in this place, surrounded only by my enemies. My own fears have overpowered me. I want to cry out to God, I need to feel His embrace, the warmth I once felt not so long ago. I can't sense God around me, He might not even hear me. Why would He? I failed Him again.

I feel as He's turned His back on me, I made more mistakes. I should have known better. Why would He give me another chance?

"You're right!" I hear Fear say. I forget they can hear my thoughts here.

"Why would He forgive you again? You will just continue messing up, falling back into the same sin over and over again," he laughs.

"Ahh, this is perfect, don't you think?" Shame asks Fear. She walks closer to me now.

"Didn't it feel good to be wanted by these guys you've surrounded yourself with?" I sob as Shame teases. I think back to my first time with Logan, and then the other night.

"You know, you wouldn't have been able to stop yourself if Logan would have taken you back to his place instead of yours! I mean who can blame you? He is gorgeous!" she laughs.

Wouldn't I? I think. I'm not as strong as I thought I was. It was just a fantasy, I hoped to have been doing better. But I really wasn't, I was just lying to myself, I'm weak. Poor Ryan invested so much time in to helping me, and I let him down as well. He should just let me be.

I hold my knees to my chest as I cradle myself. I try to find comfort…but nothing feels right anymore. I'm alone, and I'm trapped…I just want to stay in this hole. I don't deserve to be out there.

"Can't face your God now, can you? Not with all you've done. Oh let's not forget about what you did to Alex!" Guilt begins.

In between my sobs I say, "I…defended…myself!"

Guilt laughs. *"But you led him to that point. You kept leading him on. What was he to do? How can he restrain himself from touching you? You accepted his invites, he is only a man. It was your fault he acted the way he did. Then you shamed him for it, in front of all his friends. You ruined his life, you're to blame!"*

No, this can't be my fault too! He was forcing himself on me, I had to get him to stop. I look over my knees and see Alex standing in front of me. I sit up to get a better view. I'm confused, how is he here? He has a black eye, and a busted lip. I haven't seen Alex since the party the other night, he looks worse than I do.

"Look what you did to me Angelisa!" he accused.

"I didn't want any of this to happen," I tell him standing to my feet.

"I just wanted you to give me a chance, you had someone BEAT ME UP, in front of everyone!" he shouts taking a step closer to me.

"Alex, I just wanted you to respect my decision. I only wanted friendship." I hesitate before taking another step closer to him. The look in his good eye scared me.

"Our first night together, you let me kiss you. Then upstate you push me away, you even had your boy toy waiting for you outside. The other night, another guy, but you kept telling me you weren't interested in dating and yet I seen you with two guys already!"

The angry look in his eyes makes me take a step back.

"Ryan is just a friend, and Logan is the reason I didn't want to date. He was my boyfriend and he left me." Taking another step back, "He hurt me, I'm afraid to let people in. I don't trust myself to do the right thing. Alex, it really isn't what you think!" I tell him as calmly as I can.

"I'm sorry Alex, I never meant for any of this to happen. But if you would've respected my—"

Alex hits me across the face with the back of his hand, just like he did the other night. I fall back and hit the ground. I place my hand on the side of my face, as I look back up at him, he begins to laugh as he walks closer to me.

"Alex," I say his name, hoping he can see reason.

I don't want to fight him. Deep down, I don't see him as a bad guy, I just always thought him to be immature. But I was right to do what I did wasn't I? I told him to stop, I didn't want to kiss him. I didn't want to hurt him, but I had no other option. Alex's face begins to fade, Guilt stands in his place now.

"Oh you had plenty of options, you could have not gone to that party. Or not have joined him outside!" Guilt continues to torture me.

"Angelisa!" I hear a voice call out to me.

"Angelisa!" I recognized that voice, the voice of God.

"Oh He came for you, but he's not going to save you, you shamed Him as well. If I were you, I would hide!" I listen to Guilt.

I get up and run away from the voice of God. I run through the trees, it's so dark and the tears that fill my eyes make it hard to see.

"Angelisa!" I hear Him again, He sounds closer. I have to pick up the pace. I try to hide in the cluster of trees, trying to find a covering but these trees are dead, they don't offer much shelter.

"Angelisa! I'm here!" He says, but this time He sounds further away. Guilt appears next to me.

"Keep running, before He finds you!" he tells me. I do as he says, I don't know how long I run for but I have to stop to catch my breath. I sit by a tree.

"Keep going, He'll find you!" Guilt says. I get up and start to run again, but then I stop.

"What are you doing, He's getting closer, RUN!" he shouts.

"Why are you telling me to run, why are you helping me?"

He stares at me for a moment...he waves his hand and a bassinet appears before me. I stare at it, wondering why it's here. A baby begins to cry, I can't help myself, I take a peek.

The baby is swaddled in a pink blanket. She's beautiful, she's crying so hard her face is as red as a tomato.

"What's wrong with her?" I ask Guilt.

"She wanted to be born. She'll never get the chance now!" he answers.

"Who is she?" I look up from the baby to Guilt.

"Don't you recognize her?" I look back down to the baby. So many emotions run through me, again I cry as realization sets in. She's my baby! The one I lost.

"You may see it as you lost her, but reality is you were planning on making her go away anyway weren't you?" he asks me.

The day of me in the hospital begins to play in my mind. I was so upset at Logan I wanted to erase every trace of him from myself.

"I wasn't going to go through with it!" I shouted.

"You were! You didn't want anything of Logan's around you...including the unborn child!" I watch as he walks closer to the bassinet, she? Anger said 'her' was my baby a girl?

"She's beautiful, isn't she?" he asks. The baby stops crying when our eyes meet. She reaches her hand up, *"mama,"* she says.

My heart breaks. I reach my hand to hold hers, but she vanishes.

"NO!" I shout. I search the bassinet, hoping to find her. She's gone.

"My baby, I'm so sorry," I whisper.

"You went in to the hospital to kill her!" Guilt says.

I hold on to the bassinet as I slide down to the floor, it too vanishes.

"I wasn't...I changed my mind. I was going to walk out and go home, but I miscarried. I wanted my baby!" I look up to him.

"That's a lie you tell yourself to help you sleep better at night," he tells me.

"Angelisa!" I hear God again.

"Run!" Guilt yells.

I stumble to my feet and begin to run. I can't face God right now. What if He thinks I wanted to kill my baby too? I did... at first, but I wasn't going to go through with it.

"Angelisa...remember the enemy is a liar!" I hear Ryan's voice. I stop running.

"What are you doing? Keep going, He's close," Guilt says. I turn to face him, Guilt was just taunting me, and now he wants to help me to run from God? It doesn't make sense.

"Angelisa, don't flee from me! I'm here for you!" God says.

"Yes He's here for you alright, to give you your punishment! You need to keep running!"

I take a step closer to Guilt, face to face, "NO! You don't want me to get close to God do you? You making me run away from Him because of you, not me! You're trying to keep me separated from God!"

I think back to a conversation I had with Ryan one time. Guilt separates you from God. It's why Adam and Eve hid from Him, it's why Judas killed himself, his guilt for betraying Jesus Christ for silver.

His guilt was so much that he thought it better to take his own life. I will not make that mistake. I've failed, yes, but God is love! I can turn this around. Guilt looks at and smiles before he fades away.

I run back toward the voice calling my name.

"God!" I call out with no response.

Where did He go? "God!" I keep running to where I ran from. The sounds of laughter fills the silence. They're back, Fear, Shame, and Guilt although Guilt doesn't scare me as much anymore. Anger is in the distance, he hasn't come to bother me like the others...yet. He might be plotting something bigger.

"God?" Fear asks through his laughter. *"God, you call? Why would you do that? You think He will look past all the damaged you just caused? Just think, all those people right now in your house. They came to argue because of what you've done!"*

I think about what he's saying, but I also think about what they're doing right now. Brian, Rebecca, and Lady may have come to argue. Ryan just wanted to talk, my parents and Evie believe me. Logan and Val and the others, I'm not too sure why they came over. But they are all together now, holding hands I assume since Ryan told them to join hands.

They're all from different backgrounds, but they are all together in one accord, praying for me. Maybe this weekend had to happen this way, maybe God allowed it to happen to bring all these people together.

Through my tears I face Fear, "I call His name…" I say pointing up. "…Because He loves me, because He saved me. I'm ready to face Him for my actions!"

As I say these words, I feel as if a veil is lifted from my eyes. I'm in the center of a circle of people, everyone that was in my house when I passed out. I also see Ryan's friends, Jason, Ivy, Marissa, and Mike. They all may have come over for different reasons, but they are all here for one now. They all have their eyes closed, I'm happy to know that although Val has no idea of what's happening, she's here for me.

Ryan is in front of the others. I can see him still praying with his eyes closed. But here he is dressed like a warrior angel. His wings tuck behind his back, his sword in his right hand and his shield in his left. A true soldier of God stands ready for battle. His friends look like soldiers as well.

I still feel broken inside, ashamed of what I've done…what my actions have caused the people around me.

"This means nothing!" Fear disrupts my thoughts. He lifts his arms up, the leaves on the ground begin to move as the wind begins to blow. Fear wields the wind around us. His favorite trick I assume. The whirlwind he summons separates me from the others. I can still hear Ryan praying over the sound of the wind, I don't know why he doesn't open his eyes.

The last time we were here together, we were able to talk to each other. That is until Fear separated us and tried to inflict as much fear and guilt in to me. Ryan couldn't help me then either. Maybe this is something I'm supposed to face on my own.

As Fear waves his hand, an image of me appears of the night at the party. I see myself dancing and laughing with Alex. We were having a good time, why did it had to end up like it did? I watched as Alex led us out into the backyard, his expression as he walks behind me…I didn't realize. He was watching me, with lust in his eyes. I watched as he looked toward one of his friends and crossed his fingers like a silent plea. He was hoping to get lucky I assume.

"Why are you showing me this? I wasn't in the wrong here!" I shout at Fear, but instead I'm faced with Alex once again. He says nothing in response, Alex waves his hand, the scene changes to the part where Alex had me pinned to the wall. I see myself trying to push him away, but then I relax and let him kiss me.

"Looks like you were beginning to enjoy yourself with me. You let me in and then you changed your mind." Alex tells me.

"I had to bring down your defenses so I was able to get away. I wasn't leading you on, I bit you to free myself!" I tell him.

"I thought you had finally stop fighting yourself to be with me," Alex looks at me with disappointment.

"I don't care what you thought, you were forcing me to kiss you! You pinned me to the wall!"

"But you knew how I felt about you. You accepted my invite to go outside, we danced, we talked, and your body was telling me something different."

"You said you wanted to be friends, I believed you. I was dancing to the music, not trying to lead you on!" I shout. I begin to feel frustrated because Alex is making me feel as if I'm the one to blame. I can't help but to feel responsible somehow. I know it was never my intention to lead Alex on. I never wanted to kiss him, and I told him no. But he just kept insisting.

"If that Ryan guy wouldn't have showed up that night, upstate, you would have stayed with me. After all, you do have a reputation. You want to lie to me, that's fine…but don't lie to yourself. You did like me, if you didn't you wouldn't have let me kiss you the first time." He reminds me.

Another image appears before me, when Alex is on the floor after Logan had punched him.

"You see what your actions caused?" he asks. "You skipped the part where you hit me!" I tell him.

"Oh that, that was just a reflex. No need to replay that scene, although it was entertaining for me!" he laughs. I feel tears run along the sides of my cheeks.

"Let's skip ahead to what your fear was after this, shall we? Hmm, after Logan took you home, you feared Lady was watching. That she would tell everyone about your night with Logan, that she would ruin your chances with Ryan!" I did fear that she will tell people her way. I did fear Ryan's reaction, but not for the reasons they think.

"You wanted him that night!" Shame jumps in.

"You cannot deny it—"

"STOP!" I yell! "I missed him, yes…I did not want him in that way!"

Shame laughs at me.

"You kissed him, after you kissed Alex! Who was next? Ryan? I don't blame you, they are all yummy aren't they…" she pauses as she takes in the image of her own words.

"But is that something God would like? You shamed Him!"

My cries are back, I fall to my knees dropping my face into my hands. I need to gain control, I need to get out of here.

"Oh darling, you're here until we let you out!" Shame laughs.

27. Why Have You Left Me?

I begin to search my thoughts, I need to feel at peace. I know what I've done was not intentional. I need to think, there is a way out of this. I have grown a lot in the past few weeks. I will not let myself be devoured by these spiritual wolves.

Looking up to where Ryan is, I remember what he told me once about the armor of God. You have to put it on daily. Just because we gained it once, doesn't mean you can't lose it. I begin to search my thoughts, I've been so down on myself. I haven't prayed, I haven't looked for God because I was ashamed. That is why I am not wearing my armor.

"Doesn't it make you angry to see Ryan armed? God must be really mad at you to strip away all of yours, and you were so close," Anger finally speaks.

"It's ok to react, let your anger loose. It's ok to be mad at God, in fact...isn't He to blame? He allowed this to happen to you, didn't He?" Anger continues, playing on my emotions.

I could be angry with God, He could have helped me, but instead He let things happen.

I look up to the dark sky, "WHY?" I shout hoping God can hear me. I continue to cry out, hoping to hear or see some kind of sign He heard me. But there was nothing.

Anger kneels next to me, *"He's left you!"* he says in a low voice almost sounding concerned for me. *"Are you angry yet?"* he asks. I shake my head no, I'm not angry...just hurt.

I thought I was strong, able to handle my past. I still can't believe that in defending myself, I lost a reputation I was trying to build. A new life with new beginnings. Then Logan comes back and it just messes with my mind, my emotions. I am angry, at myself. I put myself in that situation. I let out a scream of frustration.

"Yes!" Anger, enjoying the sounds of my screams. *"Focus that anger on someone, how about your friend? This all started with Rebecca didn't it? All the lies she spread about you, she even tried to come between you and your new friend. How does that REALLY make you feel?"* he continues.

Rebecca appears before me, *"here is your chance for some revenge Angelisa. Attack her now, let you anger lose. Why should you contain it?"* I consider Anger's advice.

Why should I contain myself? She did start all this, instead of her lying we could have helped each other. But she rather put me through the floor. I scream as I stand to my feet. Meeting Rebecca face to face, she stands there staring at me with a blank expression.

"Why, Rebecca?" I push her as I question.

"Why did you turn your back on me?" I push her again.

"Why did you lie?" I shove her. She has no reaction.

"Ignite that rage Angelisa, and we'll let you leave here." Anger tells me.

I scream again as I charge Rebecca to the ground. She doesn't fight me back, she just lays there. As I stand to my feet I watch as she lays emotionless. Why isn't she responding?

I scream again, "Rebecca!" I feel my lips move.

Moments later I hear her voice. "I'm here Angelisa." she says.

I feel soft hands take mines from Ryan's.

"Rebecca?" I ask.

"Yes, I'm here!" she answers. I grip her hands as tight as I can.

"How could you do this to me?" I shout. I feel her trying to pull away from my grip, but I tighten my hold.

"Angel, I'm sorry I—"

"Too late for sorry!" As I tell her, the spiritual version of her remains the same; emotionless. I straddle her between my legs and begin to hit her.

"Only my friends call me Angel, as far as I'm concerned we're no longer friends. You destroyed me with your lies!" I grab her hands tighter pressing into her chest.

"Yes, let that rage take over!" Anger encourages me. I can tell he's enjoying the scene.

"Angelisa, don't give in to this anger." I hear Ryan. I try to look over to where I saw him praying. The wind surrounding us has thicken, making hard to see through, but I can see a figure of him just outside the whirlwind.

"You have to forgive, Angelisa. Let go of your anger." he tells me.

As I look back down to where Rebecca is still laying, I wonder where beating her will get me? She's not even fighting back here, I expected her to have some kind of reaction.

Searching for the real Rebecca outside these winds is useless. I was angry with her for a long time, she was part of my downward spiral. Who I became after my miscarriage was me trying to escape the person she made me out to be. I want to be angry at her, I should be…but I can't. She's only a pawn in this game my enemies are playing. Yes Rebecca spread rumors, but I have made bad decisions myself. I'm mad at myself.

I feel so helpless here. I fear I will never get out. I loosen my grip on her hands. Rebecca vanishes from under me.

"Get angry again!" Anger yells. I'm not sure what he expects me to do, I can barely stand from the pool of my own self-pity.

"LORD!" I shout again toward the heavens.

I shut my eyes, and just let the tears trail down my face.

"Why have you left me Lord?" They all begin to laugh again.

"I repent Lord, I confess my sins unto you. My desires, my anger, please…forgive me! Don't let me go, I need you more than ever." My voice trails off as my suppressed emotions begin to resurface in my mind.

I don't know how long I stay there crying out to God, asking for forgiveness. I've made mistakes in my past, but the one I believe I made recently was, I didn't seek God. He should be in the center of my life, in every decision I make.

My new friends have taught me that we often make decisions on our own and when things go south we blame God. He is a just God and will not keep anger towards us. We're human, and He knows humans make mistakes because our flesh is weak. It's what we do with those mistakes that make us. We're not perfect, and He doesn't expects us to be either, but we need to strive to be. I hear a voice in my mind telling me to get up!

The enemy is a liar! You are stronger than they are because you are the daughter of an almighty God!'

The voice gave me motivation. Suddenly, I have hope. I am the daughter of a king, Jesus Christ saved me when He died on the cross for my sins.

God loves me, He loved His creation so much that He gave His son for us to have eternal life! God is love! God loves me!

Yes I messed up, but my God is just, and He forgives. I will continue to try to live a righteous life. One that God would be proud of, one that my sister can follow in my footsteps. I need to be an example for her. I will stand firm on the word of God, I will not leave room for doubt of His love for me.

I stand to my feet, wiping away the tears from my eyes. I look up to the sky, "Lord!" I raise my hands in surrender. I realized, I have been trying to fight in my own strength. I need to rely on Him, I need to believe that He will show me a way out.

"Forgive me, I come before you now, understanding that you are my strength. You are my rock. I no longer feel alone Lord, for I know you are with me!"

As soon as I make this declaration, I see my armor take its place upon me. My belt wraps around my waist, the breastplate to my chest, and the steel shoes on my feet that gives me peace. The shield of faith latches on to my left arm. I see two new pieces come my way. A helmet of salvation, to protect my mind against the lies of the enemy. And lastly, the sword of the spirit which represents the word of God.

"NO! It cannot be!" Anger shouts.

"It is!" I answer him. "You will no longer play on my weakness, or on my emotions!"

Here I stand in the spiritual realm, ready to counter attack my enemies. I swing my sword slicing Anger on his arm.

"You think, this is over? Let's see how you fight us all!" I turn to face Alex, I wonder why he's still here. I don't move as I stare at him. Something is not right with him.

Alex suddenly becomes two, and each one transforms, one into Fear and the other Guilt. They combined themselves to make me feel fear and guilt at once.

A weapon appears in each of my adversaries hands. Guilt swings a long chain and throws the end with a cuff at me, but I am able to dodge it the first time. He swings it again this time it is able to latch itself on to my wrist. The chain represents a stronghold, but I no longer feel guilt for my past. I can't change what I've done, I can only learn from it.

I can become stronger because of it. He begins to yank on the chain causing me to lose my balance, but I regain control. I pull back the cuff is still on my wrist.

I face Guilt, "I forgive myself." I tell him. The cuff opens and falls off it can no longer stay attached to me because guilt no longer holds me down…I forgave myself.

As soon as I am released from the chain that once bound me, I'm faced with Fear. He stands there staring at me with a stern look. In his hand he bounces an atmospheric ball, he smiles as he prepares himself to throw it my way. The ball takes on a metal form and a laser beams from it. I'm so stunned by this object I froze as it came closer. The laser light aims at my chest, I look down at it and watch as it rises to my forehead. I'm not sure what it supposed to do, I raise my shield and knock it down to the ground.

I look over to Fear again, he throws more of those metal spears my way. The lasers are not on these, they're just hitting me. I block off as many as I can with my shield. They're coming from every angle now, I have to run for cover.

I look back and there is one ball with its laser on. When I turn my gaze to the direction I'm running in I hit my head on a tree branch, it knocked off my helmet. I look behind to find another laser ball aimed at my head. Suddenly I'm frozen in place. The laser is searching for something.

A scene from my mind plays before me, one of my sister. I watch as I see Evie drinking at a party with a cigarette in her hand and a guy kissing on her.

"No!" I shout.

"You see? You still have fears, you can't overcome them all. This is the example you left for your sister." Fear tells me as he walks closer to me.

I watch her as she dances and drinks with a guy. This is not the example I wanted her to follow, this is not the life for her. My sister walks up to me handing me a beer, I reach out a hand to take it but then I realized my sister didn't look like herself. I grab the beer from her hand and toss it. She vanishes. She wasn't real, another game Fear is playing with me. It was a fear I had, but my sister is not me, she's strong…stronger than I am.

The scene vanishes and I see the atmospheric ball hovering in front of me, I hit it with my shield.

I look in Fears direction, "your mind tricks won't work anymore!" I tell him reaching down to grab my helmet and putting it back on my head.

"You can't stop me." I tell him as I adjust my helmet.

"It may have taken some time for me to realize who I am."

"And who might that be?" Fear asks.

"I'm a warrior. I will not stop fighting. Especially to be a better example for my sister!"

He laughs, as Shame makes her way to me. *"A warrior she said?"* Shame joins in Fears amusement.

"Even soldiers fail, you may be a warrior right now…but you may not tomorrow. When you come face to face with your first love. What will you do then? Have your way with him than ask God for forgiveness? How many times do you think He will forgive you?"

A black whip materializes in her hand as she speaks. I watch her as she aims the whip at me. I block it with my shield.

"You think I'm still weak. That's your mistake, I am stronger than you give me credit for!" I respond back to her as I keep dodging her whips.

"You weren't very strong yesterday…were you? I believe it was you that made the move on him, was it not?" she asks.

"I did, but I am not the same person I was yesterday… am I?"

"You were moments ago, I bet I can get you there again. You humans with your emotional roller coasters, always up and down. You can't stay steady for long!" she retorts. She bends down throwing her whip to grab on to my feet trying to knock me down. I jump up and it misses.

"You're not going to get me, I don't feel shame anymore. The past is the past, I can't change it...so why dwell on it?"

Suddenly I have new hope, I feel light, whatever was weighting me down is lifted and I feel free. The atmosphere has shifted, strongholds are loosened and now I can truly see. Not only have I been called, I have been chosen. What I have experienced was not only for me to go through, but also so I can help others who have suffered like I have.

I drop my sword when I see the whip come back toward me, I intend to grab it, to yank it out of her grasp. The whip stings my hand when I reach for it, I couldn't hold it. I lower my shield and try again. With both my hands I'm able to catch it and pull it out of her hands.

"You think you've won?" she asks.

Rocks begin to fly my way. Without my shield, I have no protection, I cover my face with my arms as I try to reach for it.

Of course she hasn't won, she hasn't fought me yet." I hear Anger answer Shame's question.

I duck behind a large tree stump. I peek over the stump and find Shame standing behind Anger.

Anger is controlling the rocks. He's trying to knock me down, I throw myself to the ground so I can retrieve my shield. I crawl to avoid getting hit by the flying rocks, but I must not be doing a good job because I can feel the stings on my arms as they pass me.

I look back over my shoulder to Anger. He's walking with his arms stretched out guiding the rocks my way. He has a smug look, he must think I'm on the ground because I'm hurt, or afraid, he shouldn't under estimate me either.

When Anger comes close enough, I turn on my back, and jump to my feet with my shield and my sword on hand. I bend down low and swing my sword slicing his legs causing him to fall.

I stand over him, "I am not what people think of me." I tell him with a conviction so deep inside.

"The thoughts of others don't control me, I forgive those who wronged me!"

Shame stands not too far from Anger. "As you said before, human emotions are like roller coasters…I may have made a few mistakes in the past few days, but I'm only human. I learn from them, I will not live feeling as if I don't belong where I am right now. I will not feel shame when I walk into the house of God. I will not feel shame when I return to the physical realm and have to face everyone in that room. My past will not determine my future!" I tell her proudly.

She says nothing to me as she stands there with her arms crossed across her chest. Fear and Guilt walk to stand behind her. Anger stands to his feet beside her. They all look at each other and nod. They must have a plan B.

I watch as they close the distance between them, they've combine themselves into one being, in a full armor covering their face. The only thing I can see through their armor is a set of eyes, they look human and angry. This knight of my enemies charges toward me and we begin to fight once again. The knight of this realm matches my every move. I begin to wonder how I will ever be able to beat it.

Blow for blow, sword to sword. It begins to feel like a never ending battle. I take a few steps back and the newly combine knight does the same. If it's matching my every move, I need to trick it. I charge toward it with my sword, the knight does the same, in the last second as I reach the knight I spin clockwise and stab my sword through the knight's left underarm. The knight drops its shield and falls to its knees. I stare at the fallen knight at my feet feeling victorious. I was able to fight off every attack, I feel as if a weight was lifted from me.

I am able to leave the spiritual realm and join everyone else in my living room. I open my eyes, I quickly shield them from the brightness. I see Ryan's worried eyes first.

"Thank God," Ryan says as I try to sit up. I stare at Ryan for a moment before I look at everyone.

"We've been praying here for you!" he tells me.

I glance around the room, I'm happy. I see my old friends, my new ones, my family, and even Brian and Lady. Everyone was able to push aside their feelings to pray for me in my time of need. I'm sure some didn't understand what was happening, but the fact that they were here willing to help in any way they could was a joy for me to see.

I turn my attention back to Ryan, "I know," I tell him. "I heard you, I saw you there, wings and all." I smile at him, and he smiles back.

"Wings?" I hear Val ask.

I hear someone clear their throat, I face everyone else in the room.

"What happened to you?" Logan asks.

"I will answer your question, but before I do," I look at Mario who is still holding Val's hand while everyone had let go.

"Mario, how's Alex doing?" I ask him. He gives me a strange look, just like the others that were there that night.

"Why the heck do you care how he's doing? We want to know about you right now!" Logan jumps in.

"I care Logan, I know you don't understand. But there's something I must do, trust me! Mario, can you call him to come over?" Mario's face doesn't change.

"You're not going to have him jumped, are you?" he asks.

"No, I'm not!" I answer with a short laugh.

"You can't be serious!" Logan jumps in.

He looks to Ryan, "you ok with him coming over here?" he asks Ryan.

"It's her call, I won't let him hurt her." Ryan answers.

"Logan, you'll understand. Please everyone, sit down. I have a lot to say," I wait for everyone to be seated.

"This is not easy for me, but I need to clear up a few things. Rebecca, Brian, may I speak to you in private?" I ask, because what I need to say is not for everyone to hear, but I need to clear up a few things with her father.

"Mom, Dad, can you join us in the kitchen?" they nod.

"Please make yourselves at home, I'll be right back." I tell the others.

As everyone settles in a seat around the kitchen table I begin to speak.

"Rebecca, I can no longer carry this lie for you. I let you talk and put me down, but it has to stop. I don't want to be stuck in the past!" I tell her.

She looks at me, hoping I won't talk about it. But because of these lies, her father and others think of me as a bad influence.

"Brian, I had a boyfriend yes. Logan, we were kids and things moved pretty fast between us, I won't deny it. But Logan has been the only guy I've ever been with. I did not have a relationship with God at the time, therefore I had no conviction.

I was a teenage girl in love, and I did things I thought would please him. The night you saw me, coming from the broom closet…I wasn't there for me. I went there to find Rebecca because I was worried about her when she left the dance. I'm sorry Rebecca, but it's time you clear my name." I let out a breath I didn't know I was holding in.

"Rebecca, is this true?" Brian asks his daughter.

Rebecca begins to cry, "Yes dad, it's true. I was so embarrassed when you caught me, it was easier to blame Angelisa. You already thought ill of her, so what was one more act?" she finally confessed. My mom places her hand on mine.

"I know we haven't seen eye to eye Brian, but I just want you to know…I am not the same person as I was back then. I have truly found God, and I have been changed. And I am sure you know, that just because we are Christians, it does not mean we will not fail. We are only human, and I am still young. I'm bond to make a few more mistakes, but I will tell you that I will always try to live a godly life." I confess.

"I…I'm sorry Angelisa. I shouldn't have judged you, I made mistakes as well. I hope you can forgive me." Brian tells me.

"I have let you down as an elder of the church, as a man of God. I repent. God forgive me, for judging your daughter harshly."

I nod, because I don't want to hold any bitterness toward him or Rebecca. I turn my attention to her.

"Rebecca, I would like for us to be friends again, or at least be civil to one another. We have a lot of history before boys came into our lives," I tell her.

She stands from her seat, makes her way toward me. "I'm so sorry! I was afraid!"

We both hug each other for what seem like hours. We cried on each other's shoulders. When we finally pull away, Brian clears his throat. "I think we should invite Lady to this little meeting. We should clear things up with her as well." Brian instructs.

"We should," I agree. My mom walks out into the living room and returns with Lady.

"Those young people in that living room need to find Jesus," Lady complains.

"You're absolutely right. There are four of them that don't know who Jesus is, and it's my mission to introduce them to Him." I agreed with her.

"Will you be dating them too young lady?" She retorts. I shake my head. But before I can respond, Brian fills her in on what we just spoke about.

"No? Not Rebecca!" she response to Brian. She looks at me as if she wants to tell me something, but thinks twice about it. I still don't feel this new information will make her like me. I just hope she will stop her murmuring. We talk a little more in the kitchen before I excuse myself to go back with my friends.

"Hey guys!" I say as I enter the room. Everyone sitting together talking like they're all friends now. I still can't believe I have Ryan and Logan sitting in my living room right now.

"Mario, did you speak to Alex?" I ask.

"Yeah, he's not sure about coming. He doesn't want to see you." he answers. I nod with a tight lip grin in understanding.

"So all that stuff you tried to teach me back then about backdoors and spirituality is real?" Logan asks. A look of confusion must have crossed my face, "Ryan filled us in." Logan answers my unasked question.

"Yep, it's real. I was trying to teach you about something I knew nothing of. But now I know it's real, I walked through it. Ryan's been helping me with that." I answer him. Logan looks over to Ryan, then back at me, he nods.

I fill in Logan, and the others about my journey. I still don't mention anything about the baby. Only my sister and Ryan know about that, I'm not sure how Logan will deal with that information. Jason managed to turn this get together into a bible class.

Rebecca joined us, and we all fellowshipped together. As the night came to an end, Jason made it a point to invite everyone over tomorrow for more bible fellowship. They agree to come, guess I'll be bringing home three coffee boxes this time.

Everyone makes their way outside, to my surprise Alex is parked in my driveway. He stops walking when he sees Logan, they both lock eyes. Logan was about to go up to him, but Ryan holds him back.

"What are you doing?" he asks Ryan.

"She wanted him to come, remember?" Ryan answers.

"Yeah, well maybe you would feel differently if you would've seen what I did!" Logan replies.

"I feel you, but she wanted him here. We have to respect that." Ryan tells him.

I walk to Alex alone. "Hi," I say. He keeps his head down, and his hands in his front pockets.

"Hey," he tells me.

"About the other night..." he doesn't look at me. He's ashamed.

"Alex, I know you're not a bad guy," I tell him. He looks at me in surprise.

"Angelisa! I hit you! How can you say that?" he asks.

"Do you feel bad about it?"

"Of course I do! I've never hit a girl before. I don't know what came over me?" he answers.

"And I can understand that. I know you had a few drinks, and maybe once again I gave you the wrong impression—"

"No you didn't. I just really liked you. I just couldn't understand why you kept turning me down. But I should have never forced myself like that. I'm so sorry, Angelisa!" He takes a step forward, but quickly moves back as he looks behind me.

When I look over my shoulder I see Ryan holding Logan back.

"Logan is still upset, we use to date." I tell him.

"Is he the reason why you don't want to date now?"

"Yeah, it was a hard break up."

"He must still care about you to come at me the way he did."

"Alex, I wanted you to come here, because I wanted to tell you...I forgive you. I think you should calm down with the drinking, and focus on who you really are." I extend my hand to him to shake.

I would hug him, but I'm afraid of the guys' reaction. He takes my hand and we shake. I walk him over to Mario and Val. I tell them that we're cool and I hold no resentment. Mario and Alex give each other hard pat on the back as they hug the way guys do.

Jason and the others stood behind to make sure things didn't get out of control. As Alex heads out, with Mario and Val, Jason and the others follow. Logan and his cousin are still here, and so is Ryan. I feel bad I still don't even know Logan's cousin's name. I walk over to the three guys sitting on my steps.

"Logan? You never introduce your cousin, he's been through an eventful night at my expense and I have no idea what his name is." I tell him.

"Oh, I'm sorry his name is Carlos, Carlos, this is Angel." Logan finally introduces us.

"Hi, no offense but its Angelisa," I correct Logan. I catch Ryan smiling out of the corner of my eye. He must remember our first conversation about my name, and how I feel about it.

"Nice to meet you, Angelisa!" Carlos tells me.

"Likewise," I respond.

Logan stands up, "we should be heading out," he walks over to me and hugs me.

"We should talk soon," he whispers in my ear before he kisses my cheek.

I just nod as we pull apart. Carlos and Logan walk to their car leaving only Ryan behind. When I turn to face him, he was staring at me.

"What was that about?" he asks.

"He wants to talk that's all," I answer.

"Are you going to get back together?"

I don't say anything right away. I'm not sure what I want right now. But I think a relationship with Logan is not such a good idea at the moment.

"I'm still not into dating right now. I want to be more in tune with God, and I think he would be a distraction." I answer.

"Is that an answer only for him, or will every guy be a distraction?"

"Do you think it's a good idea to be dating anyone right now? Wouldn't it be a distraction?" I ask.

"Depends, you have to be able to balance. You can't let a relationship get in between you and God."

"What is it you're waiting for?" I ask him realizing that he's still single.

"I'm waiting on God. I've dated, but I don't want to just date anyone. I want to find the one God has chosen for me." he turns his face away from me and looks up to the sky.

"Does every Christian do it like that? Is that the way?"

"No, you don't have to. But it's always good to include God. I just decided I rather wait on Him." he looks back at me and smiles.

"Well it's something I will consider. Maybe I can finally start dating soon, we'll see. Thank you by the way."

"For what?"

"For being here for me, praying for me, teaching me. I try to picture how the other night would have ended up if you and your uncle never spoke to me. In my loneliness, I might've dated Alex...even if I didn't like him in that way."

"It was all in God's timing. He knew what He was doing and when to do it. But you're welcome." I almost forgot about my black eye until I smile at Ryan's response. I touch my eye, wipe a single tear that shed.

"Still hurts huh?"

I nod. "I'm ok."

We stay a while discussing the events of the day, and the weekend.

"Ryan, I stabbed the knight, then I was able to leave the spiritual realm. Is it over?" I ask. I assume it is, but I sense I'm still missing something.

"Did you see who was under the helmet?" I think for a moment. It never occurred to me to remove the helmet.

"No, should I have?" I questioned.

"I think you should have been able to see who you were fighting."

"I assumed it was just the four spirits combined, I never really thought to check."

"You said you were only able to see the eyes, and you said they looked human. They were defeated for now. You have to continue to pray. They will try to come back for you." he tells me.

"Then why was I able to leave?"

"Because *this* battle was over."

"I wanted to leave when I got there."

"I know, but it's something you needed to go through. We're always going to be fighting a war, this was just a battle." Ryan answers.

"The thought of having to go back in there to fight again...it was terrifying Ryan." I sign.

"I know, but you're a strong warrior now. I know you can handle whatever comes your way. Don't let your guard down, keep praying and reading the word. Remain strong."

I let what Ryan says sink in. I shouldn't be afraid, I have God on my side.

"Hey," Ryan bumps me to get my attention.

"I'm going to head out. But if you feel you need to call me at whatever time, don't hesitate. I will answer. I'm here for you." he reassures me.

"Thanks Ryan, I hope I can get some sleep tonight." We both stand, Ryan pulls me into his arms.

"Just remember you're a warrior now. Stay strong!" he whispers as he kisses me on the top of my head.

28. Fresh Anointing

After my conversation with Ryan, I kept thinking about who was under that helmet in the spiritual realm. At the time I didn't think it was important but now I'm not so sure.

I thought since I saw when Fear, Guilt, Anger and Shame merged together that it was just them. But after Ryan and I spoke, I remember the set of eyes looking back at me from under the helmet. They were human and familiar, they looked surprised and angry at the same time.

I may not know whose face was under that helmet, but I know who ever or whatever it may have been I am ready for it. I have to deal with my emotional problems, facing the past and forgiving those that wronged me. I also had to ask for forgiveness for the mistakes I've made.

I laid in my bed, tossing and turning. Sleep was far from me, after everything that happened today my mind is racing. I reach for my phone, maybe some music would calm me. Ivy made a playlist for me last week, and I haven't been able to listen to it.

As the first song starts to play, I feel my mood begin to change. It always amazes me how music can adjust your emotions. I keep that in mind, and practice precaution to what I listen to.

I close my eyes to really focus on the words. The beat of the song is soft but catchy. As the lyrics begin, I find myself surrounded by darkness but I'm not afraid. She begins to sing, wanting to see His face. A light flashes before my eyes. She wants to know the love in His heart for her; me.

I want to feel how much He loves me. I feel warmth encircle me. I'm not alone, I can feel the love of God surround me. His love for me is so strong it feels like fire burning in me. The emotions that flow through me overwhelms me; I begin to cry. He loves me so much, no matter what I've done, no matter how far I've fallen, He will always love me.

I fall to my knees as the song keeps playing, still surrounded by darkness. A light flashes with every verse she sings. I feel a presence in front of me. I know someone is standing there.

I open my eyes and stare at the ground in front of me. As the flashing light keeps to the beat of the song, I can see His form. His scarred bare feet on the ground. I realized then, why the love of God felt so strong. My heart is about to explode from this experience.

I reach for His feet and cry uncontrollably as the realization of God's love stands right in front of me; Jesus Christ. I pull myself together after what seemed like hours of baring my soul as I wept before Him. I open my eyes and find Him in the exact same spot, I allow my eyes to travel up the rest of His form. His apparel is just like God's when He had appeared to me before; white pants, white button-down shirt. His hair cascades over his shoulders as He looks down on me. His face is still unclear to me since it's still dark.

"I love you Lord!" I cry out to Him. Tears stream down my face, as I lower my gaze back to His feet.

I want to walk with Him, follow Him where ever He would lead me.

As the light continues to flash, I can see as He extends His hand for me to take. I place my hand in His, He helps me to my feet. I feel as if I'm moving in slow motion as we begin to walk. He leads me down a path I cannot see. But I trust in Him enough to know He will not lead me wrong. I think to myself, I want to see His face. I want to see into His eyes.

I turn my head to look at Him. He stops walking to completely face me. He holds my gaze, as He tightens His hold on my hand. I feel a surge flow through me. He's transferring a fresh anointing to me. I feel it swirl through my body, my spirit, it's in me and all around me.

We walk side by side; He lifts my hand and twirls me as we walk. I laugh because it reminds me of a gesture a parent does to their child as they walk down the street. He brings me into His embrace and I am in awe. I hold on to Him never wanting to let go. I raise my head from His chest to look over His shoulder as I felt some one was watching.

Fear is standing in the distance. I thought I defeated him. He doesn't say or do anything other than just watch as Jesus and I continue to hug one another. In a blink of an eye he's gone. I have a feeling he will return, but he has no hold over me.

Jesus takes my hand and twirls me a few times more before the song comes to an end, then He's gone leaving me in a brighter place.

The next song plays, the singer is talking about being enclosed in a garden. As she continues to sing, I begin to understand the meaning, I am not my own. God is my garden, I should live from the inside out. Her words led me to a garden just as the sun begins to set. I stand there watching the sun, an amazing view. The sun light casts a soft glow, feeling peaceful.

"Hello my daughter," I jump as the voice startled me.

With my hand over my heart I turn around to face the familiar voice.

"Hello Lord." I tell Him lowering my sight, the brightness surrounding Him blinds me.

"You had an interesting night, how do you feel?" He asks.

"Not finished. I thought I would feel complete when I stabbed the knight and he collapsed to the ground. But now as I think back, and after talking to Ryan, I feel there was more for me to do. I'm ready for whatever comes!"

"You will always be fighting. The enemy is not going to leave you alone because you won *one* battle. There are more to come. For each level there's a new devil. Have you heard that phrase before?"

"I think I have, but I never really understood what it meant until now. So you saying, I defeated my enemies for now, but as I reach a new level I will be challenged again?" I ask Him.

"The enemy is always going to find a way to knock you down. He will stop at nothing, he wants to see you fail. I will be honest with you. The closer you get to me, the more your faith in me will be tested. The more I want to give you, the more he will try to make you wave in your relationship with me. He will use anything or anyone as a distraction, you must keep your spiritual eyes and ears open." He answers.

"I thought it will get easier once I completed this battle, but it will never stop will it?"

"It will get easier, the closer you get to me. But you can't give up hope. Your journey is only beginning, I have plans for you. Someday soon you will see what it is. Oh," He smiles. "Get ready!" He says.

"Ready for what exactly?" I asked Him, hoping He will elaborate.

"And ruin the surprise?" He laughs.

"You need to loosen up a little, trust yourself. Don't be afraid to let people in." He advices me.

My expression must show my confusion, He continues.

"Angelisa, I need you to try to look through my eyes. See things the way I would. Always keep your spiritual eyes open. No matter what comes next, know I am always with you." I feel the warmness of His embrace envelop me and when I open my eyes, its morning.

I must have fallen asleep, but God did speak to me. What did He mean?

Am I uptight? What did He mean by loosening up? I honestly thought I was letting people in. I forgave Rebecca and Alex. I don't mind being friends with them after everything that has happened. I'm willing to try to be friends with Logan, if only we could leave our past in the past.

I have Val. Now Ivy and Marissa, Jason and Mike, we're all friends. And of course Ryan, he's one of my closest friends right now. My phone buzzes, I swipe my phone on and see a message from Ryan.

Ryan: *"Hey, you up?"*
Me: *"Just opened my eyes, what's up?"*
Ryan: *"I had an idea about the word I'm supposed to bring to your church next week. Can we meet up later?"*

Before I answer, I wonder what his idea may be and if it involves me?
Me: *"I'm working today, can you pass by?"*
Ryan: *"Ok, I'll be there to pick you up."*
Me: *"See you then!"*

I start to get ready for work, before I walk out my bedroom, I thank God for this fresh start and new beginnings. For the first time in a long time I finally feel ready to face whatever comes my way.

I glance over to where my mirror is and I see a quick flash of myself fully armed. Although I cannot see it, I know I am wearing the armor of God all the time. I must always be ready because I never know when the enemy will attack. I smile at my reflection and head to work.

When I walk into Caffeine, I don't see it as I once use to. I no longer see grumpy morning people waiting for their coffee. All I see now are people in need of Jesus Christ. I vow, whenever an opportunity presents itself, I will talk about Jesus. I shouldn't keep my salvation to myself. I want everyone to be able to encounter Jesus.

As people line up to make their order, I smile at each costumer. I have such a peaceful joy inside me I can't contain it. The customers smile back, and I'm happy.

"Medium coffee, black." A familiar voice orders. I raise my head from the register to see Ryan smiling back at me.

"You look happy today!" He complimented.

"It's a blessed day Ryan!" I smile. "You're early, I have another hour left until my shift is over." I tell him.

"That's ok, I brought my laptop to keep me company until you're ready." he winks. I hand him his coffee; he walks to his usual table. He pulls out his laptop from his backpack, a notebook and a bible.

"How did you get that guy to speak to you?" My coworker Sarah ask as she walks up to me.

"I don't know, we just did. We're friends." I answer.

"Really? Elizabeth and I have been trying to talk to him but unless it's about ordering his coffee, he doesn't say anything other than *'have a blessed day!'* Maybe he might say more than yes please, or no thank you, since you two talk!" I consider her statement, I can certainly understand her frustration.

It's how I felt before Ryan and I became friends. I smile as I remember that day. It feels so long ago, but it's been almost two months. Amazing how much my life has improved in a short amount of time.

"He's friendly, it's just when he's studying something he doesn't like to lose focus."

"Makes sense, I guess." She shrugs.

"So are you two just friends...or are you more?" She grins.

I know she's hoping I say *'no, we're just friends,'* but acting like she knows there's more to us.

I smile, because we are just friends. But I wouldn't mind if he would want to be more—I think.

"Just friends!" As far as I know he's waiting on God. I'm not even sure how that works exactly. I've heard a few women in my church talk about waiting on God, and they've been waiting for years. I make a mental note to ask Ryan about how that process works.

"Well if you don't mind, I would like to visit his table to ask him if he needs a refill!" She chirped.

"Knock yourself out, I'm taking a bathroom break." I answer her.

She gets all giddy as she heads over to Ryan's table. I'm curious to witness what happens but I don't. I go into the back and check my texts on my phone.

"Hey," Elizabeth says as she comes in.

"Hey, you need me upfront?" She smiles as she shakes her head.

"No, Sarah said you can pack up, she'll cover the remainder of your shift."

"My shift is almost over, I don't mind finishing up." I'm confused.

"Just get your stuff. Apparently you have something important to do and you should go and get started. Take advantage, Sarah doesn't usually cover for people. I would jump at the opportunity."

I begin to gather my things, still confused as to why my coworkers insists on me leaving minutes before my shift is over. I walk back out to the front and find Sarah still talking to Ryan, I guess things went well. I hesitate walking over to him, a hint of jealously I suppose. We're only friends, I doubt he'll want anything more...I hope I'm wrong. I still have Logan to deal with and Ryan knows it.

Relationships should be the last thing on my mind right now. Besides, I think when God presents Ryan His chosen for him...it will be someone just as spiritual as him. He should have someone to be able to help him not someone he may feel he always needs to help. I'm not on Ryan's level. I shake off the thought, it saddens me.

Ryan notices me, he starts to pack up his things and stands. Sarah takes a step back from his table, smiling at him.

She faces me, "bye Angelisa, see you tomorrow!" I wave good bye. I wonder what they spoke about.

Ryan makes his way to me, "ready to go?" I look up to him. I want to ask him about Sarah, but I decide against it.

We walk outside to his bike, Ryan holds out his keys to me.

"What?" I ask.

"I think, you should drive!" He tells me dangling his keys for me to take.

"I don't know how to ride a motorcycle!" I shake my head.

"You shouldn't be afraid to try something new!" Trying something new, taking a leap of faith. What was it God told me, *loosen up?*

I take his keys and hop on his bike; he explains the brakes and how to start it. He hops on the back, placing his hands on my waist. I try to ignore the sparks I feel when he does. I start the bike, and I take off slowly at first. I want to make sure I get a handle on it before I go faster. Ryan encourages me, and I speed up. I don't go as fast as Ryan does when he rides it, but it's pretty fast...at least for me.

We make it to my house in one piece, and I'm relieved.

"How was it?" He asks me as he hops off removing his helmet.

"What a rush!" I beamed. "Why did you want me to drive it?"

"It's always good to try new things!" He smiles, "and the idea I had was that you will help me give that word in your church next week!"

"WHAT?" I exclaimed. "Ryan, I don't think I'm ready for that!" Why would he think I can do that?

"Did you think you couldn't ride my bike?" He asked.

"I did think that actually!"

"And yet, you did! So why do you think you can't give a word? I think that you're more than ready. And you won't be doing it alone. I will start it off and I will be right there with you. Think about it Angelisa!" He encouraged. I consider his request.

It would be different, and a way to finally get everything out in the open. *New beginnings,* I remember what I thank God for this morning. This really will be a new beginning. It's time I step out of my comfort zone.

"Fine, on two conditions," I tell him. He looks intrigued, he crosses his arms over his chest. "Shoot!"

"One, you have to help me prepare."

"Done! Second?"

"You start calling me Angel!"

"Have I reached *friend status* with you Angelisa?" He laughs.

"Of course you have, you could've called me Angel a long time ago Ryan."

"Good to know, but I think I'll stick with Angelisa…at least for now." he winks.

"Well, I thought I tell you…I don't mind you calling me Angel." I smile.

Ryan and I pray for a while before we jump into studying the word. He pulls out his bible and a notepad. I do the same. He reads a verse and I immediately understand what it means and how to break it down. I can't help but notice this verse is perfect for what I've been through. As Ryan and I end our studying for the day, my doorbell rings. Ryan and I both look at each other. I walk over to the door and open it; Logan.

"Hey, I'm here for that bible class your friend Jason told me about yesterday!" he says.

I completely forgot about our bible study today. I nod and invite him in.

"Everyone else should be getting here soon." I tell him.

Logan walks up to Ryan to greet him. I wonder if Ryan remembered about tonight.

Shortly after everyone else shows up, even Rebecca. She looks unsure at first, but once I invite her in and give her a quick hug I see her ease up. Ryan smiles at the both of us. Jason takes over the lesson today. I look around, I'm glad to see everyone here. Val and Mario came too. I'm happy that my experience has brought us all together. Peace comes after the storm.

29. The Past is in the Past

It's Friday, I feel nervous. Tonight is the night Ryan will be preaching in my church, and wants me to join him. He thinks I should speak of what I've experienced these past few weeks. I've never been on the altar before. Ryan assures me that everything will be fine. He had requested that we fast together this morning. He said we should be in one accord spiritually since we would be ministering together.

Fasting is just what I needed, weakening my flesh so that my spirit may be strong. It was a beautiful experience when we prayed together this morning on the phone before I had to go to work.

Ryan led us into prayer and then I prayed after him. I was always afraid to let him hear me pray, I felt intimidated by him. I know I shouldn't feel that way, but to be around someone so anointed can have that impact on you, especially if you're not sure of yourself.

I know who I am now, but I also have my moments of doubt, I just don't let it fester too long. If I give root to my doubts, I would never do what I should. Of course I discuss my doubts with Ryan, and he said I should cancel the spirit of doubt in the name of Jesus every time.

I had wondered how I would be able to work and still pray at the same time. Ryan told me, that we pray without ceasing. Keeping our spirits connected to God all times, allowing the Holy Spirit to lead. I'm always talking to God now, and He talks back to me in many different ways.

When I got home, I began to pray to end my fast. My spirit was led to my favorite garden. The smells of flowers surrounded me, and the warmness embraced me. I felt as if God was hugging me. I smile at the thought.

I praise His name and I see a bright light encircle me; the Holy Spirit. His presence is all around me, His peace. Suddenly, an angel descends in front of me, I smile. It's not an angel, only Ryan. It's how I see him, as my spiritual guarding angel. Now I finally understand why he has wings. God allows us to see things in ways our minds would understand it. Although Ryan said he loved wings as well, may be its how he sees himself.

In the distance behind Ryan something catches my eye. A cluster of trees I've never noticed before now. They are so tall, they look like redwood trees. I'm drawn to them, something about them seems familiar, like I've seen them before.

"Angelisa, what is it?" Ryan ask me.

"I feel I've been here before, something about those trees." I answer.

"It reminds me of something, I'm just not sure what it is or where I've seen them," his eyebrows furrowed.

"It's probably nothing." he says.

"I guess."

"Are you ready for tonight?" Ryan asks.

"Not really, but I'll manage. Maybe once I'm there it will fade." I answer.

"I think you will be just fine." he bumps me. I shrug.

"Come on let's end this fast." He takes both my hands and begins to pray.

"Heavenly father we come before you in one accord as we're about to end this fast. I pray that we will not leave your presence, that our spiritual eyes and ears remain open. We ask Lord that you may soften the hearts of those who have harden them. Prepare their way tonight so that the word you gave us may penetrate their hearts and minds. Give us the courage we need to carry on your message, that we may not be led by our emotions but by your spirit Lord God. In Jesus name we pray, Amen!"

Once Amen was said, I'm back. I head down to the kitchen to make a sandwich. Then I head back to my room to go over my notes. I've never preached before, never even taught a lesson. I just hope I don't choke.

***

My family and I drive to the church. My heart is pounding so hard in my chest, I fear it may bust through. When we arrive at church, I'm surprise to see Val, Mario and Logan here. When I reach them they greet me with hugs and kisses.

"What are you guys doing here?" I asked pleased to see them.

"Ryan told us we should be here to support you." Val answers with a grin.

"So what are we supporting exactly?"

I lean in to whisper in her ear, *"It's a surprise!"*

She laughs and nods her head. I lead them inside and we all sit together.

A few minutes after, Jason, Ivy, Mike and Marissa take the seats behind us. But Ryan is not with them.

"Where's Ryan?" I ask Jason.

"He should be here soon." he replied.

My sister starts to sing with the choir behind her. Everyone stands to their feet joining in the worship. I look over to where Rebecca is, she's standing with her father. She looks back at me and waves. Things with us have gotten better, but it's still not as it used to be. Someone taps me on the shoulder, I turn my attention behind me.

"Ryan! You're late! I'm nervous enough as it is!" I scoff.

He laughs, "Sorry, I got caught up!" I smile at him.

After the worship, Rebecca does a pantomime with another girl to a Spanish worship song. Once they're done my sister grabs the microphone to sing a solo. Tonight is youth night, every youth that wants to participate has a part. A few more youth go on after Evie, then Pastor Edward takes the microphone.

"God bless everyone tonight!" he says as he surveyed the congregation.

"I am very happy to see so many new faces here tonight. We have visitors from Revival Church with us. Always nice to see you, you're all welcomed. Would anyone of you like to say a few words before we present the preacher of the night?" Pastor Edward asks.

I look over my shoulder to see if any volunteer. Jason stands and walks up to meet Pastor Edward.

"Bless you pastor, thank you for this opportunity!" he tells him.

Jason looks over the crowd. "It's very nice to be here. I've seen motivated youth up on this altar tonight. Evie," He looks over to where she's sitting. "That was a beautiful song." He addresses the rest of the congregation. "My name is Jason Gomez, I'm one of the youth leaders at Revival Church, along with my girlfriend Ivy! Stand up Ivy so everyone can see you!" he grins. Ivy stands and waves her hand then takes her seat again.

"Ivy is God's gift to me, I love you babe!"

"Aww!" I hear all the girls say. I look back at Ivy, *"that is so sweet!"* I whisper.

"I know!" She says never taking her eyes off Jason. She blows him a kiss.

"So, I just want to tell the youth here, trusting in God is not an easy thing to do, but it's worth it. God has blessed me with many more things, he's given me a spiritual family, and those guys back there…Ryan, Mike and Marissa. The five of us always help each other in whatever we can, we pray for one another. We're a team, and we've recently added Angelisa to our family, along with her friends.

Take a look at the person next to you…whether you're blood related or not, that person next to you is your brother or sister in Christ. You need to help each other. You never know what they may go through, you should always keep them in your prayers. We are a family, no matter if we're from different churches, we are one in the body of Christ. Angelisa," he stares in my direction.

"You've been chosen. You're special, as well as all of you." He looks over to the pastor now.

"I don't want to take too much of your time, Pastor." Jason concludes.

"Thank you Jason," Pastor Edward takes the microphone from Jason.

"I've actually always known Angelisa was special. I tell her all the time, isn't that right Angelisa?" he looks over at me, and so does everyone else.

I just nod. I don't like being put on the spot, but soon I will be up there so I better get over it.

"Without any further do, I would like to ask our preacher of the night to please come up here. Brothers and sisters in Christ, please welcome Ryan Rivera!" Everyone begins to clap as Ryan makes his way up to Pastor Edward.

"Thank you Pastor for the invitation. Thank you everyone, but let's give God the praise!" Everyone claps louder.

Ryan didn't discuss with me how I would be joining him. My heart begins to beat nervously.

"Pastor Edward invited me to preach a few weeks ago, I accepted obviously." Ryan jokes, everyone laughs.

"Recently God had entrusted me with a task. As my spiritual brother, and leader Jason said: *'trusting in God is not an easy thing.'* I also made a request to God not so long ago, I'm still waiting on that. But God gave me a mission in the meantime. Still waiting on God, I must continue His work." Ryan stops and turns to address Pastor Edward.

"I have a little surprise for you Pastor," then he looks back at the congregation.

"And for all of you…the word I have to give to you today will be given partly by me, and partly…" he pauses for dramatic affect I assume.

The anticipation is nerve-wrecking.

"By Angelisa Cruz! Angel will you come up here?" Sure, now he calls me Angel.

I feel as if all the air in my lungs have escape me. I feel my cheeks heat up, I hope it doesn't show. I stand and walk up to meet Ryan. I hear some people murmur as I pass, others clap. When I meet Ryan, his smile widens.

"I met Angelisa about two months ago." He begins, he doesn't take his eyes away from me. He's making me feel more nervous.

"God placed her in my path, He showed me just how special she is." My cheeks feel so hot, I hope it's not noticeable. His smile widens, so I assume it shows.

"We have spent a lot of time together, discussing the bible, praying. She even beat me at the skating rink, she can skate very well." he laughs.

"Anyway, Angelisa has the first part of the word tonight!" He hands me the microphone, as I grab it, I face everyone.

There are a lot of people here tonight, I hadn't noticed how full this church is right now. Ryan senses my nervousness and leans in, *"just start with the scripture,"* he whispers. *"You got this!"*

I nod.

"Hi, I'm a little nervous, please bear with me." I admit.

"If you would open your bibles to Isaiah 43:2." I give them a minute to look up the verse.

"Can we all stand as we read the word of God?" I watch as everyone does.

"*When you pass through the waters, I will be with you; and when you pass through the rivers, they will not sweep over you. When you walk through the fire, you will not be burned; the flames will not set you ablaze.'* Amen.

This verse has touched me, I have gone through a series of tests recently. I have come to realize that I wasn't alone although I felt I was.

Most of you have heard some things about me. I must assure you, they're not all true. I grew up in this church, always hearing *'you're special, God has a plan,'* I never truly understood that until recently.

I may have grown up in this church, I may have learned a few things, but one thing I never had was a relationship with God." Feeling a little bit more comfortable I stand up straighter.

"See, it's important for us as Christians to have a relationship with God. Coming to church, working in a ministry doesn't necessarily mean you are saved. It doesn't mean you have a golden ticket to heaven. I've learned in the past couple of months that there truly is a spiritual war. And I also learned that God wants a relationship with us in church as well as outside.

This is not easy for me, to stand up here and tell you what I'm about to say. Although the rumors were not true, they affected me in a way that it made me give up.

For the past two years until recently, I was dead inside. I felt abandoned by many of you. I needed help, but most of you judged me. I felt I had nowhere to turn. I'm not angry, nor am I judging you. The past is in the past. But in order to explain to you why this verse is so important, I need you to understand where I was.

I felt no one here would have been able to help me, so I raised up walls around myself. After I broke up with my boyfriend, I felt alone, I had no friends. Once I started college I slipped more into the world of parties and drinking. And one day, not even that filled the void I felt, I had become completely numb. I had a dream, I saw myself dressed as a soldier fighting a giant creature..." I trail off.

I look at Ryan, suddenly I remember why those trees looked so familiar earlier. It was from my dream. I shake it off, I can't speak of that right now.

"I killed the creature then I woke up. That night I felt the need to pray, I had no idea if God would even hear me. Who was I after all…a sinner?

That was the first time I had prayed in years, in that moment I had open the door to my heart without even realizing. Since that night God had been giving me dreams and visions. I had no idea what they meant, but I knew it had something to do with me.

That week, I met Ryan briefly. It wasn't until he showed up here with his uncle, that my life completely changed, and I began to see that God loved me no matter who I had become. This guy right here," I say pointing at Ryan who is still standing next to me.

"He helped me become who I am today. I have encounter God. He told me I needed to have a relationship with Him. Ryan showed me how to do that, he showed me how to pray, how to study the word. During that time I was being attacked by the enemy. He was angry because I was no longer on his team. It was not an easy process, but I was able to finally close the back door.

I never knew what that meant, I had to learn to forgive myself and allow God to cleanse my soul. I have faced my guilt, and overcame! I have faced my fears and I overcame! I have faced shame, and guess what, I overcame! I also had to face something I didn't realize I was harboring; anger. I had so much anger buried deep down inside, it wouldn't allow me to move on.

Then I noticed I had to forgive. I may have been wronged by many, but I had to also forgive. Once I did that, I felt as if I was completely broken, and I was able to allow the love of God to heal me.

God was always with me, He allowed me to go through the things I went through so that I can be broken. But He never left me, I just couldn't see Him because I was blinded by my own emotions. I stand here today, a new person! I have been transformed, and I now know what it's like to have a personal relationship with God. And let me tell you, it's an amazing feeling to always walk with the Father.

Now I pray and I'm led into the spiritual realm and I feel His presence all around me. I won't tell you that I'm perfect, I'm sure I'll make mistakes, but we don't have to be perfect. We just have to trust in God.

King David wasn't perfect, he made many mistakes. But yet we know him as a man after God's own heart. He loved God, and asked for forgiveness when he made errors.

Another thing," I turn to face Ryan, who is still standing beside me.

"Sorry, I know I'm talking a lot now," I tell him. He gestures for me to continue. I face the congregation again.

"What Jason said earlier about we all being family, it's important in your walk with Christ. You need to be there for your brothers and sisters in case they fall.

I recently had a spiritual attack, and my friends from Revival Church, and my other friends where there for me. Also, Brian, Rebecca, Lady, and my family as well. They were all doing spiritual warfare for me while I was under attack. You may never know what attacks your sisters and brothers are under. Don't judge, just pray!" I hand the Microphone back over to Ryan. I'm about to walk off the altar when Ryan grabs my arm.

"Hold on," he whispers.

"What Angel has gone through was pretty hard. There were times she wanted to give up. The enemy tormented her, but she realized who she was in Christ. It's important that you know who you are in Christ." He faces me.

"Angel, I was never meant to preach tonight. This was you, I was just supposed to help you get here," he smiles.

He looks over to Pastor Edward, "sorry Pastor, but you know when God speaks, we must obey," he says.

I smile at Pastor Edward because he doesn't look disappointed, he looks pleased.

"Before we close…" Ryan addresses the crowd.

"Is there anyone here today that feels they need to reconcile with Jesus Christ tonight? Maybe you lost your way, or you're not as close to God as you should be, please come up so I can pray for you," he pleads.

A few people come up, but not the new faces, not my friends. I lean in to whisper to Ryan, he smiles and hands me the microphone.

"You know what to do." He tells me.

I take the microphone, "If you're here for the first time, or you just haven't accepted Jesus Christ as your Lord and savior and would like to…please come up. I will show you how to open your heart to Christ."

My friends stand, walk up to where I am, along with a few others. I tell them to repeat the prayer of salvation with me.

"Lord God, I come before you asking for your forgiveness, recognizing that I am a sinner. I confess with my mouth and believe in my heart that Jesus is Lord. I declare that by the blood of Jesus I am saved and forgiven. I invite you in to my heart and my life. I ask that your Holy Spirit may guide me, in the name of Jesus I pray, Amen!"

I look at them all, "and now you are saved." I glance around for the 'closing back doors' team.

"Closing back doors, we have seven new souls!" The team comes up and leads them to the back room to explain the process to the new souls.

I look over at Ryan, he and the others from Revival Church are praying for the youth that came up to reconcile their relationship with God. As everyone has been prayed for, Ryan calls up Pastor Edward.

As he walks up, Ryan and I start to head back to our seat.

"Hold on there you two." Pastor Edward calls.

"Angelisa, I am so proud of you!" He embraces me in a fatherly hug.

I begin to shed tears as so much emotions flows through me. I feel accomplished, even though I know my war isn't over. I will face many more battles, but I will be ready.

"Ryan, thank you! You have helped develop this girl. I always knew she would one day preach on this altar, and I am just over joyed!" He grins.

He takes Ryan into a hug as well.

30. God's Chosen

Since I had preached in my church last week, Pastor Edward thought I was ready to be active in the church. He wanted me to be part of 'Closing Back Doors' again. He said I had lived the experience and believed I was more than ready to help new souls learn who Jesus is. He met Jessenia, apparently she spoke highly about me to him and suggested I would make a good leader. Of course, me being me, I doubted I was ready. But Ryan told me I would never know unless I tried.

I decided to accept the Pastor's offer on the condition that he will check in on me. I didn't want to get lost in working in a ministry. He told me even leader's need learning, and he was putting a class together that was just for leaders. Just because you're a leader doesn't mean you can't be taught new things, and sometimes you just need to be reminded that leaders are just people that can fall as well as any new believer.

Being a Christian doesn't mean you're over all the temptation, it just means you open your heart to Christ. Your eyes would be open, and you would see things maybe others can't. It's like a veil is lifted from your eyes and you see all the wonders of the creator, along with all the evil. You'll see the need, and the lost, the pain and hurt, and the blessings. Most of all, the presence of the Holy Spirit all around you as a guide for your life.

On my way back to college to start my third year, I wondered if there was a Christian club. If not I thought maybe I should start one.

"What you're thinking about Angel?" Val asks me. I didn't realize I was staring at her glove compartment.

"Nothing…well I was thinking if there wasn't a Christian club on campus that maybe I would start one, what you think?" She takes a moment to answer.

Val was assign to me after she confessed Christ. My pastor thought because we already have a relationship it would be better for the both of us. He had also decided that girls should work with girls, and the guys with the guys. That way, what happened with me would be less likely to happen again. And also after souls were consolidated, he wanted a full report. He wants to make sure every leader and new believer are on the same page.

"I think it would be a good idea Angel. But you have to make it appeal to their interest. Parties are so enticing. You need to be able to draw them in," she answers.

"Oh, of course, I have you!" I winked.

"I…you'll always have me Angel!" She tells me with a shy smile. "I promise Angel, I'm by your side through thick and thin. You're more than a friend to me, you're like the sister I never had," her tears begin to well as she speaks these words. And so do mine,

"I love you Angel, more than you know!" I reach over and hug her, "I love you too Val. Thanks for always being there for me!" She laughs.

"Always! Now, let's get out of this car and start our new journey!"

We both laugh as we get out of the car and head to our separate classes.

As I take a seat in my first class of the day, Alex takes the seat next to me.

"Hey, I'm Alex nice to meet you!" He holds out his hand for me to shake. I look at him and question if he's lost his mind.

"Hi?" I say as I place my hand in his, I decided to see where he's going with this.

"Sorry, I just thought maybe we should have a fresh start. I'm willing to try being your friend this time and nothing more, if you'll let me. I realized I was a jerk and I apologize for what I've done to you. That wasn't me and I never want to be that guy again. Would you allow me a fresh start to show you who I really am?"

Everyone deserves a second chance, "ok Alex...that was an interesting introduction." I laugh.

"We can start over. But just to be clear, it's only my friendship you will receive. I'm not interested in anything more." I tell him.

He smiles, "just friends, I promise." He settles into his seat a little more relaxed.

"Besides I think you have your hands full with your ex from the party, and that other guy from my...other party..." he trails off.

"Seems you always had someone watching over you. I can tell those two guys care for you deeply. You always had someone there to protect you from... me." He tells me shifting his gaze to his books.

"I guess I did. But you're ok now, right? I don't need to be protected from you anymore, right?"

"Nope, I'm good, I promise." he replies.

"Good, so how have you been?"

"Not so great, I had to reevaluate myself. That guy I was to you is not who I am, somehow I lost my true self. I let my popularity get to my head. But Mario had been talking to me about God and I'm feeling better."

I'm kind of surprise Mario has been introducing God to Alex, I'm glad.

"That's great Alex, maybe you will join us in church?" I ask hoping he would accept.

"Well, is your ex going to your church?"

"He went back to school."

"I'm not ready to deal with him yet, but I wouldn't mind." he laughs.

"You're safe, Logan has accepted Jesus Christ, and besides he's away in college right now!" I laugh.

The professor walks in, our class has begun. I'm happy that Alex has decided to change his ways. I really do see God at work. If I hadn't gone through what I did, Val, Mario, Logan and even Alex might've not have found God. God always has a plan, He never gives more than what we can handle. The hardest part is learning to trust in Him.

***

After I finished my classes for the day, Val and I head over to the diner. Val request a table for two, but then I see Jason, Ivy and Mike. Jason spots us and waves us over. Val and I join them.

"Hey guys!" I say greeting them.

"How was class today?" Jason asks. Before I can speak, Val jumps in to tell them my plans of a Christian club.

"Wow, that's great!" Ivy tells me.

"I think so too!" I hear a voice from behind me; Ryan. He winks at me with a smile on his face.

"Hey Ryan! Eavesdropping?"

He laughs. "Val was kind of loud!" I look over at Val.

"You really were kind of loud." I tell her, and she laughs.

Ryan joins us, I go on to tell them about what Alex told me earlier. Val was more than happy to hear he would try to make it to church. She and Alex were friends before I came along. I know she's glad to have her friend back. Maybe on different terms this time.

"Well maybe I can help him, introduce him to the life of a Christian, a life with God," Mike jumps in. I nod.

"That would be nice, I'll let him know." I answer. Once Alex sees how cool these guys are, it might help him be more receptive.

"So what's the plan tonight?" I ask. Everyone turns their attention to me.

"What?" They all laugh.

"Well," Jason begins to answer me.

"Maybe we should go down to the beach, have a barn fire, share a word, and pray. It would be the perfect setting." I can just picture it. It will be very spiritual.

"Yeah, Val invite Mario and Angelisa invite that Rebecca girl. I'll tell Marissa. This is a great idea!" She leans into Jason and kisses him on the cheek.

I thought it was sweet. I watch them together, they seem so perfect for each other.

"You ok?" Ryan whispers in my ear. I jump in surprise. He laughs, "Sorry I didn't mean to scare you. You looked lost in thought," he says. I look over at him.

"It's nothing." I tell him. What was I going to say? That I missed being in love? I do sometimes. But I'm not ready, I don't know if I'll ever be.

"You know you can talk to me about anything, right?" He asks. I nod. But I can't talk to him about this, not yet anyway.

"So Angel, what you want to do for your birthday this year?" Val asks me. Once again turning everyone's attention to me. I look at all of them.

"I don't think I want to do anything Val," I answer.

"Are you joking?" Ivy asks.

"You have to celebrate, how old will you be?"

I face her way, "Twenty. But I don't really want to celebrate. Parties scare me, I don't know if I can handle it right now." I answer.

"There are other ways to celebrate, and it's about the people you invite. Your party, your rules." Ryan jumps in.

"Exactly!" Ivy cuts in again.

"This is so exciting Angelisa, you have to believe in yourself. You have overcome a lot, it's time you trust yourself." Ivy reaches over the table and grabs my hand. She looks in to my eyes expecting an answer.

"I'll think about it!" I tell her. She giggles in excitement.

"I'll plan something for you. You trust me don't you?" Ryan asks.

I turn my attention to him. Searching his eyes for a moment before I answer.

"Of course I trust you!" His lips curl into a smile. There's that smile, the one he gave me when we first met.

I hear Mike clear his throat. I realized Ryan and I have been staring at each other longer than we should have. What is it about him that makes me feel this way? We break eye contact; I feel my cheeks begin to heat up. Val has a grin on her face.

"So," Jason tries to break the silence.

"I think we should start going. Let's meet at the beach around eight o clock. The beach gets cold at night, bring a sweater or a blanket. Ivy and I will get what we need. Ryan you know the spot we like to go, have the others follow you!" He says. Ryan nods.

We all head out to the parking lot. Ivy and Mike climb into Jason's car.

"Hey, I'm going over to Mario's to let him know about tonight." She tells me once we reach her car.

"I'll give you a ride Angel, if you want?" Ryan asked. He parked his bike right next to Val's car.

"Yeah Angel, you should go with Ryan. I'll meet you at your house by 7:30pm and follow you guys to the beach!" she smiles.

Ryan is standing behind me, for some reason I'm afraid to turn and face him after Val encourages me to go with him. I stare at her car as she drives off. I turn around.

"I guess I need a ride," he smiles handing me my helmet. I say *my* because he has a spare helmet on his bike since he's been driving me around. At least I assume it's mine.

When we arrive at my house, I hop off, so does Ryan. I thought he might want to go home to get a few things for the beach. But he walks me to the door.

"Are you ok Angel? You seem…distant." He tells me.

"I'm fine." I answer.

"Do you want me to go? I can pick you up later!"

"No, you don't have to go!" I answer quickly. He smiles looking relieved.

"You want to talk about it?"

"Talk about what?" I ask

"About whatever is on your mind. You seem distracted."

"I'm not, I'm fine." I tell him trying to convince myself.

I've always felt drawn to Ryan, but for some reason today at the diner, I felt something different. I think I do like him. But I can't allow myself to fall for him. He's waiting on God, the first reason, and second I may not be ready for a relationship. I can't allow myself to be distracted.

"Angel, I know something's bothering you. If you don't want to talk to me about it, that's fine. But don't tell me that you are fine."

"Have you done a barn fire at the beach before?" I ask him trying to get him to drop the subject. Sensing my intention, he decided to go with it. He puts his hands in his pockets, breathes in.

"No, this would be our first." he answered.

"Well then, it will be a first for all of us. Something maybe to start for others to follow!"

"Something like that. It's a good idea to show people that God isn't contained in four walls. We can praise Him anywhere. On the beach we would be free, I think it's going to be beautiful." He answers looking up to the sky.

I watch him, studying him. What exactly did he mean when he said he's waiting on God?

"What are you thinking about?" He looks back at me.

"Nothing."

"I should go, I'll pick you up later." he begins to walk away.

I want so much to reach out and grab his hand, tell him to stay. But I can't do that. I don't know what that look meant in the diner. But I can't allow this to distract me, and I won't be one to distract him. How I may be feeling for him may just be one sided. I can't have my heart broken again. So I let him go. I'll see him later anyway. Who am I to get in the way of what God has for him?

I go to my room, I decide to take a nap.

"Thank you Lord, for this day," is the last thing I say before I fall asleep.

I find myself climbing stairs in the middle of ruins. Its dark, only the moon to light my path. I see a creature, it's large. I look down at my clothing, I have my armor on, but no sword. When I reach closer to where the creature is floating, I hear a voice say, *'we're not done with you.'* I jump up in my bed.

I knew I wasn't finished. But does that mean, I'm still battling my same fears? It can't be, I overcame them. Someone rings the bell.

"Angel!" Evie yells.

"Your friends are here!" I grab my throw blanket from my bed and head down.

"Thanks Evie," I kiss her on the top of her head.

Val is at my door, Rebecca and Mario by her car. Ryan is on his bike. I close the door behind me. I don't know whether I should go in Val's car or ride with Ryan. Considering how Ryan and I left things earlier I consider going with Val. I stand between both Val's car and Ryan's bike. Ryan hands me my helmet, and I take it. I give Val my blanket.

When we reach the beach, the sun is just beginning to set. Jason and the others were there already standing side by side. Each of them holding hands. We join them, holding hands as well.

Ryan takes mine in his, I can't help the electricity that flowed through me as our hands touched. I felt complete as if my hand belonged there, in his. I quickly shake off the thought. If my dream was true, I'm not finished fighting.

We stand there all joined by our hands watching the sun set. A new beginning, a new chapter is about to begin, and I am ready to embrace it as God's chosen.

And we know that God causes all things to work together for good to those who love God, to those who are called according to His purpose.
Roman 8:28

***

Want to know what happens next?
Book two coming soon

Epilogue:

The Enemy

As Angelisa fellowships with her new friends, laughing and praying. The enemy is watching, observing. He decided to watch her up close, so he disguises himself as a human man. Standing near the beach. The Holy Spirit stands next to him.

"You lost, devil...go home." the Holy Spirit tells him. The devil doesn't say anything at first, he watches her more intently.

"I have another plan, one she might not be able to win. I will have her in my domain." he answers calmly.

He turns to face the Holy Spirit, "she may have won this battle, she can conquer in the supernatural, but will she still believe it's worth it if she truly loses everything in the physical? I will attack her physical world, let's see how she would handle it then." the devil tells the Holy Spirit.

"I assure you devil, she is a warrior of God, and you cannot touch her. She has me to fight in her corner!"

The devil looks back at Angelisa, then back to the Holy Spirit, "I know I cannot touch her, but I will *rattle* her world. Let's see what will unfold!" he vanishes.

Epilogue:

Ryan

Angel wanted something simple to do for her twentieth birthday. I wanted to throw her a party, one that she wouldn't feel guilty about afterwards. But I had to respect her decision.

I was able to convince her to play pool. Sitting here watching her laughing with the girls across the pool table, makes me happy. When I first met her, she seemed so guarded and sad. Now four months later, she's a different person.

"She's beautiful isn't she?" Mike asks as he takes the seat next to me. I've been caught staring.

"Who is?" I ask trying to play it off. I shift my gaze towards the pool table.

"Don't act like you don't know who I'm talking about. You haven't taken your eyes off her." I hope she hasn't notice.

"I don't. I was just thinking about my next move."

"Your next move with Angel?"

"The game."

"Right. So if you're not going to make a move on the girl you've been staring at all night, mind if I step in? I'll pray for her. She would be perfect for me, wouldn't she?"

I know Mike is just pressing me. He knows how I feel about her even though I never confessed it to anyone. I've invited all of our friends, I even invited *Logan*. I had to think twice about it.

They have history, and although she says he's in her past, I know he's not. He loves her, and I think she still does too. It sucks for me, but I'll wait. When we first met, she stood out to me, something special.

"You can pray for whoever you want Mike, it doesn't mean that's the one God has for you." I answer.

"Ryan! It's your turn." Angel reminds me.

I walk up the pool table, positioning my cue stick to the cue ball. I look for my solids. I hit one into a pocket and then another. I glance over my shoulder because I feel someone staring.

Angel averts her gaze when our eyes meet. I smile returning my attention to the pool table and shoot. I missed this time, she distracted me.

"You're up Angel!" I tell her stepping out of the way.

"I hope I can get one in this time. I suck at this game." She tells me. I wonder if she's secretly asking me to help her.

"Want me to give you some pointers?"

"If you don't mind." She answers looking towards the pool table, avoid eye contact with me. I take in a deep breath.

I look back at Mike, he's laughing with Jason. I'm sure he's enjoying this. I step behind her, not getting too close. I don't want to provoke any unintentional desires.

Placing my hand over hers on the cue stick, I tell her, "Position the cue stick to the cue ball. Aim it in the direction you want it to go. Placing your left hand under the cue stick to guide it. And use your body to guide the end of the stick to keep it steady."

I step back once she's set up. She hits the cue ball which hits the stripe ball she was aiming for and it goes into the pocket.

She jumps up and down excitedly, then wraps her arms around my neck still jumping and thanking me for teaching her. I place my hands on her back and laugh. Looking over her, I see Mike and Jason nodding in approval. I shake my head.

Ivy and Val come in with a cupcake and a firecracker candle singing happy birthday. Angel releases me.

"Sorry for invading your space, I was just—"

"Excited? It's cool. Happy birthday!" I lean in slowly to give her a kiss on the cheek, then I take a step back. The girls surround her, and the guys join me behind them.

"Too bad Logan's not here!" Mike teases.

Jason nudges him. I know he's messing with me again. He wants me to tell her how I feel. But I have to wait, it's not time for us…yet.

Luckily for me, Logan couldn't attend. I shouldn't say *luckily*, because I know one day, she will be mine. She's God's *chosen* for me.

A note from the Author

Angelisa has reach a level she never thought she could. She is finally able to be the soldier God has called her to be. Obstacles are only stepping stones to reach a greater purpose. Many people make the mistake of thinking that since we are saved we won't have to deal with temptations or conflict. It is the exact opposite. While we walk in this world not having a relationship with God, the devil leaves us alone. He begins to attack when you have realize there is a God, and you need Him. The enemy will then start his attacks on you and play on your weakness, he will try everything in his power to bring you down. He will make you doubt yourself, make you feel as if you have no authority.

The events in this book were exaggerated to give readers a visual. But the spiritual realm is a real place, there is a spiritual war and whether you want to fight in it or not, you're already in the middle. Think about whether or not you want to be fully armed to fight in this war, or if you rather stand defenseless.

Whatever you may be going through, don't think you have to do it alone. Don't ever think that the life you live now is too far from God. He will always listen to your prayers. Open your heart to Him and you will see a brighter future.

I started writing this story one way, but the more I wrote, the more I saw God's hand at work. I realized I to needed restoration, there were areas in my life that still needed to be worked on. And that's when I realized, it doesn't matter how long you've been a Christian, you will always be challenged in your walk with Christ.

The bible says in Romans 10:9-10 NLT

"If you openly declare that Jesus is Lord and believe in your heart that God raised him from the dead, you will be saved. For it is by believing in your heart that you are made right with God, and it is by openly declaring your faith that you are saved."

If you are not a follower of Jesus Christ, or you are unsure of your relationship with God…say this prayer.

"Lord God, I come before you asking for your forgiveness, recognizing that I am a sinner. I confess with my mouth and believe in my heart that Jesus is Lord. I declare that by the blood of Jesus I am saved and forgiven. I invite you in to my heart and my life. I ask that your Holy Spirit may guide me, in the name of Jesus I pray, Amen!"

If you are a Christian but feel lost or confused about your relationship with God simply pray. Ask God to help you find your way back. Tell Him you want to restore your relationship with Him. It may feel distant and awkward at first, but just like Angelisa, God hears you. Everyday talk to God, read the Bible and you will see those dry bones take life again.

If you said any of these prayers, find yourself a Christian church if you don't already attend one. It is important to surround yourself with people who can help you spiritually. You may also contact me via email or social media:

Author.dianaperez@gmail.com

Instagram: @AuthorDiana.P

https://www.facebook.com/authordiana.p/

Remember you are never too far from His grace.

About the Author

Diana Perez was raised in New York by an amazing family. She was raised in a Christian home being the only girl among three loving brothers. She is a woman of deep faith and credits God for seeing her through the challenges that she has faced.

From a young age, Diana always had a passion for writing. She kept journals inspired by her experiences and later began writing short skits and poems. Her love for writing brought her to share and write plays for her church. It was this love for writing that inspired her to fulfill her dream of creating and writing her first novel.

"Into The Realm: The Battle Within"

Diana lives in New York with her supportive husband and two children. She enjoys time spent with family and friends. Diana enjoys reading paranormal romance novels and also watches various genres of TV shows and movies, but her favorite kind is supernatural drama.

References

Chapter 3
"By their fruit you will recognize them." Matthew 7:16 NIV

Chapter 11
"A person standing alone can be attacked and defeated, but two can stand back-to-back and conquer. Three are even better, for a triple-braided cord is not easily broken." Ecclesiastes 4:12 NLT

Chapter 14
"For God has not given us a spirit of fear, but of power and of love and of a sound mind." 1Timothy 1:7 NKJV

Chapter 14
"A final word: Be strong in the Lord and in his mighty power." Ephesians 6:10 NLT

Chapter 15
"But those who wait on the Lord. Shall renew their strength;
They shall mount up with wings like eagles,
They shall run and not be weary,
They shall walk and not faint." Isaiah 40:31 NKJV

Chapter 20
"But seek first the kingdom of God and his righteousness, and all these things will be added to you." Matthew 6:33 ESV

Chapter 22
"...Man shall not live by bread alone..." Matthew 4:4 ESV

Chapter 24
"For this is how God loved the world: He gave his one and only Son, so that everyone who believes in him will not perish but have eternal life. God sent his Son into the world not to judge the world, but to save the world through him." John 3:16-17 NLT

"Jesus answered them, "It is not the healthy who need a doctor, but the sick. I have not come to call the righteous, but sinners to repentance." Luke 5:31-32 NIV

"Repent, then, and turn to God, so that your sins may be wiped out, that times of refreshing may come from the Lord," Acts 3:19 NIV

Chapter 29 and Cover
"When you pass through the waters, I will be with you; and when you pass through the rivers, they will not sweep over you. When you walk through the fire, you will not be burned; the flames will not set you ablaze."
Isaiah 43:2 NIV

Chapter 30
"And we know that God causes all things to work together for good to those who love God, to those who are called according to His purpose." Romans 8:28 NASB

Made in United States
North Haven, CT
23 January 2022

15173029R00157